THE SILENT VULCAN

THE SILENT VULCAN

James Follett

This first world edition published in Great Britain 2002 by
SEVERN HOUSE PUBLISHERS LTD of
9–15 High Street, Sutton, Surrey SM1 1DF.
This first world edition published in the USA 2002 by
SEVERN HOUSE PUBLISHERS INC of
595 Madison Avenue, New York, N.Y. 10022.

British Library Cataloguing in Publication Data

Follett, James, 1939-
    The silent Vulcan
    1.   Human-alien encounters - England - Sussex
    2.   Susses (England) - Fiction
    3.   Science fiction
    I.   Title
    823.9'14 [F]

    ISBN 0-7278-5712-6

*The Author and Publishers acknowledge with gratitude permission from the Daily Mail
to reproduce their article "A UFO? Actually it was just our alien friends in the North"
from the edition of 03February 1996.*

Typeset by Palimpsest Book Production Ltd.,
Polmont, Stirlingshire, Scotland.
Printed and bound in Great Britain by
MPG Books Ltd., Bodmin, Cornwall.

Prologue

Statement broadcast on an emergency radio transmitter by Asquith Prescott, Chairman of Pentworth Town Council, made in March on the day after the appearance of the Wall:

"Good evening, ladies and gentlemen. I doubt if there is anyone in the Pentworth area who isn't aware of the extraordinary fate that has overtaken our community. As from last night we have been enclosed by a seemingly impenetrable and invisible dome, six miles in diameter and effectively imprisoning some six thousand of us within an area of thirty square miles, with many suffering the anguish of separation from loved ones.

"We are lucky in having the services of Councillor Robert Harding, who is a senior government advisor on scientific matters. It's thanks to him that I am able to talk to you now. He has examined the Wall and has confirmed what many of you have suspected all along – that it is definitely not of earthly origin. It is also certain that the centre of the dome is Pentworth Lake. It is to the credit of the good sense of the people of Pentworth that there has been no panic. Whoever these creatures or beings are, or what their purpose is in coming here, or how long they intend to stay, we can only guess. But at least we know from the design of their amazing force wall that they mean us no harm. But the loss of all our public utilities and our total isolation is causing massive problems for all of us.

"But our immediate concern is our air quality. It has got steadily worse today – therefore, even if the dome lasts only a day or so, we must deal with the problem now. In the interests of us all, particularly our children, do not use your cars, or motorbikes, or any form of combustion engine unless it is *absolutely essential.* Only emergency vehicles are exempt. The same goes for barbecues and bonfires: a total voluntary ban until we have more information from our advisors. Clean air must be our first priority."

Prescott spoke for a further three minutes in which he urged those with bottled or LPG gas, or methane digestors, to form communal cooking groups for those without – such gases gave off very little carbon and sulphur; those with good boreholes to provide an outside tap for others to use. He urged utmost economy with water in household tanks and on no account were lavatories on main drainage to be flushed. In all he covered a further five interim emergency measures, including a request for all food shops to sell only perishable stock, and concluded with:

"If the crisis continues we will call on everyone in the setting up of voluntary groups to deal with day-to-day and long-term problems. The British have always been good at rising to challenges such as these which I am laying before you. Our best qualities shine in adversity. Father Adrian Roscoe and his Bodian Brethren have already responded by providing free cooked lunches today and will do so again tomorrow at Pentworth House between midday and 2 p.m. They will also be making a start on deliveries of fresh bread and milk tomorrow morning. Initial priority will be given to families with children. With such public-spiritedness and your fortitude and willingness to make sacrifices, I am confident that we will over-come all our problems.

"Thank you for listening to me. I will talk to you again at the same time tomorrow. Goodnight and God bless you all."

Statement by Councillor Bob Harding at the first meeting of Pentworth's Emergency Council:

"The Wall is definitely *not* the product of human technology. Of that there is no doubt. That leaves extra-terrestrial technology. It would seem that the claims of those who say that they saw an object in the sky last Tuesday may have been accurate after all. The ufologists who scoured the area on Wednesday and Thursday looking for this so-called Silent Vulcan didn't find anything because they didn't investigate Pentworth Lake, which is the geographic centre of the Wall. An excellent choice of hiding place for a flying saucer, spacecraft, Silent Vulcan – call it what you will. We can send probes to the planets and submersibles to the greatest depths of the oceans, but we do not have the instruments to probe very deep swamps."

In answer to a question about the likely place of origin of the invaders, Councillor Harding said:

"We know enough about the solar system to rule out all the planets. That leaves our galaxy – the Milky Way. Our nearest star is Proxima Centauri. A type M red dwarf flare star whose light takes 4.3 years to reach us – just over one parsec. For the sake of argument, let us assume that Centauri has a planetary system and that's where our visitors are from. We know that they can't be from anywhere nearer, and the probability is that they're from somewhere a good deal further away. Certain characteristics of the Wall – we now know from a check on the sewers and an old lead mine that it's actually a sphere – indicate that our visitors are not in possession of the sort of super-advanced technology as favoured by most science-fiction writers. It is advanced enough – but, from what I've observed, I doubt if they're much more than three hundred years ahead of us.

"Certainly enough to give us serious problems. I'm going to make another supposition and give our visitors' spacecraft a capability of one fifth of the speed of light – around sixty thousand kilometres per second. Allowing for periods of acceleration and deceleration, the journey from Centauri to Earth would take them about twenty-two years. A round trip of forty-four years. An awesome time span but within the realms of possibility for a survey expedition by a determined people with inquiring minds. The scientist in me rebels at all this stretching of a theory but I've started it, so I'll continue. I believe that our visitors had problems with their spacecraft when they went into orbit around the earth. Rather than remain in orbit and risk detection and possible destruction by us, they searched for a haven. Where better than a deep swamp? And as an added safeguard, they threw up an enclosing protective sphere around themselves. They then broadcast for help – they certainly generated a lot of broadband radio noise around one hundred megaHertz on Thursday and Friday, which led to the drowning of two Radio Communications Agency investigators. The visitors' SOS is now on its way to Centauri and will reach it in four years and four months. Assuming that HQ can launch a rescue mission right away, we can expect to be reluctant hosts to our visitors for the next twenty-seven years. On the other hand, they may be from the heart of our galaxy, in which case they, and us, will have to wait many thousands of years."

First draft of a speech by Councillor Bob Harding for the opening of the May Day Carnival held in Market Square, Pentworth, two months after the appearance of the Wall.

In September 1991, eight men and women said goodbye to Mother Earth and locked themselves into an artificial 3.1-acre ecosystem in the Arizona desert for two years. Their giant greenhouse-like building was called Biosphere 2 – the earth being Biosphere 1. It was, in many respects, similar to the situation confronting us in Pentworth. Biosphere 2 was airtight and contained everything needed to sustain life. Plants would make food and oxygen, insects would pollinate the plants, and algae and bacteria would break down waste and purify the water. The purpose of the project was to investigate ecosystems that would be needed to support crews on long space voyages, or in colonies on planets such as Mars.

Biosphere 2 included a miniature rainforest, some swamp, a four-million-litre "ocean" with a wave-making machine, desert, savannah and marshland. There was a farm with goats, pigs, and chickens. Additionally, there were fish in the ocean, and about 4,000 species of reptiles and insects in the swamp and forest. There were even birds. Everything was put in place to create a supposedly ideal environment for the eight "biospherians" in which they would grow their own food, recycle water, while completely cut off from a sustaining outside world from which they would receive only sunlight.

It didn't work. The crew ended up competing for food with their livestock. For example, egg production went down but the hens ate just as much. The goats and pigs didn't breed nearly so prolifically. This meant that animals slaughtered for food were not replaced. Weeds flourished, taking valuable nitrogen and nutrients from the soil resulting in the biospherians expending more energy in weeding than they were able to replace by eating their crops.

The all-important lesson learned in the case of Biosphere 2 was that we don't know, as yet, how to engineer a system that provides humans with the life-supporting services that natural ecosystems produce for free. *Our Earth remains the only known home that can sustain life.*

Biosphere 2 wasn't big enough to permit the drumbeat of nature to resonate. For example, their species of frog relied on the splatter of heavy rain to announce mating time. There was no rain, the frogs didn't breed, therefore there were no tadpoles to feed on water weeds to provide food for the carp that would be eaten by the crew. The food chain wasn't so much broken – it was never even started.

The crew were forced to provide a huge input of work to do the job that nature does for free. You can build synthetic ecosystems as small as you want, but the smaller you make it, the greater role human operators have to play because they must act out the

5

larger forces of nature. A scientist on the project said that the subsidy we get from nature is incredible. I want you all to remember those words, "The subsidy we get from nature is incredible."

The breeze taking away the smoke from that barbecue is doing a job that we could not replicate without a million horsepower of electric fans. Not only is the breeze carrying the carbon from the barbecue's charcoal across the fields to feed plant life, but it's also taking moisture, such as our sweat, with it at the same time. It then rises over Pentworth Lake, and gives up its harvest of moisture to the colder air so that it falls as rain . . . Perhaps as much as a tonne of our body waste has been purified, transported, and redistributed since I started talking . . . All without any effort on our part. The subsidy we get from nature is indeed truly incredible.

Pentworth within its ten-kilometre sphere is over a million times the size of Biosphere 2. It is just large enough for the cycles of nature to operate – at least we have the natural water purification process of evaporation and condensation at work – we have rainfall and some-times heavy dews. We have plenty of water locked within our dome. Like the earth's water, it is our only water. Like the earth's water, we won't lose it, but we won't get any more; therefore we have to take great care of it.

And that applies to not only water, but all our raw materials. We do not know if the Wall will remain in place for a year, or ten years, or ten centuries. Therefore we must conserve and, above all, recycle. We have about a tonne of metals per person, which ought to be more than enough. But anything we make from those metals must be built to last. Obsolescence cannot become a component part of our economy. The regulations on separation of household waste before collection, on the avoidance of pollution, the strict controls on fires, may seem irksome, but by following them we are ensuring, not only our health, but the health and well-being of future generations. That we are entrusted with the present does not give us the right to raid the future.

One

The triangular-shaped mound protruding above the sediment was at a depth of 120 metres and almost in the precise centre of the broad expanse of Pentworth Lake.

"*That*," said Bob Harding with suppressed excitement while staring at the echo-sounder's display, "has to be the Silent Vulcan – our visitors' UFO."

A breeze tugged at the Zodiac inflatable boat that the two men were sitting in, causing it to jerk against its tethers. The boat was moored at the intersection of three marker lines that had been stretched taut across the lake and kept afloat with an assortment of beach balls and plastic bottles spaced at regular intervals.

Bob Harding's companion in the boat was Detective Sergeant Mike Malone. Both men were wearing shorts and T-shirts. Malone was in his mid thirties. He was lean, muscular and bronzed. His passions were jogging and philosophy – interests that suited his temperament because he could indulge them alone. By contrast, Harding was round-shouldered and pale skinned. He was a former government scientific advisor who had taken early retirement to set up an electrical repair shop and workshop in Pentworth. Now he was the reluctant Chairman of Pentworth's governing council and therefore the most powerful man in the community. It was a post that had been thrust on him a week earlier after a successful coup masterminded by Malone. Harding supported the coup – the former Chairman of what had been Pentworth Town Council, Asquith Prescott, had used the emergency to gradually acquire almost dictatorial powers since the appearance of the Wall. His early moves, such as strict controls on air pollution and the setting up of the morris man police had enjoyed wide support because they had been necessary, but Asquith Prescott had gone on to seek absolute power in league with Adrian Roscoe. His ruthlessness had led to him being deposed and Bob Harding being installed as acting-Chairman.

Bob Harding was a mild-mannered man with no taste for power; he was quietly determined to restore normal democracy to Pentworth and step down at the first opportunity. The trouble was that to undo quickly the damage caused by Asquith Prescott required stroke-of-a-pen dictatorial powers similar to those that Prescott had employed to put them in place.

Malone squinted up at the blistering sun and adjusted the position of the parasol so that the echo-sounder's screen remained shaded. Harding used a digital camera to take another close-up picture of the anomaly in the centre of the display. He checked the image he had captured on the camera's liquid crystal display.

"Damn. Still too much hand shake," he said, not concealing the tremble in his voice.

Malone said nothing but continued staring at the echo-sounder's screen. Harding's excitement was understandable. If the hazy pattern of green shading on the screen *was* the Silent Vulcan, then it was the first visible evidence of the UFO's awesome presence other than the Visitors' ten-kilometre diameter Wall that had dominated all their lives for six months since March.

The Wall had proved impregnable. It had resisted repeated attempts to break through it. Even a coordinated onslaught by the massed forces of nearly 400 trucks, cars, and tractors distributed around the thirty-kilometre perimeter of the Wall had been unable to overcome its terrible yet strangely benign power. As the vehicles began thrusting, the Wall had given way gently at first, and then had gradually pushed back with an irresistible equal and opposite force. But no one had come to harm as a result of contact with the Wall. On the night of its appearance, a woman had unwittingly driven into it at high speed. Her Jaguar had been brought to a controlled standstill. "It was like hitting a wall of foam rubber mattresses," the baffled woman had later reported.

Equally extraordinary was that the unreachable world beyond

the invisible Wall consisted of wind-blasted steppes – a bleak vista of frost-hardy sedge grasses, and a few wind-stunted trees struggling to survive in hollows and valleys. Small herds of woolly mammoths had been seen grazing the strange landscape, and a retired school teacher, a nun, had even seen a sabre-toothed cat on several occasions. Bob Harding and other amateur astronomers had identified the night sky as that of northern Europe of 40,000 years ago. The strange world beyond the Wall had become known as Farside – a name also used for the modern world that now, after six months of isolation, seemed lost forever to the imprisoned people of Pentworth.

Some even thought that the real world had ceased to exist, and a steadily increasing minority believed that the Wall was a punishment by God. Then there were those who liked the new life, as it was called. They liked the simplicity, the clean air, organically grown food, the freedom from motor traffic and above all, the community spirit that the Visitors and their Wall had produced.

Harding had a hazy plan to attempt to communicate with the Visitors in their Silent Vulcan. There were so many questions to be asked. Where were they from? Why had they come? How long did they intend to stay? Why had they created the Wall? Did they realise the heartache and misery it was causing?

There were so many questions clamouring for answers – the most immediate being how to communicate with the Visitors. Harding had no idea but he was confident that he would think of something. Knowing exactly where they were helped.

A distant whistle blew. Malone glanced up and saw a volunteer lifeguard signalling to a bather who had swum outside the roped-off safe bathing area. The small beach that the governing council of Pentworth had created using wagon-loads of sand was dotted with sunshades. Beyond the bathing area around the beach where children were splashing with their parents was a steep shelf which fell away to the unplumbed depths of the lake.

Millennia before, water made acidic by decaying vegetation had leached down through the upper strata of sandstone and washed away the underlying limestone leaving a vast cavern. Eventually the land had collapsed to form this curious lake. It was typical of the supposedly bottomless swallow-holes of Sussex. In the case of Pentworth Lake, the upwelling from underground springs had kept the bottom sediment in a state of low density and near-constant agitation so that no one knew the lake's true depth. Since the appearance of the Wall there had been a decrease in evaporation and a corresponding decrease in the formation of rain clouds within the dome which had allowed the sediment to settle. What rainfall there was proving adequate for the needs of 6,000 people, but only just.

Harding took another picture, this time steadying his forearm against the car battery that powered the echo-sounder. He stowed the camera for future downloading of its images to his laptop computer, and used a pair of dividers to measure the fuzzy triangle against the echo-sounder's scale. "It's 6.2 metres along each side," he said to Malone. "A near perfect equilateral triangle. And it's at the precise centre of the Wall."

Malone's wide-set, brooding eyes continued to regard the echo-sounder's image of the strange mound. His quick mind applied the philosophy of Occam's Razor to the problem, quickly analysing and discarding explanations of the phenomenon. Debris? Unlikely – it was too big. A practical joke? Also unlikely because Pentworth Lake was on the patrol route of the morris man police, now under his command. A Luftwaffe bomber had crashed in the lake during World War II and had never been recovered. But something as flimsy as aircraft wreckage nearly three quarters of a century old could not account for such a large, regular structure. Several other possible causes failed at the fences of his remarkable reasoning powers. Bob Harding's conviction that the object at the bottom of Pentworth Lake was the so-called Silent Vulcan UFO was the only one that made sense.

"It looks too small to be an inter-stellar spacecraft," said Harding.

"How large should an inter-stellar spacecraft be, Mr Chairman?" queried Malone.

"Well spotted, Mike. I'm reverse engineering from the size of the brain cell. That is, assuming our Visitors are a

10

carbon-based, oxygen-dependent life form, which I'm pretty sure they are, they would have to have a brain of a certain size, which means lungs of a certain size, which means a heart and associated organs of a certain size. They could be smaller than us, but I doubt if they would be significantly so. In the intelligence league tables, size does matter." He switched off the echo-sounder.

"Unless the Silent Vulcan is a robot vehicle – unmanned, or rather, unaliened," Malone observed.

"That's a real possibility."

"And one that will make your ideas to communicate with them that much more difficult."

"The real difficulty would be persuading the Council to vote the resources to carry out any plan," Harding replied.

A telling reply, thought Malone. It illustrated the difference in leadership style between the retired scientist and the recently usurped Asquith Prescott. If Prescott decided he wanted to do something, he went right ahead and did it. Democratic decision-making had gradually become an inconvenience as far as Asquith Prescott had been concerned.

"Anyway," Harding continued. "If the Silent Vulcan is manned by machines, they must have an extremely high level of cognitive ability to control their UFO – to respond to emergencies and so on. You can't use radio remote control if the time to exchange signals runs into years. The unmanned landers sent to Mars had to do a lot of their own decision-making. And that's where the radio delay is only a matter of minutes."

Malone gazed across the lake to where David Weir's sheep were grazing the steep rise that led to the sandstone outcrop known as the Temple of the Winds. His mind went back to the night before the Wall had appeared in March when he had nearly caught a strange, crab-like device that had been following him as he jogged home. It had been about the size of a large dog. He had come within a metre of throwing himself on it when it had sprouted contra-rotating helicopter-like rotors and disappeared into the night sky. Several other locals had seen it. One had dubbed it the "spyder" and the name had stuck. There was no doubt that it was a machine – and a

11

highly intelligent and capable machine at that judging by the speed of its reactions when he had tried to catch it.

"I'm not too keen on your breakdown theory: that they're waiting for some sort of on-site repair visit," said Malone at length. "Their spyder machine seemed to be bloody reliable to me, and I expect the rest of their systems are the same."

Harding grinned at the police officer. "I'm not too keen on it myself, Mike. I only advanced it as a possibility."

"So let's assume, Mr Chairman, that their arrival is deliberate. In which case the policeman in me demands a motive for their visit. It can't be primarily to gather information, because they must know that their Wall has had a sufficiently profound effect on the environment and our behaviour to invalidate much, if not all, of their data. They've turned us into a twenty-first century community of six thousand people, but isolated from the rest of the world, and having to come to terms with the farming and transport and day-to-day living of the early nineteenth century. Our behaviour is hardly typical. So I ask myself why they're here."

"Perhaps they want to find out how we manage under stress?" Harding suggested.

The squelch on the police PMR radio clipped to Malone's belt opened. It was a report by a morris men police patrol to say that a search party had left Pentworth House. The groups sent out by Adrian Roscoe's Bodian Brethren from their Pentworth House headquarters were a daily occurrence. Malone's standing orders were that such search parties were to be monitored but not interfered with provided their behaviour stayed within the law. The duty operations officer at Pentworth police station acknowledged and the radio fell silent.

Harding started packing the echo-sounder, neatly coiling its transducer lead. He commented, "The scenario much loved by science-fiction writers of the past, starting with H.G. Wells and his *War of the Worlds*, was the takeover of the earth."

"By trapping a little town like Pentworth in the middle of a ten-kilometre diameter spherical force wall?"

"Maybe Pentworth's Wall is a prototype?" Harding ventured. "Maybe there will be, or already are for all we know, thousands of such force wall spheres all over the world?

12

Millions, perhaps. Every community in the world isolated from its neighbours. Divide and conquer."

Malone shook his head. "Too clumsy."

"Why?"

"Vikki Taylor. A sixteen-year-old girl who had a terrible accident as a toddler that resulted in her losing her left hand. She's visited in her sleep by the spyder and within twenty-four hours she's regrown a perfect left hand."

"And gets condemned as a witch because of it," said Harding with quietly suppressed anger. "The reason I took on this job you've foisted on me is because of what happened to Vikki Taylor and Ellen Duncan."

Malone regarded Harding steadily. "Any intelligence capable of growing a new hand on a human being isn't going to indulge in brute force tactics if they want to take over the world, Mr Chairman. They'd make the human race sterile and simply walk in one hundred years or so later when we're extinct."

Two

Vikki Taylor was no longer self-conscious about her miraculous new left hand and used its perfect forefinger to slide an "S" across the Scrabble board and add it to the front of Ellen Duncan's "HAG". Ellen glared at Vikki. The teenager's lovely green eyes, round and sparkling with sweetness and innocence, gazed mischievously back at the older woman while Vikki sucked pensively on the offending forefinger.

"You can't have that," said Ellen shortly. "We agreed – no rude words."

"Course I can have a shag," said Vikki defiantly.

"Now you listen to me, young lady. This is my cave and I make the rules. If I say that that's a rude word – it's a rude word. No argument."

"I think it's a type of duck," said Claire Lake, looking up from a magazine she'd read at least ten times during the three weeks she'd spent incarcerated in the cave with Ellen and Vikki.

Ellen said hotly, "Of course it is, you stupid woman! And what do you mean by 'type'? What other types are there? There's only one type of—"

"*Duck*," said Claire more succinctly, trying not to laugh. In the three weeks she had learned to love the older woman dearly, and also to respect her quick temper.

"Duck?" Ellen queried, momentarily thrown.

"Quack. Quack," murmured Vikki. She caught Claire's eye and struggled to keep a straight face.

"Methinks my plonker is being pulled," said Ellen sourly.

"Depends on how well you're getting ducked," said Claire.

The illumination from the low-wattage twelve-volt bulb

14

hanging from the cave's roof was sufficient for Claire to receive the full benefit of Ellen's disapproving glare. They stared at other.

Ellen was the first to break. Her mouth played catapults and she made an involuntary noise through her nose. Within seconds the cave was echoing with the laughter of the three fugitives. For a few precious moments the women forgot their bizarre circumstances, their fear of discovery and certain death at the hands of Adrian Roscoe and his cult's growing band of fanatics temporarily set aside.

Claire pulled a grubby handkerchief from her bra and wiped her eyes, wondering if the baby growing in her womb could sense her laughter.

Suddenly Ellen realised the danger that the noise posed and urgently shushed for quiet.

The three women sat still, listening fearfully for the slightest sound indicating that the concealed entrance to their cave had been discovered. Like the figures in the amazing 40,000-year-old Palaeolithic hunting scenes that decorated the walls, they were virtually naked. The soul-sapping humidity in the cave made wearing anything other than minimal underwear intolerable.

The most spectacular painting was a life-size woolly mammoth surrounded by diminutive human figures armed with spear throwers. The unknown prehistoric artists had cunningly exploited natural protuberances in the rock face to give the stricken beast a startling three-dimensional quality. The detail in the dazzling mural was remarkable. Long individual strands of the creature's hanging woolly coat seemed have been achieved by using the chewed end of a stick to create streaks in the red ochre pigment. Even the mammoth's mighty crossed ivories bore the chips and abrasions of a long life spent breaking up ice to get at the succulent grasses underneath.

Despite the three weeks that Ellen had been cooped-up in the cave, she had never tired of sitting in a canvas camping chair, gazing at the woolly mammoth and speculating about the artists who had lived 400 centuries ago.

400 centuries . . . 40,000 years . . .

An unimaginable time span. The paintings were at least

35,000 years old when Abraham obeyed God's command and set out from Ur in Chaldea, and when the early pharaohs ordered the building of their pyramids.

The cave was on Ellen's land, about halfway down the steep slopes that led from Pentworth where she had run her little herbal remedy shop in North Street. Pentworth Lake, where Mike Malone was sitting at that moment in an inflatable boat, discussing the Silent Vulcan with Bob Harding, was under a mile away. The strange lake was also on Ellen's land.

Ellen had discovered the cave with David Weir, a local farmer and a fellow councillor on Pentworth Town Council, to whom she rented land for grazing his sheep. The steep slopes were unsuitable for any other type of agriculture.

Their on-off relationship had developed as a result of their shared interest in palaeontology and the periods they had spent working together on the excavation of a local flint mine. They had discovered the remarkable cave and its unique paintings the previous March. They had concealed the opening in the side of the hill as best they could with turf and were about to announce their discovery when the Wall appeared. Realising that they stood little chance of protecting the cave during the emergency, they decided to keep the discovery a secret for the time being. It was as well they had done so because it was just the place to hide the three women after they'd been rescued from the clutches of Adrian Roscoe and his Bodian Brethren. Before the daring rescue, David Weir and Mike Malone had secretly prepared the cave for a long occupancy by the fugitives, packing it with supplies, providing battery lighting and a radio, some furniture, and even an Elsan chemical toilet behind a shower curtain.

"So I'm entitled to my shag?" Vikki queried.

"That's not the sort of question a nice, innocent fifteen-year-old Catholic girl should ask."

"Sixteen now," Vikki replied, smiling sweetly. "And maybe not so innocent either."

Ellen added the word's score to Vikki's running total and made her own move.

"It's also a type of tobacco," said Vikki. "Being a herbalist, you ought to know that."

"You know perfectly well that I never sell tobacco products in my shop. You're now nearly a hundred points behind."

Vikki bent her head over the Scrabble board and concentrated on her letter tiles. Ellen experienced a little pang of jealousy at the way the young girl's golden hair kept its sheen. Ellen's long, dark hair needed frequent treatment with conditioner to maintain its lustre. It was lank and lifeless, sticking to the film of sweat that covered her shoulders and breasts.

Ellen reflected that the horrific ordeal that she and Vikki had been through had changed the girl. She was no longer the shy schoolgirl who had worked Saturdays in her shop. Of course, suddenly acquiring a real hand after spending most of her life with a series of prosthetic hands would change anyone. But Vikki now accepted her miraculous new left hand although she still occasionally held her fingers half-clenched – the default position of her old artificial hand.

During their first few days in the cave, Vikki had acted the typical teenage girl – sulky and obdurate. Ellen realised that she could pin-point exactly when the change had taken place and the cheerful, more adult Vikki had emerged. It had happened a week before, the morning after the coup, when they had gathered around the radio and listened with the volume turned down to Bob Harding's conciliation broadcast. All three had been overjoyed at the time, thinking that their period of hiding in the cave was over. But the days had slipped by with no visit by Mike Malone or David Weir to tell them that their long ordeal was at an end. Ellen and Claire had been depressed but Vikki's spirit and general outgoing demeanour had continued to rise.

"I think I'm stuck," Vikki announced. "Come and help me, Claire. We can't let age triumph over youth."

"Cheeky madam," Ellen reprimanded. The old, respectful Vikki would never have talked like that.

Claire smiled, pulled up a camping chair beside Vikki and studied the girl's letters and the board.

A brave woman, thought Ellen.

Claire Lake was twenty-five. Her inclusion in the cave had surprised Ellen and Vikki because she was known to be one

17

of Adrian Roscoe's principle organisers among his team of so-called solar sentinels.

One night, when Vikki was asleep, Claire had given Ellen a detailed account of her life. Her background was fairly typical of the many young people that the cult leader had ensnared. Her story was one of an unhappy middle-class upbringing, an unwise marriage, being abandoned by her husband, losing a baby that she had ached for, and a drift into homelessness, hopelessness, and alcohol before she saw the Bodian Brethren's recruiting Winnebago-cum-mobile-canteen when it had visited Brighton. Like many before her, she had fallen under Roscoe's influence and joined his community in Pentworth House.

The simplicity of the cult's belief had a certain appeal. In 1772, the German astronomer and mathematician, Johann Bode had published what became known as the Titius-Bode "law" – a simple mathematical relationship between the planets and their distances from the sun. The later discovery of the planets Uranus and Neptune at the distances predicted by Bode's so-called "law" tended to give it much credence. The trouble was that there was no fourth planet between Mars and Jupiter, which Bode's formula said there should be. Then, in 1801, the first of the asteroids were discovered. Astronomers soon found hundreds once they knew where to look for them, all dotted around the sun in a belt between Mars and Jupiter with a collective mass that added up to what may have once been a modest-sized planet. The discovery confounded the scientific community of the nineteenth century because the law suggested that the placing of the planets was due to divine intervention rather than the random nature of celestial mechanics.

Adrian Roscoe took the theory one step further by claiming that God had revealed his law to Johann Bode as a terrible warning. The fourth planet had rejected God and had been destroyed as a consequence. Roscoe preached that the same thing would happen to Earth unless man rid the planet of Satan and his abominations. To avert this calamity, he had leased Pentworth House, filled it with down-and-out young people recruited by himself and Nelson Faraday, and established a

18

solar temple in Pentworth House containing representations of all the planets. Relays of his solar sentinels sat cross-legged 24/7 in the temple, praying for the salvation of the earth.

He turned the appearance of the Wall to his advantage by claiming it was the work of God – that Pentworth had been isolated because it harboured witchcraft and other abominations as a warning of the fate in store for the entire planet.

Adrian Roscoe had discovered that Claire had a flair for organisation and had given her a management job in his estate's dairy – specialising in the production of top-quality ice cream for the London hotel and restaurant trade. For the first time in her life, Claire felt fulfilled, useful. She was experiencing what she thought was real friendship. Everyone sharing their problems. At first she didn't even mind the sex – sometimes three or more altogether. Sometimes just girls together; sometimes a mixture. To Claire, everyone was giving and receiving. And then she had caught Nelson Faraday's eye. It was her youthful, schoolgirl looks that appealed to him and he claimed her for his own – subjecting her to all manner of brutal sexual depravities that had her crying herself to sleep in pain and humiliation most nights.

Claire had resolved to escape from the sect when she discovered that she was pregnant. That Nelson Faraday was most likely the father didn't matter; having lost one baby, she was fiercely determined not to lose this one.

Then the Wall had appeared and wrecked her plans. Roscoe's imprisonment in Pentworth House of Vikki Taylor and Ellen Duncan and his condemning of them to death as witches convinced her that the sect leader was insane. In desperation she had had a secret meeting with Mike Malone and begged him to help her. He promised to do so and, in return, she had courageously returned to Pentworth House as a spy. She risked her life to provide Malone with information on Roscoe's public execution plans for Vikki and Ellen – information that enabled the police officer to plan the daring rescue of Ellen and Vikki from the Temple of the Winds where Roscoe had planned to scourge them before having them burned alive.

Ellen considered the inscrutable Mike Malone to be a man of the highest integrity. Guaranteeing the safety of Claire and her unborn baby in order to rescue herself and Vikki meant that the same guarantee extended to herself and Vikki. Which also meant that all three would have to remain in hiding until Malone was one hundred per cent certain that Adrian Roscoe's power had been irrevocably broken.

Claire's help enabled Vikki to close the gap in her Scrabble score. So good to see Vikki smiling, Ellen thought. But why? What had brought about this profound change in the girl? What was it that she had said a few minutes ago about not being so innocent?

Oh, for God's sake! Stop acting the over-anxious den mother!

The curious appropriateness of the analogy amused Ellen.

But not enough to dispel her concern about Vikki's altered personality.

Three

W hile the three women played Scrabble, eager children were helping the two men stow the deflated Zodiac dinghy and their equipment on a horse-drawn cart. Harding's efforts were hampered by a four-year-old who considered he had an inalienable right to ride on the retired scientist's shoulders and pull his ears while his steed shook hands with parents and did his best to answer their questions, even some pointed queries from an elderly couple who favoured the new life and the renewed community spirit it had engendered.

Malone watched with interest. There was no doubt that Harding was well-liked. But Prescott's easygoing bonhomie and wealth ensured that he had a core of influential supporters. The difference was that Prescott had gone out of his way to be seen to be popular, even to the extent of arranging for groups of his supporters to hang about outside Government House to cheer him when he appeared, whereas Bob Harding always seemed genuinely surprised and touched by the warmth that greeted him during the seven days he had been Chairman. Malone reflected that he and his fellow conspirators had made a good choice. A bloody civil war between the town and the country had been averted, although the grievances were still there – particularly over Pentworth's food shortages and the widespread belief in the town that farmers and growers were withholding supplies.

"Papa One-Six. Mr Malone? Do you copy?"

Malone raised his PMR radio's speaker-microphone to his lips. "Go 'head, One-Six."

"Free to speak?"

Malone moved away from the cart. "Go ahead."

"Are you still at the lake, Mr Malone?"

"Yes. Yes." Malone disliked revealing his location. Adrian

Roscoe's Bodian Brethren were more than capable of retuning their Motorola Handie-Com radios to listen to police channels.

"The Bodian search party from Pentworth House is heading your way, Mr Malone."

Malone glanced up and picked out a distant group of eight figures skirting the far end of Pentworth Lake. There was something familiar about the confident stride of the leader and the way he swung his long staff with every step. The flash of Roscoe's ice-blue eyes was apparent even at this distance. Malone cursed inwardly. It seemed that Adrian Roscoe had gone back on the terms of Bob Harding's amnesty that there would be no more search parties organised from the Bodian Brethren's HQ at Pentworth House. "I can see them," he answered. "Any reason for drawing my attention to them? Over."

"They're being led by Adrian Roscoe. Also Nelson Faraday is with him. They were discharged from the hospital this morning."

Malone acknowledged, said that he didn't require back-up and cleared the channel. He moved to the footpath that the approaching group were using and stood facing them, hands clasped behind his back, waiting.

Nelson Faraday was the only member of the group not wearing a gown. He was dressed in his customary black but not his leather trousers and crimson-lined black leather cloak. They had been damaged in the fire at Government House that had been the opening shot of the coup. Like Adrian Roscoe, his hands were bandaged.

All those in Asquith Prescott's palatial Government House office when Harvey Evans had fired a marine distress rocket through the window from his microlight aircraft had suffered varying degrees of burns. Asquith Prescott's injuries had been the worst. The former Chairman of the Governing Council of Pentworth had displayed a remarkable degree of courage when the conflagration had erupted in his office by rolling Vanessa Grossman in a carpet. The only fatality of that fateful night had been Harvey Evans when his microlight aircraft had crashed into the building, setting the roof on fire and destroying Pentworth Radio's simple broadcast studio. The moment transmissions had ceased, Bob Harding had come on air using a spare transmitter in his workshop to announce that Asquith Prescott's rule was over.

The group drew level with Malone and stopped. Adrian Roscoe's intense blue eyes flared at the police officer from a gaunt face set deep in the cowl.

"Good morning, Mr Roscoe," said Malone affably. He made a point of never using "Father" when addressing the sect leader.

Roscoe leaned on his staff. The sleeve of his gown fell away showing that his arm was bandaged to the elbow. "What do you want, Malone?"

"I hear Dr Vaughan has just discharged you and your Man Faraday here from hospital." Faraday scowled and said nothing. Malone continued, "Naturally I'm concerned that you're up and about so soon. Shouldn't you be resting?"

"I do not rest when there is God's work to be done." The rich, resonant tone of Roscoe's voice combined with his unblinking blue eyes made him a formidable orator.

The six other members of the Bodian Brethren in the party remained standing a little way back, hoods pulled forward, eyes downcast. Of all the social misfits that Roscoe had recruited to his cult movement before the appearance of the Wall, they were the biggest and most intimidating. There was little that intimidated Malone but the police officer could well guess their impact on farmers and residents in outlying areas.

"If you would step aside, please," said Roscoe coldly.

"When you've told me what you're up to."

"That is none of your business."

Malone stared dispassionately at Roscoe. "Please yourself . . . There's no hurry. I'll have all of you taken into custody. I'm incredibly busy at the moment, so you'll have at least three days' wait before I get around to questioning you. You're in breach of an undertaking you gave last week to stop these intimidating search parties for Vikki Taylor and Ellen Duncan."

"I've told you. We are on God's work," Roscoe snapped.

"I trust he pays well."

"As you well know, Claire Lake has disappeared. She's a

prominent member of our brethren. I take her safety seriously, Malone, even if you don't."

"She's over eighteen and has every right to leave your cult if she so wishes," Malone observed.

Bob Harding joined the group and looked inquiringly at Roscoe and Faraday. "What's the problem, Mr Malone?"

"It would seem, Mr Chairman, that Mr Roscoe has forgotten the terms of your generous amnesty – that his search party charades for Vikki Taylor and Ellen Duncan would cease."

"I agreed that I would no longer concern myself with the whereabouts of those two devil's acolytes until they reappear, as they eventually must," Roscoe responded, not taking his icy gaze off Malone. "I did not promise to set aside my concern for the safety and mental state of a young girl whom I rescued from the gutter when she was contemplating suicide."

"She's not contemplating it now," said Malone evenly. "So you can go home or be arrested."

Harding frowned. "Do you know where Claire Lake is, Mr Malone?"

The policeman was undecided about answering the question. It didn't take a genius to guess that the three missing women were together. He had no doubt that Adrian Roscoe was using his supposed concern for Claire Lake as a cover for continuing his hunt for Vikki and Ellen. The cult leader's hatred of Ellen Duncan, whom he was convinced was a witch and responsible for Pentworth's troubles, was more than mere paranoia – it was a burning obsession that had led to Ellen and Vikki falling into his clutches and being tried as witches and found guilty of witchcraft. The crazy trial in Pentworth House's manorial court and the condemning to death of the two women had been a major factor that had led to the coup of the previous week. He decided to side-step the question.

"I know someone who knows where she is." It was an economic but truthful answer.

"And is she well?" Harding asked.

"Safe *and* well, Mr Chairman," Malone replied, returning Roscoe's hard gaze.

"In that case, Father Roscoe," said Harding. "I'm prepared to accept Mr Malone's word on the matter and I require you to do the same. There must be no more search parties. If you persist, you are in breach of the amnesty and will be arrested. All of you."

"The girl is confused and emotionally unstable," snarled Nelson Faraday, speaking for the first time. "Father Roscoe is not the sort of man to turn his back on his responsibilities."

"Claire Lake *was* confused and frightened," Malone corrected, staring dispassionately at Faraday. "Brought about by the sexual perversions that she was forced to take part in when she was in the supposed care of the Bodian cult." Malone decided to play a bluff. He returned Roscoe's icy stare. "I have a full statement from her and corroborative statements from two other members of your cult. I have enough evidence to arrest both of you on several charges of abduction and rape, and I won't hesitate to do so if you continue with these absurd search parties."

Malone's gamble paid off. Roscoe appeared to be undecided for a moment. Malone knew from what Claire Lake had told him that there were at least two other supposedly staunch members of the Bodian Brethren who were unhappy with conditions in Pentworth House – particularly the hours they now had to work on the estate's farms to take advantage of the long hours of daylight.

With a parting glare at Malone, Roscoe turned abruptly and strode back along the footpath with Faraday and the sentinels trailing behind.

"First time I've ever known him to capitulate without a fight or a compromise," Harding observed.

"For which he'll exact a price, Mr Chairman," said Malone, watching the dwindling group.

"Oh, I don't know. He's been effectively neutralised. There's no reason why Ellen and Vikki, and this Claire Lake can't come out of hiding."

"You cannot neutralise a fanatic short of killing him," said Malone categorically. "Nothing will shake Adrian Roscoe's crazy beliefs. Adrian Roscoe sees his fanaticism as a God-given tool to save the earth. To him Ellen Duncan and Vikki Taylor are satanic apostles and he will stop at nothing to destroy them. That's why I maintain that they must remain in hiding."

25

Four

D avid Weir jumped down from the hissing, throbbing second love in his life and helped his farm manager, Charlie Crittenden, shovel anthracite beans into her roaring firebox.

"Steady on, Charlie," said David, anxiously eyeing the smoke belching from the huge traction engine's tall smoke-stack. "I've only got a permit to burn a couple of hundred kilos."

"'Tain't no good testing our 'Brenda' proper unless we can run her half an hour at full pressure, Mr Weir," said Charlie. The muscles in his brawny, tattooed arms bulged as he used a long, heavy iron to break up a lump of clinker in the firebox, exposing the nearly white-hot core of the fire. Charlie heaved his bulk up the traction engine's step plates to the driver's position, taking care to avoid the spinning flywheel, and checked the pressure gauges. "One hundred and eighty p.s.i. and steady," he announced. "Never had her up to that before."

David was pleased. "Brenda" was the prize in his Temple Farm's collection of now-valuable ancient machinery – a monstrous Charles Burrell showman's engine – a steam-powered traction engine that had, in its day, met the electricity needs of a travelling funfair. The huge dynamo mounted on top of the engine's boiler, when driven by a belt from the steam engine's flywheel, had provided enough electricity to run bumper cars, big wheels, whips, ghost trains and all the thousands of lights that were a traditional part of travelling fairs of the first half of the twentieth century. When David had found her she had been rotting in a field for half a century. He had bought the wreck on the assurances of Charlie that it would be possible to restore it.

Charlie knew his traction engines. The former traveller and his family had funfairs in their blood. The Crittendens had settled their caravans at Temple Farm before the Wall had appeared.

Five years previously, David had sold his share in a London art gallery, bought Temple Farm, and used his boundless energy to turn the farm into a theme farm – a working museum based on pre-Industrial Revolution agricultural practices and equipment. His acceptance into local society had been confirmed when he had been voted on to Pentworth's former town council. He had been a leading conspirator in the rescue of Ellen and Vikki and the *coup d'état* a few days later that had overthrown Asquith Prescott. He and Mike Malone were the only people in Pentworth who knew where the three women were hidden.

He walked around the engine, keeping clear of the steam screaming from the stuffing boxes that were still leaking and required Charlie's skilled attention. The machine was a sorry sight: a piebald mass of red blotches where primer had been applied to the worst of the rust patches on her boiler. All that was left of the long canopy that had extended the length of the machine and its massive dynamo were a few upright supports. The dynamo had been removed to have its bearings rebuilt and its armature rewound.

The Wall had put paid to David's plans to restore the showman's engine to her former gleaming glory. The only thing that gleamed about her now was the brass plate engraved with the venerable machine's name. The plate had been restored by Charlie's wife for the occasional outing, as when, a few weeks before, "Brenda" had taken part in the massed but fruitless assault on the Wall by nearly 400 vehicles.

"Two hundred p.s.i.," said Charlie, jumping down and regarding the hissing monster with a critical eye. "She's holding up real nice, Mr Weir." The traveller went around with a pot of paint, marking pipework joints that still needed attention. "Just a few little jobs and I reckon we can mount the dynamo in a couple of days."

Five

S ome fifty creatures of the night paused in their business of staying alive and watched the spyder emerging
from the shallows of Pentworth Lake. It walked across the
artificial bathing beach on eight curiously articulated legs.
Emotions among the creatures varied from the speculative to
the apprehensive, depending on their assessment of the strange
creature's likelihood of eating them or vice versa. It was at
least twice the size of an alert dog fox who, having once
tangled with a small but ferociously determined cat, decided
that small rodents and chickens offered a less hazardous
diet. The fox slunk off into the shadows, which was as
well because the spyder had detected its presence in the
infra-red part of the spectrum and had a formidable array of
self-defence armaments to call on if needed.

The few people who had seen the spyder on its previous for-
ays, who included Mike Malone, had likened it to a mechanical
crab. The name "spyder" had been coined by the first person
to see it and the term had stuck. It was not an entirely
inaccurate name because the device was primarily intended
for surveillance, although its many secondary abilities were
phenomenal.

The previous March, a few hours after the Visitors' arrival, it
had gone to Vikki Taylor, asleep in her bedroom, and examined
the stump where the teenage girl had had an accident as a child
that had resulted in the loss of her left hand. The spyder had
even studied the artificial hand on the girl's dressing table,
sending back information to its makers deep in Pentworth
Lake. They had divined the purpose of the prosthetic hand and
instructed the spyder to identify, isolate, and trigger the stem
cells that had determined the growth of Vikki's hands when

she was in her mother's womb. The operation was carried out while Vikki slept. The result was that Vikki had, to her dismay, grown a new and perfect left hand within the space of a few hours. The spyder's makers could not have foreseen the problems that the new hand would cause Vikki, ending up with her being branded as a witch and condemned to death.

The spyder needed less than a second to check its systems to ensure that none had been impaired by water penetration during its ascent from the depths of the lake. Its back opened like a clamshell and contra-rotating rotors were extended and unfolded. The rotors started spinning, rapidly winding up to full speed and raising a cloud of swirling sand. The whine of its motors deepened as the rotors bit on the humid night and the extraordinary machine lifted vertically to a height of 500 metres.

Hovering cost energy. Without pause, the spyder set off southward. The direction was unimportant because instead of watching humans, this time it was going to examine the thirty-kilometre circumference of the Wall where it reached the ground. The spyder's makers disliked using their machine's flight capabilities because displacing air to keep it airborne meant that it made a certain amount of noise. It was unavoid-able. Like all intelligent creatures throughout the universe, they were bound by universal laws of physics; they had great ingenuity but they could not work miracles. Their machine's eight crab-like legs meant that it was admirably equipped to move over the roughest terrain but that would have taken too long for tonight's mission and would have meant spreading the reconnoitre over several nights, increasing the chances of it being seen.

The spyder flew on in a straight line, its whining rotors thrashing the humid night air. After a few minutes, it detected the presence of the Wall where it sliced across a field. It banked hard left within a few metres of the Wall's invisible presence and began its counter-clockwise examination, storing a continuous stream of data in its memory for its controllers. No intervention was required on their part for this task. Their machine had been instructed; it was capable of acting on its own initiative and generally looking after itself.

It flew at a steady twenty knots to conserve the charge in its energy cells. Occasionally it passed over isolated farmhouses, and singled some out for closer attention by slowing down. Startled occupants emerged and stared up at the night sky, looking for the source of the strange whining sound, but saw nothing.

Six

A n hour later, Mike Malone, jogging his way home to his rented flat at Tillington after ten hours on duty, heard the spyder and knew what it was. He stopped and gazed up into the darkness in the direction of the unseen machine's progress.

He was dressed in the same Day-Glo-marked running kit that he had been wearing on the night in March when the Wall had appeared, although he had been unaware of the manifestation at the time. That was the night he had first encountered the spyder. He had been jogging home, as he was now.

He had good hearing, his pounding trainers had made little sound and he had heard the clatter of the spyder's legs on the metalled road. Thinking that it was an injured animal and a possible danger to motorists, he had allowed it to follow him to a point where the road was flanked by steep retaining walls and therefore the creature was less likely to escape. Whereupon he had wheeled around and sprinted. He had actually been within a whisker of hurling himself on the machine but, to his astonishment, it had suddenly sprouted helicopter-like rotors and shot straight up into the darkness.

The memory of that eventful night was stark in his mind as he stood scanning the sky.

So what are you up to tonight, my mechanical friend?

He resumed jogging. This time with a purpose. His strides shortened and his pace quickened as his powerful, well-trained leg muscles drove him up the hill. At the crest of the rise he stopped and unclipped his PMR radio. He knew that this was a good spot for simplex radio communication with the police station. He held the speaker-microphone to his lips, listened to ensure that the frequency wasn't in use, and identified himself to WPC Carol Sandiman.

31

"Anything I need to know about, Carol?"

"Four calls from TKs, Mr Malone. All the same thing. Members of the public reporting hearing an aircraft. I've assigned all reports to the same serial."

"It's the Visitors' spyder," Malone replied. "Mark the positions of the telephone kiosks on the map and let me know where they are."

A morris police patrol asked permission to break in and reported that they had heard a machine pass by overhead. They gave their location as the A283, Blackwoods Farm.

"Isn't that on the Wall's northern perimeter?" Malone wanted to know.

"Affirmative, sir. We're right by the Wall markers now. Whatever it was, it must've been nearly touching the Wall because it passed by above us. Quite low, too. We felt a downwash as it went by."

Carol Sandiman came back with the location of the public telephone boxes. The calls had been received from Lodsworth, Halfway Bridge, Seaford . . .

"All on the Wall's perimeter?" Malone questioned.

"Yes, sir. They make a neat circle on the map."

Malone thought fast. He considered turning out the Zodiac dinghy with its outboard motor in the hope of catching the spyder when it returned to Pentworth Lake. But what would be the point? Most likely they would be too late, and even if they were early, the chances were that the spyder could evade them easily.

"If there's a unit in the vicinity of the lake, tell them to keep a lookout. I think that's where our flying machine will return."

The policewoman acknowledged.

Malone resumed his homeward jog while turning over these latest events in his mind. The obvious conclusion was that the spyder was carrying out an inspection flight of the Wall. If so, why? Were they about to modify the confounded thing? So far it had been a benign presence – no one had come to any harm as a result of contact with the Wall. Nor had the spyder harmed anyone. Quite the contrary if anything when one considered what had happened to Vikki Taylor. Which brought Malone back to the perennial question of why had the Visitors come? What purpose was served by incarcerating some 6,000 people in a ten-kilometre diameter, impenetrable sphere, and moving that sphere back 40,000 years in time?

Among Bob Harding's many theories was that they were in some form of celestial zoo or that the rest of their universe had been destroyed and that the Visitors had arrived to save Pentworth. Malone prayed that the latter theory was incorrect. His two kids were Farside, living with his ex-wife. He missed them with an intensity that his friends and colleagues barely suspected. And when he wasn't thinking of them, his thoughts automatically returned to Ellen Duncan, and her fellow fugitives, Vikki Taylor and Claire Lake. But mostly he thought about Ellen Duncan and the time on a hot afternoon when he had carried her up the narrow stairs to her bedroom over her shop. That all three women had to remain in hiding to escape the religious fanaticism of Adrian Roscoe offended Mike Malone's sense of justice – he was a staunch believer in the rule of law, but even he was forced to accept that the only way to destroy the Bodian Brethren would be to cut off its head.

Seven

A t 2 p.m. the sun beating down in Market Square was at its hottest and the hundreds of documents that had been saturated by fire hoses, now spread out on trestle tables in front of Government House, were drying in a matter of minutes. The four-storey building was the former courthouse and one of the largest buildings in Pentworth town. It had been pressed into service as government offices shortly after the start of the emergency.

Diana Sheldon was busy, fretting over documents that needed pressing, chivvying her staff, making sure that they returned dried papers to their correct filing boxes, and generally driving herself each day to point of exhaustion by mid-afternoon.

But Diana was happy. Having been ousted from her job as Town Clerk by the ambitious Vanessa Grossman, she had been reinstated by Bob Harding immediately after the coup and was determined to fulfil her promise to him that she'd have Government House's administration back to normal within two weeks or less. Fortunately the damage caused by the fire at the onset of the coup was less than had first been feared.

A blackened rafter crashed down from the roof of Government House where carpenters were repairing the ravages of the fire. It narrowly missed a methane-powered steam generator that was recharging the bank of batteries in the basement of Government House that provided the building with an electricity supply. The charred timber raised a cloud of charcoal dust that settled on her precious documents.

"You're supposed to use the chute!" she yelled up at the foreman.

"Too big!" he replied, and another burnt timber crashed on

34

to the ancient flagstones. More black dust was kicked up as charcoal burners tossed it on to a horse-drawn wagon. Nothing was wasted in Pentworth.

Market traders hurriedly covered their displays of unrationed salad vegetables and soft fruits. It was mid-summer – high-carbohydrate foods were relatively scarce although the signs were that all the main crops would be early. A bonus of Pentworth's isolation and the greenhouse effect of the Wall was that the community now enjoyed a humid Mediterranean climate that stimulated rapid growth.

Diana considered that many of her small army of girl clerks were inadequately dressed – distracting the repair workmen – but the girls worked hard, so she held her peace. They were certainly more useful than the men in her charge.

She spotted Dennis Davies, the chief librarian, struggling ineffectually to unlock a heat-scorched steel filing cabinet. She homed in on him.

"Having problems, Mr Davies?"

The librarian smiled sheepishly. He was a confirmed bachelor, with a soft spot for the greying Town Clerk that went back many years before Diana had gone grey. For some weeks he had been nerving himself to invite her to have a drink or a meal with him. It was all a matter of choosing the right time. Probably when she had gone white.

"The heat appears to have damaged the lock on this cabinet, Miss Sheldon," said Dennis.

Diana seized a crowbar from a toolbox and jemmied the filing cabinet's top drawer open in about five seconds. She opened a folder at random and riffled through the documents, testing them between her thumb and forefinger. "All bone dry," she declared, slamming the drawer shut. "What's the situation on the second floor?"

"All the books are OK, except about a hundred volumes in the paperback romances section got soaked beyond repair, but I don't consider that a great loss."

Diana smiled. After the Wall had appeared, one of the first actions of the Emergency Council had been to require everyone to donate their books to the newly established library which would become the repository of all the community's

35

knowledge in case the Wall remained in place for many years, which Bob Harding had considered a possibility. As a result Dennis had became custodian of over a million books and magazines. Most of the clerks now sorting out documents in Market Square were girls who had been hired to write out the index cards.

"I would've thought you'd regard the loss of any book as a misfortune, Mr Davies."

"I'm sure they'll be replaced," said Dennis. "There are so many duplicates among the romances. Books, videos and DVDs are still coming in from the refuse sorting depot. I was wondering if you'd ask Radio Pentworth to make an announcement asking people to stop putting them out with their rubbish until we get things back to normal."

"Ask them yourself, Mr Davies. As Chief Librarian, you don't need my authority. You know that their studio is now located in the Doll's House Museum for the time being?"

"Yes, indeed."

"A big mistake housing the radio station in Government House. It compromised its independence."

"Yes, indeed. A painfully learned lesson, if I may say so." He hesitated. "Do you have any idea now when we'll get back to normal, Miss Sheldon? Only, the indexing is badly behind."

Diana glanced up at Government House and the smoke stains above the top-floor windows of what had been Asquith Prescott's prestigious office. "Sorry, Mr Davies, but I'm going to need your clerks for a few more days salvaging and refiling this lot. As it is, we seem to have lost about ten per cent of all our admin records – more due to water damage than fire damage. Who would've thought our two fire engines could dump so much water on a blaze, and so quickly, too?"

"Miss Sheldon?"

Diana turned to the girl who had approached them. "Yes, Mary?"

The girl held out a sheet of paper covered in coloured bars and blobs. "A test print from the colour laser, Miss Sheldon. It seems to be working OK. In fact the complete Mac system is all OK. It's just that the monitor case is a bit melted but it's working."

Diana was pleased. That Pentworth Council could still print the promissory notes that were now used as money within the community was one worry less.

Eight

D r Millicent Vaughan was an iron-willed, greying lady who had been the senior doctor in Pentworth's largest group practice. The Emergency Council which had been established after the Wall appeared had tasked her with the setting up of a small hospital which she carried out with her usual brisk, no-nonsense efficiency that bordered on the ruthless.

Much as she respected Bob Harding, she didn't spare him from her wrath when he paid his first visit to the disused church that had been scrubbed whistle clean from crypt to roof and redecorated before she had deemed it acceptable as a hospital.

"You've got to get Ellen Duncan back working in her shop," she raged at the retired scientist, having cornered him in her office. "She's Pentworth's best herbalist – correction – our only herbalist, and we desperately need her back in production. The dispensary is running dangerously low on supplies."

"I'm sorry, Millicent, but Mr Malone is concerned for her safety."

"Because you granted that madman, Roscoe, an amnesty! Malone arrested him and you let him go!"

"It was that or a civil war, Millicent," said Harding quietly.

"It was a surrender!" Millicent snapped. "Pure and simple. You give an inch to loonies like him, and they take a mile."

"And his supporters would've taken lives," Harding countered. "At least we've disarmed them. It's given us time. As you know, Roscoe controls some ninety per cent of our methane supplies. We couldn't afford to disrupt that. Look, Milly – if you're unhappy with me as Chairman—"

"I didn't say that."

"You can always refuse to ratify me as Chairman at the

38

next full Council meeting. To be blunt, Milly, I don't want the bloody job. And if a majority don't want me either, then I'll be more than happy to stand down and let David Weir take over. And let us not forget that you discharged Roscoe and his sidekick yesterday."

"I didn't discharge them, I threw them out. Roscoe started preaching his avenging God rubbish to patients and staff, and that animal, Nelson Faraday, had two of those Bodian girls visit him. Bringing him gropes rather than grapes."

Bob Harding couldn't resist a smile at that.

"It's not funny! My staff nurse caught them. *Two* girls dressed up as schoolgirls. I don't give a damn what they get up to in Pentworth House – no worse than when Turner used to stay there, I daresay – but I won't have such things in my hospital. You're going to have to dissolve that absurd sect; get the girls out and married off. Three deaths and only one birth in the last ten days. We need an intensive campaign on the radio to get more babies on the way. We'll all die out if the Wall stays for several years."

Pentworth's birth rate, or lack of it, was fast becoming Millicent Vaughan's principle theme. Harding considered that he had enough issues to deal with without getting embroiled in that sensitive problem. He changed the subject. "I've actually come to see Asquith. How's he been?"

"No trouble. His burns are healing well. He's a much-mollified man since the coup. More like the old Prescott. Still a prick, but no longer an egotistic prick. I'll get someone to show you up."

A ward orderly showed Harding into Prescott's room. The landowner was listening to Radio Pentworth on headphones which he tried to pull off with heavily bandaged hands.

"So how's things, Asquith?" asked Harding, helping disentangle the patient's hands and arms from the headphones.

Prescott managed his usual ebullient smile despite the dressings around his face and head. He bore no ill will towards the man who had succeeded him. "Apparently my hair has started growing back. I won't be permanently bald as I had feared."

"Is that all you've been worrying about?"

"It's all I've preferred to worry about," Prescott replied with some feeling. He nodded to his hands. "All clearing up, but I'll be a marked man for life."

"You rolled Vanessa Grossman up in a carpet. That was a brave thing to do."

Prescott's florid features twisted into a scowl. "I should've let the scheming bitch die. She deceived me, Bob. They all did."

That's right, blame everyone else but yourself, thought Harding. "Including Roscoe?"

"Particularly Roscoe. He tricked me into signing those warrants for the arrest of Ellen Duncan and the Vikki Taylor girl."

Harding knew that that was an over-simplification of what had happened but he hadn't come to see Prescott to start another argument. He came straight to the point. "Do you have any influence over Adrian Roscoe?"

Prescott laughed and winced in pain. "None. Never have had. The only way to exert any influence over him is to tap into the direct line he thinks he has to God."

"As you know, the reason I granted you all an amnesty is that I saw it as a way of averting a civil war. Also Roscoe controls Pentworth's main supply of methane from his piggerys' digestors. I felt that I couldn't afford to put that supply at risk. In your case, I decided on an amnesty because you did a lot of good in the aftermath of the Wall's appearance. The emergency measures you pushed through were necessary. The anti-pollution directives; setting up the morris police force. I'm not sure about Vanessa Grossman, but in Adrian Roscoe's case, I now believe that the amnesty was a mistake."

"There is something that would influence Roscoe," said Prescott. "One thing only."

"What's that?"

"A bullet between the eyes."

Nine

Ten years earlier, Roger Dayton's reaction to an enforced early retirement as director of a major yacht chandlery business in Chichester had been to fulfil a life-long ambition by renting out his house and paddock for two years and sailing around the world with his wife and cat. His fifteen-metre deep-keel yacht didn't do any sailing now but sat on blocks in his paddock, its winter home that now looked permanent.

"Go easy, you idiot!" he snapped at the elderly man who was scouring a rust patch on the hull with a wire brush. "You use just enough pressure to clean the rust away, not wear a hole through the hull."

Typical ex-officer know-all, thought Lennie Hunter. But he held his peace. He enjoyed his Saturday job working on the yacht. Better than his boring weekday job working in the supplies depot. Directed labour, just as he was getting used to his retirement. For one thing he was outdoors here. For another the Dutch steel-hull yacht was a fine craft – well worth putting up with Roger Dayton's bellicose moods for the extra pay, now that his pension had been slashed. "I think we're going to need the scaling hammer on this patch, Mr Dayton. I reckon it goes right under the paintwork."

"Rubbish, man. She's rock solid." Dayton seized a hammer and rapped it sharply on the hull. There should've been a ringing sound, but the blow resulted in a dull thud. He struck the hull harder and a large flake of paint fell away, exposing more corrosion. "Dammit," he muttered. It didn't occur to him to apologise to an employee, which was why his fellow directors had pushed him into early retirement. "What in hell caused that? She had new sacrificial anodes last year."

"Could be a hundred and one things, Mr Dayton. A blowhole

41

in the steel plate, a welding seam with a weak spot that's gone acidic. Happens to the best Dutch hulls. Some self-etching primer and filler and she'll be fine."

"I haven't got any primer, you idiot!"

"Good afternoon, Mr Dayton."

The yachtsman spun around. Bob Harding was standing near the yacht's bow.

"Your wife said you were here," Harding explained. He held out a package wrapped in dried grass and fastened with raffia. Dried grass was now Pentworth's primary packaging material for anything fragile. "Your echo-sounder, Mr Dayton. Returned with thanks. It's a fine instrument."

Dayton grunted his thanks and took the package. "As you're now Chairman, I would've thought you'd be far too busy to go running around on trifling errands."

"I promised you to look after your echo-sounder, therefore I considered it my responsibility to see that it was looked after and returned to you. Would it be possible to borrow it again, please?"

Dayton shrugged and offered the instrument back to Harding. "In that case, you might as well hang on to it."

"That's extremely kind of you, Mr Dayton," said Harding gratefully, taking the echo-sounder back.

"Well at least you haven't seen fit to commandeer it. Not like that DS Malone who took my distress rockets."

"Mr Malone was enforcing an order requiring all explosives and firearms to be handed in," said Harding mildly. He had had this argument before with the belligerent yachts-man.

"I wasn't told they'd be used for a bloody *coup d'état*!"

"Nor was I," Harding replied gravely. "Strange, that. But apart from the death of Mr Harvey Evans, which was a terrible accident, it wasn't bloody."

Dayton pointed at six ponies grazing at the far end of the paddock. "And what about those?"

"They're ponies."

"I know that! I didn't mind three grazing my paddock so much, but there's now six of them!"

"I'm sorry, Mr Dayton. We're short of grazing. Every scrap

of land has to be pressed into service, as I'm sure you're aware."

"My paddock is not a scrap of land, dammit. But *six* of the damned things! They scratch themselves on my yacht!"

"Using the sharp end, presumably? They obviously recognise quality."

"This place is turning into a police state."

"Better than a policeless state," Harding observed. He added, confident that Dayton hardly listened to anything that was said to him, "Well – I mustn't let you take up any more of my valuable time. Thank you for the echo-sounder. I'll take great care of it."

"Did you find anything?" Dayton demanded as Harding turned to leave.

"Did I find anything where?"

"In the lake. With my echo-sounder!"

"I'm writing a report now. It'll be on the news in the next day or so." Not wishing to annoy Dayton more than he already had, Harding added, "Actually, we did find something. The lake silt's settled now. We certainly detected some sort of anomaly which may or may not be the Silent Vulcan. We couldn't have done that without your echo-sounder."

"So what are you going to do about it?"

Harding looked blank. "What would you have me do about it?"

"Well I don't know! You're the new big white chief, for God's sake!"

"Yes – but I hardly think—"

Dayton took Harding by the arm, led him a few paces away from his yacht, and pointed at it. "What do you see, Mr Harding?"

"A boat. It's hard to miss."

Dayton hated his beloved yacht being called a boat but he let it pass. "A dream, Mr Harding," he said with unexpected passion. "Sailing around the world with my wife was only half of that dream. The other half is to take part in the round-the-world single-hander. Not to win, but to take part, you understand . . ." Dayton paused, staring at his yacht. "It's all I've ever wanted to do . . . It's next year. That's why I bought her here. So I could fit her out as I wanted her fitted out rather than entrust her to a bunch of clueless marina fuckwits. If I miss next year's race, there won't be another for five years, and by that time they'll probably say I'm too old. In fact, I know they will . . . Taking part in that race is something I've dreamed about all my professional life, Mr Harding. I want nothing else. I will settle for nothing less."

Harding nodded sympathetically as he turned to leave. "I understand, Mr Dayton. I really do."

"How deep was your mystery object?"

"One hundred and twenty metres," Harding replied. "Surprising how deep Pentworth Lake is." He was about to add that it was deep enough for Dayton to sail his boat on, but decided that that would've been unnecessarily cruel.

It is doubtful if the dour yachtsman would have heard the comment if he had uttered it. Harding watched Dayton's stooping figure cross the paddock towards the house. His mind racing as it formed an outrageous plan, Dayton gave Lennie Hunter a curt order to carry on and went in. His wife was working in the kitchen. She called out but he ignored her. She, too, had been looking forward to him taking part in the single-handed round-the-world yacht race.

A few minutes rummaging in his workshop and Dayton found what he was looking for: an empty aluminium firkin – the beer keg was a leftover from his sixty-fifth birthday party that would have been returned to the caterers were it not for the Wall.

He heaved the heavy keg on to his workbench and stood back to study it critically. Originally it had held forty-one litres of beer. He opened the tap and released a dribble of stale lager. He tested its weight again. My God – it was heavy for aluminium. Obviously it had a substantial wall thickness, designed to withstand a lot of rough handling. His surmise was proved correct when he unscrewed the bung and checked the keg's wall thickness between his thumb and forefinger. At least eight millimetres as near as he could judge. His heartbeat quickened. There seemed little doubt that it would be ideal for the crazy plan that was taking shape in his mind. As a former naval gunnery officer he had had some experience of the simplest and crudest armament that most of the world's navies possessed.

Depth charges.

But Dayton was thinking about the possibility of one depth charge.

One with its hydrostatic fuse set to detonate at a depth of 120 metres.

Ten

D espite her age, Sister Mary Thomas Selby was remarkably adaptable. Half a litre of water, no more and no less, was just right for her morning cup of tea even if were home-dried nettle tea, and even if it did mean having to wait until 11 a.m. when the sun was high enough to boil the careful measure of water in her kettle without a long wait. Her eyesight was good, so she had no trouble using a long hazel staff to hook the kettle on to the arm in the centre of her four-metre diameter solar dish. A painful twinge in her hands due to her arthritis. Of course, at her age she was entitled to one of the charcoal burners but she had found working the air pump plunger difficult, and having to fiddle about with charcoal granules was a messy business. After all, the radio was always going on about the need to strictly limit all fires – something about having to keep carbon locked up in trees and only releasing it in controlled quantities. Everyone seemed to be coping with the solar dishes that were popping up everywhere like grotesque silvery flowers, and so could she.

Selby Engineering was stencilled on the dish in large letters. Tony Selby was her nephew. She was proud of him. As a child he had been just like his father – her brother – always making things. He had taken over his father's engineering business at the age of twenty-three and had invested heavily in new machine tools. With new shapers, capstans, lathes, mills, stamping presses, injection moulding equipment and a wide variety of other tools, Selby Engineering and its one hundred employees had been able to tackle any business that came their way. Immediately following the Wall crisis they had doubled their staff and turned out these solar cooker dishes by the score – from which they had acquired skills in papier-mâché moulding. They had followed this with solar water-heating panels, methane lamps, and charcoal cookers – all well-designed and built to last, and with good spares support because Pentworth could not afford to waste materials or labour on planned obsolescence. They had even designed and built a pair of steam-driven twenty-kilowatt methane-powered generators to supply their plant's power needs. She knew from her nephew's increasingly rare visits now that his dependence on Adrian Roscoe to keep his factory going rankled considerably.

She sat at her garden table to wait for the kettle to boil, enjoying the warmth of the sun. Looking up at the huge, silvery dish on its lattice framework mounting of lashed chestnut saplings took her mind off the strange and abrupt change of scenery not ten metres from where she was sitting. The dish was such a clever device. In her teaching days she had often used papier mâché in her craft classes at St Catherine's to make the heads of glove puppets, but she had never imagined that her talented nephew could use it to make such an extraordinary range of items. Even her shiny new telephone, installed last week, was made of moulded and lacquered pâpier maché.

Himmler, the Taylors' Siamese cat, rubbed around her legs. He wasn't so much a cat as an ever-empty, ever-hopeful stomach on legs, and had the retired nun down as sucker No. 4 on his morning breakfast round, for it is a truth, universally acknowledged, that a hungry cat of good breeding must be in want of a breakfast. Or, in Himmler's case, several breakfasts.

She reached down and rubbed his head. Himmler responded with his standard emotional blackmail tactics of endearing loud purrs and sticking his tail up when stroked to ensure that Sister Mary's hand didn't fall off the end of his back.

"Still no sign of your Vikki then, Himmler?"

His many years' experience as a skilled scrounger had taught Himmler that old ladies talking to him was a sure sign of victory. Breakfast No. 4 was a few affectionate head butts and a couple of pitiful meows away.

Sister Mary missed Vikki. Such a sweet girl. Always cheerful despite that awful handicap of her left hand, always happy to run little errands such as on Saturdays when she had only to phone Ellen Duncan's herbal shop and Vikki would drop by with the order on her way home. At least those misguided Bodian Brethren sentinels had stopped coming around now, pestering her, poking about in her outhouses – looking for Claire Lake, they said, because they were worried about her.

Sister Mary prayed that the rumours that Vikki was safe were true.

A movement caught her eye. She turned her head and stared at the Farside sabre-toothed cat padding stiffly and silently across what appeared to be the end of her lawn. The fur around its jaws was matted with blood and feathers. It stopped and wiped its fearsome fangs on the desiccated sedge grass, twisting its head from side to side and using its paws to help with the clean-up, its movements almost identical to those made by Himmler after a cadged breakfast. The creature was thin, badly emaciated, its ribs showing through its lustreless fur. She doubted if a bird would provide it with enough sustenance. It paused and raised its head. The nun shivered. The baleful yellow eyes, the pupils reduced to slits in the bright sunlight, seemed to be staring straight at her.

Himmler saw the big cat. He made a strange noise in his throat and decided that he had pressing business on the roof of the cottage. From the safety of the chimney stack, he subjected his distant cousin to death from a thousand glares, and puny growls interspersed with bouts of furious chest-washing that jingled the silver bell on his collar.

Unlike Himmler, Sister Mary had seen the female big cat on several occasions. After her first fright, she had always felt some empathy towards it. Like her, it was old and stiff. But this was the first time it had stopped so near the Wall that sliced through her property. For several seconds the two stared at each other across the awesome gulf of 40,000 years. She wasn't afraid. Living so close to the Wall had given her confidence in its strange powers but she couldn't help a stir of apprehension as the malevolent eyes seemed to bore into her. She wondered if the cat could see into her world as clearly as she could see into its world. Well – there was one way to find out. Pulling herself out of the garden chair required a little effort. She grabbed the hazel staff and advanced on the sabre-toothed cat like a medieval pikeman. The tip touched the Wall and caused that strange blackening at the point of contact. The resistance and the size of the black patch increased as she pushed harder. It was like poking a pillow. Jabbing caused the black patch to flash, which the big cat would be certain to see. But it resumed its unconcerned washing and even ignored her kettle which had started whistling.

During a talk on the radio Bob Harding had speculated about the possibility of interaction between the present-day world of Pentworth and the bizarre world of Farside and its wind-desiccated steppes and stunted trees of prehistoric northern Europe. She wondered if she should tell him about this, but it was negative information and Bob Harding was now Chairman of the Council; he would be far too busy these· days. The sabre-tooth got bored with washing and stalked off, disappearing down a steep rise in the undulating landscape.

Himmler came down from the roof, pleased with himself for having vanquished a fearsome foe, and resumed his demands for a fourth breakfast.

The crunch of wagon wheels in the lane intruded on Sister Mary's thoughts. She unhitched her boiling kettle, and grabbed a carrier bag containing her empty milk bottle and her portable radio. She went around the side of the cottage to greet her visitor. The twice-weekly visits of the morris man refuse collector was always a welcome event although conventional household refuse was now a thing of the past. Her radio had said before its batteries died that this week all light bulbs were to be rounded up.

"Good morning, Mr Norris," said Sister Mary, making a fuss of the new arrival's pony.

"Morning, Sister," said Russell Norris, jumping down from his cart. He touched his broad-brimmed morris straw hat, and opened his post chest. A big man. Two metres of muscle and good humour. This wasn't his normal duty but Malone had assigned him to warn off Adrian Roscoe's search parties that had been concentrating on this area.

The morris men visited every one of Pentworth's 1,800 or so households at least twice a week. In the months since the

Wall had appeared, they had evolved into postmen, refuse collectors, pollution inspectors, bread and milk delivery men, and now policemen – all rolled into one. Most important of all, they were government representatives – a valuable point of contact between the people and the governing council which acted as a rapid conduit for grievances and ensured they were addressed quickly. They were strict enforcers of government policy and had the power to exact fines for all breaches of the emergency regulations, such as lighting bonfires without a permit, although such powers were rarely needed now.

"And another fine morning it is too," Russell continued cheerfully. "Just two letters and they look like bills."

She took the folded sheets – envelopes were rarely used now – and broke the seals. "Bills," she said ruefully, thrusting them into her apron pocket. "No refuse, Mr Norris. But I've found some more books."

"Hang on to them until next week, Sister. It's still a bit chaotic at the library."

"How are things in town?"

"Getting back to normal," said Russell, taking Sister Mary's empty milk bottle and her radio. "The Pentworth House bakery is back in business. And methane supplies from Pentworth House are back to normal. Some sort of deal Mr Harding did with Father Roscoe. I'll be back on normal policing duties tomorrow."

"Ridiculous doing any sort of deal with those cultist loonies. They should've all been arrested."

The morris man wasn't going to be drawn into discussing government policy. "Have their search parties been around recently?"

"No. I think that sign has put them off." The nun indicated a notice that had been fixed to the side of her cottage: "TELEPHONE AVAILABLE HERE FOR EMERGENCIES".

Russell replaced the batteries in the radio and tossed the discharged cells in a collection bag. Pentworth's precious stock of dry batteries were looked after by a special government depot. He opened the food pannier and took out a full bottle of milk and half a loaf of bread. "Will this do you until Friday?"

"Oh, lovely." Sister Mary put the milk, bread and her radio in her carrier, and dug in her pocket for a ten euro promissory note. "I saw my sabre-toothed tiger again just now."

"Have you been leaving saucers of milk out for it?"

Sister Mary laughed. Russell Norris declined her invitation to have a cup of tea. He was behind schedule. Before driving off he promised that his replacement would move her solar dish to a more optimum position now that the days were getting shorter.

Sister Mary returned to her cottage. Her memory failed her for a moment when she looked around her kitchen for her kettle. Of course – it was on the garden table and would have to be brought back to the boil. Such a fine morning, why not have tea outside? And why not the Indian Tree china? A little treat wouldn't go amiss. That meant going into the front room where she kept her china cabinet. She hesitated at the door. It wasn't that she was frightened of the Wall – not after all these months – rather that seeing the vista of the distant windswept steppes instead of the fireplace and bookcase where the Wall had sliced through a third of the little room reminded her of what she had lost: the missal given to her by her father when she had taken her first communion; family photographs from three quarters of a century ago that helped guard against the cruel memory thief of old age. Oh well . . .

She opened the door and froze. She stood rooted on the threshold, clutching the doorknob for support. Her first rational thought to emerge from her sudden whirl of confusion was that her eyes were playing tricks. But she was blessed with good eyesight. Maybe her mind was failing? And she knew that that couldn't be the case because it was all so real. The room was intact, no missing corner. Her crammed bookcase, her ornaments, the much-missed, precious photographs, the clock on the mantlepiece that had belonged to her grandmother – all were where they had been last March before the Wall had materialised and taken them from her.

Telling herself that maybe she had dozed off and was dreaming, she shuffled to the mantlepiece and reached out trembling fingers, fearful that her sense of touch would contradict what her eyes were telling her. The clock's hard, ebony case felt as it had always felt when she used to wind it each week. She noticed that there was dust on the mantlepiece – something she would never normally allow.

But this isn't normal!

Yet it was. Everything was. Even the pain in her hand as she picked up the worn key and held it at a slight angle to prevent it slipping as she wound the clock. It started chiming immediately as if to make up for the lost hours. She spent the next few minutes in a daze as she explored her long-lost mementoes before realising that she couldn't keep this astounding news to herself.

The pain in her finger joints was hardly noticeable as she turned the little crank handle on the telephone in the hall.

Pentworth's manual telephone exchange was in the basement of Pentworth Museum. Carol Hopkins saw the exciter lamp flash for Sister Mary Thomas's number and answered the call immediately. Because of her age and the fact that she lived alone, Sister Mary had been supplied with the first of the new telephones intended for private use now that all essential services and government offices had been connected.

"Good morning, Sister Mary," said Carol brightly. "Is everything OK?"

"Is that Carol?"

"It certainly is. Who do you want to speak to, Sister?"

"Well . . . I'm not sure."

Carol was alarmed. The elderly nun sounded ill. "Do you need a doctor?"

"No . . . I'm fine . . . Or am I?"

"I'll put you straight through to the hospital."

"No. No – I'm OK. Really," Sister Mary insisted, her voice suddenly regaining its strength. "I think I need someone in Government House. Carol – you won't believe this, but the Wall has gone."

Eleven

Pentworth's entire police committee consisted of Bob Harding, David Weir, and Mike Malone, with Diana Sheldon taking the minutes. A protracted hammering session by carpenters led to them abandoning their room in Government House in favour of the more agreeable atmosphere of an outdoor committee room in the form of a table under a parasol outside the Crown. It was 10.30 a.m. and Market Square was in full bustle. A pub lacks the formality of a committee room, so the members reverted to first names. A waiter brought their drinks, which David paid for, being voted the bloated plutocrat landowner.

"I didn't think you drank on duty, Mike," said Diana reprovingly.

Malone looked indignant. "I have a strict rule to always drink less on duty."

"Having made him Chief of Police," said David Weir, "I daresay we can allow him one small abuse of power."

Malone grinned. He admired David Weir despite an occasional pang of jealousy because of the young farmer's relationship with Ellen Duncan. It was, Ellen had once told Malone, a very on-off relationship.

"Quite remarkable," said Bob Harding reading some reports that Malone had supplied. "Last month's crime figures down sixty per cent over the same period last year before the Wall."

"And some crimes, such as public order offences, now virtually non-existent," said Malone, downing most of his drink in one swallow. He was becoming addicted to the locally brewed malt. He noticed two people enter the square from the direction of Pentworth House. There was nothing unusual about them other than that they were eating hamburgers. Meat and bread were strictly rationed.

"Having nearly two hundred and fifty police officers on the payroll probably has something to do with that," Diana commented.

Malone smiled. "Don't forget, Diana, that many of them are also postmen, countryside wardens, social workers, food inspectors, agricultural hygiene inspectors etcetera. I never did like the old system of over-specialisation and job specifications. Those that the community pays to be up and about in the community should also have wider responsibilities to the community. It makes for efficient use of our limited manpower, and it provides people with more interesting and rewarding jobs. *And* we have full employment."

The four were silent for a few moments. Malone watched another couple cross the square, also eating hamburgers. A passer-by spoke to them. One of the hamburger eaters pointed in the direction of Pentworth House.

"Nearly all our pre-Wall social problems stemmed from one thing," Malone continued. "The reluctance of society to employ people and to spend money on its own infrastructure. We sacked thousands of customs officers, police officers, tax inspectors, immigration officers. The British set out to destroy their bureaucracy because they believed that it was a Bad Thing. They forgot that a bureaucracy is society's means of getting through a great deal of routine business in an expedient manner. Worse, the process involved the wholesale dumping of an entire stratum of experienced middle-management. Men and women with the skills to see trouble looming and deal with problems before they became serious. Capable people shunted into early retirement, or driven to it because their supporting bureaucracy had been taken away from them and their workloads became intolerable; people whose only sin was to climb a little too high up the salary ladder. As a result all manner of services started spinning out of control. Health, education, the police, public transport. And even big business suffered and hitherto well-run major corporations suddenly found themselves running up debts they couldn't control and worse, didn't have the management skills to control."

"Marconi," Harding commented.

"To name one major mess," said Malone. "The joke is that little money was saved in the long run because large numbers were sucked into the new slamming-stable-door industries of regulation and inquiry. At the same time, fraudsters and con merchants had a field day because the Treasury pressurised police forces into disbanding fraud squads."

Harding tossed a report on the table. "I sometimes think Mike relishes the mess we're in because it gives him a chance to practise his brand of social engineering.

"I question that we are in mess," Malone replied. "Despite having to use horse-drawn vehicles for half the transport fleet, we actually have a better public transport system now than we had before the Wall. All villages have a twice-daily service to and from Pentworth. It may be slow, but it's reliable. Pentworth now has its own hospital, two children's clinics, and more than enough doctors and nurses because we've winkled them out of retirement. Street crime is now virtually non-existent, and no motor traffic other than the odd methane-powered bus now and then means that Pentworth town centre is actually a pleasant place to sit in the sun, drinking, and talking to friends."

"The CO_2 levels are stable," Harding commented, who rarely suffered from asthma attacks these days.

"We must be the first society to introduce draconian measures to protect our atmosphere," said Diana.

"The operative word is 'our'," said David. "We perceive it as our atmosphere because the effect on oneself and neighbours of anyone lighting a bonfire is immediate – they choke."

Malone observed, "According to Radio Pentworth's poll, clean air and organically grown food are major reasons why fifteen per cent of the population like the new life and hope the Wall remains."

"How much attention should we pay to an unstructured survey?" David asked.

"Quite a lot," said Harding. "My Suzi is very pro-Wall."

"You will marry a teenage rebel," said David, grinning. "Wasn't she arrested during some anti-globalisation demos last year?"

"My wife is *not* a teenager," said Harding sternly. "The rebel I don't deny."

"It's not only Suzi's age group who are pro-Wall," said Malone. "There's a sizeable percentage of older people who like the simplicity and the community spirit of the new life. I suspect that Diana is one."

They all looked speculatively at the Town Clerk.

Diana refused to be drawn. "We're still on Item Six on the agenda," she reminded them. "Are you agreed that the new police manning levels should be recommended to the full Council?"

"Blame the Chairman for waffling," said David.

Harding was aggrieved. "I never waffle. Mike does enough for all of us." He turned to David Weir. "So how's the work going on that showman's engine?"

Malone groaned. "Now you've started him off."

A youth clutching a hamburger sat at a nearby table and started eating.

"Where did he get that?" Diana Sheldon wondered.

Before Malone could reply there was a distant howl of feedback from a public address system followed by the unmistakable rich tones of Adrian Roscoe's voice booming across the town.

"Testing . . . Testing . . . One . . . Two . . . Three . . ."

Harding looked startled. "Now what's that idiot doing?"

"Three guesses," Malone answered, his face grim as he rose. He signalled to two nearby morris police, reached for his PMR radio and changed his mind. "Do something for me, Diana. Phone the nick and tell them from me: 'Wildfire. Papa Hotel'. They'll know exactly what to do. Got that?"

She repeated the message.

"What are you going to do?" asked Harding.

"Arrest Adrian Roscoe," Malone replied.

Twelve

M alone strode quickly towards Pentworth House with David Weir and Bob Harding, and the two morris police officers in tow. They picked up two more police officers on the way, their iron-tipped staffs ringing on the road. An assortment of housewives with prams and pushchairs, shop assistants and children sensed trouble and brought up the rear.

"My beloved people of Pentworth!" said Roscoe's amplified voice. "Children of God! Your needless suffering is continuing on the say-so of a Satan-inspired minority who persist in harbouring abominations in our midst! The Wall is the Word of our everlasting God made real! It is His retribution for our sins and it will continue so long as we continue to thwart His divine will by allowing abominations in our midst to live!"

Malone held back from entering the high gateway of Pentworth House. He could see all he wanted to see through the open gates and he had no intention of being out-decibelled in a verbal contest with Adrian Roscoe.

The scene in the courtyard in front of the mansion was exactly as the police officer had expected. The big mobile canteen that Roscoe used to employ in the days when he visited London and south coast towns to round up homeless recruits to his Bodian Brethren sect was parked in the centre of the courtyard. Two assistants, who had been serving hamburgers to an eager queue, had closed their counter temporarily while their master was speaking, and the shroud that kept direct light off the vehicle's rear-projection video screen was folding down into the closed position, much to the disappointment of some television-starved children who had been watching a Tom and Jerry cartoon. The combination of free movies and hamburgers had had the desired effect: Adrian Roscoe had a sizeable audience.

Looking like an underfed biblical father figure in his spotless white gown, he was standing on top of the vehicle, steadying himself against a huge speaker, as he began addressing his gathering of about 200. Some of them were shaven-headed heavies – private security men that Roscoe had hired to cover a party he had thrown in Pentworth House on the night that the Wall had appeared. Their continuing allegiance to Roscoe and their acceptance of Nelson Faraday as their boss owed more to their passion for the Bodian Brethren's plentiful supply of girl sentinels rather than any interest in Adrian Roscoe's message.

Their master was wearing a headset radio-microphone which left his bandaged hands free for the sweeping gestures that were an important part of what was a skilled act. The combination of Adrian Roscoe's ice-chip, unblinking blue eyes, whose gaze seemed to alight on everyone in turn, his resonant voice, repetitive rhetoric, half-truths and whole lies, and theatrical body language made for a compelling performance, but it was his voice alone that commanded attention and carried authority.

"Ask yourself this! Why should you be made to suffer for the sins of others? Why should you be made to endure separation from loved ones and from the rest of the world? Why should you suffer the deprivation and hardship of a world without gas, electricity, or television? Why should you have to suffer the indignities of food rationing? Of your children going hungry? Of forced labour? Of having to live your lives burdened with heartless laws, forever looking over your shoulder because you're being forced to live in what has become a police state. Why? I'll you why, my friends. Because the fat cats who've taken over Pentworth Council care nothing for your suffering so long as they can go on forcing you, the people, the children of God, to be their tools while they continue to profane His Word by harbouring abominations!"

"He never blinks," said Harding. "Quite remarkable."

Malone made no reply but noted with some disquiet that at least thirty members of the public in addition to Roscoe's

58

sentinels contributed to the roar of approval that greeting his words each time he paused. There were a few catcalls and whistles but the dissenters were in a minority.

"What are you planning to do?" David asked. "Just walk up and arrest him? If so, mind if I watch?"

"Well I don't plan to get into an argument with a man with a microphone. Not yet."

A convoy of four white Commer vans converged on Pentworth House and stopped short of the gates in response to Malone's signal. The high wall around the mansion hid the vehicles from the crowd in the courtyard. The rear doors were thrown open and some fifty morris police in riot gear piled out. Their equipment consisted of a mixture of makeshift shields, motorcycle crash helmets, cricket faceguards, batons and staffs. But they were all big, determined-looking men, hardened by working the fields. Malone was pleased to see that four of them were dressed in the leather jackets and jeans favoured by Roscoe's security heavies. His contingency plans were being followed to the letter.

"In fighting these apostles of hell, I, like all of us, have paid a price!" Roscoe's voice boomed from the speaker cabinet. He held his arms aloft in a gesture of supplication to reveal that his arms were bandaged to the elbows. "Like you, my friends, I too have suffered. This is what they did to me! But am I daunted? No! Have they deflected me from my determination to fight! No! With the strength of God and your strength, I will fight on, just as we all must fight on to ensure that the Word of God triumphs over the forces of evil that think they have us by the throat! But our souls remain free! I will fight! You will fight! And together we shall win!"

More applause mixed with sporadic booing.

Watched anxiously by Harding and David Weir, Malone conferred briefly with his men. The four dressed as Roscoe's security men slipped into the courtyard just as a burst of cheering greeted Roscoe's latest diatribe about the damnation that was in store for those who harboured witches and permitted them to follow the evil practices of Satanism and black magic.

The driver of the lead Commer pulled away from the kerb

and stopped halfway through the gates. The rest of Malone's men filed past the van and into the courtyard. They formed a disciplined, hard-faced line. Some sentinels who had tried to close the gates as the police vehicle nosed in were advised by the morris police that such a move would incur their displeasure.

Malone spotted Nelson Faraday's scowling face. Roscoe's lieutenant was watching the scene from an upstairs window in Pentworth House. He saw the van and the new arrivals and spoke briefly into a Motorola Handie-Com radio. Roscoe was alerted. He turned to face the main gate and pointed an accusing finger. "And here they are! The apostles of oppression and Satan are with us even as I speak!"

Malone waited beside the police van, holding the microphone that the driver had passed to him.

There was a sudden commotion around the mobile canteen. The speaker cabinet in front of Roscoe rocked and was dragged off the top of the vehicle by its cable. It crashed down on to the cobbles. There were yells and curses from the mêlée.

"This is the police!" Malone's amplified voice echoed around the courtyard. "You are required to leave immediately. The show is over. Disperse in an orderly manner or you are liable to be arrested."

Several morris police had left the line and had words with mothers with children. They saw the line of morris police and needed no second invitation. They gathered up their charges, converged on the main gate, and pushed hurriedly past the van. By singling out those likely to leave anyway, Malone's men had ensured that the exodus would be infectious. Others joined the mass of people filing out of the courtyard leaving about 150 sentinels and Roscoe's security men. They seemed bewildered by the rapidity of events but that had not affected their resolution.

Even without his public address system, Roscoe's voice had enough power to be heard all over the courtyard. But his pleas for everyone to stand firm against their oppressors were drowned by Malone repeating his warning. His blue eyes blazed hatred at the police officer.

"You are to come down from that vehicle now," Malone commanded.

Roscoe gave a defiant gesture and seemed relieved to see Nelson Faraday leave the house. He was dressed in his customary black leather outfit, cavalier boots, and cloak. The sullen expression was also part of the ensemble. He was speaking to his men as a horse-drawn haywain entered the courtyard through the arch that led to the estate's farm. It was loaded with a mixture of about twenty teenagers of both sexes. They jumped down from the wagon and were handed an assortment of agricultural tools – spades and hoes. Some even had pitchforks. They swelled the numbers gathered around the mobile canteen, chattering excitedly until silenced by Faraday. Now that Roscoe's army had a leader, they were better organised. Some helped Roscoe down from the roof of the mobile canteen. The rest regarded Malone's silent line of morris police with a mixture of eagerness and trepidation.

Malone quickly summed up the odds. The police force consisted of fifty men whereas Roscoe was surrounded by nearly 200 of his faithful, all fired with the passion of their master's compelling zealotry and prepared to do bloody battle. Bloodshed was the one thing that Malone wanted to avoid but he was prepared for it if necessary. This was a confrontation that he couldn't afford to let Roscoe win.

"Mr Roscoe, you are under arrest and will accompany me now." Malone followed with a formal caution, all delivered over the police van's public address.

On a word from Faraday, his army spread out, forming a barrier between the police line and their leader. They advanced as one until the wicked tines of several levelled pitchforks were within three metres of Malone's men. Roscoe pushed through his line and confronted Malone. He folded his arms as best as his bandages permitted. His demeanour one of supreme confidence.

"What's the charge, Mr Malone?"

"Public preaching for starters, contrary to your amnesty conditions," said Malone curtly. He was about to take the offered handcuffs from the driver but realised that he could hardly handcuff a man whose wrists and arms were heavily bandaged.

"This is private property," said Roscoe, smiling, but the deadly blue eyes boring into the police officer were icy. "Your so-called amnesty," he almost spat the word out, "said nothing about our spreading the message of the Divine Johann Bode on our own property."

"Public preaching is just the beginning," said Malone cheerfully, returning Faraday's scowl with a bland smile. "There's a whole string of public order offences plus contravention of emergency by-laws relating to unlicensed food preparation and distribution. In fact it will be a lot less work if we make out a charge sheet listing what you're not being charged with."

That was as much arguing with Roscoe that Malone was prepared to tolerate. He moved forward. Faraday seized a pitchfork from a supporter and pressed the tines against Malone's jacket. His eyes were wary having had previous and painful experience of Malone's lightning reactions and formidable martial arts skills.

"You're also under arrest, Faraday. Threatening a police officer with a deadly weapon." Malone started forward but Faraday pressed the pitchfork even harder against his chest. There was an angry response from Malone's men, some took a threatening pace forward, but generally they held their ground and would not do anything until their senior officer gave the signal.

"Lesson One," said Malone affably, "is never to allow your opponent nearer your weapon than you are."

Despite being braced for a fast reaction, Faraday was not prepared for what happened next. Malone seized the pitchfork's tines and twisted them to one side with such force and speed that the implement's haft was jerked from his grasp. Malone spun the pitchfork through an arc like a skilled drum majorette and drove the butt end of the haft into Faraday's groin. He gave a scream of anguish and brought his hands down in a belated gesture of protection. The pitchfork whirled again and struck Faraday on the right forearm with enough force to ensure that everyone heard his radius and ulna bones snap. Roscoe's motley army surged forward. Some of them went sprawling over Faraday who was writhing on the ground, howling.

"Go! Go! Go!" Malone snapped.

Those morris police without shields held their staffs in the horizontal position and charged, adding to Faraday's problems as he was trampled. A girl sentinel brandishing a pitchfork screamed as she was impaled through the leg by her own weapon. A morris man went down, clutching his head, blood streaming through his fingers. Six morris men darted forward and dragged Adrian Roscoe clear of the mêlée while another four provided a shield. The police pinned Roscoe down, ignoring his yells of pain as they doubled his arms behind his back and secured his wrists with a cable tie.

"Save the Father!" Faraday managed to scream as he was dragged to his feet. Ten heavies threw themselves on the group of morris men that were dragging Roscoe towards the van. The scrum collapsed – a seething mass of humanity, waving arms and legs, crash helmets rolling across the cobbles. Despite the odds, Malone's men managed to retain their grip on Roscoe but they were singled out for a determined assault by a second wave of some twenty sentinels. They had dispensed with their weapons and relied on brute strength and sheer weight of numbers to haul their leader away from the morris men. With several of his men having sustained injuries and two lying alarmingly still on the cobbles, Malone realised that the situation was fast getting out of control. His force, although better trained and disciplined, was no match for the sheer numbers of the opposition. He ran to the van, raised the microphone to his lips and pressed the PTT button. Just as he was about to speak, a women screamed out behind him. She was out of breath but her voice was loud enough to be picked up by the microphone and relayed across the battleground above the uproar:

"The Wall has gone! The Wall has gone!"

Thirteen

It was a cliché. Ellen Duncan knew it was a cliché yet the marking off on the calendar of the days that the three women had been imprisoned in the cave was a daily task that brought the day of their freedom, or otherwise, one day nearer.

Or otherwise?

Think positive, she told herself.

"Twenty-four days now," said Claire Lake listlessly, reading Ellen's thoughts as the older woman stared at the calendar.

Ellen didn't reply. It was her own business calendar – emblazoned with "Earthforce" in letters that matched those on her shop sign. How she missed her little herbal shop – the pervasive smell of mixed herbs, the rows of neat little rosewood drawers, the jangle of the Victorian bell whenever a customer entered, the nightly updating of her website so that her loyal mail-order customers across the country knew exactly what she had in stock. And what of her customers in the town? How was Dawn Linegar's mother coping with her daughter's epilepsy without the regular supply of a decoction that Ellen prepared from heartsease?

"Only twenty litres of water left," said Claire.

"What?"

Claire repeated her daily stocktaking finding.

"Shit," Elaine muttered. "Well – nothing for it but to stop washing."

"Jesus Christ!" Vikki wailed. "As if we don't pong enough as it is!"

"Dried beans – about a kilo," Claire continued. "Dried eggs – half a tin. Still two big tins of corned beef and ten tins of baked beans. All long out of date. Charcoal's nearly gone. Enough for about four more hot meals and that's it."

"They've forgotten us," Vikki declared.

"Don't be so stupid, young lady."

"For fuck's sake, will you stop calling me that!"

Ellen checked an impulse to let fly at Vikki. God – how the girl had changed. "David and Mike haven't forgotten us," she said calmly, and hoped she sounded convincing.

"They're the only two people who know we're here," Vikki retorted. "Supposing something's happened to them?"

"Don't be ridiculous. What could possibly have happened to them?"

"The same thing that nearly happened to us!"

"Sanitary towels," said Claire, who had learned to ignore the bickering between Vikki and Ellen. "They're the one thing we've hardly touched. We've only used six. Not that I need them, of course."

"Okay. We'll have them on toast tonight," said Ellen drily.

Vikki fell back on her camp bed, holding her hand to her mouth to prevent herself laughing out loud.

"We're out of toast," said Claire, and joined in with Vikki's silent mirth.

Ellen couldn't contain herself and was hardly able to suppress her fit of the giggles. Laughter – the best medicine so it was claimed in the *Readers' Digest*s she'd now read a dozen times. But something was nagging at the back of her mind.

Not that she ever counted them, but she was fairly certain that the six sanitary towels were ones that she had used.

Fourteen

Sister Mary Thomas was quite flustered by the visit by no less than the Chairman of Pentworth Council and the Deputy Chairman. What should she call Bob Harding? Mr Harding or Mr Chairman? Well, it had always been Bob in the days when he used to repair her toaster and other appliances but that seemed inappropriate now. She settled for Mr Chairman. She knew David Weir slightly as the owner of Temple Farm who had upset local sensibilities when he had turned it into a working rural museum, and tourists and schoolchildren started arriving by the coach load. She decided that she would never have become a nun had she met such a good-looking man seventy years before.

"Through here. Just through here," she said, ushering her guests into her tiny cottage. "I'm sorry about the mess, only I didn't have time to tidy up."

Harding assured her not to worry. Sister Mary paused at the door to her little front room and fretted about being shown up as an utter fool if she had been mistaken. But she knew that she wasn't mistaken. She had looked into the room at least a dozen times since phoning Government House. A dreadful thought occurred to her. Supposing it had only been temporary and the Wall was back?

She pushed the door open and felt a wave of relief. The room was complete. She stood aside for Harding and Weir. They paused on the threshold, staring into a perfectly normal, low-beamed room, cluttered with the memorabilia of her long life.

"And the Wall was where?" asked Harding, entering the tiny room and looking around.

Sister Mary pointed along the floor. "About there, Mr

Chairman. That bookcase and the fireplace and the dresser all vanished last March when the Wall appeared."

"I believed you were offered to be rehoused at the time?" David queried.

"Oh yes, but I refused. I mean, what would've been the point? The Wall didn't seem to be doing any physical harm and it didn't hurt to touch it. Just a tingling and that strange black patch would appear when you tried to push against it."

Bob Harding took two photographs of the room with his digital camera. He examined the very fine layer of dust on the bookcase and ran the tip of his finger through it. Sister Mary was suddenly embarrassed. "I wanted to dust before you came but they said at Government House not to touch anything until you'd been."

"Shouldn't there be more dust than this after six months?" David enquired.

Bob Harding shook his head. "Household dust is mostly particles of dead human skin. We're shedding it all the time. Where there's been no human contact, there's never that much dust. All those movies showing rooms or vaults that have been abandoned for years with everything covered with a thick layer of dust have got it wrong." He paused to study the clock on the mantlepiece. "Had it stopped, Sister Mary?"

"Yes. I wound it up. Oh dear. Did I do wrong?"

Bob Harding gave the elderly nun a warm smile. "No – of course not. A perfectly natural thing to do. Can you remember the time it had stopped at?"

"No. I'm sorry."

"No matter. Can we take a look at your garden, please?"

Sister Mary showed her guests into the garden. Bob Harding unrolled some large-scale survey maps of the Wall's perimeter that had been prepared when it had appeared. He weighted them down on her garden table. He and David studied the expanse of lawn. The sudden change from neatly mown grass to unkempt lawn marked the original line of the Wall. But further down the lawn and away from the house, was the usual bleak vista of a wind-desiccated Farside, sedge grasses yellowing in the harsh summer sun.

"Well, Sister Mary," said Harding. "It would seem that the Wall is still there but in a different position."

"I'm so dreadfully sorry – ringing you like that. But I saw that it had gone from my front room and my first thought was to call Government House. I was so excited, I didn't think to check the garden."

"You did exactly the right thing," Bob Harding assured her. "This is an extraordinary event."

Sister Mary smiled her pleasure. "Can I make you some nettle tea? I've plenty of hot water in my thermos."

"That would be very welcome, Sister."

The nun looked embarrassed. "I'm terribly sorry, but I'm out of biscuits. I always seem to get through my week's ration by Wednesday."

Harding and David assured her that just tea would be fine. Sister Mary bustled off to her kitchen. The two men took the map that covered the sector where Sister Mary's cottage was located and walked warily towards Farside. Harding stooped to examine the boundary between the mown and unmown grass.

"Looks like normal six months' growth," David observed.

"That's what I thought," said Harding. "Curious." He stooped and plucked a handful of the long blades of grass which he examined closely. "This is modern grass. Cultivated. Sister Mary's original lawn." He paused and stared at the enigma of the Farside landscape of pre-history. "It means, David, that the real world of the twenty-first century is still there. Maybe the Farside world we're seeing is an illusion after all."

They walked on a few paces, hands outstretched. They crossed a twin-rutted farm track and walked on for about twenty paces. The sudden resistance and blackening where their palms made contact told them that had found the Wall's new position. They spent the next thirty minutes plotting the Wall's altered line with a series of Xs pencilled on one of the maps. They returned to the table where Bob Harding joined up the Xs by lightly sketching in a neat, freehand curve. The result was that the smooth curve of the Wall's five-kilometre radius, hardly noticeable as a curve on the large-scale map, now bulged out around Sister Mary Thomas's cottage to form a blister that was decidedly noticeable.

"So we now have a bulge in the Wall," said David slowly. "But I'm damned if I can make anything of it."

"Mike Malone's surmise about the spyder's little sortie the other night being a survey of the Wall was probably right," Harding commented. "It looks like . . ." His voice trailed away. He thumped the table suddenly and jumped up. "We're a couple of blind fools," he said, heading rapidly towards the bulge. His tall, stooping frame and long legs obliged David to break into a near-jog to keep up. Harding reached the farm vehicle track and, unmindful of the damp grass, knelt to study it closely. "Fools that we are," he said angrily. "It looks like such an ordinary track that we didn't notice it."

David followed the two deep ruts of the track in each direction and saw that it was only about a hundred metres long from where it emerged through the blister in the Wall. It ran for a distance, and disappeared again into the opposite side of the blister.

"Tyre marks," said Harding triumphantly. "Recent, too, I'll be bound. You're a farmer, David. What sort of agricultural vehicle cut these ruts?"

David looked closely at the tyre marks, particularly where they where clearest at the grassy edges of the ruts. "Well, they've certainly not been made by tractors unless it was one of those giant French jobbies. And I don't know of any farmer around Pentworth who had one. None of our fields are big enough. West Sussex isn't Lincolnshire."

"Definite proof that the outside world still exists, wouldn't you say?" Harding aimed his camera at the ruts. "I'd say that those tyre marks are recent. Very recent."

"Well, if it is proof, this track must've been damn close to what had been the outside perimeter of the Wall," said David.

Harding nodded and stood. "Let's take a look at that Ordnance Survey map."

The two men returned to the garden table and unfolded an OS map of the area. They studied it closely. The scale was large enough to show Sister Mary's cottage as a tiny block. There was no sign of a track on the map.

"My guess," said Harding, "is that it's a new track made by military vehicles and that it goes right around the outside perimeter of the wall."

"Mr Chairman!" It was Sister Mary, standing by her kitchen door. "A phone call for you from Government House."

Harding took the call, listening intently to what Diana Sheldon had to say while making notes. He finished the call and said to David: "We've got another hole in the wall. Blackwoods Farm, near the A283."

Forty-five minutes later the two men were standing in a small valley while talking to Eddie Blackwood, whose family had worked his farm for several generations. He was a big, no-nonsense man who relished the return to farming that emphasised crop-growing. In his case the Wall now bulged outwards to avoid a cluster of low, clinker-block pigsties which hitherto the Wall had sliced through.

"Them Silent Vulcan folk, whatever they are, ain't done me no favours by shifting their Wall," he said. "Them pigsties ain't bin used for twenty year. I was gonna knock 'em down and use the breeze blocks on my side to build a composting tower." He paused and grinned. "If the supplies depot don't want all that chain-link, I can make use of it."

He was referring to an extraordinary feature that had been revealed by the repositioning of the Wall – at the foot of the slope stood a 200-metre length of chain-link fencing that was like no fencing that the three men had ever seen before. It stood four metres high, secured to massive columns that gleamed with the whiteness of new concrete. They were spaced at four-metre intervals, set in concrete. The galvanised chain-link was of a heavy gauge, secured to stout horizontal wires that were held taunt with bottle screws at frequent intervals. The bright sunlight caught the gleaming edges of the coils of razor wire that decorated the top of the fence. As if that wasn't enough, there were more horizontal wires mounted on ceramic stand-off insulators. A rotting copse of an adult deer at the foot of the fence spoke of the electrification's effectiveness. Beyond the fence was a three-metre gap and then another fence that consisted of coiled razor wire, as high as a man, supported on sturdy timber cruciforms. A few metres further on was a

70

twin-rutted track similar to that which they had seen at Sister Mary's cottage.

"I think we'd like to take a closer look please, Mr Blackwood," said Harding quietly.

"Sure thing."

The two men followed the farmer single file along a narrow path between large plots in which rows of peas were catch-cropped between furrows of earthed-up main crop potatoes.

"Didn't see it right away," Blackwood said over his shoulder. "Early morning mist that were slow to burn off."

Mindful of the size of the ceramic insulators which indicated the voltage they were designed to carry, Harding and Weir kept a respectful distance from the massive fence.

Blackwood laughed. He grasped the chain-link and shook it. "Don't worry. It's as dead as that deer. I chucked a wire over it. Nothing. The Wall chopped off its power when it spilled over it, I reckon."

The three men walked to the western end of the fence where it was cut off abruptly to give way to Farside. Harding took a photograph of David Weir creating a black patch on the Wall where it appeared to touch the fence.

"I detect the efficient hand of the Royal Engineers in all this," said Harding. "This fence is built to last, and that worries me."

"Why isn't there a length of matching fencing at Sister Mary's place?"

Harding shrugged. "Who knows? Building thirty kilometres of fence of this quality is a big order, even for the army. They're probably concentrating first on spots where the public have easy access."

"Or maybe they've left Sister Mary's part clear for experiments in breaking through the Wall?"

"Your guess is as good as mine," Harding replied.

"Must've cost a fortune. The outside world doesn't seem to have our more laid-back attitude to the Wall."

"You can't blame them for not taking chances. Don't forget that they don't have our experience of the Visitors – little as that is."

71

They walked towards the fence section's eastern extremity where it passed through the Wall.

"What do you suppose the outside world sees of our world?" David wondered.

"Who knows?" Harding replied. "My guess is that they see what we see – Farside – a world of forty thousand years ago."

They drew level with the back of a large sign.

"Wonder what it says?" Harding mused.

"That's what I wondered," said Blackwood. "Why not take a look?" With that the big farmer dragged aside a large section of the chain-link that had been cut through. "Got busy with the croppers soon as I saw the sign. Sorry – but that was before Government House told me not to touch anything."

Harding and Weir ducked through the opening. They read the sign in silence, each wrapped in his own thoughts. The corners of the board were marked with vivid lightning flashes above a skull and cross-bones. Harding raised his camera and clicked the shutter. The actual sign was curt and to the point. It said little yet spoke volumes:

PENTWORTH EXCLUSION ZONE
DANGER EXTREMELY HIGH VOLTAGE
ATTEMPTS TO BREACH THIS FENCE WILL
RESULT IN DEATH
MINISTRY OF DEFENCE

Fifteen

Tony Selby, of Selby Engineering, was extremely pissed off. He and four of his employees had better things to do than labour with billhooks in the midday sun, searching for what was supposed to be the equivalent of Cleopatra's Needle in a small haystack.

He paused in his task of hacking at brambles and mopped his forehead. "Councillor Baldock," he said wearily. "You are one big dumb pillock. How the hell could you lose something as big as you say it was?"

Dan Baldock was a waspish little pig farmer, much given to indignant bristling. He bristled indignantly at his old school friend's accusation. "It *was* nigh on thirty year ago, and I resent being called big. Anyway – I don't use this field. Too small and too close to the town for my pigs. People don't appreciate honest smells no more."

There was a yell from the lower corner of Baldock's Field where two of Selby's men were up to their chests in the midst of a huge bramble thicket. One of them waved.

"Found it!"

Selby's team walked down the slope to the thicket where his two employees were gorging themselves on plump blackberries and looking very pleased with themselves. They used their billhooks to drag the brambles aside, exposing grey, lichen-mottled concrete.

"That's it, all right," said Baldock morosely, scraping at the moss. He repeated his excuse about it being nigh on thirty years ago.

The six men set to work with renewed vigour. Thirty minutes sweated labour, hacking at the thick suckers and dragging them clear using industrial gloves, was enough to expose a huge slab of concrete. It measured about ten metres square and stood a third of a metre high. They gathered in the centre of the slab and contemplated the conical concrete obelisk-like structure that protruded from the slab's exact centre. It was about a metre high and the same in diameter at its base.

"That's the cap," said Baldock.

"I guessed," said Selby sourly, eyeing the squat obelisk with distaste. He needed tools and sent a man up the hill to the field's entrance to fetch their pony and cart.

Baldock produced a yellowing newspaper cutting that bore a photograph of a gang of men in Conoco overalls and hard hats. They were standing at the foot of a robust tower-like derrick. The caption said: "Conoco Drilling Team's Lucky Strike". Underneath was a sub-headline: "Significant natural gas find say experts".

In fact there was little luck in the find. In the early 1980s, after weeks of painstaking surveys, Conoco had drilled a series of exploratory test bores across Southern England. The purpose of the exercise was not so much to set up production, but to assess the United Kingdom's resources of mainland natural gas and oil. When finished, the derricks were dismantled, the test bores were capped, and Conoco went back to more lucrative exploration contracts in Alaska and the Far East.

"Funny," said Baldock, studying the tree line in the photograph's background, "but I could've sworn that this thing was at top of the field – not down here."

"Age and senility creeping up on you, Dan," was Selby's unkind retort as he selected a sharp bolster and a club hammer from the toolbox that had been dumped beside him.

With sharp taps of the heavy hammer on the bolster, he quickly scored a vertical line down the obelisk in the hope that it would act as a fault line that would fracture easily and simplify the task of breaking the concrete away from whatever was underneath. But Conoco's engineers had done their job well by adding a fibrous binder to the concrete's mix necessitating progressively harder blows to weaken it.

"They certainly didn't want it tampered with, did they?" Selby commented.

They took it in turns with the bolster and club hammer.

Gradually a huge valve, protected with several layers of hessian like a mummy, was revealed. It required treating with respect, using smaller tools to completely expose it. After that the rest of the concrete came away easily in large chunks.

At the end of an hour's work they brewed tea using a portable solar heater and contemplated their handiwork. In the centre of the rubble and chippings stood a massively proportioned device that looked like a large fire hydrant. The shut-off valve at the top of the heavy casting consisted of a recessed hexagon drive. At the side was a large threaded male outlet protected with a screw-on plastic cap. Selby removed the cap, checked the thread's pitch and profile with a set of gauges, and measured its diameter.

"Seventy-five mill," he announced with some satisfaction. "Should be a doddle."

He treated the recessed drive with penetrating oil and left it to soak in while he rummaged in an old ammunition box. He had come well-prepared; the box was filled with an assortment of pipe couplings, adaptors, and even pressure gauges. It took him only a few minutes to screw an adaptor on to the valve and add a series of reducers that terminated with a pressure gauge. He carefully tightened the assembly with spanners. The gauge reading would give no indication of the size of the gas field that they were sitting on, but the pressure would give a good idea of what they would have to handle. They didn't even know what the gas was. Baldock's newspaper cutting didn't say, council minutes covering the period had been destroyed in the fire, and none of the locals who had provided casual labour for Conoco could recall.

Let it be methane, Selby prayed as he searched for a socket wrench that fitted the valve's drive. He needed the biggest socket in the set.

Selby Engineering had learned a great deal about the characteristics of methane gas from that produced by Pentworth House's piggery digestors. Although Adrian Roscoe's monopoly on the gas was being eroded by the increasing number of digestors that were being built on farms as a means of extracting useful energy from slurry, their output, valuable as it was, was nothing compared with the prodigious quantities

75

that Roscoe's 5,000 pigs could produce. Several buses and other public service vehicles had been converted by Selby's company to run on the stuff as a means of conserving Pentworth's irreplaceable stock of polluting petrol and diesel oil. Methane was a valuable hydro-carbon fuel, a greenhouse gas in its free state, but which burned without producing excessive pollutants. It was also valuable in the manufacture of ammonia, which was needed by the new ice-making plant. But not enough methane was being produced. What was needed was a major find which would end Adrian Roscoe's powerful political and economic hold over Pentworth that he had already shown he was prepared to use.

"Right. Everyone off," Selby ordered. "Take yourselves and the pony and cart at least two hundred metres away."

"What are you expecting?" Baldock demanded.

"I've no bloody idea."

"Supposing it does blow up, Mr Selby?" enquired an employee.

Selby grinned and glanced up at the sky. The clouds that formed at night and provided Pentworth with regular rainfall had virtually dispersed. "You'll need a hot air balloon to scrape me off the inside of the Wall. Now piss off."

Once they were a safe distance away, Selby tapped the socket into place on the valve and inserted a tommy bar. He kept an eye on the pressure gauge and applied a gentle force to the tommy bar. He didn't expect the valve to budge, and it didn't. Nor did gentle thumps with the heel of his palm have any effect. A judicious tap with a hide mallet was the same. He slid a length of steel tube on to the tommy bar to increase the leverage and went through the process again. It crossed his mind that maybe Conoco well-cap valves had left-hand threads. Shearing the hexagon off its spindle would be a disaster.

A slightly harder blow with the mallet resulted in the valve giving a fraction. Either that or the tube was bending. The needle remained on the stop. Another blow and the valve gave about a degree but the results were out of all proportion to the tiny amount of movement. The needle whipped around to the stop with an audible clunk, and the pressure gauge exploded with a deafening report, spraying the field with glass and fragments of metal. Gas blasted through the remains of the pressure gauge. Although shaken, Selby had the presence of mind to pull on an industrial glove and deflect some of escaping gas upwards with his hand. The searing cold of the expanding gas stabbed through the glove's thick leather. It attacked the atmosphere's eighty per cent relative humidity and created a cloud of swirling fog. He bent over the valve and sniffed cautiously before closing it.

There was no odour.

Methane! It could only be methane! Glorious, wonderful methane!

The others came running in response to his gesture of triumph.

"Methane," said Selby in answer to their questions. "And I've no idea how much. But a lot, I reckon. It blew that fifty-atmosphere pressure gauge to glory. And Adrian Roscoe's monopoly."

"What's fifty atmospheres in old money?" Baldock demanded.

Selby laughed delightedly. "Seven hundred and fifty pounds per square inch – probably a lot higher if the speed at which it took the gauge out is anything to go by."

The team celebrated their momentous discovery with more tea. None of them could have guessed that the far-reaching consequences of their find would result in Pentworth taking the first steps towards a civil war.

Sixteen

M ike Malone was not one to allow his behaviour to indicate his moods, but there was no mistaking his feelings as he strode into the operations room in Pentworth police station, stuck his feet on a desk, and loosened his tie. WPC Carol Sandiman poured a cup of tea from a vacuum flask and placed the police station's last biscuit in the saucer. "It went badly?" she enquired, placing the tea before Malone.

"Magistrates' courts," he said bitterly. "There ought to be a law that gives police officers the right to shoot one magistrate before they retire."

Carol smiled. She admired Mike Malone and had mentally awarded him a 10 on the F scale when she had first met him. "A great idea," she said. "Trouble is I'd probably abuse it and take out at least three. Just how badly did it go?"

"Hasn't it been on the radio yet?"

"Not yet."

"The charges relating to food distribution were dismissed. He produced evidence showing that the beef in the hamburgers were allowances that his bloody sentinels had donated. The bread rolls were rejects from his bakery. The hamburgers were given away free of charge on private property therefore the beneficiaries of his largesse were his guests."

"Any good news?"

Malone sipped his tea, his expression morose. "Faraday's got a plaster cast on his right arm the size of a marrow. He's not a happy man."

Carol smiled.

"A two thousand euro fine each for resisting arrest," Malone continued. "Police objections to bail for assault and incitement refused. Bail conditions were that his preaching activities must be confined to the inside of Pentworth House or any privately owned building. Which reminds me. Roscoe's not going to be happy about the methane find when the news is released. I want you to organise a three-man twenty-four/seven guard roster on the well head, please. It's being fenced but I'd feel happier knowing that we're keeping a permanent watch on the thing."

The policewoman frowned. She turned to the wall map and found Baldock's Field, near the southern end of the High Street. "Three men round the clock is stretching us," she observed. "How about two men? Armed?"

Malone hesitated and decided that the suggestion made sense. He nodded. "Okay, Carol. Make sure they can handle shotguns."

"That won't be difficult with our local yokel force." Carol's phone rang. She answered it, listened, and called out to Malone. "Mrs Anne Taylor is here, sir. She'd like to see you."

Malone drained the teacup. He had been expecting the visit. "Okay – I'll see her in the interview room."

"Would you like me present?"

"No – I'm sure Mrs Taylor can be trusted to restrain herself."

Anne Taylor was shown into the interview room. She was in her mid-thirties and bore a striking resemblance to her daughter. The same green eyes as Vikki – now lined and lustreless from worry and lack of sleep – the same golden hair. On a happier occasion, at the May Day carnival, Anne Taylor had told Malone that she was a little tired of being thought of as Vikki's older sister. The police officer knew that Anne's husband was Farside and that her enforced estrangement from him because of the Wall was no great hardship because their marriage was on the point of breaking up anyway.

Malone smiled reassuringly at his guest. "I saw you in court just now, Anne. I confess I was a little worried in case you were going to buttonhole me outside, which was why I cleared off quickly. I didn't mean to appear rude."

The green eyes regarded Malone steadily. "You told me not contact you in public, Mike."

"And you've been very good."

"But I had to go to court. I wanted to see Roscoe imprisoned."

"Which makes two of us."

"It's been nearly a month now."

"You don't have to remind me."

"Well, I think I do," Anne replied with a flash of anger that
she immediately regretted. "Oh hell . . . Mike – I hate having
to say this because it must make me seem ungrateful. I can
never thank you enough for rescuing Vikki, but I know my
daughter. Wherever it is you've got her hidden, after all this
time I worry about her mental state."

"Would you believe me if I said that the mental state of all
three women is uppermost in my mind?"

Anne met Malone's gaze and looked down at her hands.
She nodded. "You must think I'm so ungrateful."

"I think you're a good mother who's naturally concerned
about her daughter. Believe me, Anne, I'm going to break
Adrian Roscoe and his cult. It's my number one priority, but
until I do so, Vikki and Ellen, and Claire Lake must remain
in hiding. That they have to do so, I regard as a failure on my
part. And I hate failure."

Anne looked at the police officer with renewed hope. "Do
you have a plan . . . ? I'm sorry, Mike – don't answer that –
a stupid question."

Malone came out from behind the desk and sat in a chair
beside Anne. He took her hand and smiled encouragingly.
"Actually, Anne, I've about ten plans. My concern is to
choose the one that'll work with a single blow. That fiasco
in the magistrates' court just now was a result of events beyond
my control."

"But Vikki's well?"

"Yes." It was a white lie. Knowing that Roscoe had his
watchers and informers everywhere, Malone and David Weir
had deliberately avoided making contact with the three fugitives. "Anne – the August Market Square carnival is coming
up. I'd be pleased if you'd do me the honours again."

Anne stiffened and pulled her hand away. "Do you really
think I should go gallivanting while Vikki's in danger?"

"She's not in danger where she is and I don't want you to

do any gallivanting," said Malone seriously. "Just indulge in some wild dancing in that little white dress you wore at the May Day do. I'm pretty sure Vikki would approve. I know I would."

Anne's first reaction was to snap Malone's head off but, when she met those wide-set brown eyes, she realised that she couldn't get angry with this man.

"And it'll do you a power of good," Malone added. "I daren't tell you what seeing you in that dress again would do to me. I might even misappropriate police methane to run you home in the wee small hours just to have those gorgeous legs beside me."

"Why do I get the distinct impression that your intentions are not honourable?"

Malone looked pained, put his hand on his heart and said, "I give you my solemn word as a police officer and a gentleman that they're not."

Anne could not help smiling. She nodded. "I don't really feel up to socialising but it's a date, Mr Malone."

Malone stood. "Excellent. We'll firm up nearer the day."

Anne rose. "I'll look forward to it, Mike, but I can't promise to be the life and soul. At least Roscoe's search parties seem to have stopped."

"He's had enough warning shots across the bow," Malone replied.

"No amount of warning shots are going to stop a mental case like Adrian Roscoe," said Anne emphatically. "Nothing short of a broadside and his being sunk without trace will achieve that."

When he was alone, Malone thought about Anne's parting sentence. The worrying thing was that she was so damnably right.

Seventeen

B ob Harding looked quickly in turn at each of the ten councillors seated around the conference table. The meeting was being held on the ground floor of Government House in a room that sometimes served as a juvenile court. A large-scale map of the area showing the Wall was spread out on the table. "Has everyone seen all the photographs?"

There were nods of assent. Harding turned the laptop computer around to face him and called up the next picture he would be referring to.

"I'm sorry not to have printed them out, but we need to be extremely careful with our stock of bubble jet ink. We can't expect Selby Engineering to make everything."

"That's good news," said Tony Selby wryly. "I've been getting so depressed recently."

There was a ripple of laughter around the table.

"Firstly," said Harding briskly to the gathering. "Thank you for coming and I apologise for the short notice but there have been a number of recent events that need urgent consideration. I take it you've all read my somewhat terse report. Unless there are any objections, I'm suspending standing orders so that Mr Selby may give his advice if needed. Standing orders will be reimposed automatically during voting arising out of the agenda. Town Clerk – you need only minute decisions."

Diana Sheldon stopped making shorthand notes.

"There's no 'any other business' on the agenda, Mr Chairman," Millicent Vaughan observed.

"I think these two items are going to take long enough, Councillor," Harding replied, knowing that Millicent would use any opportunity to voice her concerns about Pentworth's low birthrate.

There were no objections, so Harding pressed on: "Item One. As you all know by now, the Visitors have carried out several modifications to their Wall."

Councillor Alec Morton had an immediate objection. He was a humourless, retired bank manager. His glasses gave him a studious, owl-like expression. He appeared to be the elected spokesman for three other councillors known to share his support of Adrian Roscoe's extreme views. "We don't know that we have any so-called Visitors, Mr Chairman."

Harding tapped his laptop. "You have just seen the echo-sounder screen shots I took in Pentworth Lake, Councillor Morton."

"I've seen pictures of a vague shape that could be anything. As you know, there is a wide body of opinion that the Wall is the work of God. We're a predominately Christian community, therefore we accept that evidence for the existence of God is all about us. The evidence for the existence of these supposed Visitors is non-existent."

"What about their spyder thing?" asked Dan Baldock. "Quite a few of us have seen it now. It may have wings but I don't think it's the Archangel Gabriel."

"The purpose of this meeting is not a theological discussion about Life, the Universe and Everything," said Harding quickly, not caring if he antagonised Morton's group and certainly not wishing to give them a platform. "We're dealing with reality to try and solve the problems of this world which God has given most of us the intelligence to deal with. I'm sure God is more than capable of looking after the next world. If you and your like-minded councillors think a prayer meeting would be more useful, then by all means feel free to withdraw from this meeting and hold one in the next room. Any decisions you receive from higher up, please minute them, and we'll be pleased to consider them."

Morton and his three colleagues braved out the laughter, stony-faced.

"Until now," Harding continued, wondering if his comments had been wise, "we have not really known if our old world still exists. One theory has been that the world suffered a cataclysmic disaster and that Pentworth was deemed worth saving by the Visitors by moving it some forty thousand years into the past." He paused and smiled wryly. "A bizarre theory to explain a bizarre event. I've no quarrel with bizarre theories provided they're dumped when they're disproved."

He turned the laptop computer around so that the meeting could see the photograph he had taken at Eddie Blackwood's farm of the Ministry of Defence fence and the notice board. Harding tapped the screen with his pencil. "That, ladies and gentlemen, is irrefutable proof that our old world still exists and that it is aware of the disaster that has overtaken our community. That alone must give us hope."

There was a silence in the room. The unspoken thought was that if the outside world, with all its formidable resources, couldn't breach the Wall, then Pentworth with its limited resources stood no chance. But at least the outside world still existed and was aware of their plight.

"There is something else we must consider," Harding continued. "These recent modifications to the Wall suggest, and I stress 'suggest', that the Visitors are planning to stay. It's pure supposition but that's the way it looks." He pointed to the map. "There have been four modifications and all of them have one thing in common: the line of the Wall has been altered to avoid buildings."

"Considerate of them," said David Weir sarcastically.

Harding called up a picture of Eddie Blackwood's disused pigsties. "These pigsties were bisected by the Wall but they haven't been in use for some years. It seems that the Visitors' surveillance techniques did not, or could not, discern that. It has me wondering what else they don't know about us."

Dan Baldock snorted. "If they're intelligent creatures then it behoved them to find out first the trouble that their bloody Wall would cause us. Not go tinkering with it afterwards. What they've done to us is tantamount to a hostile act."

"Perhaps we should try telling them?" Harding suggested.

A councillor opened his mouth to speak and promptly shut it again. Harding had the meeting's full attention.

"Perhaps they don't know the mess we're in?" Harding added.

"Surely it was up to them to find out?" David Weir interjected.

"You're thinking in rational human terms, Councillor Weir. While I believe that the Visitors are rational, the chances are they are not human and therefore don't share our values. This manifests itself to us as naivety. I imagine that information is common currency throughout the universe, therefore we should at least make an attempt to contact them."

Millicent Vaughan was scathing. "So we go down to the bottom of Pentworth Lake, bang on the side of their Silent Vulcan, or whatever it is, and tell them that they're being a nuisance?"

Harding beamed. "I couldn't have put it better myself. That's exactly what I do mean."

"How?"

"That's what I've given a lot of thought to and why I'll be asking the Council for fifty thousand euros to fund a contact programme. But before I propose that, Tony Selby has something important to say that might have a bearing on how you vote. Tony Selby. You needn't stand up."

The engineer quickly substituted the rumours about the methane well discovery in Baldock's Field for hard facts. For once the rumours were insignificant compared with the truth.

"*All* our energy needs!" an astonished councillor echoed. "Surely not?"

"It certainly looks like it," Selby affirmed. "What little information we've uncovered in the library suggests that our well taps into the same field as Conoco's other test bores around Surrey and West Sussex. Even allowing for the fact that the Wall extends underground to form a sphere, don't forget that it reaches down to a depth of five kilometres. That's an enormous volume. I'd say we're sitting on untold billions of joules of heat energy that are there for the taking. As a bonus, it's pressurised at around seventy atmospheres. An extraordinarily high pressure. It's CNP – compressed natural gas. We don't have to compress it for bulk storage. We transferred some into the gas cylinders we fitted to one of our fire engines and the vehicle's clocked up over one hundred miles so far on one fill-up and is still going strong."

85

There was a silence as the full import of Selby's words sank in. Most of those present had seen the crimson fire appliance being driven around and had assumed it was being used for training. The unspoken thought was that the discovery would spell the end of Adrian Roscoe's power.

"So we can connect up the well to the gas mains?" Millicent queried. "Give the entire community proper cooking facilities again?"

Selby shook his head. "That's something we can't risk, Doctor. Methane is an odourless, poisonous and extremely volatile gas. Without a regulated, steady-flow low-pressure distribution system such as you have with big gasometer tanks, its supply to households is out of the question. We can't risk domestic users having blow-outs."

"Not much chance of that with our food rationing," a councillor observed.

Selby continued, "The other reason is that methane, although clean-burning, is a greenhouse gas in its free state. We can't risk it being released unburnt into our atmosphere. That's why its usage has to be strictly controlled and why buses, police vehicles and ambulances we've converted to run on methane need regular and thorough checks."

"So how can we use it to benefit the people?" asked Alec Morton.

"We turn it into electricity," Selby replied. "Pentworth has got ten generators of various sizes, all converted to run on methane. At least we don't have a fuel problem any more. Our largest jennie is an old two-hundred-and-fifty-kilowatt Centrax job that belonged to Adams Plant Hire. Trailer-mounted. We've been using it at Selby's when we need extra juice for urgent production runs. Continuous use has been out of the question – it burns methane like there's no tomorrow. But we can certainly use it now for some sort of public service electricity supply."

"Like what?"

"Street and shop lighting," said Harding promptly. "Don't look so surprised. Using electricity for lighting is incredibly effective. A hundred-watt light bulb in a room transforms the room. Serious work can be done. Whereas a hundred-watt

86

appliance is useless – just about enough to run an aquarium pump. And don't forget that most of the shops in the town are also manufacturing units now – just as they were in the nineteenth century. Farriers, tanners, garment-makers, candle makers, bakers, wheelwrights, and so on. They've been managing fine with natural light so far, but winter's coming, already the hours of daylight are getting noticeably shorter. Production is going to be badly hit in the winter."

"Would there be enough to supply the villages?" Dan Baldock asked.

Selby shook his head. "Out of the question. Electricity's horribly lossy stuff. Two hundred and forty volts mains voltage generated in Pentworth would only be about one hundred volts when it arrived at Tillington, if that. That's why National Grid voltages are stepped up to megavolts for distribution across the country. Even that results in high losses, and more losses when shoving the stuff through voltage step-down transformers at the consumer end."

He pointed to Pentworth on the map and made a circle around the town centre. "This is the highest concentration of shops, small factories and homes in the entire area enclosed by the Wall. That's the sensible area to provide a public electricity supply. Even then two hundred and fifty kilowatts is going to be spread very thinly. We can disable every second and third street light around the town centre easily enough, and fitting current limiters on electricity meters so that no one can draw more than two hundred and fifty watts won't be too difficult. We could even get the street lighting working for next Saturday night's Market Square carnival. Have a special switch-on ceremony."

"We could run open-air movie shows in Market Square!" said a councillor. "Seaford College have got an enormous video projector."

Suddenly everyone was bubbling over with ideas. Harding held his hand up. "Let's not get ahead of ourselves," he warned, and added, "Although regular movie shows might not be a bad idea. I've never been happy with the Bodian Brethren and their mobile canteen showing children's cartoons at village fêtes."

"We should be grateful to Father Roscoe for the valuable

87

service he provides with his mobile canteen," said Councillor Morton frostily. He glared around at the meeting, ready for an argument.

"Decent movies would make a change from his Tom and Jerry cartoons," said someone caustically.

"And the plays on the radio."

The comment and the burst of laughter that followed defused an awkward situation; the live productions of the amateur dramatic society on Radio Pentworth were the butt of many unfair jokes.

"I don't wish to pre-empt our hard-working food committee," said Harding. "But this changes our entire agricultural policy. This year's shortages are largely due to the need for this season's crops to provide seed stock for next year. And that, in turn, has been dictated by the amount of land we can physically cultivate with our limited population. The heavy horse-breeding programme, that was started after the Wall appeared, won't be effective for three years – we're desperately short of heavy horses."

"Look at all the tractors we can convert now that we've got unlimited methane," said a farmer.

"But *can* we convert them?" Harding queried. "How many man-hours does it take to convert an internal combustion engine to run on methane, Mr Selby?"

Tony Selby scribbled a few notes. "For a petrol engine – about a hundred man-hours, Mr Chairman."

"A fortnight's work for one man," said Harding.

"And double that for a diesel. They're a pig to convert."

"And all of our tractors are diesel," Harding finished.

There was a silence in the room. All the councillors were aware of Pentworth's labour crisis – the community did not have the work force to undertake all the work that the community needed done for its smooth running. To counter the inflationary dangers of the demand for labour outstripping the supply, the concept of retirement had virtually been abolished. The staff manning the telephone exchange's manual switchboards were mostly retired, as were the hospital laundry staff and the heroic men and women who looked after the many septic tank public toilets. In outlying areas they were little more than well-managed earth latrines. School children with little or no aptitude for academic work had been drafted into training schemes as assistants to cartwrights, wheelwrights, leather workers, carpentry shops, etcetera, even cooperage because barrels were now essential for long-term food storage. There were over one hundred vital trades that needed labour, and to get that labour had resulted in long discussions in various council committees and the passing of emergency legislation that had initially encountered a good deal of resentment. Much of that resentment had disappeared as people discovered the pleasure of making things for the benefit of their fellow man, particularly when there was direct feedback from the user. Tony Selby had long-recognised this; his small team that made the solar cooker dishes would spend a week producing a batch and the following week installing them. It was a technique that he had extended to many products. It made for contented customers and a work force that felt fulfilled.

Tony Selby now employed over 250 people and another hundred part-timers whose skills were also needed elsewhere. Hot, low-humidity days, good for drying paper at the paper mill, could cost him half his part-time staff. He had work in hand to provide employment for 500 people and the work that was expected of his company was steadily increasing each day.

Harding cleared his throat. "Of course, we have to tread carefully where Mr Adrian Roscoe is concerned. He's Pentworth's main supplier of methane, so we can't afford to alienate him until we have a better idea of what the well-head can produce. I suggest we issue a statement to Radio Pentworth saying that we have an unassessed find – which is the truth."

He paused. "Moving on. We have to make some attempt to communicate with the Visitors. At the risk of stating the obvious, all our policy-making, our planning, depends on what they are planning. Will they be gone next week? Next year? The next century, or the next millennium?"

His words were a chilling reminder of his statement to the first meeting of the Emergency Council following the appearance of the Wall. In particular his warning that if the Visitors were from the nearest star, Proxima Centauri, then they might

89

be stuck with Visitors for nearly thirty years. But if they were from the centre of the galaxy, that they could be unwilling hosts to the Visitors for many decades – centuries even.

That had been six months ago. What Bob Harding had not told anyone was that since then he now believed that the Visitors came from Sirius – the Dog Star.

Long before the trouble with Vikki Taylor had blown up, the schoolgirl had come to see him in his workshop-cum-observatory to ask him questions about Sirius. She said it was for a school project. How far was the star? What was known about it? Did it have any planets?

He had told her what he knew: whether or not Sirius had planets was unknown. That the dog days of summer were so called because there was a period during the height of summer when Sirius rose and set with the sun, and that ancient superstition believed that the combined forces of the sun and Sirius were responsible for the days of summer madness.

At the time, he had thought nothing further about the visit until the shock revelation during the witchcraft trial when Vikki had demonstrated her real left hand to a stunned courtroom, claiming that the Visitors were responsible for it and that they had talked to her.

Had they told Vikki that they came from Sirius? If true, it was worrying.

Sirius was approximately ten light-years from earth – over twice the distance of Proxima Centauri.

Eighteen

Lunchtimes were always quiet in the supplies depot. Lennie Hunter's five colleagues usually took themselves off to the Crown while the beer was cheap. More European Union barley that had been held in store at the time of the Wall's appearance had been found to be on the point of germination and had been sent to Pentworth Breweries for making into malt beer.

Lennie disliked his job in the disused school with its former classrooms crammed with rows of laden Dexion shelving, but he didn't have much choice in the matter. There were no proper pensions now for the physically fit. You had to work for those grubby bits of paper that Government House printed in lieu of money. He would've preferred outside work like his Saturday job working on Mr Dayton's yacht, but the labour allocation committee had said he was a border-line case for agricultural work, and that Pentworth had no use for his boat-building and chandlery skills. So here he was, stuck in the supplies depot doing a job that was mind-numbingly boring.

Last week it had been spectacles that had been handed in. This week it was putting light bulbs into storage. A small mountain of them that got no smaller. His movements as he filled a big cardboard box were mechanical. First a layer of chopped hay, then a layer of light bulbs laid on the hay so that they weren't touching. Then another layer of hay, and so on. Like packing fruit. The carton he was filling was big and tough – it had once held a wide-screen television. Funny to think that such cartons were now more useful than their original contents.

"See you in an hour, Lennie! Don't work too hard!"

It was Lennie's boss. He heard a door slam and he was alone. He went to the chief storekeeper's room and took the key to the chemicals store – a separate building across the playground that had once been the school's metalwork shed. After six visits, Lennie knew his way around the bins and carboys although he had no business there. The particular bins he was interested in were marked "Potassium Nitrate – Saltpetre". The depreciations caused by his visits meant that the bins were now considerably lighter than they should be but, with any luck, it might be weeks before the shortage was noticed, and perhaps not even then; the depot's records clerk was way behind because she was even older than Lennie and was often off sick.

He pulled the two long polythene tubes with their supporting harness out of the legs of his trousers and hung them on a hook so that he could fill them with the white powder using a scoop and a funnel. It was slow, painstaking work. He took great care not to leave evidence of his visit by spilling any on the floor. Each tube held two kilos of the stuff. Mr Dayton said that today's consignment was the last and that he had enough. Which was a pity because the twenty euros that the yachtsman paid Lennie for each delivery had come in useful. Mr Dayton had said that he needed the stuff to salt down a black-market pig that he had been promised.

Lennie wet his finger and picked up the few grains of the potassium nitrate that he had spilled. He tasted them and decided that it was going to be an incredibly salty pig.

Nineteen

M ike Malone jogged into Temple Farm's farmyard and stopped beside "Brenda", breathing easily despite the sweat streaming from his saturated headband. David Weir and Charlie Crittenden were too preoccupied with the huge dynamo they were positioning on the traction engine's boiler to notice his arrival.

"Good morning, Charlie, David," Malone called out.

David was pleased to see the police officer. "Can you manage for a few minutes, Charlie?" he asked the traveller.

"No problem, Mr Weir." Charlie nodded a greeting to Malone.

David Weir climbed down from the traction engine. The two men sat at a table in the shade of a barn where there was a small keg of cider waiting.

Malone tugged off his sweatshirt and downed half the contents of the tankard that his host placed before him. He looked quizzically at the traction engine. Little attempt had been made to make the ancient machine look pretty. It was the same mass of dappled blotches of red primer as when he had last seen it. "I'm surprised you've got time to mess about with that rust bucket, David."

"Charlie and his boys have rewound the dynamo," said David defensively. "Amazing what those guys can do. Bob Harding wants it over at the power station he's setting up in Baldock's Field near the methane well. Standby power for the Centrax jennie."

"What use is direct current?" Malone queried.

"It'll be fine for ordinary lighting. We've rewound the dynamo and faffed about with the regulator to punch out mains voltage."

Malone helped himself to more cider.

"Anne Taylor told me she'd been to see you," said David.

Malone nodded. "Naturally she's worried about Vikki. I didn't tell her anything. Is that why you wanted to see me?"

"Ellen, Vikki and Claire have been in the cave for nearly four weeks now. They must be down to the last of their water and food."

Malone gazed hard at the farmer. "You haven't made contact with them, have you?"

The question annoyed David. "Of course not. We agreed that that would always be a joint decision."

"Just as well," said Malone. "Roscoe's still got some of his pus stains trying to keep tabs on me."

David grinned. "They must be getting fit."

"How about you?"

"They've been hanging about. One was careless with his binoculars the other day. Look, Mike – we've got to resupply the girls within the next few days."

"Or, better still, let them out," Malone replied.

David stared. "How? You've always maintained that they have to stay in the cave until you're a hundred per cent certain of their safety."

"There's one way of being a thousand per cent sure," Malone replied enigmatically.

David was silent for some moments as Malone's words sank in. "And how does that equate with your lofty principles about the rule of law and order?" he enquired.

"Stauffenberg's dilemma," said Malone.

"What?"

"Count von Stauffenberg. A member of Hitler's staff. In July 1944 he placed a bomb under a conference table that Hitler was using. His dilemma was whether or not a lesser evil was justified to end a greater evil."

David said nothing, wondering if he would ever understand Malone.

"The analogy is alarmingly close," the police officer continued. "Although Adrian Roscoe is not a head of state and although his influence is such that he could probably persuade the more unhinged of his followers to commit murder, I think his crusading zeal is such that he'd see it as a commission from God demanding his personal action. If anyone makes any move against Ellen and Vikki, he'll be the one to make it."

"How about Faraday?"

"Nelson Faraday doesn't share in Roscoe's fanaticism. Faraday's fanatical interests centre on girls – the younger the better, the livelier the better."

"And Roscoe prefers older women?" David suggested.

Malone nodded. "It seems likely."

"Such as Ellen Duncan?"

"From what she told me of his behaviour – yes."

"Which means that you and Roscoe have something in common," said David.

Malone was too experienced as a police officer to show a reaction to anything that caught him unawares. The remark took him by surprise and he wondered how much David knew about an hour he had spent one afternoon with Ellen in the little flat above her shop. "I have a weakness for dark, strong, mature beer and dark, strong, mature women," he admitted.

"You'd be better off with strong, mature blondes," said David. "Anne Taylor told me how much she likes you. Lousy judgement, but a lovely woman."

Malone laughed but wondered if David's remark was an oblique warning-off regarding Ellen. "What concerns me is that if the Wall continues as now seems likely, Ellen and Vikki will never be more than ten kilometres from Roscoe at any time. That frightens me."

"So what's your Stauffenberg plan?"

Malone had a natural reticence about discussing half-formulated ideas but David Weir had already shown that he was capable of the sort of thinking that Malone approved of, and it was important to keep the farmer's confidence. He quickly outlined his thoughts.

David Weir was quiet for a moment when Malone had finished. "Your mind moves in strange ways, Malone. The idea has the advantage of being so utterly bizarre that it's certain to catch Roscoe wrong-footed. Everyone will be wrong-footed if it comes to that. Whether or not it's sufficiently bizarre to push Roscoe into pre-emptory action and into making a serious mistake is another matter."

"I'm taking a calculated risk that Roscoe's hatred will cloud his judgement. Also my rough plan has the advantage of keeping the initiative with us," said Malone. "We write the menu; we determine events and not Roscoe."

"You realise what will be on that menu?"

"Only too well."

"Could you do it? Pull a trigger on a man? Shoot to kill?"

"I've been trained." Malone knew it was a feeble, evasive answer.

"I know you can shoot straight," David replied. "But how many live human targets did they provide on your training? If it comes to that, how much were you taught about what the SAS call 'over penetration'? Unlike them, you don't have much choice of a weapon. You're thinking of that gun you took off Faraday?"

Malone nodded. "A Smith and Wesson .45."

"Which is little more than a hand-held cannon. You might not just kill Roscoe. Have you thought about that?"

Rather than answer the question, Malone finished his drink and stood. "Duty calls, David. Great cider. Thanks."

David Weir remained deep in thought for a few moments after Malone had left.

Count Klaus von Stauffenberg's plan had failed – a failure that had unleashed a bloodbath of reprisals that had ended all opposition to Hitler, and Stauffenberg and his fellow conspirators had ended up dangling on meat hooks.

Twenty

The swimming-pool filter housing stood in a clear area of Selby Engineering's plant that was normally used for stripping Pentworth's hundreds of unwanted vehicles for scrap and usable spares.

The barrel-shaped housing was moulded in bright yellow glass fibre. It had been intended for a new swimming pool at Seaford College. It rested upright on wooden blocks and stood three metres high and a metre diameter at the broadest part of its girth.

Harding stood on a stepladder and held the steel tape against the top of the housing for Tony Selby, who was entering its measurements into a notebook. The engineer did a mental calculation and looked quizzically up at the scientist. "Its displacement is nearly two metric tonnes, Mr Chairman."

"I hate being called that," said Harding, climbing off the stepladder.

Selby grinned. "To make this thing sink, Bob, is going to mean hanging some two thousand kilos of weights on it." The engineer mounted the stepladder and put his hand through the large opening at the top of the filter that would normally be used for filling it with sand when it was installed. He jumped down. "About twelve-mill wall thickness. Quite strong. It's designed to take an internal pressure of three Bar. Being round, it can probably take an external pressure equivalent to a depth of sixty metres. Say six atmospheres."

"The Pentworth Lake anomaly's at twice that depth," said Harding.

"I did say probably. Once we've cut the hatch opening and can get inside, we can build up the wall thickness to about twenty mill. We've got plenty of chopped strand matting and resin." The engineer hesitated. "I doubt if pressure is going to be the problem, Bob. It's going to be the question of strong enough fixing points so that it'll take two tonnes of bags of rocks as ballast on the outside."

"Need there be as much as that? After all, it's three metres high. I'm tall but not that tall – all I'd need is a ledge to sit on. How about putting in some sort of floor with car batteries underneath for the lights? I'm going to need plenty of external light. At least a thousand watts or more. A cluster of sealed beam car headlights on some sort of rack would be ideal."

Selby made some notes. "That's not a bad idea, Bob. Taking the batteries with you would avoid the problem of voltage drop down a cable, and ten or so car batteries on board would certainly cut down on the amount of external ballast needed."

"And how about a net-type harness made of cable to go around the thing to take its weight?"

Selby considered and nodded. "Good thinking." He made another note.

Harding was pleased. The problems of getting himself down to the Silent Vulcan were disappearing.

"But we'll still need some external ballast and some sort of quick release mechanism operated from inside so that you can dump the ballast in an emergency if we can't winch you up for some reason."

"It would shoot up like a bloody cork!"

"Better that than being stuck on the bottom."

"My original model was for a free roaming submersible," said Harding ruefully.

"It's just not practical, and certainly not possible on the budget the Council voted you," Selby declared. "We'd have to make water and pressure-proof pods as motor housings. Rudders and hydroplanes, controls and God knows what else. The bathyscaphe approach in which you're winched up and down from a raft like a conker on a string is going to give us enough headaches as it is, yet it's a much simpler design proposition, and a damn sight cheaper in terms of man-hours than turning this thing into a submarine."

"How long will it take you?"

"Top priority?"

"Top priority," Harding affirmed.

"Everything we do is top priority."

"You were at the Council meeting," Harding reminded the engineer.

Selby considered. "About two days to do the structural work." He rapped the side of the housing. "Fit the hatch-cum-porthole about here – luckily you're a bit of a beanpole. Another two days for the electrics – rigging the lights and so on. Put in a telephone. Then at least a day for testing. The only way of doing that would be to send the thing down empty for a couple of hours."

"Can you foresee any difficulties?" asked Harding.

Selby laughed. "Nothing but difficulties all the way. The biggest problem is going to be fixing you up with some sort of air supply and a CO_2 scrubber. Then we're going to need a pontoon for winching you up and down. Something big and stable."

"How about oil drums lashed together with scaffold poles?" Harding suggested.

"Great minds think alike," Selby replied. He hesitated. "One thing that comes to mind. Assuming you do find the Silent Vulcan or whatever it is, how are you going to communicate with it or them?"

"I'm working on that," said Harding stiffly.

"Meaning, you don't know?"

"Meaning, I haven't a fucking clue," Harding admitted.

Twenty-One

L ike all successful ocean-going yachtsmen, Roger Dayton was resourceful, good with his hands, and a good organiser. All these talents were needed for this final stage in the manufacture of his home-made depth-charge: producing the hydrostatic fuse – the device that would detonate the depth charge when it reached the right depth.

A visit to the library in the town had enabled him to glean all he could about the manufacture of black powder – one of the simplest explosives of all to make. It consisted of sulphur, saltpetre and charcoal mixed together in equal quantities. The sulphur had presented a problem until he decided to risk persuading some market-gardening friends and acquaintances to part with enough of the stuff, saying that he needed to fumigate his greenhouses. The saltpetre was the result of Lennie's light-fingered lunchtime exercises at the supplies depot. Charcoal was the least problem – it was plentiful and merely required grinding the requisite amount to a coarse dust. What required careful organisation was his use of his little four-stroke 1,000-watt Honda generator. As far as Dayton was concerned, it was part of his yacht's fittings and therefore he had seen no reason for declaring it or the ten litres of petrol in its tank. It produced just enough power to run his lathe provided he didn't try to cut too much. Biggest risk was the 1,000 euro fine if he was caught running an internal combustion engine without a permit, plus confiscation of the generator.

With the puttering of the Honda hardly audible under its layers of yacht mattresses, he used his workshop lathe to bore a large hole right through the firkin's threaded aluminium bung. It was a stepped hole to provide the seating for the spring and diaphragm that formed the hydrostatic valve. There was little chance of his wife interrupting him. She knew that the "DON'T DISTURB – THIS MEANS YOU" sign on the workshop door meant her in particular. Anything that kept her moody husband out of the house was fine by her.

He screwed the spring and pressure diaphragm into place in the bung and added a short length of copper tube to house the switch and plunger. The device was crude but simple. Water pressure acting on the diaphragm would act against the spring, gradually pushing it in as the depth charge fell to the bottom of Pentworth Lake. He had already calculated the spring rate needed for the spring to operate the micro-switch at a depth of 120 metres. The micro-switch would trigger the percussion-hammer plunger and so fire the Very pistol distress flare cartridge into the black powder.

The crucial percussion hammer was a model of simplicity – it was the coil and plunger from his battery-operated front door chimes. In normal use, pressing the button energised a coil causing the plunger, which formed the core of the coil, to fly out and strike a chiming plate, then recoil on to a second plate, giving out the characteristic ding-dong note of door chimes. In Dayton's depth charge, he had machined a point on the plunger which would strike the percussion cap of a distress cartridge. The marine rockets and flares which he had handed over to Malone some weeks before had all been out of date and due for replacement. He had kept quiet about his stock of current cartridges.

He assembled the detonator and tested it using a live Very cartridge from which the charge had been removed. Pressure applied to the diaphragm set into the bung with the aid of a bottle screw triggered the fuse and caused the hammer to hit the Very cartridge's percussion cap. It emitted a satisfying crack as the tiny mercury-fulminate charge exploded.

Five more tests with the hammer striking the defunct cartridge case convinced him that everything was working perfectly. The entire detonator, complete with battery, switch, coil and a new Very pistol cartridge, all neatly housed in the length of tube, was ready.

He hefted the empty firkin aluminium keg on to the bench

and spent five minutes pouring the black powder into the keg until it was nearly full, shaking the keg occasionally to ensure that the powder settled properly. He had already carried out tests in a large water butt and had mixed the right weight of black powder needed for the keg to sink at half a metre per second. Next the detonator tube mounted on the bung was inserted and screwed home on to a fibre washer. The angle of the bung meant that the live cartridge was aimed right into the centre of the charge.

Perfect.

A final tighten with a "C" spanner so that the bung was flush with the outside of the keg and the job was done.

He sat back and contemplated the home-made depth charge. Other than the now hardly noticeable hydrostatic diaphragm set into the bung, it looked just like an ordinary aluminium beer keg.

Thirty kilos of black powder, with a generous air space to aid oxidising when the stuff was ignited, ought to make one hell of a bang when the casing burst. If the Silent Vulcan lying at the bottom of Pentworth Lake was already severely damaged, as some theorists had suggested, it certainly would be by the time he'd finished with it. Hopefully, the aliens and their Silent Vulcan, together with the mechanism that maintained their accursed Wall, would be destroyed.

Twenty-Two

D avid Weir's "Brenda" moving through Pentworth was a major event. The huge showman's engine, with steam and smoke belching from its smokestack and steam hissing from its stuffing boxes, had attracted a retinue of excited children and parents by the time Charlie Crittenden was cranking the steering wheel to turn the ponderous engine into Baldock's Field where the methane well-head was sited.

Among the small crowd following the showman's engine was Nelson Faraday. His right arm was in a sling, obliging him to use his left hand to operate the camcorder which he used to keep Adrian Roscoe posted on events in and around the town.

A hard standing consisting of a raft of felled pines had already been prepared for "Brenda". When Charlie had surveyed the site he had vetoed the plan by Selby Engineering's power station team to park the engine on the soft ground of the field near the big Centrax mobile generator so that it could share its methane-piped supply. Charlie had declared that the traction engine would probably sink up to its axles, so rather than build a road, it was decided that the showman's engine station would have to be sited near the entrance to the field, at the top of the rise overlooking the well-head, and supplied with its own piped methane. Workmen were already filling in the slit trench that had been cut for "Brenda"'s pipeline.

The small crowd watched in fascination as Charlie reversed the showman's engine on to the bed of pine logs. The huge rear wheels, taller than a man, graunched the heavy timbers into the ground as the monstrous machine settled into its new permanent home. Once in position, Charlie opened valves to allow the steam to escape, and wound the handwheel that

103

clamped the brake shoes against the wheels. Carl, his eldest son, jumped down and helped Selby's men to drag old railway sleepers into place as chocks.

Eventually most of the onlookers got bored, but Faraday remained to record the hot ashes in the machine's firebox being dumped and quenched with water. A hose was played on the firebox to cool it and the Selby team set to work to bolt into place the methane adaptor that they had made.

Faraday's final shot was to roam the camcorder over the entire scene, taking in the methane well-head, now protected by a sturdy fence, the concrete section garage that served as a control room, the Centrax generator, and the new line of pine poles leading to the town that engineers were rigging with insulators and cables. He zoomed the camcorder on the two morris police on guard duty. They were armed with shotguns. The switch-on ceremony of the town's street lighting was planned for the coming Saturday evening carnival in Market Square.

Twenty-Three

The children's walkie-talkie was under Ellen Duncan's pillow so she didn't hear its call tones. Nor did she hear David Weir's voice.

"Ellen! This is David. Do you copy?"

But Claire Lake heard something. Her camp bed creaked as she propped herself on one elbow, brushing her long blonde hair away from her ears while listening intently.

The cave was illuminated by the glow from the tiny ten-watt light bulb powered by a truck battery which the cave's three occupants kept on during their sleep time. Day and night had no meaning in the cave but Ellen had wisely insisted that their sanity depended on their observation of clock time and the maintenance of their eating and sleep patterns.

"Ellen. Can you hear me?"

Claire slipped quietly from her bed. Her shadow flitted like a black cloud across the Palaeolithic hunting scenes that decorated the walls of the cave.

She glanced at Vikki Taylor. The teenager had taken to sleeping naked. The fingers of her left hand, as always, were slightly clenched. The floor's rough, ill-fitting flat stones that had been laid 40,000 years ago, were a welcome coolness beneath Claire's feet as she crossed to Ellen and gently shook the older woman awake – not without some trepidation because Ellen's temper was becoming even more uncertain of late. The seemingly unending long days of boredom and deprivation of natural light were getting to all of them. They had been incarcerated a month in the cave.

"Ellen . . ."

"Piss off."

"Ellen – I think it's David Weir calling you."

Ellen was immediately wide awake. She sat up, her dark, matted tresses falling about her shoulders. "What?"

"The radio. I thought I heard David Weir's voice."

Ellen snatched the tiny transceiver from under her pillow, raised it to her lips, and squeezed the press-to-talk button. "David?"

"Thank God. I thought the bloody thing was broken. I've brought you fresh supplies. I'm coming in. Don't answer."

Outside the cave, David Weir turned the radio off without waiting for a reply. The output power of the pair of children's walkie-talkies was only a few milliwatts, their range a mere 200 metres, but Adrian Roscoe's accursed Bodian sentinels had radios. Mike Malone had warned that their sets were tuneable to the family radio frequencies used by the kids' walkie-talkies.

There was a waning half-quarter moon that bathed the harsh outlines of the sandstone scarp of the Temple of the Winds in a strange, ethereal light. David didn't need his torch to see what he was doing other than for a quick inspection of the turf around the hidden entrance to Ellen's cave. Some of the more inquisitive of his southdown sheep gathered around to see what he was doing. He made no attempt to shoo them away; if there were prying eyes in the shadows, he was a good farmer checking the welfare of his flock.

Before setting out from Temple Farm with a wagon loaded with supplies for the three women, he had taken every possible precaution to ensure that he wasn't followed. He had even spent three hours before darkness fell repairing gates and fences. Hopefully any watchers would get as bored as quickly as Titan did. The big shire horse was happy hauling a heavy coulter plough but loathed being between the hafts of a wagon.

David Weir was alarmed when he studied the steep bank where the turf concealed the entrance to Ellen's cave. He passed it often enough in daytime while looking after his sheep but had always avoided as much as a casual glance at it. Roscoe's spies were everywhere. Easing the turf away confirmed his suspicions. Not only were the turfs incorrectly positioned, but they came away too easily – after a month in the good, humid growing conditions they should have knitted together more than they had done so. Midges swarmed around him as he used a trowel to clear away the soil.

The stink from the nearby ginkgo tree that Ellen had planted to deter deer from the terracing in which her crops had grown was overpowering.

It took only a few minutes to clear the soil yet he was drenched with sweat by the time he reached into the narrow opening to pull the piece of supporting hurdle clear. It came away unexpectedly easily because Ellen was pushing it from inside.

"David!" Ellen scrambled out of the opening and threw her arms around his neck. "Bloody hell," she said. "I never thought I'd would ever be so pleased to see your ugly face. I thought we'd been abandoned."

"Let's get inside, m'dear," said David curtly, pushing Ellen away. "That nightie's like a bloody beacon."

"Wonderful," said Claire, poking her head and shoulders out of the opening and inhaling. "Is that what fresh air smells like?" She withdrew hurriedly as David bundled Ellen unceremoniously into the entrance.

Vikki had pulled on a nightdress and was sitting on her camp bed by the time David, Ellen and Claire entered the main cave. Ellen switched on the main lights and turned to confront David. She was on the point of berating him for his cavalier behaviour but checked herself when she saw his grave expression.

"David? What's the matter?"

"Someone knows about this place. The turfs have been disturbed."

"But that's impossible," said Ellen. "There's only you and Mike Malone that know about it. And he would never tell anyone."

"Has he been here?"

"No. Of course not."

David glanced around the cave. The shock effect of seeing those extraordinary hunting scenes would never wear off.

David explained to the three women what he had found outside.

"Perhaps it was a fox or rabbits?" Claire suggested.

"Foxes and rabbits may dig holes," said David, "but they don't put the turf back."

"Maybe you're mistaken," said Vikki, speaking for the first time.

David shook his head. "I know exactly how I packed that turf."

Ellen looked at Claire. "Do you know anything about this?"

Claire shook her head.

"Vikki?"

The sixteen-year-old avoided Ellen's eye. "What?"

"Don't 'what' me, young lady. Do you know anything about the entrance being disturbed?"

"No."

Ellen knew Vikki well. The teenager had worked Saturday mornings in her herbal shop and they had been imprisoned together in Pentworth House to await being burned at the stake as witches. She knew that Vikki was not given to lying. The slight hesitation before the teenager replied, and that she was avoiding eye contact was all Ellen needed. She stood over the girl.

"Look at me."

Vikki's gaze remained on the floor.

"*I said, look at me!*"

Vikki looked up, and flinched away from Ellen's hard stare.

"Do you know about the entrance?"

Silence.

Ellen's stinging slap across Vikki's cheek knocked the girl's head back.

"I don't think that will achieve—"

"Stay out of this, David," said Ellen quietly. She saw a tear roll down Vikki's cheek and knelt to put an arm around the trembling girl. "You do know, don't you, Vikki?"

The young girl gave a little shuddering gulp and nodded. "I'm sorry, Ellen. Really I am. But I couldn't help it."

"Start at the beginning, Vikki. You've been out while we've been asleep, haven't you?"

"Yes," Vikki whispered.

"When?"

"The night of the coup."

"Why?"

"They called me . . ."

"Who?"

"The . . . the Visitors . . . They spoke to me. Called me. They said I was to go to the lake . . ."

Claire and David stared wide-eyed at the teenager.

"How did they call you?"

Vikki looked up at Claire and David. She touched her forehead with her left hand and jerked it away as if the recently regrown fingers were traitors.

Ellen took the hand in her own and held it tightly. "You're saying that you heard words in your head?"

Vikki didn't reply. Ellen realised that the girl was probably intimidated by having three people gathered around her. She said to David, "Wouldn't it be a good idea if you and Claire brought the supplies in?"

"Oh, for God's sake," Claire snapped in frustration. "Surely it's safe for us to leave this place now? What have we to fear now from Roscoe and his gang?"

"You've been listening to the radio?" David asked.

"Of course. What else is there to do?"

"Then you know about the conditional amnesty that Bob Harding granted Roscoe and the others?"

Claire grimaced. "Seems like a cop-out to me. He tries to murder Vikki and Ellen, and now it looks like he's getting away with it."

"If it's any consolation," said David. "Bob Harding isn't too happy about it. The trouble is that Adrian Roscoe has the best part of a hundred and fifty followers in Pentworth House and probably three times as many supporters in the community. Also he has control of the grain silos and most of our methane production." He looked speculatively at Claire. "You were one of the Bodian Brethren. You were the only one with the guts to run away."

"You know the reason for that," Claire retorted. "I don't want my baby born in that place."

"So how loyal do you think the others are?"

Claire thought about the question and admitted that maybe David had a point. She added, "But there'll be a confrontation sooner or later. All the amnesty does is buy us time."

"That's exactly what I said to Bob Harding. He replied that time was the one thing that was needed. Maybe the Visitors will suddenly up sticks and go tomorrow. We simply don't know. Meanwhile all three of you are safe here until we can be one hundred per cent certain that Adrian Roscoe and his followers won't do anything stupid." He grinned at Claire. "I like that nightie but it's best you get changed into something dark and let's get the wagon unloaded before Titan takes it into his head to go back to Temple Farm without me. Sometimes I feel like shooting that damned horse if he wasn't so valuable."

Vikki smiled. She knew that the others would eventually learn that she had left the cave and had been dreading this moment. Now she was relieved that it had come. David gave her a friendly squeeze. "Not to worry, Viks. No harm done. You tell Ellen all about it."

Ellen sat beside Vikki on the camp bed. "So how did all this happen, Vikki?"

"It was the night of the coup. I didn't know that at the time, of course. I just heard this voice in my head . . ."

Twenty-Four

*V*ikki . . .

$\quad$ Vikki was dreaming. It was her going-to-sleep dream that she'd always used since her imprisonment. It started with her concentrating on being in her little bedroom that her father had worked so hard to make perfect for her when she had only one hand. Electric curtains, wardrobe doors and drawers that opened at a touch. She imagined herself curled up, with her arm around Benji, a threadbare bear that had shared her childhood for as far back as she could remember. As sleep came, so the dream continued as a gentle diffusing from harsh reality into another world that ushered in Dario – the name she had given to the magnificent Zulu warrior in full impi regalia depicted in a life-size poster on her bedroom wall.

Dario was always there. Safe, reliable, beautiful Dario. Those strong arms around her, holding her against his powerful body, protecting her from the terrors of the night. The most potent aspect of her fantasy was that she had only to reach down to take hold of him for that wonderful body to be hers to command.

Beloved, sweet Dario.

Vikki . . .

The dream was gone in a cruel instant. Vikki's eyes snapped open. She stared up at the roof of the cave, lit softly by the low-wattage bedside lights that Ellen and Claire were reading by.

Vikki. Can you hear us?

It was the same voice in her head that she had heard before when it had summonsed her from her bedroom to Pentworth Lake. But it was stronger – the concepts that formed in her mind as words were much sharper. But Pentworth Lake was not as far from the cave as her bedroom was.

111

"Yes." She said it as an almost mute whisper.

Come to us, Vikki.

"I can't."

The girl was aware of a sensation of puzzlement until she concentrated on her surroundings.

You are trapped?

"In a way – yes."

Vikki turned and looked at her companions. Ellen was already dozing off. She switched off her bedside light and muttered a general goodnight. Claire did the same and Vikki was left in the feeble glow of the low-wattage night lamp that provided just enough light for toilet visits and to relieve the frightening totality of the darkness that would otherwise prevail in the cave. It would be at least ten minutes or more before her companions were sound asleep.

We understand. But you will come to us. He is ready.

"Yes," Vikki whispered to the darkness. "I will come."

The minutes slipped by. Vikki dozed off despite her trepidation about the strange voice in her head.

Vikki . . .

The tip of Dario's tongue was making rings of searing ecstasy around her nipples. She woke with a start. She hadn't meant to doze. She listened intently. Claire and Ellen had switched off their reading lights so that the cave was lit only by the solitary night lamp. The women's regular breathing told Vikki that her companions were asleep.

Come to us, Vikki.

"I'm coming!" her lips mimed in reply.

The glow of the night lamp enabled Vikki to dress in jeans and a T-shirt, and push her feet into her trainers without knocking anything over. Lacing the trainers could wait; the voice urging her to go to Pentworth Lake was an insistent clarion call of such intensity that she was sure Ellen and Claire would hear it.

But they didn't stir as Vikki arranged her pillows so that it looked as though she were asleep under the sheet. She took Ellen's penlight torch and a bread knife, and ducked into the narrow passage that led to the blocked entrance. David Weir and Malone had sealed the cave's entrance so that it could be opened from inside in an emergency. Sometimes, when her longing to be free became a torment, she would often come and sit close to the hurdle that retained the turf covering and listen to the sound of birdsong. Sometimes she had heard people passing by, talking. On one terrifying occasion she had sat in petrified silence as she listened to a group of voices discussing which farmhouse they would be raiding next in their search for the fugitives. They were so close that they must have been sitting on the grass outside the cave entrance.

She listened carefully now in case lovers were nearby or a morris patrol was in the vicinity, enforcing the curfew for under-eighteen-year-olds. A barn owl hooted mournfully but there were no other sounds, so she carefully sprung inwards the hazel wands that held the hurdle in place. Using the bread knife to cut a hole through the turf large enough for her to wriggle through was easier than she expected.

A breeze kept the smell of Ellen's ginkgo tree at bay, so that the draughts of night air she breathed seemed to sting with their purity after two weeks shut up in the cave. The sweet air and the realisation that she was now free for the first time since Nelson Faraday had arrested her in Ellen's herbal remedy shop was a heady brew, quickly displaced by the summonsing voice that told her that she wasn't free. Not yet.

She reached through the opening to reposition the hurdle, clenching the penlight torch between her teeth. The turf had to be packed into place in exactly the right position. To be doubly sure that she left no traces she even brushed the grass upright around the cave entrance. A sudden movement out of the corner of her eye gave her a scare until she realised that it was a group of David's southdown sheep that had strayed from the main flock.

Vikki. Come to us.

"Yes," she answered. "I'm coming."

She set off towards Pentworth Lake. Her progress startled small creatures of the night, which bolted into the darkness at her approach.

She was within 200 metres of Pentworth Lake when she heard the microlight passing overhead. She paused to stare up at the black sky. There was nothing to see. Only the angry buzz of the little air-cooled engine to mark the aircraft's passage. She knew nothing of the planned coup that was about to wrest power from Asquith Prescott or why Harvey Evans was flying his microlight at night. The tiny aircraft was armed with nautical distress rockets and heading towards Government House. Mike Malone's scheme was that the exploding rockets would create a diversion that would distract the armed guards around Government House long enough for him to arrest Adrian Roscoe, Asquith Prescott, and all those who had usurped Pentworth's democratic government for their own purposes. All Vikki knew was that the sound seemed to be heading towards the faint lights of Pentworth. She felt a sense of foreboding and shivered.

Vikki!

"Yes – I'm coming."

She resumed her journey but her pace lost its certainty. Why was she here? What could she do? Her footsteps faltered when the grass gave way to sand. She could hear the gentle lapping of the breeze-stirred lake.

She concentrated on the words: I'm here.

No answer.

I'm here! Was it possible to *think* louder?

The sharp yap of a vixen answered as though it had read her thoughts. She flashed the feeble beam of her torch along the black line of the water's edge. Doubts assailed her. Perhaps she had dreamed that she had been summonsed to the lake? She would have to return to the cave and face Ellen and Claire in the knowledge that she had compromised their safety by venturing out. The darkness was almost total and she suddenly felt very alone and afraid. Her torch dimmed. Shaking it caused it to brighten for a few seconds, and then it went out for good.

This time her mounting sensation of dread caused her to call out, "Hallo! I'm here!"

"Who's that?"

Vikki gave a gasp of fear. The voice that had answered was very close, male, deep, with a strange, resonant quality. She wanted to turn and run, but without the torch she would be certain to fall and injure herself. She preferred not to think about the terrible consequences of being caught in daylight

114

with a twisted ankle or a broken leg. The radio station had reported that Pentworth House was offering a huge reward for her capture.

Suddenly a faint glow suffused the lake. She wheeled around and watched the rocket climbing into the sky above Pentworth. It was a signal flare; it burst into a brilliant white light that seemed to hang motionless in the night haze. At this distance the light it created was the equivalent of a full moon.

"You must be Vikki," said Dario.

Twenty-Five

A rnie Trinder had no idea why he said that to the girl standing by the lake – the words swam into his head. The tall West Indian and his colleague, Nevil Rigsby, were Department of Trade and Industry radio interference inspectors who had been sent to Pentworth the previous March to investigate powerful radio emissions that were interfering with the aircraft navigation beacon at Midhurst. Their direction-finding equipment had led them to the flooded lake that had been made doubly treacherous due to surface run-off water from the South Downs in the wake of recent severe storms. Much to their surprise, their equipment had indicated that the transmissions were actually coming from the lake. Convinced that all they had to find was an electronic bug planted by someone with a warped sense of mischief and a good knowledge of radio, they had waded into the lake's swamped margins to search for an antenna.

The soft bed had given way beneath them. Both men were weighed down with heavy direction-finding equipment. They had struggled desperately to extricate themselves from the clinging mud but their frantic thrashing aggravated the situation. Trinder's last clear memories were hearing Rigsby's panic-stricken screams and the thought that he would never see his family in Jamaica again. And then the waters had closed over him and his body sank into the depths.

Although he had no sense of the passage of time, he knew that a long period had passed when something akin to consciousness began seeping back.

He was at the centre of a strange blackness that pervaded every corner of what he supposed was his reason. He was dead. He knew he was dead. He accepted that he was dead.

And yet . . .

Yet if he were dead, how could he be possessed of the self-awareness to know that he was dead? It didn't make sense. Nothing made sense. Not even the blinding lights that were suddenly floating above him. Pictures flitted in and out of his confused mind like moths attracted to and yet wary of a lamp.

There was an image swimming before him, blurred and indistinct. Concentrating on it required very little effort because there was nothing else to see. The picture cleared yet he was no wiser until he realised that what he was seeing was a cross-section picture of the human eye. But it wasn't a static picture: patterns of light, possessed of a strange energy, were racing along what he supposed was the optic nerve and flooding portions of his brain. Trinder had no medical knowledge but he knew that no earthly science could produce such vivid 3-D images of a complete neural system and exclude everything else. He blinked. An instant later all the neural activity in the image flicked off and back on again and he knew that what he was seeing was himself – his own eyes – his own retinas responding in harmony with the strange, impenetrable lights.

Your optical facilities are fully restored.

They were not words in his mind but concepts expressed by whoever they were beyond the lights. He could not see them but he could sense their awesome presence.

And so it went on like that. Drifting in and out of consciousness. And the returns to what he assumed were periods of consciousness were always accompanied by the strange, unspoken yet insistent command-concepts.

Lift your left leg.

Lift both arms.

On one occasion even his reproductive system came under intense scrutiny.

Trinder had no idea how long this went on for. Weeks . . . Months perhaps. He didn't know or care. Then the presences beyond the lights wanted him to speak. So he spoke:

"Am I dead?"

He sensed their uncertainty.

Your companion . . . We did our best . . . We are not like you. We cannot work miracles.

He assumed the presences were referring to Rigsby, and tried to ponder the meaning of this curious answer but he was tired. All he could manage was to repeat:

"Am I dead?"

A picture of a wristwatch formed in his mind. The hands suddenly advanced an hour. It was like one of those simple conventions used in old movies to indicate the passage of time. It amused Trinder. Why not show him an ashtray filling slowly with cigarette ends? But the image served its purpose and he knew how long he had to live.

"An hour? Why bother?"

So that you may bear a gift.

Another enigmatic answer that he could not get them to clarify no matter how hard he concentrated.

She will probably call you Dario.

"Who will?"

You will know.

"Is that my name?"

It is now.

"But I'm Arnie Trinder."

You were. But now you are Dario. You even look like him. Her name is Victoria. You must call her Vikki.

"I will die in an hour?"

A pause, then:

We don't think you ever die.

Another maddeningly meaningless answer.

"What will happen to me afterwards?"

Trinder sensed that they were keeping something from him. He formed the question again in his mind, trying to shape his meaning with forceful images.

We do not know. That is why we are here.

And then images were strong, insistent.

It must be up to Vikki if she wants you and if you want to. There must be no force. This is important. You are two people exercising their free will. We can only provide an opportunity.

Suddenly they were gone and he was alone. Sensations

118

flooded into his body. Normal sensations: the pressure of his body lying on his back; a cooling breeze. He even heard the buzz of midges. A wave of external stimuli washed over him with the shocking suddenness of a fall into a river. It was as though bodily feelings had been held back by a dam that had been suddenly breached.

Arnie Trinder opened his eyes and sat up.

It was night. A lake was beside him. Pentworth Lake, but no longer the expanse of swamp that he recalled when he and Nevil Rigsby had stumbled around its margins. There were distant lights in the direction of Pentworth, but not the harsh, steady glow of electric lights as one would expect of a small town. These were individual points of weak light. He climbed to his feet and realised that his body had undergone profound changes. He was taller, his muscles more pronounced, his chest deeper. His lankiness was no more, and his clothes were uncomfortably tight. The dry sand gave way underfoot in a manner that he attributed to his additional weight. Extraordinary as these changes were, he accepted them.

A rocket climbed into the sky over the town and burst into a bright flare that hung like a miniature sun. Its distant glare was enough to illuminate the tall girl who was standing only a few metres away. Her golden hair was gathered into a ponytail. She hadn't seen him and was staring towards the town and the flare. Trinder was momentarily confused by contradictions. He knew this girl, and yet he had never seen her before.

"You must be Vikki," he said.

Twenty-Six

V ikki's head snapped around and her eyes went wide with shock when she saw the figure of the man standing not ten metres away. His jeans, sweatshirt and anorak looked uncomfortably tight, as though they had been made for a smaller man.

Recognition was instantaneous. "Dario!" she exclaimed.

"Hallo, Vikki." Trinder smiled and held out his hands.

Vikki rushed at him and threw her arms around him. His body felt hard and unyielding as she remembered it in her dreams. "Oh, Dario . . . Dario . . . I knew you would come. I just knew."

To Vikki's irritation, he seemed to be distracted. "Look." He pointed.

She didn't want to take her eyes off the man she knew as Dario for an instant, but she turned and gazed at the sudden orange-yellow glow that permeated the haze over Pentworth. It grew brighter by the second. They could see flames leaping into the sky, silhouetting intervening rooftops.

Vikki wasn't interested. She reached up and kissed the man she knew as Dario, tracing his finely sculptured aristocratic features with her left hand as she had done on many occasions in her daydreams. When she touched his lips, his incredibly white teeth parted to gently grip her fingers, drawing them in, sucking slowly while pushing the tip of his tongue between her fingertips, melting away her reason.

All Vikki would ever be able to recall with any clarity of the next ten minutes was the divine moment when she threw back her head and uttered a primeval cry that was neither ecstasy nor pain, but triumph.

As they dressed in silence, Vikki became aware of a mounting sensation of joy. It was almost the same feeling of euphoria she remembered when her new hand was growing. But this time there was a difference; this time pictures formed in her mind with a vivid, almost frightening clarity of what was happening to her body. She saw a huge globe surrounded by millions of wriggling, tadpole-like creatures, their tails lashing furiously. One broke through and the cell divided instantly into two cells. They, in turn, became four cells, swelling rapidly to maintain their size.

And four were eight . . . Then sixteen . . . thirty-two . . .

They heard the harsh crackle of distant gunfire.

"There is much to be done," said Dario softly.

Together the couple started walking hand in hand towards the orange glow that was lighting up the sky.

The night breeze sweeping across Pentworth Lake created surface ripples which meant that the disturbance caused by the spyder as it emerged from the water went unnoticed. It advanced purposefully up the beach. Its sensors could see into the infra-red – its surroundings were as day. It located Trinder and Vikki and set off to shadow them, its curiously articulated legs not making a sound as it moved across the grass. It had little difficulty absorbing the lights of the night so that its body reflected none, rendering it virtually invisible unless one knew exactly where to look.

Dario's awesome masculine presence beside Vikki suddenly made her feel awkward and uncertain. She felt strangely detached from her body, hardly able to believe that she had actually allowed this majestic being beside her to make love to her, that she had wanted him to make love to her and had almost forced herself upon him. But she felt no remorse. There had been a rightness about the loss of her virginity that transcended all the mores of her Catholic upbringing.

"It looks like Government House is on fire," she stammered.

"Government House?"

"Don't you know?"

"Know what?" asked Trinder.

There was the sound of a fire engine's siren. The flames clawing into the sky were now clearly visible.

121

Vikki! Stop!

The command was louder and stronger than Vikki had ever known. It burst like a roman candle in her head.

She stopped. Trinder wanted to know what was the matter.

"There will be people about – going to see what is happening."

Trinder was puzzled. "Does that matter?"

"There are wicked people in the town who want to kill me. They will kill you, too."

"I'm already—" He broke off, appearing to be confused.

"Already what, Dario?"

Trinder's teeth gleamed in the gloom. "Dead." He added hastily, "Vikki – my name isn't Dario. It's Arnie Trinder." He added, awkwardly. "About just now – I'm sorry . . ."

Go back, Vikki! Go back your hiding place!

Vikki drew Trinder's head down and kissed him. "There's nothing to be sorry for. It was what I wanted."

"But I'm not your boyfriend. I'm not Dario."

Vikki smiled. "I know that." She took his arm and steered him back to the path that led towards Ellen's cave and the brooding scarp of the Temple of the Winds.

"We must hide before anyone finds us."

"Where?"

"I will show you."

They walked through the cloying humidity of the night, talking in low tones, unaware that the spyder was trailing some thirty metres behind them. Vikki explained to Trinder about the cave and was astonished to discover that he knew nothing about the Wall or the misfortunes that had overtaken Pentworth since the previous March. They climbed the steep path that led towards the buff that Pentworth was built on and stopped near the concealed entrance to Ellen's cave.

"What's that smell?" Trinder asked.

Vikki put her hand over her mouth to suppress a giggle and explained about Ellen's ginkgo tree.

"Sure does stink."

"We must be very quiet so as not wake them," said Vikki, kneeling and pulling the turf away from the cave's entrance.

"I can't stay with you," said Trinder, crouching beside Vikki and helping to remove the hurdle.

The girl stopped work. "Why not?"

"I have to return to the lake. They're calling me back. It's very strong. When they call, you have to obey."

Vikki remained intent on clearing the loose soil from the opening so that her companion would not see her silent tears. "I know," she said dully.

"You'll need me outside to make good here," said Trinder. "I'm sorry, Vikki, but I must go back."

Vikki brushed the soil from her hands and entwined her arms around Trinder's neck, burying her face against his shoulder. "Hold me, Dario. Hold me tight. Just for a while."

They remained like that for a minute, not speaking until Trinder eased her gently away and cradled Vikki's head in his hands. He considered her the loveliest creature he had ever beheld and wanted the moment to last forever, but the summonsing voice in his mind was becoming an insistent clarion call that he could not ignore.

With one final, lingering kiss, Vikki wriggled into the opening. She turned for one last look at her beloved Dario but Trinder had pushed the hurdle into place.

He spent a few minutes pressing the soil back into place with his bare hands and repositioning the turfs as best he could, unaware that the spyder was watching him from a few metres away. Satisfied that the entrance to the cave was properly concealed, he brushed himself down and set off at a fast pace for Pentworth Lake.

The spyder paused to inspect the cave's entrance and moved off to follow Trinder at a distance.

If the machine's makers had not known before where Vikki had been in hiding, they knew now.

Twenty-Seven

Ellen was silent for some moments when Vikki stopped talking. She didn't doubt a word of the teenager's story. The evidence that the Visitors were possessed of extraordinary abilities was the Wall, and Vikki's perfect left hand.

David and Claire had finished dragging supplies into the cave and were lining up the five-litre containers of fresh water near the cooking area and generally tidying up, creating work while Ellen and Vikki were engrossed in conversation. David refilled the base of the Selby burner ring with carbon granules and checked that the forced-draught hand plunger was working properly.

"His name wasn't Dario," said Ellen firmly, concerned about Vikki's hold on reality. "You must get that out of your mind."

"I know. But I'll always think of him as that."

"You make it sound as though he is dead."

"I think he is," Vikki answered, keeping her voice steady. "He seemed to think he was."

"Do you know who Trinder was?"

"No. But I think I've heard the name."

"He was one of the two men that were drowned in my lake."

Vikki's green eyes opened wide. "Yes – I remember now. But that was months ago. Before the Wall appeared."

"It was the day before the Wall appeared. And their bodies were never found."

Vikki remained silent.

"And you let him make love to you?"

There was defiance in Vikki's nod. "I wanted him to."

"And he didn't use a condom?"

"No."

"How many days since your last period started?"

The girl thought for a moment before answering.

"Which means that they couldn't've chosen a worse time," said Ellen ruefully. "Or a better time . . ."

"They?"

"*They!*" Ellen snapped. She jumped up and stood over Vikki. "They? The Visitors or whatever they are! You *could* be pregnant, for God's sake!"

The outburst caused Claire and David to stop what they were doing and gape in surprise.

"I think I *am* pregnant!" Vikki retorted. "In fact I know I am."

"Don't be absurd, child."

"*I tell you, I know! I don't why I know! But I do!*"

Ellen realised in that moment just how much the events of last month had changed Vikki. Being tried and condemned to death as a witch because she had grown a new hand, the amazing rescue from the scourging at the Temple of the Winds, several weeks imprisoned in this cave . . . And now this. The once demure schoolgirl who used to work Saturday mornings in her shop was no more. This was a new Vikki. More determined, more decisive, more certain of herself, more mature.

Claire sat beside Vikki and took the girl's hand. Vikki snatched it away. "I'm not some child that needs comforting," she said, as though underlining Ellen's conclusions.

"We've finished unloading everything," said David awkwardly, wishing he could think of something more sensible to say. "Should be enough to last you another two weeks."

"I think we're going to be stuck in here a lot longer than that," said Ellen grimly. She sank into a canvas chair and regarded Vikki thoughtfully.

"I don't understand," said David, looking at the three women in turn.

"Think what Adrian Roscoe will make of this if it gets out," said Ellen. "Consorting with the devil . . . The seed of some Satanic messiah growing in her womb."

"That's not true!" Vikki flared. "We made love because *I* wanted to!"

"You made love because the Visitors forced you!"

"No! They kept telling me that I didn't have to but I ignored them! It was my choice!"

Ellen saw the intensity in Vikki's eyes and realised that she had made a mistake. "I'm sorry . . . I should not've put it like that. But that's how Adrian Roscoe will see it. This stupid amnesty won't be enough. It'll only be safe for us to come out when Adrian Roscoe is dead and his Bodian cult destroyed."

Twenty-Eight

"Well all I can say," said Andrew Dayton, as he stood with his arm around his wife, waving goodbye to the pony and trap that his father had hired, "is that the miserable old bugger must be mellowing in his old age."

His wife laughed at the thought. Roger Dayton mellowing? It was a ridiculous notion. She tugged on her husband's arm. "Come on. A whole Saturday without the kids. Let's make the most of it."

"Maybe he's finally accepted that his yachting days are over?" Andrew wondered.

"Not the way he was moaning last week, he hasn't," said his wife. "And if he has finally taken a liking to his grandchildren, Allison will knock it out of him in an hour."

She was wrong about her father-in-law. Any liking that Roger Dayton thought he might manage to muster for the shrieking ten-year-old was knocked out of him before they reached the end of the road. Peter, his younger grandchild, was quieter and therefore more tolerable, but the sad truth was that Dayton had much the same love of screaming children that he had for tropical Force 12s.

"Can't this thing go any faster, Grandpa?" Allison demanded, banging the side of the trap and causing the pony's ears to twitch. "We'll never get there at this rate."

"We're going fast enough," said Dayton morosely, wondering if he'd last the day.

"Daddy's car could do a hundred miles an hour!"

"Those days are over, aren't they, Grandpa?" said Peter seriously.

"They're gone for good, stupid!" Allison yelled.

"You never know, Peter," Dayton replied. "They might come back."

127

"Mummy said that she hopes they will never come back," Allison declared. "She said she likes the new life."

"No, she didn't," said Peter. "She said only if they could find a way of growing chocolate."

"It doesn't grow, stupid!"

"Yes, it does, too!"

The rest of the journey proceeded in that vein, with Dayton wishing he had the pony's ability to swivel his ears away from the uproar.

"I can see the sea!" Peter yelled.

"It's the lake, idiot!"

Pentworth Lake's artificial beach was already dotted with family groups, bright parasols, and children splashing and shrieking around the water's edge under the watchful eye of a lifeguard perched on a high chair. Any bathers venturing beyond the line of brightly coloured floats that marked the shelf where the lake's bottom fell away into the depths earned angry blasts on his whistle.

"Sorry, sir. No animals allowed on the beach," a beach marshal told Dayton.

Peter pointed to the reeds at the far end of the beach near the tree line. "Could I use the pony to take the trap over there, please? It'll be in the shade. I'm under strict instructions to keep my granddaughter out of the sun."

"I go all blotchy and disgusting in the sun," said Allison proudly.

"You're blotchy and disgusting without the sun."

Peter's observation earned him a sisterly rebuke – a hard punch on the nose. He started howling.

"No problem, sir," said the marshal. "But please bring the pony back right away."

Dayton thanked him. One problem out of the way. The pony plodded across the soft, dry sand, hauling the laden trap. The edge of the beach he selected was close to the reeds, in the shade, and therefore unpopular. The nearest family were some fifty metres away. Happy and excited, Peter and Allison unhitched the pony and led it to the pony park – a grassy field provided with water troughs and rows of woven sunshades.

While they were gone, Dayton checked his aluminium firkin

128

depth charge. It was wrapped in a travelling blanket under the trap's seat. It could stay there for the time being. He laid a ground sheet on the sand and settled in a camping chair. A model yacht scudding across the lake caught his attention and his mind wandered to his own yacht, stranded in his paddock, twenty miles from the sea.

Soon, he promised himself. Soon.

The children were back. Laughing and whooping. They changed into swimming costumes and kept rushing in and out of the water, demanding that Grandpa admire their swimming prowess or time them in races, their sibling rivalry forgotten during the hot, idyllic afternoon. They were particularly delighted with the second-hand inflatable boat in the shape of a duck that Grandpa had bought for them at the Mothercare shop. It wasn't big enough for two children, therefore its possession was the cause of so much renewed dispute that Dayton felt impelled to call them to order for lunch. They ate their picnic – mustard and cress, and tomato sandwiches washed down with home-made fizzy apple juice.

"Let's do something different," said Dayton.

"Like what, Grandpa?"

"Well now, you two. How would you like to make a car?"

"One that can do a hundred miles an hour?" asked Allison hopefully.

"One that does nought miles an hour but is big enough for both of you to sit in."

The notion appealed to the children's imagination.

"Get the buckets and spades," Dayton ordered cheerfully. "And then cold water and plenty of it. We've got to make the sand wet so that it keeps its shape."

Under their grandfather's guidance, the children damped the sand in an area near the reeds and set to with trowels and toy spades to dig out the footwell.

"It's got to be bigger and deeper," Dayton insisted. "This is going to be a low-slung racing car. You don't want it rolling over on bends, do you?"

The children laughed delightedly and dug deep and wide. They were seeing a wholly unexpected side of their usually dour grandfather. Peter built up the bonnet, making it progressively longer as he learned the pleasure of moulding the damp sand while Allison produced four passable half wheels. Peter was proud of his headlamps.

Once finished, they spent a happy two hours in their two-child imagination-powered car, roaring around Goodwood and arguing over taking turns to drive while Dayton read and dozed. At 5 p.m. he announced that it was time to go.

"You two go and fetch the pony," he ordered. "While I fill in the hole we've made. We don't want people falling in it, do we?"

"Can't we take the car home, Grandpa?" Peter wailed.

"'Fraid not," said Dayton solemnly. "It's run out of petrol."

This struck the brother and sister as hilarious. They ran off laughing to collect the pony.

Dayton's movements were brisk but not overtly hurried. The nearest family had packed up and left. He deflated the toy boat, opened the trap's rear door and dragged the heavy keg from under the seat. It was a comfortable fit in the sand car's deep footwell. He tucked the folded boat down the side of the keg, and pushed in the car's sides and bonnet on top of the cache. He was levelling the area with his feet, having carefully memorised the spot, when the children returned leading the pony.

"Where's the blow-up boat, Grandpa?" Peter asked as they were packing the trap.

"I've put it away for next time," Dayton replied absently. He was thinking that the biggest risk was discovery of his cache by hobbyists with metal detectors, although the use of batteries for such activities was now illegal. Besides, metal detector nerds concentrated on popular picnic spots on the main beach. "Best I look after it. That way it won't get torn to bits by you two fighting over it."

During the ride home, Dayton reflected that only the final phase of the operation was left in his plan to destroy the Silent Vulcan – the actual dropping of the depth charge on the first moonless night. So far everything had gone much better than he had expected. He had been dreading this particular day and was somewhat surprised by the realisation that he had actually enjoyed himself.

Twenty-Nine

The conversion of the swimming-pool filter into Bob Harding's bathyscaphe was progressing smoothly, so Tony Selby ordered work on the raft to begin. There was a desperate shortage of wagons and horses now that the first of Pentworth's main crop vegetables were being gathered, therefore dismantling the scaffolding that covered the façade of Government House and moving it to Pentworth Lake was a two-day operation.

The basis of the raft was several wagon-loads of empty liquid-fertilizer drums and assorted oil drums. Each one had to be tested for leaks by the team of scaffold erectors who had volunteered for the job of assembling the raft while working waist-deep off the beach. The drums were clamped in place by scaffold poles to form a pontoon that was ten metres square. Beach marshals were hard-pressed to keep children and their families away from the strange construction and were eventually forced to declare the beach and the lake closed to the public.

Tony Selby arrived to inspect the pontoon towards the end of the first day's construction when the decking consisting of builders' scaffolding planks was being bolted into place. The team were resourceful and had devised solutions to many problems that had arisen.

The engineer strode around the anchored raft, his keen eye missing nothing, and was pleased with the work. In the centre of the structure was a rectangular opening about three metres square which some of the hot, weary workers were using as a swimming pool. On each side of the hole were two securely braced towers, four metres high, fashioned from short lengths of scaffolding. The tops of the towers were spanned by a stout steel "I" beam that would be taking the weight of the bathyscaphe once the winch and pulley block were in place.

Selby congratulated the team on their handiwork: the pontoon was sound and stable. He told them and a Radio Pentworth reporter that tomorrow the bathyscaphe and winching gear would be brought down and that he hoped to complete the unmanned test dives that day.

He returned to his pony and trap and was about to drive off when he thought he heard a once familiar sound: a sound that belonged to past winters.

It was the distant baying of the local hunt's foxhounds.

Thirty

D avid Weir cursed roundly and began the long climb up
the narrow path that led to the sandstone scarp of the
Temple of the Winds. His sheepdog wagged its tail furiously
as it trotted at his heel, pleased that it had finally persuaded its
master where the missing sheep were. The sun was a bloated
ripe fruit hanging above the western horizon. David would
rather have left the search until morning but decided that he
couldn't take chances having a dozen valuable ewes milling
around on the dangerous sandstone scarp.

He was sweating by the time he emerged on to the flat
plateau and was immediately transported back to the night of
the rescue of Ellen and Vikki from Adrian Roscoe's clutches
at this very spot.

His collie was right. The missing sheep were in a huddle
near the sheer drop where Ellen and Vikki had nearly fallen
to their deaths. The ewes started bleating the moment they
saw David. Trust the stupid creatures to remain silent while
he was searching for them below. He bade his dog to remain
where it was and went cautiously forward, whistling. It only
needed one sheep to start towards him and the rest would be
certain to follow. Sure enough, an older ewe responded. She
trotted sheepishly towards David, bleating piteously, and the
rest followed. God knows how long they had been up here
where there was hardly any grass. On a signal, the dog circled
around the flock, keeping low, and flattened itself to the ground
near the edge in case the senseless creatures decided to double
back. David herded them towards the path. Once the lead ewe
picked up the path, the other sheep followed her without further
encouragement from him or the dog.

David was about to fall in behind them when he heard a

sound that chilled his blood and had him reaching for his folding binoculars.

It was the baying of foxhounds.

He ran towards the wooded end of the plateau where the great slab protruded from the slope and scanned the backs of the row of distant houses and shops that fronted North Street. He tracked down the terraces where Ellen Duncan grew her crops of herbs and, with a sinking heart, found the foxhounds within a hundred metres of the cave's concealed entrance. There were ten of them milling around in apparent confusion. One broke away, running furiously, and the rest followed. Then they all pulled up short and resumed their aimless milling, sniffing here and there, tails high, working overtime.

David searched the lengthening shadows and found the horsemen. There were two of them. He doubted if the master of the hounds was one of them – it was most likely a kennel lad. The local hunt had their kennels on the Pentworth Estate and paid a nominal rent to Adrian Roscoe. But there was no mistaking the figure on the second horse. His right arm was in a sling.

It was Nelson Faraday.

David nearly stampeded his sheep on the narrow path as he pushed hurriedly past them. His only thought was to contact Mike Malone as soon as possible.

Having sent his collie home, it was forty minutes later and nearly dark by the time he found a private house with a telephone that the owner allowed him to use to call the police station.

"I'm very sorry, Mr Weir," said the duty officer, "but Mr Malone isn't available."

David read that as police speak for Mr Malone isn't here. "Can you get a message to him, please. He's always got a radio with him. Tell him that it's extremely urgent he meet me at—" He stopped himself.

Where? For God's sake!

"Ask him to please return to the police station and tell him I'll meet him there."

"If you could tell me what it's all about, Mr Weir—"

134

"I'm sorry, I can't," said David. "But if you tell him who called, he'll understand." David suddenly realised that he didn't have Malone's private telephone number. "If you give me his number, I'll call him direct."

"I'm very sorry, sir. We can't give out that information, but I'll see that he gets your message."

David hung up and waited a few seconds for the telephone operator to disconnect the line before turning the crank handle again.

"This is David Weir," he told the operator. "Would you put me through to Mr Michael Malone, please."

"I'll put you through to the police station, sir."

"I've already been on to them. I need to call him at home."

"Do you have his number?"

"No," said David, guessing what was coming.

"I'm very sorry, but I can't connect you unless you have his number."

David wasted several minutes arguing and nearly ended the conversation by slamming down the receiver, but it wasn't his telephone and the papier-mâché handsets were not designed to withstand abuse. He thanked the householder and left.

He was undecided for the moment. His instinct was to go to the cave and make sure that the women were safe, but he realised that that might be what Faraday was hoping for. It would be best if he headed for the police station.

It had been dark nearly two hours when he arrived at the police station, half running, out of breath, just as a police Range Rover pulled up outside and Mike Malone jumped out of the passenger seat. Malone explained that the last mile of his homeward jog took him through a radio dead spot and that he had called for a vehicle the moment he received David's message. His face was tense as he listened to the farmer's account.

"You're sure the dogs didn't find the entrance?"

"Not while I was watching. But they were milling about the area, so they obviously had picked up something. I didn't go to investigate in case that was what Faraday wanted."

"Dogs," said Malone bitterly. "That's something I didn't think of."

"It doesn't look like Roscoe has until now," David replied. "Actually, I don't think that foxhounds would be much use, even if Roscoe had articles of their clothing—"

"Which he has," Malone interrupted. "And he'd certainly have stuff that belonged to Claire Lake."

"Yes – but the hounds are trained to go after fox or deer scent. It's not as if they're bloodhounds."

"How sure can you be?"

David shook his head. "Not very. I don't have anything to do with the hunt."

"We play safe," said Malone. "There's sure to be a hound in the pack that's smarter than the rest."

Malone thought fast. His first inclination was to do nothing. But David's concern was infectious and Malone conceded that he too was too worried for the safety of the three fugitives for doing nothing to be considered as an option. Particularly Ellen's safety.

"We'll take the Range Rover," Malone decided. He dismissed the driver and took the wheel. It was the same vehicle that Asquith Prescott had had armour-plated on the inside when he had been Chairman. David jumped in beside him. To his frustration, Malone drove at a moderate speed and ignored his pleas to step it up. "We're just a routine patrol," he told his passenger. "This way we don't draw attention to ourselves."

Using the vehicle meant taking a longer route in a wide circle around Pentworth town to reach the lower slopes near the foot of the Temple of the Winds but they got there quicker than they could have walked. Malone parked on a patch of hard standing that was often used by the pony-and-trap morris police patrols for rest breaks.

Malone wound down his window and used a pair of Sussex Police-issue night-vision binoculars to scan what he could see of the sensitive area in the proximity of the cave. Not getting out of the vehicle would make it difficult for a hidden watcher to make out where he was looking.

"Nothing untoward," he said, handing the binoculars to David.

The instrument out-performed David's own binoculars.

136

After a careful search he conceded that everything looked normal.

"Let's take a saunter," said Malone, climbing out of the Range Rover. He locked the vehicle and the two men set off unhurriedly up the slope towards Ellen's cave. After a few moments Malone's calming influence got to David, so that he was able to keep step with the police officer and not try racing ahead.

They neared the cave entrance. Malone sniffed disapprovingly when he caught a whiff of Ellen's pungent ginkgo tree. "That tree sure does pong."

"Ellen planted it to keep deer and rabbits away from crops," said David absently, feeling in his pockets. "I've often used a rag soaked in diesel oil."

"That's it, then," said Malone. "You said the hounds were milling about as if they were confused. Hardly surprising. That tree stinks to high heaven."

Malone's deduction raised David's hopes. "Damn it," he muttered. "I haven't got the walkie-talkie with me. Bugger. Bugger. Bugger."

"Stop panicking," said Malone, unclipping his PMR radio and rotating the channel selector. "Family Radio Service Channel 1, isn't it?"

"For God's sake, Malone! You'll be heard all over Pentworth on that thing!"

Malone unscrewed the transceiver's stub antenna and pushed down the power attenuator button. "Try not to get too excited, David. This thing has a range of only a few metres without its aerial. Let's get closer."

They walked on and stopped outside the entrance to the cave. Malone raised the PMR's speaker-microphone to his mouth. "Ellen? Copy?"

Silence. Malone opened the set's squelch and tried again. "Ellen. Do you copy?" Again, silence other than the low hiss of white noise. He passed the microphone to David. "Maybe she's refusing to answer because she doesn't recognise my voice?"

David called twice but there was no answer. Malone flashed his torch for David's benefit as the farmer knelt and pulled at the turfs. "Oh Christ," he said. "They've been disturbed."

"You were here a few days ago," Malone pointed out.

"And I didn't put them back like this!" David snapped. "They've been pulled out and put back – recently."

Malone knelt beside him. "You're sure?"

"Of course I'm bloody sure! Christ – look, man! They're all loose! They've only just been pushed roughly back into place!"

The police officer was able to pick up a sod without encountering any resistance. He conceded that David had a point but his companion wasn't listening. He burrowed into the hillside like a rabbit and pulled out the hurdle. "Torch!" he snapped.

Malone handed him the torch and David wriggled through the hole. He was gone less than two minutes. Light danced around the opening as he crawled back and pushed his head and shoulders out. He held the torch before him, so that it lit up his haggard expression.

"They've gone!" David croaked, his voice cracking. "Those bastards have found them!"

Thirty-One

The moon was in its last quarter and provided adequate light for Roger Dayton to see that the pontoon construction site on the beach at Pentworth Lake had been provided with a small caravan and, as near as he could judge from their voices, two watchmen. Every few minutes they played a powerful light on the giant raft, the humidity of the night defining a beam that would be more than capable of sweeping the entire lake if the watchmen heard anything suspicious.

Dayton melted back into the trees. He hunkered down and consulted a map with the aid of a penlight torch to work out a route so that he could approach his buried depth charge without crossing the main beach. His original plan had been to carry out tonight's operation in a few days' time when there would be no moon, but the news reports on the radio about the coming bathyscaphe operation decided him to bring to bring D-Day, as he thought of it, forward. In a few days' time there was a chance that the pontoon would be permanently located in the middle of Pentworth Lake, possibly with men on it. Dayton didn't want any deaths on his conscience. The Visitors didn't matter. They were aliens and therefore not human, and therefore not protected by law.

Legal niceties were important to Roger Dayton. He wanted to take part in the single-handed round-the-world yacht race the following year, not spend it in prison. The position of the watchmen's caravan on the beach worried him, but his depth charge would be exploding at a depth of 120 metres and black powder, although lethal enough, was hardly a high velocity modern explosive. From his experiences on naval exercises, he knew that there would be an eruption on the surface but doubted if there would be much of a tidal wave. It was a calculated risk

139

that he decided was worth taking. He set off to find the track that led to the northern end of the lake.

He found the track without difficulty and walked along its grassy verge where his trainers did not make a sound. It was as well he did so because he heard approaching voices and had to crouch in the undergrowth, thankful that he was wearing a dark tracksuit. He had even stuck black tape over the stainless steel strap of his yachtsman's wristwatch.

The two-man morris police patrol were deep in conversation as they passed his hiding place. He waited until they were a long way off and resumed his walk. He came to the bend he was looking for and left the track to push through the undergrowth in the direction of the lake. He emerged near the dense reeds that bordered this part of the lake and skirted them cautiously. The ground was soft underfoot. The distant lights of the watchmen's caravan were duplicated on the lake's still surface. The reeds ended and he was on the beach. A quick check with the torch enabled him to locate the spot where he had spent the day with his grandchildren. The tracks left by the pony and trap he had hired for the trip were still visible in the sand.

The sand was dry, soft enough for him to dig down with bare hands. He found nothing, quickly suppressed a mild sensation of panic, and carefully checked his surroundings. Maybe a little to the left . . .

His fingers encountered the cold, hard surface of the beer keg. A little more digging and he was able to roll it out of the hole and recover the inflatable toy boat.

He sat cross-legged and inflated the boat by mouth. It took him longer than he expected and it made him a little dizzy but the nausea soon passed. He stepped out of his tracksuit. Underneath he was wearing swimming trunks. Rather than exert himself unnecessarily, he used his feet to roll the aluminium keg down the beach to the water's edge.

There was the initial shock when entering water but he had known worse. In fact the water was not nearly as cold as he had expected. He carried the keg until he was up to his waist and placed it carefully in the centre of the toy boat. It took the home-made depth charge's weight comfortably.

He was a good swimmer and made steady progress using

breaststroke to avoid splashing, nudging the toy boat and its deadly cargo along using his chest. He lifted the line of bathing area marker buoys and swam on towards the centre of the lake. He felt the surface water becoming noticeably colder – probably something to do with convection currents bringing up colder water from the depths.

What he judged to be the centre of the lake was extremely cold. He rested by holding on to the toy boat. He would need his strength for a fast swim back to the shore. He watched the luminous dials on his wristwatch, finger poised on the stopwatch button. The depth charge was weighted to sink at half a metre per second and would therefore take 240 seconds – four minutes – to reach 120 metres when the hydrostatic fuse would fire the Very pistol cartridge into the charge. In this cold, and therefore denser, water the keg would most likely sink at a slightly slower rate but he couldn't take chances: he would have to reach the shore and get clear of the scene in well under four minutes.

He watched the second hand crawling around the watch face. He felt his heartbeat quickening when it reached the figure 8.

9 . . . 10 . . . 11 . . . 12 . . .

Dropping the depth charge was simply a matter of tipping the toy boat over. He pressed the stopwatch button and struck out for the shore using a fast crawl. He blundered into the bathing buoys and experienced momentary panic when he thought he'd become entangled in the line. He broke clear and swam on, putting all his strength into his strokes with his arms and avoiding splashing with his legs. His hands grazed on the bottom. He scrambled to his feet, dashed across the beach to snatch up his trainers and tracksuit, and headed into the undergrowth. Brambles slashed at his bare arms and legs but he ignored the pain as he continued his plunge deep into the thickets. He came to a small clearing and threw himself flat. It took him a few moments to get his breath back and focus his eyes on his watch.

160 seconds.

Not bad for an old-timer, he thought. He donned his tracksuit and laced up his trainers.

200 seconds.

He stood and stared at the centre of the lake, his breathing getting easier.

220 seconds.

Come on! Come on!

240 seconds . . . 250 seconds . . .

Obviously the cold water had slowed down the keg's sinking more than he had anticipated.

Five minutes slipped by. He left his cover and walked cautiously down to the water's edge as if his being closer would somehow trigger his failed depth charge.

"What's your game, sunshine?"

He wheeled around and was blinded by a powerful flashlight. He recognised the voice as belonging to one of the morris police he had avoided earlier.

"Dayton, isn't it? Our intrepid yachtsman. What are you doing here? Pining for the lonely sea and the sky?"

Despite his conviction that they could hear his heart hammering, and bracing himself to run if the depth charge went off, he managed a casual smile and replied that he was out for a late-night jog.

"Didn't you see the sign?"

Innocently, "What sign?"

"The lake's closed. It's been on the radio."

Dayton heard a PMR radio squawk. The morris policeman who hadn't spoken moved away and muttered something inaudible into his radio.

"I'm sorry," said Dayton. "I had no idea."

"Got your ID?"

"Sorry – there aren't any pockets in this tracksuit."

"We're wanted, grade 1," said the second morris police officer curtly.

"You'd better head back, sir," said the first morris policeman to Dayton, waving his torch in the direction of the road.

Dayton set off for home, wondering what had gone wrong with his depth charge. It could be any number of things, the most likely being that the fibre washer under the bung had leaked and water had saturated the charge. The morris policeman had recognised him, so perhaps it was just as well that it had failed.

Thirty-Two

A lthough Malone had had little time to organise the raid on Pentworth House, the plans were going well. By 1 a.m., three hours after the discovery that Vikki, Ellen and Claire were missing, he had mustered a hundred-strong force crowded into Pentworth police station. Rather than risk a telephone operator in the exchange tipping off Roscoe that something was up, all the men had been summoned by radio, using a code word, or by a door-to-door knock-up.

Malone used a pointer to indicate photographs taped to the wall. "Ellen Duncan, Vikki Taylor and Claire Lake," he said. "They're the three women that we have reason to believe have been abducted to Pentworth House. Sorry the pics are a bit small. We won't be leaving here for another two hours, so you've got plenty of time for a closer look. The primary purpose of the operation is to recover these three women, unharmed. Please keep that in the forefront of your minds at all times." He moved the pointer to pictures of Roscoe and Faraday. "These gentlemen need no introduction from me. They are to be arrested. Do be careful with Faraday, he's nursing a broken right arm, courtesy of myself, and may be a little fragile. I should hate him to get even more bones broken."

Laughter greeted Malone's words.

"He can be dangerous," he warned, and turned to a large-scale plan of Pentworth House's floors. "Okay. How many of you know the interior layout of Pentworth House?"

Carol Sandiman noted the names of those who put their hands up and quizzed them in low tones about their knowledge.

"Pentworth House is too big for shock entry tactics to be

effective," Malone continued. "It's no good breaking down doors and charging in like a herd of stampeding bison. We need to get all our teams on to all the floors and have the place secured before they know what's hit them. This is going to be a strict softy-softly op. Pentworth House has a lot of bare board corridors, so you'll all be wearing bits of torn-up blankets over your shoes and boots. No staffs – they'll just get in the way. Whatever you've got in the way of body armour and night sticks."

"How about some tooling-up, sir? We've got plenty of kit."

"Definitely not," said Malone. "I'm certain that all their firearms were handed over as part of the amnesty deal. We've certainly accounted for all of them. If a gun goes off, we'll know it's not one of ours. Your best weapons are surprise, followed by your torch, followed by Captor." He held up an aerosol of the concentrated onion gas. "But we've only got ten aerosols, so I'll be issuing most of them to the group that will be dealing with Roscoe's heavies."

Malone spoke for a further twenty minutes, outlining the details of the operation and answering questions. Many of the queries raised highlighted potential problems for which countermeasures were discussed and decided upon.

At the end the men were divided into three primary groups. Those with a knowledge of Pentworth House's layout were distributed among all the groups. Alpha group, under Russell Norris, was tasked with securing the grounds before the main assault on the house started.

Each group spent the remainder of the time with their respective commanding officer going over their objectives. Carol Sandiman distributed squares of blanket material that were securely lashed to footwear. She also issued each man with several cable ties for use as handcuffs.

At the appointed hour, the hundred black-clad morris police filed into the passage at the side of the police station and packed themselves into the three Commer vans. Malone drove the third van – Charlie group. All three vehicles left by different routes to avoid a convoy being seen driving through the town centre. Malone was determined not to lose his principal weapon of surprise. He took the most indirect route eastward out of the town, circled around using narrow roads before heading north on the A283 for half a kilometre. He drew up outside a row of cottages – a spot well-known to local children – where a part of the eighteenth-century wall that completely surrounded the Pentworth estate had crumbled away to virtually nothing.

The other two Commers were already parked and empty. Malone and his thirty-man team poured silently over the remains of the wall and worked south, skirting the crops, moving purposefully towards the dim points of light that marked Pentworth House. They kept close to the wall and reached their rendezvous spot. At first Malone thought he'd made a mistake about the location until someone tapped him on the shoulder. It was Russell Norris – the big man came from a long line of poachers and knew a thing or two about countryside stealth.

"Six prisoners, Mr Malone. Patrol guards. All trussed up and oven-ready. They didn't get a chance to use their radios."

Malone was pleased. He knew about the guards but not their whereabouts. "Well done, Norris."

After a brief conference, the teams set off, converging on the big mansion. Malone led his team towards their allotted rear door in the stable yard. He produced a crowbar and jemmied the door open, making little noise.

As expected, Pentworth House's common ways were lit by low-wattage bulbs from a methane-powered generator. His team made hardly a sound as they mounted the narrow flights of servants' stairs that led to the fourth floor – the top floor where most of the bedrooms and dormitories were located.

A sudden uproar from the floor below and yells of "Police!" served as a trigger. Malone's Charlie group burst into the largest dormitory. One of Roscoe's prize heavies leapt naked from his bed and charged blindly into the flashlights. A squirt of Captor and he went down screaming, clutching his face. Someone switched the lights on. Malone's deadly feet dealt with two would-be assailants, more screams, a girl sobbing in terror, clutching a sheet to herself, and suddenly it was all over. The room's occupants saw what had happened to their writhing colleagues and surrendered without further resistance.

Malone left four officers to deal with the prisoners and charged into the corridor which was filling with the occupants of the neighbouring dormitory. They were no match for the dazzling flashlamps and were quickly overpowered and herded into the first dormitory.

As Malone had hoped, the remainder of Roscoe's guards on the top floor came to him, converging on the uproar. Overpowering them, with heavy boots taking advantage of bare toes, was achieved within minutes although one tiresome thug, with more muscle than brains, had to be pinned down by four officers before they managed to wrentch his arms behind his back and secure his wrists. Lashing out with his feet caused a painful connection with a bed. He lost all interest in further struggling and comforted himself with howls of agony.

Ten minutes after he'd jemmied the door, Malone broke the strict radio silence and announced that Charlie group had secured the top floor. Russell Norris answered that his Alpha group had done likewise on the ground floor, concluding with, "We're moving them all into the dining hall."

Bravo group reported some problems and Malone sent twelve men to back them up. And then the text book operation was over. All the prisoners were shepherded down the main staircase and into the panelled dining hall, presided over by a picture of Johann Bode, the eighteenth-century astronomer after whom the Bodian Brethren were named.

Malone stood behind the table on the dais at the far end of the former ballroom. This was where Adrian Roscoe and Nelson Faraday ate their meals, with the faithful seated in rows below them. They weren't looking very faithful now. Some of the more belligerent refused to sit on the floor and had to be informed by Malone's men that it would be sensible if they did as they were told. Most of them were in pyjamas or nightdresses. Several naked girls had huddled themselves against the wall. Malone felt sorry for them. They were just frightened kids caught up in a turmoil of events they neither understood or had control over. He ordered that some sort of covering be found for them.

It was the number of them that worried Malone. Although he knew that Roscoe had over 200 followers, seeing them all gathered together, mostly young adults, was a salutary reminder of the strength of the Bodian Brethren and of the difficulty he and others faced in breaking Roscoe's power. Among them were the faces of local youngsters whose parents had come to Malone pleading for him to do something about returning them to their families and loved ones. He had had to tell them that Roscoe was always careful to ensure that his new recruits were over eighteen and that there was nothing that the police could do.

The last followers to be ushered in were the bakery staff, dressed in white overalls and looking bemused. Malone reflected that Pentworth's main bread supply was going to be late in the morning.

There were still two more to come. A commotion outside the door and Adrian Roscoe's voice, bringing down heavenly curses on his handlers, announced the cult leader's imminent arrival. The double doors burst open and Roscoe and Faraday were bundled none too gently into the dining hall by six morris police. In deference to their wounds, neither were handcuffed. Roscoe was wearing his customary white gown.

"They were claiming sanctuary in their solar temple," a morris police officer explained. "Mr Roscoe threatened us with divine retribution if we laid a finger on them. The upstairs call centre must be closed because we seem OK so far. That's everyone accounted for, sir."

Malone nodded to Russell Norris for the search of Pentworth House to begin. It was to be a very thorough search – not just Pentworth House itself from attics and roof spaces to cellars, but also every outhouse, and every agricultural building including the bakery and the piggeries.

Malone could feel the intensity of Roscoe's incredibly blue eyes across the length of the dining hall.

"Ask them to sit down," said Malone.

"Spawn of Satan!" Roscoe spat, levelling a finger at Malone. "You have profaned our temple! The constant prayers of our sentinels to protect the earth from the fate that God meted out to the fourth planet have been broken! You will pay the price in hell and the earth will be destroyed!"

A particularly large morris policeman encouraged Roscoe

to sit by kicking his feet from under him. Faraday, not wishing to add to the stress on his broken arm, sat without persuasion. The policeman held a roll of duct tape under Roscoe's nose and made it clear that he was prepared to use several metres of the stuff on Roscoe's face if he didn't belt up. The cult leader decided that silence was a sensible option.

"I expect you're all wondering why I've called this meeting," said Malone when quiet had been restored. One of the bakery staff actually laughed. "Well – you will all find out in the fullness." He scanned the sea of watching faces and found one that he recognised. Helen Costello – a tall, sensible blonde whom he had had dealings with before – one of Roscoe's senior sentinels. She was wearing a long nightdress. He caught her eye and held it. "Helen – I'd like to talk to you first." With that he rose and entered a small side room that he had already identified as a suitable interview room. A cutlery trolley served as a desk. Two morris police guided the girl into the room.

"Take the tie off her."

One of the morris police used a watchmaker's screwdriver to release the cable tie around the girl's wrists so that it could be reused. Malone waved her to a chair and indicated that the two policemen should remain.

She sat and watched him, rubbing her wrists, her expression more one of puzzlement than trepidation.

"I'm sorry to have so rudely disturbed your sleep, Helen," said Malone. "But needs must. I've good reasons for believing that Ellen Duncan, Victoria Taylor and Claire Lake have been abducted and brought here earlier tonight."

The girl looked genuinely taken back.

"I'm not saying that you had anything to do with it," Malone continued. "What I want to know is where they're likely to be hidden. It'll save my men having to tear this place apart."

Helen was startled by the news. She shook her head. "Whatever you've heard, Mr Malone, I can promise you that it's wrong. They're definitely not in Pentworth House."

"Meaning that they're being held somewhere else?"

"Meaning that you've made one big mistake. If they had been found, I'm sure I would've heard about it. No one can keep a secret in this place."

Malone was silent for a moment. He suspected that Helen was telling the truth. He spoke to one of the morris police outside the room and instructed him to keep all those he'd interviewed in a separate room. His next interviewee was Harry Shaw – an edgy young man in charge of the kennels. He sat opposite Malone and looked decidedly uncomfortable at his first question.

"You took the hounds out yesterday evening?"

"Yes. Some of them."

"Whose idea was that?"

"They need exercise now and then."

"For which Pentworth Park is usually deemed large enough. I asked, whose idea was it to take them out of the park?"

There was a longer silence before the kennel lad replied. "It was Mr Faraday's."

"Does he normally accompany you when you exercise the hounds?"

"No."

"So what was different about yesterday?"

Another silence. Malone repeated the question.

The youth looked as if he were about to reply when there was a commotion in the dining hall and the sound of Roscoe raising his voice and being abruptly silenced.

"I don't think you have anything to fear from Roscoe or Faraday," said Malone mildly.

"I told him that it was a useless idea," the youth suddenly blurted out. "He had some underwear that had belonged to Claire Lake. He thought the hounds could find her from that. I told him, maybe a couple of them might pick up her scent if they got near or lucky, but they're best chasing after a hot scent."

"So what did you find?"

"Nothing. We got as far as the end of the land where Ellen Duncan has her little fields and then they got confused. Some tree down there that gives off a terrible smell."

Malone said nothing. He was ninety per cent certain that

149

the lad was telling the truth and dismissed him. There was nothing for it but to confront Adrian Roscoe.

Roscoe started heaping curses on Malone's head the moment he was wheeled into the room.

"Yes, Mr Roscoe," said Malone wearily. "I'm sure I'll suffer all manner of agonies in hell, not least being your redoubtable company."

"You have interrupted our sacred prayers! The Solar Temple is empty! The world lies naked and helpless before Satan!"

"In that case, the sooner you answer my questions, the sooner you can get back to saving the world, Mr Roscoe."

Malone expected Roscoe to start leading off again, but he remained silent, regarding the police officer with that uncomfortable, icy stare. Malone decided to get straight to point. Watching Roscoe carefully, he said, "What have you done with Claire, Ellen and Vikki?"

Roscoe actually blinked at that. "I don't understand."

"You understand me, all right. It was a simple enough question. What has happened to Claire, Ellen and Vikki? Where are they?"

Understanding gleamed in Roscoe's eyes. "So they've finally received their retribution."

It occurred to Malone, not for the first time, that the growing numbers of Roscoe's supporters meant that the three women could be hidden in any number of locations within the thirty square miles of Pentworth enclosed by the Wall. He decided on a direct question. For all his faults, Malone didn't think that Roscoe was a liar.

"A straight question, Mr Roscoe. Do you know where they are?"

"No."

"And you expect me to believe you?"

Roscoe smiled. "Whether or not you believe me is unimportant, Mr Malone. What matters is that they have been plucked from wherever you were hiding them to face their just retribution. But, if it makes you happy . . ." Roscoe felt in his gown and produced a pocket bible, ". . . I will even go so far as to swear on this when I say that I do not know where they are."

150

Alone again, Malone finished writing some notes and wondered if there was much point in questioning any more of Roscoe's followers. The night had gone badly. He had mounted an expensive and abortive operation. Trouble ahead was more than a certainty. There was a rap on the door and Russell Norris entered with a bulky, strong-smelling bundle wrapped in sacking. He placed it on the trolley and pulled the material aside to expose three shotguns.

"Found them in the piggery, sir, buried under pig crap."

"I believe you," said Malone faintly, putting a hand to his face.

Russell felt in his pocket and placed a small cardboard box beside the shotguns. "And we found this in Nelson Faraday's room."

Malone opened the box and his black mood began to lift. Discovery of the shotguns was justification enough for the raid, but the contents of the box amounted to high-quality lily gilding. It contained about twenty .45 rounds – ammunition for the Smith and Wesson revolver that he had confiscated from Faraday before the sham trial of Ellen and Vikki.

Thirty-Three

E llen was the first to hear the baying of the hounds. She signalled frantically to Vikki and Claire for silence.

"What is it, Ellen?" Claire whispered.

"Shh!"

They listened in silence. And then they all heard the distant, muffled yapping that reached into the cave. At one point the baying of the hounds got frighteningly close and then faded away. Gradually all sounds faded and then there was silence. Ellen was the first to speak, keeping her voice to a whisper.

"Christ. The local hunt's pack of foxhounds."

"Do you think they could find us?" Vikki asked.

"Well, of course they could. That's what they're for. The three of us must stink more than any fox." Ellen looked at her watch. "It must be starting to get dark. We don't move or make a sound until I say."

The three huddled close together on Ellen's camp bed as if the older woman could provide Claire and Vikki with protection from the terror that was lurking outside, searching for them. Ten minutes of white-faced silence ticked by. Ellen began breathing a little easier.

"Looks like they're not so good after all," Claire whispered.

"Maybe they've been searching for us all day," Ellen reasoned. "And called them off when it got dark. Chances are they'll pick up where they left off tomorrow morning, fresh and raring to go."

Vikki began trembling when she thought of the time when she had been forced to stand naked before Adrian Roscoe. "I think I'll kill myself if they come for me."

Ellen put her arm around the girl and pulled her close. "No

152

one's coming for us," she said fiercely. "If they try anything on, they'll have me to reckon with."

The vehemence in the older woman's tone conveyed all the reassurance Vikki needed without her considering its likely effectiveness.

After a few more minutes the three felt sufficiently confident to begin preparing an evening meal. Ellen had always insisted that they should have at least one cooked meal each day even if the fumes from the charcoal burner did take a long time to clear, but there would no cooking tonight. Claire was tipping dried peas into a pan to soak when all three heard a sound coming from the narrow opening that led to the exit tunnel. They all stopped what they were doing and stared ashen-faced at the opening. There was a scrabbling noise, a metallic scratching sound that seemed to get louder. Magazines rustled in the sudden draught and they all felt the cooling draught on their bodies.

Ellen snatched up the children's walkie-talkie. "David? Mike? Is that you?"

She repeated the question twice but there was no answer. She seized a carving knife and waved Claire and Vikki to the far wall but Ellen's determined stance near the entrance imbued the girls with courage: Claire grabbed a knife which she tossed to Vikki and snatched up one for herself. The three women formed a crouching semicircle around the entrance, ready to hurl themselves on whatever emerged.

The metallic, grating noise got louder. Ellen wiped the sweat from her eyes with the back of her wrist and tightened her grip on her knife. I'm ready for anything, she told herself: foxhounds, Nelson Faraday, even Roscoe. This time there was going to be no submission without a fight. A bloody fight if necessary.

Ellen was deluding herself by thinking she was ready for anything: she was not ready for what emerged from the opening and moved on eight articulated legs into the centre of the cave.

It was the spyder.

Thirty-Four

For timeless seconds the scene in the cave was a frozen tableau: the three half-naked crouching women, knives at the ready, surrounding the strange crab-like device. The poor illumination in the cave enabled the spyder's remarkable light-absorbing properties to work at their best; even when looked at directly it was difficult to see the bizarre machine when it was still.

Vikki was the first to react. She relaxed and managed a twisted smile. "It's the spyder. I don't think it means to hurt us."

Ellen had caught a glimpse of the spyder on a previous occasion but Claire had never seen it before. She kept a tight grip on her knife.

"Knives won't be much use against it," said Vikki.

Vikki. Can you hear us?

Despite the spyder's proximity, the picture of foxhounds and the message that formed in Vikki's mind was incredibly weak.

Yes. But only just.

How much are those animals a danger?

Very dangerous.

Vikki looked at her companions. "It wants to know about the hounds. But I can hardly hear it. It's very weak."

Ellen and Claire exchanged baffled glances.

"It's talking to you?" asked Ellen, sitting on her camp bed and contemplating the spyder, her expression a mixture of fear and curiosity.

"Yes. It's like I told you when I went out."

Can the animals hear us when we talk like this?

No. I don't think so. They use smell. Vikki concentrated on

154

a mental picture of foxhounds sniffing about as she had once seen them doing on a hunt. She tried to focus on their noses. The voice in her mind suddenly became sharp and clear.

Where are these animals?

"They want to know where the foxhounds are," said Vikki.

Ellen gazed at the spyder, marvelling at how it seemed to become virtually invisible when it was still. "Back in their kennels in Pentworth Park by now, I imagine." God – this was all so damned surreal.

"They still keep them there," Claire whispered, not taking her eyes off the spyder.

"Those runs and the building west of Pentworth House?" Vikki asked. "Close to the park's wall?"

Claire nodded.

Vikki concentrated on an image of the kennels and the wire-enclosed runs for the hounds.

We must take you to a safe place. It is important that you are safe.

Vikki relayed the message to her companions. The spyder moved, becoming easier to see. To emphasise the point it used one of its manipulators to touch Vikki and point to the opening in the cave.

"No," said Vikki spiritedly. "I'm not going anywhere without my friends. If you have somewhere safe, then we all go or none at all."

But your safety is vital.

"So is their safety," said Vikki aloud. She plonked herself down on her camp bed. "They want me to leave without you. I don't take orders from a tin crab."

"Atta girl," said Ellen. She looked at the spyder. "Your move, I fancy, Rin Tin Tin."

The spyder became still as if it were contemplating this unexpected rebellion.

Very well, Vikki. You will all go.

Vikki gave a grin of triumph and passed the news to Ellen and Claire. "They're sending a picture of clothes . . . We're to take plenty of warm clothing."

"I only hope," said Ellen a few moments later, having pulled on dark jeans and a T-shirt and cramming clothes and belongings into a small kitbag, "that this isn't a case of out of the frying pan and into the fire."

"They say we'll be safe," said Vikki.

"But will we be free?" Claire asked, lacing up her trainers.

"Just that we'll be safe."

"Well let's hope that wherever it is it's got a bath," said Ellen, distributing some chocolate bars that David had brought on his last visit.

"You and I have to hide our hair," Vikki said to Claire as she wriggled into her jeans. Ellen waited patiently while the two girls knotted their hair under some black underwear. The spyder remained motionless during all this activity.

They crawled out of the cave, dragging their bulky kitbags behind them, and stood, breathing deeply of night air that, despite the smell of Ellen's ginkgo tree, tasted like champagne after the fetid stink of the cave. Claire looked up at the stars and the crescent moon as she hitched her kitbag on to her shoulder and gave a little gasp of pleasure at seeing the sky after so long. The spyder was last to emerge. It worked quickly to hide the entrance to the cave and moved off at a brisk speed that forced the three women to break into a trot. A small flock of sheep bleated in alarm and scattered.

"For Chrissake tell it to slow down!" breathed Ellen.

Vikki passed the message and the spyder reduced the gait of its articulated legs.

Claire wanted to know how far they would have to travel. Vikki concentrated on shaping the question in her mind and received an immediate, if puzzling answer.

"They say to the border."

"The border?" Ellen echoed, nearly tripping over on a rock. "Do they mean the Wall?"

A pause then Vikki answered in the affirmative.

"Oh, shit – that'll be at least three miles. There's hardly any moon. I can't see a bloody thing!"

It seemed that the spyder sensed the problem before Vikki had a chance to communicate. Quite suddenly a cone of light appeared with its apex some four metres above the spyder. It moved with the spyder and provided a broad spread of a strange illumination that was more than adequate provided they kept close together within the cone. Rocky outcrops that had been absorbing the sun's energy during daylight appeared to be much brighter than their surroundings, and the stony path they were following had a strange, mottled appearance.

"Oh, great," said Claire anxiously. "We must be a beacon that can be seen for miles."

"I don't think so," said Ellen. "I think we're seeing in the infra-red."

The spyder preferred moving in a straight line cross-country – they even took a direct route across a field of potatoes that could've been avoided, although the machine did alter its course to avoid trees when they entered woodland.

"Oh bugger!" said Ellen suddenly and stopped. The spyder carried on a few metres and also stopped. "We've got to go back. I forgot to leave a message for David and Mike."

"They say we can't stop," said Vikki. "We have to carry on."

"We have to go back," Ellen declared. "Christ knows what they'll do if they go to the cave and find we're not there."

"They say we can't!" Vikki insisted.

"They! They! How come they can talk to you but no one else?"

"I've asked them that," said Vikki. "They didn't answer. I don't think they know."

The spyder made an impatient clicking noise with a manipulator – the first deliberate sound it had ever made.

"We can't go back," said Claire. "Whatever the Visitors have got planned for us, it's got to be better than being dug out of that cave like a trapped fox."

Ellen shook her head in exasperation and gave in. "Come on, Rin Tin Tin," she said to the spyder. "Walkies."

The group resumed their trek.

After an hour they came to a road, glowing eerily in the light strange pool of light around the spyder.

"We're heading in the direction of my place," said Vikki. She added with a catch of excitement in her voice. "Do you think I'll be able see Mum?"

"You're the one with the direct line to Rin Tin Tin," said Ellen sourly.

"They say it's not possible," said Vikki sadly a moment later.

"Tough," Ellen muttered, and immediately regretted the remark. She put her arm around the girl as they walked along the road. "Sorry, Viks . . . I shouldn't have said that. It was cruel of me and I'm sorry."

"It's all right, Ellen – really." Vikki was pleased with herself for holding back her tears. To change the subject she commented that it was strange that they hadn't encountered any morris police patrols.

"Well, if we do come across one," said Ellen, "we'll say we're taking Rin Tin Tin here for a walk."

Claire giggled.

They trudged on. They crossed another field of potatoes that were nearly ready for lifting. Ellen paused briefly to dig into the soft ground and quickly fill her pockets with tubers. At one point they took a direct line across a nurseryman's field that had been harrowed to fine tilth for late sowing. They could easily have avoided the soft soil but the spyder seemed intent on sticking to a straight line so they had to follow it. When they reached the fork that led to her house, Vikki desperately wanted to break away and to run home, to be back with her mother, snug and secure in her little bedroom.

"It can't be much further now," she said. "Sister Mary Thomas's cottage is at the end of this lane, and that's where the Wall is. It chops her front room in half."

A dog barked nearby and the spyder stopped abruptly. It extended a whip-like sensor from its clam-shell back which reached to a height of about three metres and seemed to be probing the neighbourhood. After a few seconds the spyder seemed satisfied, the sensor telescoped into the machine's back, and they resumed walking.

"Rin Tin Tin doesn't seem to like dogs," said Ellen.

"I don't think the Visitors understand them yet," Vikki replied.

"Do they understand us?"

"I think that's why they're here. They say we're privileged."

"Just us, you, or everyone?"

"I don't know," said Vikki. "It's not always easy understanding them but they don't talk in words. They use . . ." She struggled to think of the right term, ". . . thought shapes. But I think they mean that we're all special."

Ellen snorted. "How does that fit in with them using you when you went out?"

"They didn't use me!" Vikki responded heatedly. "They've never done that. I can shut them out if I want to and they can't reach me. I have to open my mind to hear them and even then I've never had to do what they ask. What happened between me and Dario happened because I wanted it to happen."

"And your new left hand? Did they consult with you on that?"

Vikki remained silent. Ellen wanted to press her for an answer but she decided it could wait because their route was taking them past a few dimly lit houses where they could hear the faint strains of Radio Pentworth's late night concert programme. She noticed that the spyder's gait was a little slower and that the cone of light it provided had lost some of its brightness.

"That's Sister Mary Thomas's place," Vikki whispered, pointing to a nearby cottage alongside a field. The building was in darkness. The spyder paused briefly at the entrance to the field as if listening, and then they followed it single file into the pasture. The nun's solar cooker dish shone above the low hedge, catching the light of the moon. A pair of sinister orbs glowed at them from the darkness and seemed to draw nearer. The spyder stopped.

"Himmler!" Vikki cried in loud whisper. And then she seemed to be talking urgently to herself. "No! It's all right! It's my cat! Himmler!"

There was a blur of movement and the tinkle of a collar bell as the Siamese streaked out of the darkness and raced up Vikki's jeans to land in her arms. Delighted, she cuddled the cat to her breast, crooning to it while it purred like a train and subjected her chin to a sustained head-butting, ignoring her scolds for wandering so far from home.

159

The spyder made that strange rattling noise to signify impatience and they followed it obediently across the field.

"We'll walk into the Wall any minute," Vikki whispered above Himmler's insistent purring. "It goes right through Sister Mary's cottage and across her garden. So it must cross this field."

Their route took them past a clump of trees.

"So where is it?" asked Claire. "Oh." She broke off when she saw the striped Wall markers that they were almost abreast with.

They slowed their pace, to the spyder's annoyance, expecting to walk into the Wall.

"We must be on top of it now," said Ellen, holding her hand out before her.

Vikki was about to answer when something extraordinary happened: the temperature plummeted with a speed that had the three women gasping in shock, and a northerly wind keened into them with the unremitting savagery of flailing machetes. This was a cold that had not been known in southern England for many millennia; this was the desiccated cold of a wind that had had every last vestige of moisture sucked from it by the mighty ice sheet that lay to the north. Even the moon shone with increased clinical brightness in that humidity-free air.

The Wall had opened.

And the Wall had closed.

They wheeled around but there was no sign of the dark shape of Sister Mary's cottage or the gleam of her solar cooker. Instead the moon threw an ethereal light on a landscape cowering under the onslaught of that terrible wind that permitted nothing other than sedge grasses to gain a foothold in the frozen loess that made up the impoverished soil. The Milky Way was an impossible blaze of glory that was never seen from earth now save in mountainous regions.

"What's happened?" Claire whimpered, clutching her arms around herself. The moisture-starved wind snatched a great cloud of rapidly dissipating vapour from her throat.

"Just keep following Rin Tin Tin," ordered Ellen. "And keep your mouth closed. Breath slowly through your nose." Even as

160

she spoke, Ellen could feel the saliva evaporating from her lips and tongue as though she had stuffed a handful of tissues in her mouth.

Himmler leapt from Vikki's arms to escape the biting cold that seemed to be sawing his nose off. His feet encountered even worse paw-searing conditions that prompted him to race up Vikki's jeans again and thrust his nose under her armpit to reconsider his attitude to his staff and wonder whether or not he had just made a bad choice in accompanying them.

The terrible cold would have shocked anyone out of their senses but the three women had become accustomed to six months of an agreeable Mediterranean climate in which the night-time temperatures rarely fell below 17 degrees Celsius. There was so little moisture that the grass didn't even crunch under their trainers as they trailed down a steep slope but, after 200 metres, not even the thick soles of their footwear was sufficient to insulate their feet from the numbness that was stealing insidiously into them. They heard a nearby stream and wondered how water could remain liquid in that terrible cold.

"They say that we mustn't go up the slope," said Vikki. "We're to stay away from the Wall."

A dark, humped shape appeared before them. It resembled a long, rounded-top tent because that was more or less exactly what it was. The spyder's gesture with a manipulator was unmistakable: they were to enter the tent. Ellen was almost blinded by the cold. Her numbed fingers fiddled frantically with what felt like bone toggles fastened through leather loops. In her keenness to escape the wind she didn't stop to consider what she was entering. She pulled the heavy hide flap aside and stumbled into the darkness. There was a steep step down that sent her sprawling, banging her head painfully on a stone. Her cry warned Vikki and Claire who entered more cautiously. Vikki took particular care because Himmler had burrowed under her T-shirt and between her breasts to keep warm. Ellen fumbled with her kitbag and switched on her torch.

The three women forgot the cold as they took in their extraordinary spacious surroundings that seemed much larger on the inside than on the outside. More than a tent, it was a definite structure framed with pairs of massive tusks set deep into the ground in pairs, the tips of each pair of ivories lashed together at the top with stout leather thongs so that they formed an arch with a span at the level of the sunken floor of about four metres. Their clouds of breath outlined the torch's beam as Ellen shone it towards the hidden depths. There were ten pairs of tusks at intervals of one metre with the intervening gaps cross-braced with bones and lengths of ash or hazel saplings. The whole structure was covered with thick hide. It was slack yet felt rigid and unyielding with the cold when Ellen touched it. Claire took advantage of the torchlight and shut out the marrow-chilling wind by closing the flap, which could be held in place by bone toggles and thong loops that matched those on the outside.

"Rin Tin Tin's gone," she announced. She gazed at the two rows of knee-high large squares whose tops were at the level of the original ground. "What on earth is this place?" she asked.

Ellen didn't answer. She was staring at a ring of roughly shaped stones that she had struck her head on. They formed a circle around a shallow pit that was filled with fine ash.

"Looks like some sort of fireplace," said Vikki.

"That's exactly what it is," Ellen breathed. There was an icy draught blowing from the pit. She moved the torch closer and saw the opening in the side of pit. It had been formed by digging out a gully which the draught told her led to the outside. It had been bridged with wide, flat stones and then covered with packed earth flush with the floor.

"Ladies," said Ellen softly, her voice filled with wonder. "You are looking at mankind's earliest and greatest invention: the forced-draught hearth." The beam of her torch alighted on a small bale of dried moss and a pile of sticks. Beside it was a tall stack of assorted bones and skulls of foxes, antelopes and even antlers. "And what is more," said Ellen with rising excitement as she plucked moss from the bale, "we are going to have a fire!"

It proved astonishingly easy to light. One match was sufficient to get the moss burning, followed by several handfuls of the sticks. The three women's spirits rose with the warm flames that flared up rapidly, fuelled by the strong draught blowing through the underfloor duct. Himmler emerged from under Vikki's clothes and regarded the fire with approval. The hut filled with smoke that stung their eyes, but it was warm smoke that soon found its way out through a vent in the roof. Ellen added bones, gradually building up a hot but slow-burning fire that could be controlled thanks to Vikki discovering the purpose of a heat-blackened flat, round stone that could be rolled back and forth in front of the duct's opening to regulate the flow of air.

There was sufficient light from the fire now for them to explore the hut's interior without the torch. Vikki found a piece of limestone that had been roughly hollowed out and filled with what looked like lard. She lit the twist of flax-like material because it had to be a wick and was pleased when her surmise that it was some sort of lamp proved correct. The smell of burning animal fat was bad but tolerable.

"What I don't understand," said Claire, struggling out of some clothes because it was getting quite warm in the hut. "If the Visitors are so advanced, you'd think they could build something a little less crude than this place."

"They didn't build it," said Ellen cryptically. "We did. Or rather, our ancestors did. And, if you look closely, you'll see that there's nothing crude about it. Simple, maybe – but not crude." She was examining several rolls of what looked like furs that were hanging from thongs. A tug on one of the thongs resulted in a heavy roll of the furs dropping into her arms. She unrolled them on one of the raised squares of soil. The furs were still stiff with cold but separated easily. "Antelope or deer," she muttered. "And look at this! My God, it's beautiful!" She brought the huge bearskin nearer the fire so that Vikki and Claire could examine it. Himmler deemed it worthy of attack. Ellen shooed him away. The trio admired the fur and the way that the hide backing had been carefully scraped and worked to make it supple. Ellen's find prompted Vikki and Claire to do some exploring.

"Look," said Vikki.

Claire and Ellen gaped. The girl was holding a shaped yoke across her shoulders, padded with strips of fur. From each end dangled the complete skin of a small animal that had been tied and knotted at the anus, legs and feet leaving the neck open. There was no mistaking the contraption's purpose.

"Right," said Ellen, taking it from Vikki and thrusting the torch into her pocket. "I'm going to find that stream and we're going to cook something and have a decent wash."

She was gone ten minutes and returned staggering under the weight of the filled skins. Claire closed and secured the flap while Vikki and Ellen hoisted the bulging skins on to antler hooks, lashed to the tusks, that seemed to be made for the job.

An hour later they had eaten a meal consisting of jacket potatoes cooked in the fire's ashes and strips of dried beef that Claire had thought to bring. A hand-moulded clay pot served for boiling water. Ellen had packed some nettle teabags and they were contentedly sipping tea, sitting around the hearth on piles of comfortable furs. Himmler had ventured out for a brief foray and returned with a baby rabbit that he was now sleeping off, stretched out on the best place near the hearth.

Claire's gaze wandered around the interior of the long hut, lit by the yellow flames of the simple oil lamps they had found. "You said that our ancestors built this," she said to Ellen. "Who were they?"

"Cro-Magnon," said Ellen. "The same people that painted the hunting scenes in the cave. They lived about forty thousand years ago."

"You mean now, don't you?" Claire ventured. "We're Farside and Farside is in the past."

Ellen smiled and nodded. "Now," she confirmed.

"Supposing the owners come back and find us? Won't they be somewhat cross?"

"Imagine Neanderthals having their wicked way with us," said Vikki.

"They most certainly aren't Neanderthalers," Ellen replied. "And I doubt if they'll return for another three months or so." She added, "I saw four more huts like this one further down the slope. All unoccupied. This was the only one making smoke."

"Why not build them in a circle?" Claire asked.

"From what little I could see, they were all aligned to offer the least resistance to the prevailing wind. I think this village is the winter quarters for a clan of about a hundred Cro-Magnon. They've probably moved north to hunt mammoth. They were hunter-gatherers, so their movements were dictated by the annual migrations of game." Ellen paused and looked around the hut's interior. She wished she had a pad and pencils to sketch every detail of this remarkable place but knew she would have to depend on memory. "Forty thousand years ago puts them at a transitional period when they were changing from a nomadic existence to becoming settlers. This place is evidence of that. A nomadic life cramps innovation and invention because everything you make, you have to carry with you. Nomads can't build communities, and without settled communities, you can't build towns and cities and civilisations."

"Didn't they have horses?" Vikki asked. She was interested because Ellen was a good talker. Palaeontology had always been Ellen's favourite conversational topic during quiet moments when they worked together in the shop.

"Not until around 8000 BC. So these people compromised and built camps along their nomadic routes. To do that required a great, innovative leap that we can hardly understand because it seems so logical. It's worth remembering that everything that seems simple and obvious to us had to be invented. If the Neanderthal clans couldn't find a cave, they perished. And, as we know, they became extinct. Whereas our ingenious forefathers solved the problem by building their own caves like this where they wanted them."

"They hadn't invented doors and locks," Claire observed. "Weren't they worried about people stealing their things? There's a tremendous amount of work gone into this place. All these skins . . ."

Ellen smiled. "David Weir collected a lot of papers on Palaeolithic populations. Most of the universities have used computer modelling to calculate past populations by working backwards from the present. The general consensus is that there were tiny numbers of Cro-Magnon living in this part

165

of Europe." She grinned and added. "They seemed to prefer living in Spain and the South of France."

Claire laughed. "And nothing has changed. Sensible people."

"Also they probably had a culture of respecting the property of others. Just as we must do with this place. As the saying goes: we must take away only memories and leave only footprints."

"How long must we wait before we can take away any memories?" Claire wondered.

"God knows," said Ellen. She annoyed Himmler by banking up the fire. "Time for bed. We might have a busy day tomorrow."

As the three women and a cat were settling down for the night, warm under a selection of furs, three miles to the north the spyder was moving slowly through the reeds towards Pentworth Lake. Its energy cells were nearly exhausted and it could have done without the wide detour around the beach to miss the men camped near their pontoon. In its present state it could hardly have evaded capture if it were spotted without having to call upon its formidable armoury of self-defence devices. There was much that its controllers wanted done but that would have to wait until the following night.

Exhausted, the spyder entered the water, moved clear of the shallows, and sank into the depths.

At least Vikki was now safe.

So the Visitors thought.

Thirty-Five

B ob Harding was up early the next morning, busy working on his 'box', as he called it – an old lever-arch box file filled with notes and reports that Diana Sheldon had prepared for him to take home the previous evening. Instead of reading everything with his customary care before initialling the documents, he skimmed quickly through them. He wanted everything out of the way so that the day would be free for the test submersion of the bathyscaphe. He had already phoned Tony Selby, who had reassured him that the converted swimming-pool filter was already on its way to Pentworth Lake. His desk was a cleared area of workbench in his crowded workshop at the back of what had once been his electrical repair shop. Even his prized Newtonian telescope had had to go to make room for the assistants that now worked here during the day, keeping Pentworth's valuable stock of portable radios in working order. He heard the telephone ring but left Suzi to deal with it. She intercepted all his calls these days otherwise he'd never get anything done.

She came into the workshop wearing a transparent negligée that had Harding yearning for the day when he could step down from this latest responsibility that had been thrust on him so that he could spend more time with his family – a family that consisted solely of Suzi: a lovely twenty-year-old brunette – a former student at a college where he had lectured part time. Both had been disappointed by the lack of a scandal that their marriage had provoked – they had expected better of Pentworth.

"You've got another woman after you," she said reproachfully, working her seductive fingertips into her husband's collar bones.

167

"Give her a number and tell her to join the queue," said Harding.

"A nun. Is there no end to your depravities?"

"Not Sister Mary Thomas?"

"Ha. So she's still fresh in your perverted mind?"

"Suzi, angel. She's over ninety."

"She's nearer your age than I am."

"What did she want?"

"Have you heard the one about the Essex girl who was asked during a survey if she smoked after having sex? She replied that she didn't know because she had never looked."

Harding laughed. "What's that got to do with Sister Mary?"

"She's worried about smoke. Farside smoke."

Thirty-Six

It was a glorious Farside morning. By ten o'clock the sun was pleasantly hot as Ellen discovered when she threw back the hut's hide flap and gazed out at the scene before her. The stream that she had struggled to find in the dark the previous night turned out to be a broad, fast-flowing shallow river that tumbled cheerfully down to a thickly wooded valley. There was a sharp bend in the river where bones and branches, and even complete trees, barkless and scoured white, had piled up – probably accumulations from flash floods. That was something – no need to worry about the fuel they were using.

Himmler's indignant howls of profound grief concerning the lack of his customary four breakfasts woke Vikki and Claire. From their raised beds at the far end of the hut, they voiced complaints about the bright light flooding into the hut, and the smoke as Ellen made up the fire that had nearly gone out.

She ignored them and took a proper look at the hut. Around the outside deep drainage gullies had been dug to deflect rainwater towards the river. The width and depth of the gullies and the fact that they had been lined with tessellated flat stones to prevent floodwater erosion suggested that rainstorms here could be quite something. The same had been done with the other huts. Around the outside opening to the underfloor forced-draught duct was a funnel-like wind scoop made from thin hide stretched over a framework of lashed saplings. It was angled to catch the prevailing wind. The wind scoop was the simple but outstanding invention that enabled bone to be used as a fuel in areas where wood was scarce. The high temperatures that could be achieved by burning bone had laid the foundations of ceramics and metallurgy, and given Europe a technological lead that it had never lost.

She turned her attention to the hut's covering and guessed that the heavy material was mammoth or bison hide. It was as thick as her finger and hung slack and somewhat untidily from the ivory frames. The stitching used to join the heavy material intrigued her. The individually knotted stitches were visible on the inside of the hut but not on the outside. A close look where a loop stitch was coming loose revealed the secret: the fine leather thong did not break through the outside of the outer, overlapping hide but went halfway into the thick skin and doubled back inwards, through the inner hide, and was knotted on the inside. The result was a sound, watertight joint with no likelihood of water being able to leak into the hut. It was something else to commit to memory about the remarkable skills and ingenuity of the Cro-Magnon.

The hut itself was built on a slope yet the sunken floor had been excavated level and covered with matting made from woven reeds. Ellen guessed that this was the first type of artificial floor that mankind had ever walked on. The symmetry of the pairs of mammoth tusks that formed the hut's U-frames intrigued her. Most mammoth tusks recovered from the Siberian and Alaskan permafrost were misshapen. Had these early *Homo sapiens* killed so many mammoths that they had a choice of tusks? Or had they found a way of removing unwanted twists by steaming them? She made a mental note to discuss it with David, and checked herself. When would she see David again? Were they condemned to live out the rest of their lives in this Farside world?

Further exploration led to the discovery of a bulky roll of chamois leather. She untied the loose knot and marvelled at the collection of tools inside the roll: flint burins, awls, some razor-sharp flint blades with their tangs set into antler handles, and a collection of bone needles ranging in size from large bodkins to fine embroidery needles. All were individually secured in place in the roll by neatly stitched loops of chamois, just like a modern toolkit. She marvelled, not only at the practical beauty of the implements, but at the hours of painstaking work that must have gone into making them.

An itch in her scalp reminded her that there were other, more immediate matters to deal with. She stripped off, and

170

raced naked down the grassy slope to the river. She hadn't had a proper wash in a month and the attraction of the river was too much. The water was not as cold as she had expected although it took her breath away when she found a deep eddy pool and immersed herself up to her neck. She spent a blissful ten minutes rubbing herself vigorously with a T-shirt. She emerged, her skin tingling, and was about to stretch out on an outcrop of sandstone to dry herself in the sun when she noticed pug marks in the soft mud near the water's edge.

She stooped to examine them and felt a prickling of alarm at the nape of her neck. The paw marks were large – almost the width of her hand. A big cat. In fact, she thought to herself, a fucking big cat. A cave lion? The thought tightened the knot of fear in her stomach. From what she remembered of cave lion remains, they could grow to four times the size of their African counterpart. A search revealed plenty of small hoof marks, probably deer or antelope, and what were definitely the paw marks of wolves. She eyed the 200 metres distance between herself and the group of huts and told herself that the village had been built here for the same reason that animals came visiting – it was a convenient watering place. The chances were that any big cats that drank here avoided the humans and vice versa otherwise the Cro-Magnon would not have sited their village here. She had read about watering-holes in the African bush being neutral territory. It was a comforting thought but brought home the risk she had taken in coming down here at night.

A movement in the water caught her eye. A fish was trapped in shallow water between a spit of sand and the far bank, and couldn't find its way back to the main channel. A big fish, too, judging by its heavy splashes.

Ellen dashed across the river. At one point she was wading in water that reached her breasts, but she pressed determinedly on. The river bed shallowed rapidly underfoot and she raced into the narrow channel to cut off the fish's escape. Her nerve nearly failed her when she saw the carp's size. It was close to a metre in length and had a mouth that looked capable of swallowing her arm – sideways. Twice it nearly bowled her over as it darted between her feet. Ellen saw that it was likely

171

to escape so she threw herself on the creature. In one smooth movement she grabbed it by the tail, braced herself, and swung it out of the water with all the arm-wrenching strength she could muster. She succeeded in landing it on the sand spit. The huge fish gave several mighty spasms that threatened to flip it back into water but Ellen was upon it with a rock. Three heavy blows and the struggle was over. She threw back her head and uttered a primeval yell of triumph.

Whatever an uncertain future held in store for the three women, they would survive.

Thirty-Seven

"Y ou see, Mr Harding?" said Sister Mary.

Harding lowered his binoculars and stared at the pall of white smoke rising above the fold. He was standing at the nun's upstairs landing window. "Indeed I do, Sister. Perhaps it's a bush fire?"

Sister Mary snorted. "A bush fire would spread. That smoke's been coming from the same place ever since I first saw it two hours ago. Animals don't make fires. Bush fires don't stay in the same place. Which leaves only one possibility – that fire's manmade."

Harding had already made the same deduction. Animals had often been seen Farside but this was the first evidence that there were people living in that strange place.

"Maybe the Wall—" he began.

"First thing I checked," said the nun. "It's still there."

"Perhaps we'd better check again," said Harding.

They went downstairs and into the garden and encountered the Wall where they expected to find it. Harding pressed his hand hard against it. The initial yielding and increasing resistance the harder he pushed felt no different, and the strange blackening effect wherever he applied pressure was exactly as it had always been.

"Of course, there's no reason why there shouldn't be people Farside," said Harding. "*Homo sapiens* were certainly around forty thousand years ago."

"Except we've never seen them."

"They were thought to be nomadic. Perhaps they've just returned?"

Sister Mary nodded. "That makes sense. My worry was that the smoke would stop before you arrived, Mr Harding. I hope you don't think I've wasted your time. I know how busy you must be."

Harding assured her that she had done the right thing in calling him. He was about to thank her and return to his pony and trap, when they both saw the Siamese cat breast the rise.

"Good heavens," the nun whispered. "I do believe that's Himmler." The strap nearly yanked Harding's head off when she grabbed his binoculars and peered through them. "Yes – it is Himmler. His markings! And he's Farside!"

Harding retrieved the glasses and focused them on the cat. It was stalking a rook – not very skilfully because there was no cover and its tail was stuck straight up and quivering in excitement. It made a sudden dash. The rook was airborne before the cat got within pouncing distance whereupon the thwarted hunter decided some concentrated washing was called for, as though that was what it meant to do all along.

"Are you sure you know the cat?"

"I ought to," Sister Mary replied. "He belongs to Anne Taylor."

"Vikki Taylor's mother?"

"That's right. She swears that Himmler gets enough to eat, yet he comes around every morning even though their place is at least two kilometres away, bullying me to feed him. But there was no sign of him this morning. I thought he'd found himself another mug. Looks like he's found a hole in the Wall instead."

Harding declined the nun's offer of tea. She accompanied him back to his pony and trap, not speaking, sensing that the retired scientist had much on his mind.

"Thank you for calling me, Sister," he said, picking up the reins. "You certainly did the right thing. One thing, though. I think it would be best if you said nothing about this to anyone for the time being."

"How can you expect to keep it secret, Mr Harding? There're quite a few houses around here and several lanes. The entrance to that field next door opens on to the lane. Look – see the Wall markers? Any number of people are sure to see that smoke and be curious."

Harding thanked her again and went on his way, heading the pony to Pentworth Lake.

Thirty-Eight

H e arrived shortly before midday. The bathyscaphe had
already arrived and was sitting on the pontoon that was
now held in position in the centre of the lake by long lengths
of rope that extended to the shore.

"They've had to sort out some winch cable problems, Mr
Harding, so you've not missed anything." said the night watchman, helping Harding into an inflatable dinghy and pushing it
clear of the beach.

Harding was rowed out to the pontoon, where Tony Selby
and his four-man crew made a pretence of piping him aboard.
Harding shook hands with Selby and the crew, and apologised
for being late.

"We're behind anyway, Bob," said Selby. "We've had some
trouble making sure we've got enough steel cable. The stuff's
a pig to splice. All fixed now, though. And we've got the
pontoon positioned about a metre to one side of the anomaly
on the echo-sounder."

Harding examined the yellow bathyscaphe. It was resting
on several builders' scaffolding planks that had been laid
across the rectangular opening in the centre of the pontoon. A big, old-fashioned manual winch had been bolted
to the pontoon's main framework. The winch cable was
threaded through a pulley block hanging from the "I" beam
above the bathyscaphe and was secured at several points to
a robust-looking steel cable harness that the huge barrel-like
swimming-pool filter was sitting in. He had visited Selby's
plant several times to see how work was progressing but this
was the first time he had seen it completed. The principal
modification was the porthole-hatch whose diameter provided
just enough clearance for his shoulders. As expected, the

glass-fibre moulding that housed the round, clear acrylic porthole had been professionally carried out and had even been painted matching yellow.

The echo-sounder's screen was shaded by a parasol. The strange triangular anomaly that he had first seen with Mike Malone was centred precisely below the bathyscaphe. The depth was unchanged at 120 metres.

"We've filled the thing with rocks equal to the weight of the car batteries that you'll have aboard," Selby explained.

There were still tasks to be completed before the test dive could begin so Harding sat on the side of the pontoon where he wouldn't be in the way. An array of car sealed-beam headlights was bolted into place above the hatch. They would not be needed on the test dive, of course, but Selby wanted everything in place so that any likely problems could be dealt with. One of the crew went around the circle of wing nuts that secured the porthole, giving each one a final half-turn tighten. The ballast sacks containing rocks were hung on the circle of quick-release hooks around the girth of the bathyscaphe, the cleats that secured the winch cable to the lifting harness were checked, and everything was ready.

On a word from Selby two of the crew grasped the winch's crank handles and took up the lifting cable's slack. Two further turns of the winch was enough to take the bathyscaphe's weight off the planks. The scaffolding towers that supported the "I" beam creaked but took the load.

"Looks good," said Selby, giving everything a final visual check. "Okay. Let's go."

Harding jumped up and helped drag the planks clear so that the bathyscaphe was hanging above the surface of the lake.

"Okay. Start letting her down. Easy does it."

The men on the winch started turning the crank handles in the reverse direction. The locking pawl made a loud clanking as it rode over the teeth on the ratchet wheel. The water rose around the bathyscaphe, supporting its weight, easing the effort required by the men on the winch. They kept turning and the bathyscaphe disappeared, much to Selby's relief; it meant that his calculations were correct and that the thing was negatively buoyant.

The men manning the winch kept turning. The white paint on the cable that was the ten-metre marker disappeared into the depths.

Twenty metres . . . thirty metres . . . .

The amount of cable on the main drum diminished and the winch team kept turning.

"That's halfway," Selby called out as the sixty-metre marker was swallowed by the lake.

A hundred metres was paid out when all six men felt the sudden jolt that travelled up the cable and was transmitted through the pontoon. Harding's first thought was that the cable had parted but two men on the winch were struggling to hold the crank handles in check.

"Her weight's shooting up!" yelled one of the winch men.

Selby darted forward and wound on the brake. The cable held but the scaffolding supporting the "I" beam was groaning alarmingly. Harding exchanged glances with the engineer. The unspoken thought that passed between them was that something had given way under pressure and the bathyscaphe was flooding. Fortunately there was adequate reserve buoyancy in the pontoon's floatation drums to enable the structure to cope with the increased load but the now rigid cable was another matter. Selby ordered the other two men to keep clear of it. He cautiously eased the brake off and ordered the winch men to bring the bathyscaphe up. The muscles stood out on their forearms as they turned the crank handle even though the winch's reduction gearing was handling most of the load.

After five minutes steady, sweated winching the ten-metre marker appeared and finally the top of the bathyscaphe was visible just below the surface. The pontoon dipped noticeably when just a metre of the bathyscaphe was raised above the surface. Selby jumped into the water and released the ballast sacks one by one. Dropping the tonne of rocks helped ease the load on the entire rig. He pulled on a face mask, grabbed a large ring spanner and dived down to unscrew the filter housing's drainage bung. He had to return to the surface twice to gulp down air before the task was complete.

"Okay," he said, handing the bung and the spanner to

Harding. "Start lifting, but slowly – give the water time to drain out."

A minute later the porthole appeared and it was immediately obvious what had gone wrong. Water was gouting out of the shattered acrylic window. It had imploded under the ten-atmosphere pressure at a hundred metres.

Five minutes later the planks were slid under the drained bathyscaphe and it was secure. The wing nuts that held the window in place were removed. Harding examined a piece of the once clear plastic porthole, now milky and crazed along the fracture line. It was as thick as his forefinger.

"Fifteen-mill Perspex," said Selby bitterly, examining the inside of the porthole's frame with the aid of a torch. "We put twice the hundred and twenty metre pressure load on it in the workshop, too."

"Trouble is that it's such a large, flat area," said Harding. "Have you got any thicker Perspex in stock?"

"Some twenty-five mill."

"That's sure to be more than thick enough," said Harding. "Why didn't you use that in the first place?"

The question annoyed the engineer. "Because, Mr Chairman, we're trying to do this on a fixed price, and fifteen mill ought to have been more than thick enough."

"You're quite right to be angry, Tony," said Harding. "It's not your fault. Your work has been excellent. I approved the design, so the fault and the cost is down to me. I apologise most sincerely."

Selby accepted the apology with a dismissive wave. "A thicker window means we're going to have to bond in longer threaded studs around the porthole. We can do that here, today."

"So we could test dive tomorrow? Friday?" Harding queried.

"If we get started right away. The resin needs to be left overnight to cure. Yes – we should ready for a test dive by midday tomorrow."

"And the manned dive in the evening?"

Selby was doubtful. "I don't think we'll have enough time. I'd want to do a visual over every square centimetre of the filter body before your manned dive – which would be better

178

in the morning so we've got a whole day in front of us in case we have problems. Listen, Bob, what we're doing is fucking dangerous enough as it is. Let's not cut any corners."

"The Market Square do on Saturday evening isn't the usual youngsters' disco, but the August carnival," said Harding thoughtfully. "I said I'd open it. A manned dive on the Saturday morning is cutting it a bit fine."

"And there's the street lighting switch-on," Selby reminded him. "My staff have still got a fair bit of line work to get through. Let's say that we do what we can here, make the new window today and bond in new studs – that won't take too long. We carry out a test dive early tomorrow morning and your manned dive in the afternoon only if all goes well, otherwise on Saturday morning. How does that sound?"

Harding grinned. "Excellent. Tomorrow it is."

Selby gave a broad grin. "If you do manage to talk to the Visitors, maybe you'll have something to announce on Saturday night?"

Both men laughed at the prospect.

Thirty-Nine

D avid Weir found Malone sitting under a parasol at his favourite table outside the Crown. The policeman was studying some papers, his PMR radio and a beer in front of him. A loudspeaker provided by the owner of the Crown was relaying Radio Pentworth's interminable MOR afternoon music interspersed with reports on the setback to the bathyscaphe operation at the lake. Around Market Square teams were rigging sound equipment for Saturday evening's carnival. Electricians were checking the street lights in readiness for the switch-on.

"Dunno why you don't move your office here," said David, flopping on to the bench opposite Malone. He looked tired because he had been up since first light looking for the missing women.

"I might just do that," Malone replied, not looking up. "Trouble is I get to meet a worse class of people here."

"I've just come from the Wall," said David. "Quite a crowd of smoke-watchers down there now."

"So I heard on the radio," Malone replied phlegmatically. "All looking for holes in the Wall. They won't find any."

"What makes you so sure? If a cat can get through—"

He was interrupted by the squelch opening on Malone's PMR set. The policeman answered the call.

"Unit 6 at position Sierra Mike," said a voice. "Alpha Romeo's arrived."

Malone acknowledged and told the two-man morris police unit to continue monitoring the situation. Nothing else.

"Let me guess," said David. "Alpha Romeo is the code for Adrian Roscoe. Hardly an unbreakable code." He caught the waiter's eye and ordered a beer.

Malone said indifferently, "I want that little pus stain to know that I know. I want him to know that I'm watching his every move." He smiled thinly. "Seems he's decided to take a look at the mystery smoke for himself. Not that it's such a mystery. And there won't be a hole."

"What makes you so sure, Mike?"

"While you're chasing around looking for Ellen and Co, I'm sitting here doing my being a detective bit – deducing things. The most obvious deduction being that nothing can pass through the Wall unless the Visitors decide it can pass through."

"I see. So if there are people Farside, they've taken to breeding Siamese cats some thirty thousand years before the cat was domesticated?"

The waiter brought David his drink.

"Let's look at a few facts," said Malone. "We know from Vikki's new hand and the account of your visit to the cave, that she's important to the Visitors. I know Vikki. I'm certain she's telling the truth about her ability to communicate with them. Once I'd satisfied myself that the three girls hadn't been found by Roscoe, and made a bit of a prat of myself into the bargain, I reasoned that the only people other than you and I who know where they were hidden was the Visitors and Trinder."

"How would the Visitors know?"

"Simple. Their spyder followed Vikki back to the cave when she went to the lake on the night of the coup. It's damned good at moving about at night, as I can testify. It's hard to see unless it's moving, and it can fly if it has to." Malone took a long pull from his drink. "In view of their interest in Vikki, they've kept the cave under some sort of surveillance. They saw the foxhounds sniffing around yesterday evening, panicked like we did, and decided to move them to a safer place. Where could be safer from Roscoe than Farside? They got to them before we did."

David sipped his drink and shook his head. "It all seems too improbable."

Malone sorted through his papers and pointed to a location on a map of Pentworth that he marked with a cross. "An irate nurseryman called the nick just as I came back on duty. He had

181

discovered that trespassers had trampled across a field that he had just prepared for a late sowing of peas. I went out to the field and took a look. Three sets of footprints. All trainers. All the right sizes to be the girls' footprints. Also some odd marks left by what could only be the spyder. Partially obliterated by the trainer prints which meant that the spyder was leading the way." Malone smiled quizzically at David. "Draw a line from the cave to that field and keep going."

David found the cave and moved his finger across the map. It reached the cross and continued, ending at the field adjoining Sister Mary Thomas's cottage. He looked up at Malone and was at loss for a moment. "That's where the smoke has been seen."

Malone nodded. "It all fits, doesn't it? We can't see down the rise where the smoke is coming from but the chances are that it's some sort of secure accommodation that the Visitors had to get ready for the girls in a hurry."

"And the cat?"

"Sister Mary says it's Vikki's Siamese. Her home is about two kilometres away. Outside the territorial range of a cat I would've thought, but I suppose that depends on the cat. It saw Vikki and decided to join the party. My parents used to have a Siamese. It'd go for walks with you like a dog."

David was silent as he drank his beer. He set the glass down carefully and said, "You're a clever sod, Malone."

"So I've been told."

"Now be ultra clever and tell me why Ellen didn't leave a note?"

"Try an educated guess," Malone invited.

"Because the spyder wouldn't let her or it destroyed the note?"

"Great minds think alike. We don't know what persuasive powers the Visitors have given their spyder. Somehow I can't see them ordering Ellen about but we don't know. The trouble is that with the girls gone, the Visitors are now calling the shots."

David watched an electrician working on a floodlight. "Despite being scientifically advanced, I get the impression that the Visitors are incredibly naive in some respects. How sure can we be sure that the girls are safe Farside? If your theory is correct, that the girls have had to light a fire suggests that the Visitors have not thought everything through. A fire isn't exactly on a par with the technology that built the Wall."

Malone was annoyed with himself for not thinking of that. "Well – everything is down to the Visitors now," he said. He added with a determined note, "It's their move and they seem to make their moves only at night. This time I don't intend for them to make any move without my knowing about it."

Forty

There was something outside the hut.

Ellen opened her eyes. The interior of the hut was lit by the soft glow of the fire. Her first thought was that the spyder had returned but her heartbeat started racing when she heard wheezy breathing not a metre from her head on the other side of the hut's hide covering. Without disturbing Himmler, her hand reached from under the furs and groped around the side of the raised bed for the tool roll. Her fingers fumbled at the knot and felt for the largest of the flint knives. The blade was a good length, was incredibly sharp and had a dangerous point. Although terrified, she intended to give a good account of herself if whatever it was outside decided to enter the hut.

She sat up slowly and listened intently. The only sound was the soft breathing from Vikki's and Claire's gloom-shrouded end of the hut. And then she heard a licking sound near the entrance. Whatever the creature was, she guessed that it had found the flat stone that she had used that day to cut the carp into slivers for drying and smoking. There were no scraps – Himmler had seen to that, and Ellen had encouraged him, not wanting to leave anything around outside that might attract night-time scavengers. That the creature was resorting to licking stones suggested that it was hungry, and that frightened Ellen even more.

She glanced at the strings of dried fish hanging like bunting from lines she had rigged across the hut. Her curing experiments had not been too successful. Some of the pieces of fish were starting to reek. They could probably be smelt for miles. They had worried her at the time. That simple things such as plastic containers with airtight lids were something that one took for granted had brought home to her the problems that early man had with food storage.

184

Her grip on the knife tightened when she heard the creature move to the front of the hut. The flap had been well secured. She reasoned that if whatever it was decided to try breaking in, it wouldn't be able to burst through the hide that quickly and that she'd be able to get in some stabs. She felt for another knife with her free hand and crouched on the bed, ready to spring into action, absolutely determined with every gramme of her being to put up a determined fight if she had to.

Get a grip, she told herself. It's probably a fox.

But the wheezy breathing suggested it was something much larger than a fox. Eventually it moved away and then there was a silence. The minutes slipped by without any further sounds but Ellen waited for at least five minutes to be sure, poised for action, before she dared move. She picked up the torch and cautiously opened the flap a little, just enough to flash the light around outside. The big pug marks near the entrance where she had smoked the carp were unmistakable. They were the same as those she had seen that morning by the river.

She secured the flap and returned to her bed. Ellen was a practical women, not given to harbouring irrational fears despite the justification of the last few minutes. From what her rural upbringing and her abiding interest in palaeontology had taught her, she knew that wildlife tended to avoid human habitation unless driven by hunger. Whatever the creature was, the chances were that it had been just as scared as she had been. Perhaps that was how the first animals had been domesticated? By some kind-hearted soul leaving food out for a wounded or sick animal and so winning its trust?

Pondering her favourite subject was a reassuring exercise and she eventually drifted off to sleep.

Forty-One

M alone used the apartment on the top floor of the police station to catch up on his sleep. At nightfall he entered the operations room, alert and ready for anything that might happen over the next few hours.

He had nearly fifty officers on duty for what he had code-named Operation Scorpio. Every available PMR and CB radio had been brought into service, batteries fully charged and tested. All the officers had been issued with compasses. Even mundane matters such as overtime payments had been squared with Government House by Carol Sandiman.

The wall map that she and an assistant were working at was covered in marker flags, one for each of the morris police officers that were distributed at vantage points in the town and around the surrounding countryside. Each flag bore a boldly marked two-letter callsign that not only identified the officer but, more importantly, his or her location. The callsigns had been assigned for this particular operation only; anyone listening in to the police and CB frequencies would not know what was going on because Malone's briefing had included strict instructions that no one was to give their location away or pass messages likely to indicate the purpose of the operation. Also no police officer was to move from their assigned location or use their radio unnecessarily.

"This is a watch and learn operation only," Malone had told them during the briefing. "Any response needed will be by me." For that purpose he had Asquith Prescott's armoured Range Rover outside, ready and waiting.

Malone tilted his swivel chair back and studied the map. The highest concentration of flags was for the six officers he had located around Pentworth Lake. Those were the key men that had been issued with binoculars. There were four in the vicinity of Ellen's cave although they did not know of its existence, of course. There were five more grouped close to Sister Mary's cottage. These were the locations where Malone expected some sort of activity. The rest of his force were scattered thinly around the countryside. He even had five officers distributed in the grounds of the Pentworth estate. That they had not reported meant that they had managed to conceal themselves without incident. So that nothing would appear to be out of the ordinary he had several regular morris police officers around the town following their normal beat, and a few country patrols doing the rounds. They didn't have radios and were therefore unlikely to interfere in the operation.

There was nothing to do in the operations room except read. Malone made a start on Sören Kierkegaard's analysis of human freedom and personal responsibility. So far he had studiously avoided the nineteenth-century Danish philosopher. After two hours' reading he was on the point of continuing to avoid him when the wall speaker came to life.

"Lima X-Ray. Activity in centre of target area."

Carol bent the base microphone's gooseneck stalk closer to her mouth. Her answer was a cryptic, "Received."

Malone glanced at the wall map. The officer with the callsign LX was in a prime position up a tree overlooking Pentworth Lake. Confirmations of his report came in from the other watchers dotted around the lake.

"Lima X-Ray. It's the objective right enough." A pause then the police officer added, slightly disbelievingly. "It's climbing on to the structure in the middle of the target area. Seems to be taking a look around."

The operations room assistant pinned a yellow flag marked spyder on the map. Malone smiled to himself as he pictured the spyder climbing on to the pontoon. He wondered what the Visitors made of the strange platform that was moored directly above their Silent Vulcan.

"Lima X-Ray. Objective now Alpha 50 and increasing."

Alpha 50 and increasing meant altitude 50 metres and climbing. The spyder had decided to go flying.

"Lima X-Ray. Objective now Alpha 100 approx. Bravo Three-Two-Zero."

Bearing 320 degrees? North-West? Malone hadn't expected that. He crossed to the map where the assistant had moved the marker for the spyder.

A new voice came on. "Papa Tango. Objective estimated Alpha 200. Bravo 320."

"Definitely heading North-West, sir," said the assistant, moving the marker to the new position.

Two more reports came in that confirmed the spyder's flight pattern. Malone traced its likely destination. It was heading towards Pentworth House.

Five minutes passed without a report. Malone cursed inwardly. He hadn't expected the spyder to take this route and had less observers around the town.

And then another new voice reported, "Papa Golf. Objective audible. Alpha and Bravo unknown."

The assistant moved the spyder's marker again. Malone checked the operation's notes; Papa Golf's position was fifty metres from the hunt's kennels. He felt uneasy. Something wasn't right and he had an uncomfortable idea what and why.

"Papa Golf. Objective Alpha 100 and steady. Correction – slow decrease of Alpha. Bravo seems to be static."

"The bloody thing's hovering," Malone muttered.

Papa Golf came back but this time his transmission was distorted. Malone caught the odd word here and there. The strange fluctuations in the transmission were like no interference that Malone had ever heard before. It sounded as though Papa Golf's voice was being alternately squeezed and stretched by an electronic harmoniser. He moved to Carol's side, alarm bells sounding off in his mind.

"Go again, Papa Golf," said Carol. "You're breaking up."

This time the interference completely obliterated Papa Golf's transmission.

Jesus Christ! The kennels!

Malone snatched up the base microphone. "Papa Golf! Leave your target zone now! ASAP! Get clear now! Run! Go! Go! Go!" He repeated the message twice, having to make a conscious effort not to shout and cause distortion. "Jesus Christ – let's hope he heard that," he said, putting the microphone back on the desk.

Carol and the assistant were staring at him. Carol was the first to speak. "What's the matter, sir?"

"I don't know!" said Malone, showing uncharacteristic irritation. "Give him a few more seconds and ask for a welfare."

The policewoman was about to press the PPT key when Papa Golf came back, out of breath but his transmission was clear this time. "A hundred and fifty metres," he gasped. "Anyone going to tell me what's up?"

Malone studied the wall map. "Get a welfare check on all units in the park and send them to position Papa Hotel to await further instructions. They're to stay well clear of location Papa Golf."

Carol relayed Malone's instructions. Papa Hotel was the spot where his men had entered Pentworth Park the previous night. There were no reports for several minutes then:

"Papa Tango. Objective estimated Alpha 200. Bravo 220."

"South-East," mused Malone, much relieved. "Looks like our metal friend is heading for home."

His surmise was borne out a few minutes later with reports from Pentworth Lake that the spyder had returned. "Looks like it had trouble maintaining Alpha as it came in," said Lima X-Ray, concluding his report. "Power sounded down and it made heavy contact in the centre of the target area."

Meaning, it had landed with a splash, thought Malone. Should that be important? Christ knows. He was too tired to think straight.

He kept everyone on standby until dawn was seeping into the eastern sky, when there seemed little likelihood of the spyder reappearing. He thanked everyone and stood them down, knowing that he'd have to repeat the operation the following night – ructions permitting. Right now the only thing on his mind was sleep.

Forty-Two

Harry Shaw's first job in the morning on the Pentworth Estate was to attend to the hounds. Normally the rattle of his galvanised bucket was enough to set them off – a massed canine fury erupting into their wire-enclosed runs, joyously milling expectantly against the wire mesh, yapping for their breakfast as though he starved them. But this morning the kennel block was eerily silent. Not a hound stirred.

With a deep sense of foreboding, he slid back the bolt, pushed the door to enter but it wouldn't budge. Something was holding it shut at the bottom. It needed a series of hard pushes with his boot to force it open as though a heavy sack was on the floor. It wasn't a sack, it was a foxhound, and it was dead.

He pushed the corpse clear, opened the door fully, and stood surveying the terrible scene, the silence closing on his reeling mind as it sought to equate the evidence of his eyes with reality. The foxhounds were scattered everywhere, lying perfectly still. No sign of movement, not as much as a flicker of an eye or a twitch of a leg. Not only was the dreadful scene wrong, but the smell was wrong – a sweet, slightly sickly smell of roast meat, and the temperature was also wrong. It was only an hour after dawn – the sun had hardly risen – yet it was strangely warm in the long shed. He knelt and reached out to touch the nearest corpse. It was warm, so warm that he could feel the heat radiating from the animal on the palm of his hand before it made contact with its fur. He opened the animal's eye and what he saw had him racing towards Pentworth House, screaming.

The vet arrived an hour later. A frightened Harry Shaw showed him and Adrian Roscoe into the kennel block. The vet checked three of the hounds and didn't bother with the rest; it was obvious that all thirty-five animals were dead. He decided to carry out an initial on-the-spot post-mortem and lifted one of the corpses on to a table. The warmth of the hound was wrong. Instead of making the usual opening incision, he made a cut deep into a muscle of a hind leg and pulled the fur and skin back to expose the muscle's tissue. In a few minutes of shocks, the colour of the striated muscle fibre was the worst of all.

"It must have just happened before I opened up," said Harry Shaw. "They were still warm."

"Warm?" the vet echoed. "Warm? This animal isn't just warm! It's been cooked! Take a look – it's as though it's been cooked in a microwave oven!"

Forty-Three

M alone drove the heavy Range Rover across the small field next to Sister Mary's cottage and stopped. A small crowd of onlookers that had gathered near the striped marker poles along the line of the Wall that cut across the field were too intent on Farside to notice his arrival. A pony-drawn gig was nearby, its side panels sign-written with "Stayin' Alive! On 87.5!"

Near the gathering of mothers with young children was the lean figure of Nelson Faraday, looking resplendent in his black leather gear and cavalier boots. His cloak hid the sling and the plaster cast on his right arm. He was standing slightly away from the onlookers in the shade of a tree. Malone guessed that the black leather he favoured would be uncomfortably hot in the sun.

Malone left the vehicle, thrust his hands in his tracksuit's trouser pockets, and sauntered towards the small crowd at the Wall. The smoke rising above the steep, grassy fold in the land Farside was the attraction although the crowd was much smaller than the previous day when it had first been seen and had aroused considerable excitement. One of his morris police officers, in his beat uniform of straw hat, white blouse, baldric, dark trousers and buckle shoes, was standing nearby, leaning on his ash staff. He straightened when he saw Malone and decided to resume his patrol. The radio reporter was Ted Savage. A Uher tape recorder was hanging from his shoulder and he was talking into a microphone. He was known to Malone and returned his wave.

"Good afternoon, Nelson," said Malone pleasantly. "Pity we can't see down the slope. It would certainly be interesting to see what or where the smoke is coming from."

Faraday turned and did not seem overjoyed at seeing the police officer.

"How's the arm?" Malone enquired.

"Healing."

"Excellent. Try not to get the other one broken. Ah . . . I see you've brought your camcorder. Mr Roscoe is fortunate indeed to have you so willing to keep him supplied with home movies although I doubt if he finds them as satisfactory as the young girls you used to recruit for him in the old days."

"Maybe you'd like to see the last scenes, Malone? Thirty-five dead foxhounds."

"I know. I've just come from the kennels," said Malone. "A strange business."

"Nothing strange about it. Such things will happen if you permit witches to live."

Malone grinned broadly. "Come off it, Nelson. You don't believe that guff any more than I do. Will you be disgracing us with your presence at the carnival tomorrow evening?"

Faraday shrugged. "I wouldn't want to spoil your fun."

"I would derive a good deal of pleasure from seeing you having to discourage girls from hanging on to your arm."

Malone moved away to talk to the Radio Pentworth reporter when there was a sudden commotion in the crowd. Mothers called to their children. People were pointing. A woman screamed. None seemed to trust the Wall's invisible presence – the entire crowd left the field in some haste with the exception of the Radio Pentworth reporter, who remained gabbling excitedly into his microphone, and Nelson Faraday.

"Jesus Christ," Malone muttered, too astonished to think of anything more imaginative to say.

Faraday moved to a better position and raised the camcorder's viewfinder to his eye, working the zoom control with the fingers of his plaster-encased right arm.

A sabre-tooth cat had appeared on the level, grassy stretch between the far side of the Wall and the tantalising dip.

Forty-Four

"**B** oo!" said Vikki.

Ellen turned and nearly cut herself on the knife she was using to slice the carp. Vikki had used a kitbag strap to secure the upper half of a sabre-tooth cat's skull to her head. The pair of wicked incisors hung down in front of her cheeks. It was all she was wearing apart from decorative circles she had drawn around her breasts and navel with a burnt stick. "You stupid bitch! I nearly cut my finger off!"

"Sorry, Ellen." Vikki sat cross-legged, well away from the heat of the outside fire that Ellen had built. She wrinkled her nose at the carp. "It'll all have gone off soon. Breakfast was definitely dodgy."

"That's why we've got to cook and eat what's left today," said Ellen. "You must be used to fish on Fridays."

"All that went out years ago. Mummy just gives up chocolate for Lent." Vikki fell silent, thinking about her mother always upset her. The thought that her home was only two kilometres away made matters worse. She had been up at dawn, shortly after Ellen, searching along the top of the rise in the hope of finding the gap where they had come through into Farside, and had found nothing but the yielding blackness and the continuation of the vista of an alien, windswept landscape. Home was a mere two kilometres in distance but 40,000 years in time . . . She brushed away a tear.

Ellen sensed the girl's distress and changed the subject. "Where did you find that skull?"

"Down by the river. That big pile of bones."

"I don't suppose you thought to bring any wood back?"

"I've been doing nothing else all morning!" Vikki protested.

"Why do we have to have such a big fire? It's not as if it's cold in the daytime."

"I like big fires," said Ellen. "We'll need enough fuel to keep it going all night."

"What's wrong with the fire inside?"

Ellen made no reply but concentrated on cutting large slivers of carp and laying them on stones around the fire to cook. There was just enough left for generous helpings for their lunch and evening meal. Being naked had certain disadvantages when cooking so she had draped a fur over herself. She had built the fire just before dawn after obliterating the pug marks around the hut, and had said nothing about their night visitor to Claire and Vikki.

Claire, also naked, came out of the hut holding some torches she had been making at Ellen's behest. They were lengths of stout sapling, each with a bundle of dried moss and twigs tied around the end. She looked askance at Vikki's fearsome headgear and offered the torches for Ellen's inspection. "I've soaked the ends in the fat we found in those sausage things," she explained.

Ellen held one of the torches in the fire. The brand burst into flame immediately. She put it out by banging it on the ground. "Excellent, Claire. We'll need at least ten."

"You're a slave driver, Ellen."

"Fucking hell – Olympic torches now," Vikki declared.

"Language," Ellen chided.

Vikki jumped up, grinning impishly, her depression gone. "You'll be banning body language next." She grabbed one of the torches and pranced exuberantly around the fire, uttering whoops and cries, charcoal-marked breasts jiggling, golden hair flailing, the sabre toothed cat's skull askew, threatening to fall off her head. For a finale she framed her pubes with her thumbs and index fingers and performed a decidedly unladylike pelvic gyration like a nightclub lap dancer coaxing money out of a besotted punter.

"There's no doubt that our Vikki has changed," Claire observed wryly.

"Her mother will hold me responsible," said Ellen morosely.

"She felt sick this morning," said Claire. "That's one thing you can't be blamed for."

Ellen looked sharply at the young woman. "Do you really think she is pregnant?"

"Certainly seems that way." Claire touched her stomach. "I was sick as a dog when this was a few days under way."

"It infuriates me to think of the way the Visitors have used her," said Ellen tightly.

"She doesn't see it that way. She insists that she was the willing partner – her choice."

"And what about something like six thousand people trapped inside their bloody Wall? What choice did they have?"

Vikki flopped down before Claire had a chance to reply. She grinned at her companions. "Better not do too much of that," she said. "Might frighten off a caveman whose got me in his sights to drag me off to his cave and do unspeakable things to me."

"I'm considering dragging you into the hut and smacking your unspeakable bottom," said Ellen severely.

"Promises, promises," Vikki retorted.

Claire laughed and touched the huge incisors on Vikki's headdress. "Wow. Some teeth. A sabre-toothed tiger?"

"A sabre-toothed cat," Ellen corrected.

Vikki made the skull more secure and stroked the vicious canines. "How could it eat with these things? They're way over the top."

"They weren't so much for eating as for hunting," said Ellen. "It was a forest creature that depended on ambush as its hunting technique. It wasn't capable of the bursts of speed that a lioness is capable of on the open plains to bring down zebra or antelope. The sabre-tooth would climb a tree and drop on its prey, using those canines and its incredibly powerful neck muscles to rip out its victim's spine."

"Bloody hell," Vikki breathed. "Good job it's extinct, then."

Ellen was about to say something when Himmler, who had been waiting for the right moment to obtain breakfast No. 4, darted forward, seized the largest and choicest piece of fish, and raced up the slope, his collar bell tinkling.

"That sodding cat!" Ellen raged. "He's had more than all of us put together!"

"I'll get him," said Vikki. "I rescued a fillet steak from

him once." She jumped up and ran up the hill, using one of Claire's torches to speed her progress, while yelling at Himmler to stop.

The thief reached the brow of the hill and did just that. He dropped the heavy piece of fish, hoping it would sprout legs and try to run away, while keeping one eye on Vikki climbing towards him, shouting curses. He didn't like her hat, but he liked a game and decided that this was one he couldn't lose provided he got the timing right. He let Vikki get within a few metres, snatched up his trophy, and bounded along the flat stretch.

The sabre-tooth cat snarled. The creature was crouching in Himmler's path. The Siamese's reactions were superb; his change of direction and amazing acceleration was one seamless movement. His glimpse of the beast's teeth and the distressing lack of nearby roofs or trees imbued in him a sudden strong desire to garrison the nearest horizon. He became a grey streak of southbound, panic-propelled domestic cat.

Vikki screamed and froze.

Ellen and Claire saw the sabre-toothed cat at the same instant. It was within five metres of Vikki and seemed to be preparing to spring, wriggling its haunches to tuck its hind legs closer together.

"Vikki!" Ellen screamed. "Don't move! For Christ's sake keep still!" With that Ellen was racing up the slope towards the big cat with Claire following.

Vikki was incapable of moving. All she could manage were great sobs of terror as she stared into the malevolent yellow eyes. Serendipity played a vital part by paralysing her muscles, so that her grip on the torch never slackened.

The sabre-tooth cat was undecided. Her hunger was a ravening torment but she had encountered these strange, upright, two-legged beings before. They had one arm longer than the other and were dangerous. They had killed her mate and her nearly fully grown cub a long time ago but the memory hadn't faded with time. Two more were coming up the hill towards her, not running away like most prey – although she was now too old and stiff to catch even slow-moving animals. Her last meal, an injured bird, had hardly assuaged

197

her gnawing hunger whereas the overpowering warm blood scent of this puny creature promised a feast. The heady smell was a compulsive clamour that caused threads of saliva to hang from her mighty incisors that had killed so many, so effortlessly, when she was young. But caution prevailed and she hesitated, expressing her rage and frustration by snarling at this blinding temptation standing stock-still before her.

Ellen slipped on loose stones. She snatched up two large, round rocks and kept climbing. She reached the brow of the rise and rushed straight at the sabre-tooth cat. Her first rock missed, but the second hit the big cat painfully on the nose. That decided it. With a final enraged snarl of angry defeat, it turned and fled downhill, the steep slope giving it an impetus that her arthritic joints would not otherwise permit.

Forty-Five

Malone was standing not twenty metres away and had witnessed every detail of the extraordinary incident. For once his clinical rationality deserted him and he started forward, only to encounter the benign resistance of the Wall. The blackness cleared and he stood staring at the three tearfully embracing women. The image of Ellen rushing at that hellish creature, that lovely black hair and that beautiful, naked, voluptuous body that had writhed under him on a memorable hot afternoon, played over and over in his mind with a vividness that ceased when the three women, sobbing with relief and still clinging to each other, disappeared from sight.

"So we now know what the smoke is coming from," said a voice at his side. Malone turned to confront Faraday. He was holding his camcorder with his good arm like a talisman, his smile mocking. "A cauldron, no doubt. Bubble, bubble, toil and trouble. Should be some interesting footage. Or is it metres these days?"

The thought of this dreg and Roscoe drooling over a video tape of Ellen was intolerable but Malone contained his anger, keeping his voice calm. "I would like that tape, please, Faraday."

"Really, Mr Malone? And which one of those three lovely ladies is your favourite? Claire Lake? I've had that little one more times than I can remember. Passable, I suppose. Vikki Taylor? She gave me a hard time; a prissy little virgin but she didn't look it just now, did she? A skull on her head, pagan runes on her body, naked. Quite the wild little witch's acolyte." Faraday's smug grin was of someone who knows that he has the upper hand. "Or is your preference for older woman such as Ellen Duncan? If so, I admire your taste.

A splendid animal. There's something excitingly primitive about her."

"The tape," said Malone evenly. "Or do you want your other arm broken?"

Faraday lowered the camcorder and gave the radio reporter a pained glance. "Uttering threats, Mr Malone? In front of a witness?"

"A witness would add piquancy to the pleasure I would derive from hearing your other arm snap like a rotten twig. It won't be a clean break. It will be a horribly messy greenstick fracture that will take months to heal properly, if ever."

The two men regarded each other for several seconds. The radio reporter sensed trouble brewing and sneaked his microphone between the two protagonists. Faraday shrugged and fiddled to get the camcorder open – a task hardly made easy by his cloak and a plaster cast on his arm. He handed a video cassette to the police officer.

"Thank you, Nelson," said Malone, pocketing the tape. "I'll see that a receipt is sent to your HQ."

Faraday smiled thinly. "Consider it a gift, Mr Malone. I hope you enjoy it. I wouldn't want to deprive you of a chance to see some naked girls."

Malone resisted a powerful temptation to carry out his threat by turning on his heel. He signalled to the radio reporter and moved towards the radio gig, out of Faraday's hearing.

"Some story, Mr Malone," said the radio reporter. "Claire Lake was one of them. The one Roscoe was offering a reward for."

"He's not now," said Malone shortly. "You know who the other two were?"

"Ellen Duncan and Vikki Taylor, of course. Good to see that they're alive."

"Listen, Ted. I want you to do me a favour. By all means file your report about seeing the Siamese and that sabre-tooth, but don't mention the women."

The reporter looked doubtful. "It's a big story, Mr Malone. You're asking a lot."

"I know that, Ted. I wouldn't ask but the lives of those three women are at stake. Give me forty-eight hours and I'll give you the full story. Every detail. But I want your promise that you'll sit on any mention of the women until then. Don't even leave your tape lying around the studio."

The reporter had a good working relationship with the senior police officer and had considerable respect for him. He nodded and pressed the rewind key on his Uher. "I'll wipe the tape and record a new report. I'll do it now. That's a promise."

That was good enough for Malone. He spent a few minutes giving an interview about the time when he had seen a Farside family of woolly mammoths before thanking the reporter and returning to the Range Rover, well aware that Faraday's hostile gaze was following him. He was far from happy with the situation but he had done his best. If anyone had seen the women, at least the resulting stories that circulated would be treated as rumours. Pentworth had plenty of rumours. The hard evidence of the bizarre events he had just witnessed was in his pocket. Another consolation was that he now knew for certain where Ellen, Claire and Vikki were. The trouble was that Roscoe would now know, too. Although the three were safe from Roscoe, they were hardly safe from the world of Farside as he had just seen. He recalled David Weir's words when they had been drinking outside the Crown: that despite the Visitors' undoubted scientific skills (the latest demonstration being their mass killing of the foxhounds) they seemed to be incredibly naive about some things. He needed to talk to David Weir about these latest developments.

Forty-Six

"Stop! Stop!"

The two men working the winch to lower the bathyscaphe didn't need Tony Selby's yelled warning because they had seen what was happening to the splice that joined the two lengths of steel cable together. A protruding snag of the cable's plaited strands had caught on the "I" beam pulley and the strands had started to pull apart. The six men on the pontoon held their collective breath, expecting the cable to part but the weakened splice held.

"Back up," breathed Selby. "Nice and easy."

The winchmen reversed their cranking. The damaged splice moved towards the take-up drum. Harding pulled on an industrial glove and helped Selby steer the second turn of the cable over the splice to trap it. Only when the joint was safety pinned under several turns did Selby allow himself a succinct, heartfelt, "Bugger."

Harding could barely hide his disappointment as the winchmen continued winding in the cable. It was early afternoon – the entire Friday had been one setback after another and still they hadn't completed an unmanned test dive to 120 metres. First the telephone hadn't worked, then the gasket for the new porthole-hatch had leaked after reaching only thirty metres and a new one had to be made, and now this – a major cable problem when the bathyscaphe had been lowered only fifty metres from the pontoon into the depths of Pentworth Lake.

"Keep going," said Selby wearily. "She'll be secure now."

The bright yellow craft emerged into the sunlight and was rested on planks laid across the opening in the centre of the pontoon. At least they hadn't lost the bathyscaphe but it had been a near thing.

Selby and his staff pulled the cable off the winch's drum until they reached the damaged splice. Being a man who never took chances, Selby pulled off more cable until he came to the next splice and discovered that that one wasn't in a safe condition either. He swore bitterly.

"How about cleating the cable, side-by-side at the join?" Harding suggested.

Selby pointed at the overhead pulley that was hanging from the "I" beam. "It would never go though that. That block's the biggest we've got."

"Could you weld the cable ends together?"

Selby avoided looking contemptuous. "What would *you* say would be the disadvantage with that, Mr Chairman?"

Harding realised that it was a stupid suggestion. "I'd say that welding is rigid, that the whole point of cable is that it's flexible, and the welding would most likely crack and fail when the joint passed over the pulley."

"And you'd be right," said Selby, banging the winch drum angrily. "This is the only steel cable we've got."

"So how about using rope?"

"Ordinary hemp rope?"

"Yes. Have you got any?"

"Four thirty-metre lengths back at the factory. Old stuff. Now look—"

"What size?"

"About the same as this cable – six-strand I think, about seventy-mill circular."

"Sounds like ten-tonne rope," said Harding. "So let's use that."

Selby looked despairing. "Why do you think there's a saying 'money for old rope'? I'll tell you why – because old rope is worthless. It's dangerous. Jesus Christ, I can remember the stuff kicking about the yard when I was a kid!"

"So we test it," Harding reasoned. "Isn't that what the unmanned test dive is for?"

"There's another problem. It's in four lengths. Splicing manila hemp rope is a skilled business. It's got to be done properly otherwise it won't go through the pulley block. The last bloke I knew who could slice hemp rope was an old bargee. And he's been dead twenty years."

"I think I know someone who could do it," said Harding.

"Who?"

Harding looked at his watch. "We can't do much here today. You need to get over to the generator site. I've got a lot to do. Let's call it a day. I'll phone you this evening if I've found someone and you could bring those lengths of rope here first thing."

Selby spat into the water. "Whole bloody day wasted. And it's carnival tomorrow."

An hour later Bob Harding pressed Roger Dayton's door chimes button and discovered that they didn't work. He guessed that the yachtsman had been one of the few to think of handing over its batteries. He used the knocker. Roger Dayton answered the door and was a little taken aback. "Yes – it is a good afternoon," he said in answer to Harding's opening pleasantry. "I'd thought you'd be needing the echo-sounder for much longer."

"Actually we're still using it, Mr Dayton. I've come to see you on another matter."

"Which is?"

"Can you splice hemp ropes together?"

Dayton was surprised. Harding repeated the question.

"Well of course I can splice ropes! All ropes. All sizes. Even modern rubbish. For God's sake, man! I'm a sailor! I'm not some green-as-grass arsewipe, ditch-crawling, floating gin-palace weekender who thinks a chart is something that pop songs are listed on, too scared to poke his nose outside the Solent in case his GPS receiver gets wet."

"In that case," said Harding. "I've got a big favour to ask of you."

Forty-Seven

M alone turned his Range Rover into Baldock's Field and parked near "Brenda". Two armed police officers at the foot of the slope guarding the well-head enclosure returned his wave. The Centrax generator was roaring flat out as near as Malone could judge as he slid from behind the wheel. Two engineers were watching it critically. All the overhead wiring work appeared to have been completed.

The showman's engine was running surprisingly smoothly other than the rhythmic spitting of the steam exhaust and the regular snick-snick of the broad, leather drive belt taking power from the flywheel to the dynamo. The venerable machine was certainly quieter than the Centrax even though the big mobile generator was a hundred metres away, stationed downhill, a safe distance from the enclosure. There was no smoke billowing from "Brenda"'s smokestack. The loudest noise from the showman's engine was the dull roar of its methane-fuelled firebox. David Weir was too intent on his work, completing the burial of a heavy power cable, to notice Malone's arrival.

"It all looks very professional," said Malone admiringly.

David straightened. "A flat-out test run. No load, of course, but it's all looking good. Anyway, you're just the man we need. Find yourself a spade."

"That's not the sort of digging that's to my taste," Malone replied.

"Maybe this is?" David queried, producing two mugs and a bottle of beer from his pony and trap. He now knew Malone well enough to know when something was his mind. The two men sat on the railway sleepers that served as chocks against "Brenda"'s front wheels and talked for some minutes.

"Microwave cooked?" said David softly when Malone had

finished sketching in recent events. "All thirty-five hounds? The radio said that some sort of disease was suspected."

"Makes you think, doesn't it? All that power packed into the spyder."

"Looks like your theory's holding up, Mike. The Visitors decided to move the three girls somewhere safe until they'd zapped the foxhounds. Except Farside isn't so safe, is it? The Visitors screwed up. All I heard on the radio was that a sabre-tooth tiger had been seen Farside."

"The radio station is sitting on all mention of the girls."

David shook his head in disbelief. "Ellen chucking rocks at a sabre-tooth . . ."

"She scored a direct hit on its nose just as it was about to pounce on Vikki. That made it decide that taking off was the better option."

"God – that woman's got balls," David murmured.

"I'll drink to that. Vikki managed to stand her ground, which seemed to confuse the sabre-tooth. Trouble is that Faraday and his bloody camcorder saw the whole thing as well. I threatened him with a broken arm unless he gave me the video tape. Quite illegal, of course but I'd couldn't stand the thought of those sickos at Pentworth House drooling over it. Not only that, but anyone not wholly convinced that Vikki's a witch, certainly would be after seeing that tape. She was naked, covered in body markings like a shaman, and wearing a skull on her head."

"Why?"

Malone smiled. "You haven't got a daughter. My guess is that she was just horsing about when she had to chase after her cat. The unanswered question is why are the Visitors so keen to protect the three girls, albeit, in their own peculiar fashion?"

"Vikki says that she's the key," said David. "They can talk to her. Or she says they can."

"She's telling the truth," said Malone seriously.

"Oh, come on, Mike. She probably imagines she is. All that talk when I went to the cave about her meeting this Dario guy and being pregnant. You said yourself that you'd seen a poster in her bedroom of a Zulu warrior she called Dario. A young girl's fantasies can be pretty bloody potent. Strong enough for her to mix them up with reality and to convince herself that she's telling the truth. After the horrors of what she's been through, it's hardly surprising she's turned to her fantasies as an escape. I would've been gibbering by now."

"I don't think young girls fantasise about being pregnant. Anything but, I would've thought."

"I don't know," said David. "She seemed so rebellious in the cave that maybe she was just saying that to shock. Anyway, if the Visitors and their spyder can pack the sort of punch that cooks dogs, why didn't they use it to save Vikki when she fell into Adrian Roscoe's clutches?"

"I don't know," Malone admitted.

The two men talked for another ten minutes. David listened attentively to Malone's plans. They were refinements of the rough idea that Malone had outlined during their von Stauffenberg discussion. David had some grave reservations, not least being a reluctance to take on the spyder on the not wholly unreasonable grounds that anything that could microwave thirty-five foxhounds to cooked meat was worthy of respect. Eventually he was persuaded to go along with Malone's outlandish scheme. The two men crossed to the Range Rover. Malone was about to start the engine when he asked David how much power "Brenda" and the Centrax could produce.

"The best part of three hundred kilowatts," David replied. "Although we've not had a chance to test them under full load."

Malone whistled, eyeing "Brenda" and the big mobile generator. "Nearly a third of a million watts? That's quite something. I've had a thought. Tomorrow night at the switch-on, instead of turning on a few street lights and some floodlights, why not light up the whole of Market Square? All the shop fronts, the offices and flats? And plenty of extra floodlights. Last year's Christmas lights. Make it a real blaze. Could you do that?"

"I can't see that it would be a problem. But what would be the point?"

"A psychological point. It would bring home to everyone that the skids are under Adrian Roscoe. That Pentworth doesn't need him any more."

David grinned. "That's not a such a bad idea. Bob Harding's

supposed to here be soon when he's stopped messing about with his bathyscaphe thing. I'll put it to him."

Malone's parting words to David were an admonition to get a couple of hours' sleep because they might have a long night ahead of them.

Forty-Eight

Malone's Operation Cancer differed from the surveillance operation of the previous night in several respects. This time he had a much better idea of the spyder's likely movements if it appeared, and had been able to distribute his one-man lookouts more effectively. Pentworth House had been code-named Warren Farm. There was a real Warren Farm, therefore anyone turning up there without good reason was liable to find themselves held under suspicion of listening to police frequencies. Pentworth House and its estate had been ringed with lookouts – nothing was going to move in and out of that place without Malone knowing about it. The major difference was that this time Malone was not in the operations room at the police station. He and David Weir were sitting in the Range Rover that was concealed in the clump of trees in the field bordering Sister Mary's property where they had a good view of the field's entrance and the expanse of grass. The two men had cut some rhododendron fronds and propped them around the Range Rover. To their left, across a hundred metres of grass, were the Wall's marker poles. It was the field where the extraordinary scene between Vikki, Ellen, Claire and the sabre-tooth had taken place. Silent lightning spikes of a gathering storm blazed across the Farside sky, illuminating the humped horizon of the South Downs.

Shortly before midnight David slipped out of the passenger seat and stood in front of the Range Rover's camouflage. Despite the greenery, he could feel the warmth radiating from the engine. He returned to the car and said to Malone, "Still damned hot. If that spyder can see into the infra-red, then we're going to show up like a beacon. This camouflage isn't going to hide us."

"Let's deal with that problem when it arises, if it arises," said Malone.

"It's a wonder the damn thing doesn't sink into the ground."

Malone made no reply. His reason for using the armoured vehicle was that its radio had a high-gain antenna on the roof, and the radio itself had greater sensitivity than the handheld PMR sets. It was essential that he could hear the exchanges between his scattered units and the operations room without Carol Sandiman having to break radio silence unnecessarily to keep him posted on what was going on.

The two men sat in silence. The Farside lightning was intensifying, heavy clouds were coalescing although the sky within the Wall remained clear. Malone commented on the fact that there were no matching crackles from the police radio each time the Farside sky was lit up.

"We can't hear the thunder either," said David. "Yet the storm's getting closer."

Like many before him, Malone pondered the strange filtering characteristics of the Wall. They could see Farside yet hear no sounds from it. Sunlight, the light from the stars and the moon, even Farside scenes penetrated the Wall but not radio signals. The unearthly powers that the Visitors possessed had never worried him so much as they did now. Mindful of the massed slaughter of thirty-five foxhounds by the spyder, he had issued instructions to all his men at the evening briefing that they were to "run like hell" if the spyder showed any interest in them. Such was his concern for their safety that he had been in half a mind to cancel the operation.

David looked at his watch and muttered, "Midnight."

Malone switched on the broadcast radio and kept the volume low. "Stayin' Alive! . . . On 87.5!" Radio Pentworth's identification jingle, mixed with the Bee Gee's song, was hardly necessary because it was the only station on the band. But the song was now Pentworth's unofficial anthem. It was played to mark the opening of the monthly discos and children's parties that had been held in Market Square since May, two months after the Wall had appeared. The brash, confident number symbolised the mood of Pentworth and the way its

210

resourceful people were coping with the extraordinary crisis that had overtaken their community.

"Looking forward to the carnival?" asked Malone.

David considered his answer. "If it means ending this impasse with Roscoe – the answer's yes. If it means bloodshed, then no."

The midnight news bulletin included a recorded interview with Bob Harding explaining what had gone wrong at the lake with his plans to dive down to the Silent Vulcan.

"Silly old fool," David muttered. "We should never have voted him that funding."

"At least you had the chance to vote," Malone observed. "More than you would've had with Prescott running things." He turned the radio broadcast off and remarked that the food David had brought smelt promising.

David retrieved a shoebox from the back seat and passed Malone a sandwich. "Ham!" said Malone appreciatively, sinking his teeth into the fresh bread. "I'd forgotten what it tasted like." He opened the sandwich and inspected the contents. "My God! Look at the thickness of these slices!"

"I never was much good at carving," David admitted.

Malone took the shoebox and examined its contents. "For Chrissake, there must a month's ration for an entire family here."

"More like two months," said David, wondering what Malone would say when he found the hard-boiled eggs.

Malone found them and muttered something about bloody farmers and Philistines. He finished his sandwich and started on another. There were enough of them for a small feast.

"Chutney?"

"How do you manage that?" asked Malone, taking the jar and spooning the contents into his sandwich.

"Green tomatoes are plentiful at this time of year."

"Hang on. You're a sheep farmer. How come you've got all this ham?"

"I don't really think you want to know the answer to that, Mr Malone," said David, returning the shoebox and its uneaten ham sandwich contents to the back seat.

Malone grunted and decided that perhaps David was right.

The sandwiches had assuaged his hunger. He reclined his seat, and settled back, easing the loaded .45 from under his thigh. The revolver was a dead weight in his tracksuit pocket. "Might be an idea to get a bit of shut-eye."

He was nudged awake by David a few minutes after 1 a.m.

"Lima X-Ray has just reported activity in the centre of the target area."

Malone stretched. "Our spyder emerging to spin another web of mystery," he said, much relieved. He switched on the map light and unfolded his operations map. He pointed out Lima X-Ray's position at the lake.

A minute passed.

"Lima X-Ray," said the police officer to identify himself. "Objective is showing no interest in the structure."

"It climbed on the pontoon for a look-see last night," said Malone in answer to David's query.

"Lima X-Ray. Objective Alpha zero. Bravo 170."

"Zero altitude?" David queried.

"It's not flying," said Malone shortly. "And bearing 170 degrees means it's heading our way."

Thirty minutes went by without a report being heard. Malone got restless. The silence was broken by Delta Charlie. Objective was at zero altitude and its bearing was 170.

"It's covered a kilometre," said Malone, checking Delta Charlie's position on the map. He peered out of the side window at the moonlit field. "Come on, you bastard. Fly!"

The two men got out of the Range Rover to stretch their legs. "It'll be another two hours at this rate," Malone grumbled. He was edgy about his men's welfare. It was relatively easy to track the spyder's course when it was flying but on the ground it was difficult to see. The last thing he wanted was for an over-zealous police officer to get too close.

"Maybe it's frightened of heights?" David suggested.

"Well it certainly doesn't seem to like flying," said Malone. "There was that time when it took off when I almost caught it. I got the impression that it sprouts wings only as a last resort."

"But it flew last night when it killed the foxhounds?"

"And it made a crap landing in the lake when it returned.

212

Maybe flying canes its batteries or whatever it uses to store energy. Looks like the damned thing's saving them tonight and is going to walk all the way here."

"All the more energy to zap you with, Grandmother," David murmured.

"That's not funny. I'm more worried about the moon setting before it gets here."

The two men returned to the car. The next report indicated that the spyder was still heading their way and had increased its speed. Malone began to feel better. The storm that had been brewing Farside suddenly erupted with a silent ferocity that astonished the two men. The rain beat down with a savagery that tore into the shallow-rooted sedge grass along the flat stretch close to the Wall. Within minutes runnels were forming and merging into a seething cascade of water that was sweeping away grass and soil.

The two men watched the mighty deluge without speaking. The radio broke in on their thoughts.

"Foxtrot Juliet. Objective Alpha zero. Bravo 170. It just passed under me. Going at a clip."

"Foxtrot Juliet is up a tree," said Malone, consulting his map. "He's only a kilometre from here."

After five minutes Malone lowered his side windows and trained his nightsight binoculars across the field to where he expected the spyder to appear. "All we want now is a report from Zulu Mike and the thing's here."

"Zulu Mike," said the radio. "Objective Alpha zero. Bravo 175."

"It's altered course," said David.

"Looks like it's not even interested in hedge-hopping," Malone replied, focusing his binoculars on the open gate that was the field's entrance from the lane. "That course change will take it to the entrance. It doesn't like the idea of pushing its way through a layered hedge." He stiffened, his thumb making fine adjustments to the knurled focusing wheel. "It's here," he said softly, and passed the binoculars to David. "You can't actually see it, but you can see the background distortion it causes as it moves."

David adjusted the glasses. He could see nothing at first. And

213

then he spotted a rippling effect – a small patch of distortion that was moving purposefully along the grass towards the Wall markers. "Got it," he murmured, passing the glasses back to Malone. "About two hundred metres off."

After a few more seconds David could see the spyder with the naked eye. He could even make out its eight legs. It got within fifty metres of the Range Rover and seemed to merge with the background.

"It's stopped," Malone whispered. "Bugger it. I think it knows we're here."

"Didn't I say that this thing must look like a bloody beacon in the infra-red?"

"Yes, you said. I was confident that it would ignore us. It's always ignored my lookouts."

Malone kept the glasses trained on the spyder, willing it to resume walking towards the Wall but the machine remained motionless. As near as he could judge, it had turned towards the spinney where the Range Rover was hidden. It took a few steps in their direction and stopped, as if undecided or receiving instructions. Malone's thoughts were dominated by the images of the dead foxhounds. He concentrated on stopping his hands trembling. He lowered the binoculars as slowly as he could.

"I think," he whispered. "That it might be a good idea if we got clear of the area."

"Not in this thing!" David protested as Malone's hand went to the ignition key. "Let's leave it here as a decoy."

"That might not be a bad idea. Softly does it."

The two men eased the door catches open and slipped quietly from the Range Rover, their movements were smooth and silent as they edged away from the vehicle and backed deeper in the tree cover. The spyder's next move was wholly unexpected. Its shell-like back snapped open and the powerful rotors sprang from their housing. The machine was airborne in an instant. Far from being fooled by the Range Rover's heat source, it ignored it and swooped into the trees, twisting and banking, demonstrating an extraordinary manoeuvrability as it closed on the two men.

David broke from the cover of the trees and sprinted across the grass with Malone following him while struggling to yank the revolver from his pocket. He freed it, wheeled around and managed to fire a single shot at the diving spyder before the cloud of white gas enveloped him and David. The two men collapsed and lay still.

The spyder wobbled in mid-air and made a heavy landing. It moved near the two still forms sprawled on the grass and carried out what seemed like a cursory examination by touching them in turn with a manipulator. It appeared to have trouble folding its rotors. It tried extending them again and refolding them but the casing did not close fully. Finally, it seized Malone by the collar and dragged him under the trees, and repeated the process with David before continuing its journey to the Wall and the torrential deluge that was awaiting it Farside.

Forty-Nine

Ten minutes after the downpour started, Ellen was forced to do something she hated: accept defeat. It was hopeless trying to keep the outside fire burning. Such was the ferocity of the rain in that terrible storm, it seemed that the atmosphere itself had been turned to a wall of iced water. It was only a matter of minutes before the water charging through the drainage gullies broke down the sides and swept the sodden remains of the fire away.

"Useless!" she yelled to Vikki and Claire, gesturing to the hut and having to cup her hands together to be heard above the thunder of the rain drumming on the hut's rapidly tightening hide covering.

The three drenched, shivering women crowded into the hut, peeled off their clothes, and sat huddled around the hearth, not speaking. Conversation was impossible in that appalling uproar. Ellen poked at the fire to expose its hot core. The leaping flames met with Himmler's approval. He had had a bad day. After his meeting with the sabre-tooth cat, he had taken a high-speed short cut across the surface of the river and had not returned until late afternoon. His breakfast quota was seriously down on the day and the hunger he was nursing was several notches above his usual ravenous. Unlike the fire, the noise of the rain did not meet with his approval. What was the point of having humans if they didn't keep the sound turned down to an acceptable level or keep his stomach filled? He treated his staff members to a sneer of contempt and crawled under the furs on Vikki's bed in an attempt to escape the racket.

Claire repositioned one of the oil lamps and resumed work on the scoop net she was making. She had formed the frame by steaming and bending an ash wand into a loop and tying it

216

to a long, stout handle which she had shaved smooth with one of the flint scrapers. She had even mounted a cross-brace using a neat cross-halving joint. The netting she was dexterously knotting into a coarse mesh was made from an unravelled pullover that had been wound into a ball on a stick. Fortunately the yarn was a tough polyester. She was nearly finished. Ellen and Vikki watched her at work because there was nothing else to do. They had searched the other huts that afternoon in search of a similar device without success. Ellen had concluded that perhaps the fishing net had not been invented yet. While watching Claire at work, she wondered if several strands of the yarn would be strong enough to make a bow. She didn't think arrows would be too difficult to make.

The rain continued hammering down with unremitting savagery. Ellen allowed her gaze to wander over the interior of the hut. There were some leaks, but they were little more than dribbles that ran down the inside of the covering. The hides themselves had shrunk and were now pulled drum-tight over the ivory frames.

Two hours passed and the rain started to ease slightly although normal conversation was still impossible. Vikki was stretched out on her bed, making a fuss of Himmler. Claire reached the toe of the net's sock and tied the final knots. She gestured to Ellen that the net was finished and offered it for inspection. It was a robust, practical tool. Ellen gave Claire a smile and a thumbs up gesture.

Vikki sat up suddenly, staring at the hut's fastened door-flap. She slipped off her bed, caught the attention of her companions, and pointed. They both turned and looked at the flap. Vikki knelt beside Ellen and cupped her hands to the older woman's ear.

"The spyder is outside!"

"Our erstwhile Rin Tin Tin has returned?"

"Yes!"

The rain stopped abruptly. The suddenness of the silence was broken only by the sound of water rushing through the drainage gullies.

"Thank Christ for that," Claire muttered to no one in particular.

"Better let the dog in," said Ellen. She rose from the hearth, unfastened the toggles, and pulled the heavy flap aside. The oil lamps flickered in the draught and the spyder walked into the hut.

The three woman stared at the machine. It was in a sorry state. The two halves of its shell-like back were partially open and the gap was filled with mud and protruding tufts of grass and twigs. There was a deep gouge in the top of one of the shells. Mud was trapped around its manipulator joints, giving it a stiff gait as it moved. Most remarkable of all was that its light-absorbing properties had either been switched off or were not working; for once it was possible to see it clearly, even in the poor light from the oil lamps, and appreciate what an intricate machine it was.

Ellen was the first to break the silence that greeted its arrival. "Tell Rin Tin Tin," she said to Vikki, "that it's not to shake itself on pain of death."

The spyder had had a bad time climbing down the slope in the terrible deluge. Normally it would have flown but that was not possible, and its skills with its manipulators had proved of little use if the ground it was trying to secure a purchase on kept getting washed away. At one point a sudden unleashed cataract had thrown it on to its side and it had spent several minutes extricating itself. Negotiating the steep slope had been like crawling down a waterfall and had taken far longer than it had anticipated.

"They want us to leave," said Vikki.

"And go where?"

Vikki concentrated by staring at the spyder. "They won't say. Back to the cave, I suppose."

Claire looked frightened. "And be found by those hounds?"

"They say there aren't any hounds now," said Vikki.

The spyder suddenly made the rattling noise with a manipulator that it had made before to express impatience.

"We must leave now," said Vikki.

"No," Ellen firmly. "We need an hour to clear up here. We're going to leave this place exactly as we found it."

Vikki passed the message and Ellen was rewarded with a furious rattling by the spyder. Ellen sat down on her bed and regarded the machine. "Listen, Rin Tin Tin. You seem to be the product of some sort of highly advanced society, yet you can't communicate with me other than by banging a rattle, just like a baby. That pisses me off no end because it suggests you're not trying. Part of our social code is good manners. Good manners means clearing up this place. You didn't build it, you took advantage of it being here. So did we. So we're going to leave it neat as a pin, just as we found it, and there's nothing you can do about it." She jumped up. "Come on, girls. Housework time. Rin Tin Tin here can watch."

The spyder seemed resigned to the situation because it moved out of the way, watching the whirl of activity, contenting itself by making a rattling noise now and then when it considered that things were moving too slowly for its liking, such as Ellen insisting that they do their best to remove all the marks from the furs before rolling them into bundles and hanging them up. Himmler watched with deep misgivings. He knew all about housework and was poised, ready to leg it if a vacuum cleaner appeared. His staff rounded up a few scraps of food for him but they made him eat them outside, and there was nothing like enough to satisfy his gnawing hunger.

Ellen unrolled the chamois tool kit to check that all the tools were present, that there were no empty loops. She held one of the beautiful antler-handled flint knives for the last time, relishing the touch of the sharp, carefully knapped blade. The tool was a link with her ancestors. It would be so easy to slip it into her pocket, but how could she? How could she, from a world that had everything, take something from these trusting people who had nothing other than what they had made for themselves to ensure their survival? She returned the knife to its rightful place, knotted the toolroll and put it back where she had first found it, hoping that no one would see her tears.

It took less than an hour to clean up the hut to her satisfaction. Last job of all was to shake out the woven matting.

"Right," said Ellen. "Well – we've done our best but they're sure to know that someone's been here. I think it would be good idea if we left them a present each. Claire – I'm sure your fishing net, that ball of wool and your torches would be most acceptable. Vikki?"

The girl thought for a moment and removed a tiny crucifix on a fine gold chain from around her neck. It had been given to Vikki by Malone before they had been incarcerated in the cave. It was one of the few things that he had passed to her from her mother.

"You don't have to leave that, Vikki," said Ellen gently.

Vikki shook her head. "I want them to have it. This place saved our lives."

Claire smiled. "It'll probably drive them mad trying to work out how the chain was made and what it's made of."

Ellen searched through her belongings and realised that she had nothing that would serve as a present. The box of matches wouldn't last even if the hut's owners found out how they worked. Himmler, cradled in Vikki's arms, gave her an idea.

"How about leaving them that fleabag's collar?"

Cat and girl resented the epithet.

"What use would they have for a cat's collar without a cat?" Vikki queried.

"It's got all sorts of interesting things," Ellen reasoned. "A silver bell. A name and address tag, some elastic, a tiny metal buckle. Those coloured sequin things. I think someone would be very proud to have it as a bracelet."

"People are always bringing him back because he goes such long distances, searching for food," said Vikki doubtfully. "He'd be lost without his collar."

"Okay. We leave him complete with collar. He'd make someone a nice pair of gloves."

Eventually Vikki was persuaded to remove the collar and leave it with the other gifts.

"Right, Rin Tin Tin," said Ellen briskly. "We're ready."

Luckily the clouds were clearing and the moon was breaking through low in the west when they secured the hut's flap and set off up the storm-scoured slope. The climb was hard going – the rain-loosened turf kept breaking away underfoot. It was not helped by the spyder wanting to take the shortest route rather than the easiest. At one point they even had to help it out of a deep gully. The machine, never very high in Ellen's estimation, sank even lower. Vikki's climb was not helped by Himmler's decision that the best way to make the journey was under her T-shirt with his head stuck out of the neck so that he could supervise the proceedings. She shivered when they climbed up to the spot where she had encountered the sabre-tooth cat. Relieved to be on level ground, they followed the spyder to the point where they had first entered Farside.

As before, it was the sudden change in temperature that told them that they had passed through the Wall. But this time warmth and humidity engulfed them instead of cold. Himmler clawed at Vikki's shoulder as he climbed halfway out of her T-shirt, his nose twitching in all directions before his sensitive olfactory system locked on to the nearby spinney. "Bloody cat!" she wailed in pain, pausing to disentangle Himmler and his claws, and hold him more securely.

The spyder rattled impatiently and pressed on towards the field's entrance with Ellen and Claire dutifully following, pulling off their outer clothes. Vikki tried to follow but Himmler had other ideas. He wriggled furiously, launched himself out of the girl's grasp, and darted a little way towards the clump of trees, stopping to test the air.

"Himmler! Come here, you naughty cat! Himmler!" Vikki started after it, making reassuring noises, that Himmler, true to the perversity of his kind, pointedly ignored.

The spyder moved fast. It circled around and placed itself between Vikki and the spinney that Himmler was now heading for. The machine rattled furiously.

Vikki! The command exploded in her head like a roman candle. *Please follow the monitor!*

The what?

You call it the spyder. You must follow it!

Ellen turned and walked back to Vikki. "For God's sake leave that stupid cat alone," she said. "And you're upsetting Rin Tin Tin."

"He hasn't got his collar," Vikki protested. "He's too far from home."

"He'll find his way back."

Vikki ignored Ellen, the spyder, and the imperious commands. She plunged into the woods and pulled up short when she saw the Range Rover. One leap without checking if the side window was open and Himmler was in the vehicle.

"Himmler!" Vikki called, her first thought being that the cat may have landed on a naked and angry courting couple. She dashed up to the vehicle, ready with profuse apologies, and tripped over Malone's body.

Her cry bought Ellen and Claire running.

Fifty

M alone was the first to recover full consciousness. Ellen and Claire helped him to his feet. He leaned against a tree. Vikki found two bottles of water in the back of the Range Rover, where Himmler was gorging himself on the remaining ham sandwiches. An attempt to get Malone to drink resulted in him turning away and being violently sick. After that he was able to drink properly and started to feel better. David sat up and held his head. Ellen insisted that he should stand. Once on his feet, he too experienced waves of nausea and was sick. Vikki looked around for the spyder but it had gone. The voice that came to her was faint.

They are unharmed, Vikki. The gas is regulated so that just the right amount is used but only in self-defence against people – to avoid discovery or capture. It is the Law.

"So what happened?" Ellen asked when the two men were able to speak. Malone didn't reply but felt in his pocket. He walked unsteadily to where the spyder had attacked them, found the revolver, and returned to the group gathered around the Range Rover's open tailgate. Ellen and David were in a passionate embrace. He told himself that his pang of jealousy was unreasonable: the couple had been in a long-term relationship.

"Makes two of us," said Malone thickly when David complained about his headache. Between them the two men explained what had happened.

"You shot the spyder?" said Vikki, shocked.

"I remember getting in one shot at it. It was self-defence. Why? Did I hit it?"

"You certainly did," said Ellen, including Malone in her embrace. "I don't think it can fly now."

222

Malone looked around. "Where is it?"

"Gone," said Vikki.

"It's worrying to think that we might've upset the Visitors," David remarked when they abandoned the search. "We don't need any more enemies."

"You think they're friends?" said Ellen cynically.

"Their spyder could've killed us like it killed the fox-hounds," Malone pointed out, taking a long swallow from the water bottle.

"They understand," said Vikki quietly. "They say that the spyder is repairable and that we must return to the cave without it. One of you men must hide the entrance."

"They're too bloody fond of giving orders if you ask me," Ellen declared.

"Christ – orders," Malone muttered, suddenly remembering his responsibilities. He grabbed the car's microphone and gave instructions for all units on Operation Cancer to stand down.

"So what happened to you ladies?" David asked.

Between them the three women gave an account of their Farside adventures. They were astonished when Malone said that he had seen the incident when the sabre-tooth cat had nearly attacked Vikki. "And I wasn't the only one that saw it," he added, "There was Nelson Faraday with his bloody camcorder."

"But we were naked," said Vikki, suddenly ashamed.

"All three of us were," Ellen commented. She shook her head and gazed at the Farside sky. "We couldn't see anything of the real world. Nothing."

"Which *is* the real world?" Claire wondered.

"This is," Malone replied. "And unfortunately Adrian Roscoe and his Bodian Brethren are still a part of it."

"So you're going to return us to the cave?" said Vikki.

Malone shook his head. "No, Vikki. I've got a better idea. He opened a door of the Range Rover. "There's room for everyone."

Ten minutes later the Range Rover coasted silently to a standstill outside the two cottages knocked into one that was Vikki's home. Vikki was first out, clutching Himmler. She released him and stood looking at the darkened cottages, her heart pounding.

She hadn't seen her beloved home since she had cycled to Ellen's shop for her morning job where she and Ellen had been arrested by Nelson Faraday on charges of witchcraft. A flickering light appeared inside the house in response to Malone's persistent rapping on the front door.

"Who's that?" It was Anne Taylor's voice.

"Mike Malone. Sorry to wake you at this hour, Mrs Taylor, but I've got an urgent delivery for you."

"I'm sure you have. Isn't this a little sudden, Mr Malone?"

"Open up please, Mrs Taylor."

The bolts were slid back and the door opened. Vikki gave her mother no time to recover from the shock but threw herself into her arms. Their cries of joy quickly gave way to kisses, tears and an ecstatic mingling of blonde hair.

For an hour worries were forgotten as the knocked-into-one cottages rang with recounted stories, breathless exclamations, repeated hugging by Vikki and Anne, with even Himmler coming in for his share of affection although he would have preferred a breakfast or two. Malone was happy at the obvious pleasure that David and Ellen showed over being reunited and accepted that the terrible events of the last month had probably strengthened the casual bond between them into something more enduring.

An hour later Malone was sitting alone with his thoughts in Anne's modern but comfortable kitchen, its limed-oak doors and cupboards lit by several candles, listening to the excited chatter upstairs and the squeals of delight when Ellen and Claire discovered that Anne had a well-insulated tank with enough hot water left from the day's solar heating for showers. Anne compounded their pleasure when she parted with some of her precious stock of shampoo.

The unspeakable torment that Adrian Roscoe and his deranged beliefs had inflicted on these decent people, and still intended to inflict given the chance, hardened the police officer's resolve to destroy Adrian Roscoe even if it meant coming to stark terms with Stauffenburg's dilemma.

Then there was the sound of furniture being moved about,

some more chatter, and then silence. Malone was drinking his third cup of tea when Anne entered, flushed and excited, her green eyes shining with a radiance that Malone had never seen before. Without warning, she sat herself on Malone's lap and gave him a kiss of such passion that even his customary phlegmatic demeanour took some time off. She jumped up, a little embarrassed at her impetuous gesture, and paced restlessly.

"That was for bringing my Vikki back to me."

Malone looked indignant.

"Oh dear. Sorry, Mike. I've offended you."

"Don't forget I brought Himmler back as well."

The warmth of Anne's smile turned Malone's stomach to water. "There wasn't a reward for that damned cat," she replied. "David and Ellen are in my spare room. Claire's in with Vikki. They said to say goodnight to you – they're all exhausted. It suddenly hit them after their shower. They hope that you don't think they're being rude."

"How could I after what they've been through?"

Anne made fresh tea but couldn't settle. She went upstairs and was gone some time. Her expression was sombre when she returned. "I've just had a little chat with Vikki and Claire but they could hardly stay awake. Now they're both out like lights. Remember Benji? That huge cuddly bear I wanted you to give to Vikki? She's got him in bed with her, *and* that darned cat." She hesitated. "Are you sure they won't have to go back into hiding? It's the one thing that's preying on their minds."

"Positive," said Malone emphatically.

"Claire seems a nice girl. I've said that she can stay here as long as she wants to. She's terrified of Roscoe, but more scared of Faraday."

Malone hesitated and began, "There's something you ought to know about her—"

"That she's pregnant? Yes – she told me. Vikki is, too."

Malone was surprised. "She told you?"

"Of course. She always was an honest, open girl."

"She only believes she's pregnant," Malone pointed out.

"She is. I've got a kit."

There was a silence for a few moments because Malone

225

was at a loss and Anne seemed disinclined to talk unless spoken to. "Has she told you the circumstances?" Malone asked at length.

Anne nodded. "It seems my Vikki is more important to the Visitors than we imagined. So why didn't they do anything to save her when she was in real danger in Adrian Roscoe's clutches?"

"From what little Vikki has been able to tell me, the problem for the Visitors is that she's always been in crowds. Their spyder has a self-defence mechanism – some sort of nerve gas – as David and I found out tonight. It saw us as a threat and acted accordingly. The gas has to be carefully regulated and can only be used only against individuals posing a direct threat to itself. Which I suppose we were. Vikki says that the Visitors are governed by a strict code of ethics. They aren't allowed to harm people."

"And what about the harm they caused Vikki with her new hand?"

"I don't suppose they could've foreseen that," said Malone. "None of us could. They could not have seen providing her with a new, naturally grown hand as harming her."

"Which doesn't explain why she's so important to them."

"Communication," said Malone. "It seems that they can read our thoughts but Vikki is the only one who can answer them."

"What have they got to communicate?"

"Now you've got me. You seem to be taking it very well, Anne."

"Nothing really matters so long as I've got my Vikki back." She paused and smiled wanly. "I daresay the realisation that I'll be a grandmother at thirty-seven will hit me tomorrow."

"We've got to talk about tomorrow," said Malone seriously. He sensed that she was about to suggest that it wait, so he launched straight into an outline of his plan. She listened attentively, asked a few questions, but kept the most pertinent one until he had finished.

"Is it dangerous?"

"I'd be deceiving you and myself if I said that it wasn't. All

226

I can promise is that I'll do everything in my power to keep the danger to the absolute minimum."

"Have you mentioned this to Vikki and Ellen? After all, they're the ones who will be taking the risks – being exposed to danger."

Malone stood. "No. Which is why I must shoot off now to get some sleep and come back first thing to talk to them."

"It would be sensible if you stayed here," said Anne.

"Surely you've run out of bedrooms?"

Anne gathered up the cups and saucers and took them to the sink. "I have," she said, her back to Malone. "But I've not run out of beds."

There was a silence for a moment. Malone realised that he was embarrassed. He said hesitantly, "Much as I'd like to stay, Anne, I don't think it would be right. I can understand your being grateful for having Vikki returned to you but—"

Anne turned to face him. "Oh, for God's sake stop acting the thick plod, Mike. Do I have to spell it out? I'm asking you to stay because I want you to stay."

Fifty-One

S itting on the pontoon in middle of Pentworth Lake was the last place Roger Dayton wanted to be. But to refuse to splice Tony Selby's lengths of ropes together to make a bathyscaphe lifting rope would seem churlish and might attract suspicion if anything untoward happened. Not that anything would happen now. It was obvious that his depth charge had leaked or the spring he had used in the hydrostatic fuse was too strong to overcome water pressure and so fire the detonator. It could be any of 101 things that had gone wrong.

Tony Selby and his three-man crew watched in fascination as Dayton spliced the final length of rope. He enjoyed showing off his skill as he prised the heavy strands of manila hemp apart with a marlinspike, unravelled the strands and merged the two ends together, turning and plaiting the strands, interlacing them, tucking free ends deep into the rope so that they would be locked progressively tighter the greater the strain placed on the rope. Naturally he kept up a steady commentary, heaping abuse on those who didn't treat proper rope with proper respect.

"Look at the state of it," he railed. "Bruised, scuffed, and whose idea was it to use a jubilee clip as whipping? Disgraceful bodging. Call yourself engineers?" He made some final tucks with the marlinspike. "Right – test that."

Having had Roger Dayton on the pontoon for over an hour "showing him the ropes", Tony Selby now knew how to tie more than a rudimentary clove hitch. How to tie a hangman's noose for Dayton's neck would've been welcome knowledge but he contained his annoyance and lashed the free end of the rope to the pontoon's structure. His two men on the winch turned the cranks to put the splice under tension. Dayton examined the splice as it tightened. The looseness in the

228

strands pulled out and locked tight. There was no slippage. A little more tension and the rope at the splice was reduced to the same size as the rest of the rope. A perfect 150-metre length of rope had been achieved by joining several shorter pieces together with no bulges and with hardly any use of whipping twine and seizing other than to strengthen abrasions. It was a remarkable demonstration of a disappearing craft.

"That should do you, Mr Selby," said Dayton. "You could hang a bus from that."

"Bloody marvellous," said Selby admiringly, inspecting the last splice.

"Look after your rope and it'll look after you, Mr Selby. This is good rope. None of your manmade fibre rubbish. It'll last years with a little care."

"We're very grateful, Mr Dayton."

"Good. Glad to have been of service. If someone could row me ashore . . ."

"But you must stay for the unmanned dive, Mr Dayton," Selby insisted. "Besides, I'd be happier having your amazing expertise on hand in case anything goes wrong. A lot of time and labour has gone into this thing. Mr Harding will be along soon. He's busy at Government House with final preparations for this evening's carnival, but I know he'll want to thank you personally."

Selby's guess that Roger Dayton's ego would respond well to a little massaging proved correct; the yachtsman hesitated but agreed to stay.

The unmanned test dive got off to a good start. The hemp rope was fully wound on to the winch's drum and threaded through the pulley block. It proved much easier to handle than the troublesome steel cable. The rack of lights was bolted in place on the bathyscaphe and all the equipment Bob Harding would be taking down into the depths – tape recorder, camcorder, digital still picture camera and bottles of drinking water – was placed aboard. There was a final test of the telephone, the porthole was closed, and everything was ready.

Dayton helped drag clear the planks that the bathyscaphe was resting on. The winch turned and the bright yellow filter housing sank below the surface of the lake. The top remained visible until two metres of rope had been paid out and eventually it faded from sight as it dropped smoothly into the depths.

The unmanned test dive was under way.

The winch's pawl clanked over the ratchet. No problems were encountered lowering the bathyscaphe to fifty metres – seventy metres short of the depth needed to reach the Silent Vulcan anomaly. Selby allowed the bathyscaphe to hang at fifty metres for five minutes, his hand resting lightly on the rope to detect any vibrations transmitted from the depths that would herald a catastrophic failure.

"Okay," he said. "Seventy metres."

The men turned the winch until the seventy-metre marker on the rope passed over the pulley. They stopped turning when the marker was just above the surface. Selby waited, his hand on the rope again.

"We'll give it five minutes," he decided.

At the end of the five minutes the winchmen released the lock and reported that there was no apparent increase in load.

"You can tell that just by looking at the rope," said Dayton caustically. "You really ought to learn to read your ropes, Mr Selby."

"Okay. Let her down to a hundred metres," Selby ordered.

"Isn't the anomaly at a hundred and twenty metres?" Dayton queried.

"Our Chairman wants a controlled descent with him on board for the last twenty metres," Selby replied.

The hundred-metre marker was a length of red ribbon wrapped around the rope. Lowering the bathyscaphe stopped and the winch was locked when the marker was touching the surface of the lake.

"We'll leave it hanging for forty minutes," said Selby.

"Why forty minutes?" Dayton wanted to know.

"That's as long as Bob Harding will be able to stay down. The CO_2 scrubber we've installed is only good for an hour. It can't handle a longer period. So forty minutes is the maximum safe period. Right – time for tea."

230

Vacuum flasks were opened and the men sat on the edge of the rectangular opening in the centre of the pontoon, drinking from mugs and plying Dayton with questions about his round-the-world voyage. He was a good talker and enjoyed spinning yarns. The number of sharks that had followed his yacht in the Red Sea increased with every telling.

Tony Selby paid little attention but watched the red marker ribbon intently. He couldn't be certain but it seemed to him that the rope was describing a slow circle. He looked at his watch. After five minutes he was sure that the rope was indeed moving through a circle, taking just over a minute to complete a cycle. As near as he could judge, the circle the marker made on the surface was less than twenty centimetres diameter, but mentally extending that movement to what it would be one hundred metres down caused the hairs to rise on the back on his neck.

He jumped up and opened the parasol that was used to shade the echo-sounder's screen from the sun.

"What's up, Tony?" one of his men asked.

"That rope's making rings," said Selby tightly, switching on the echo-sounder.

The men gathered around the instrument. The strange triangular anomaly that Harding had discovered with the echo-sounder showed up in the centre of the screen.

"Where the hell's the bathyscaphe?" someone asked.

The screen refreshed. Selby spotted the blob and pointed. It was not below the pontoon but was deflected some twenty metres off centre. The next screen refresh showed that the blob had shifted its position. A few more refreshes removed all doubt: the bathyscaphe was definitely swinging in a wide circle, furthermore the diameter of the circle was increasing inexorably.

"So what the hell's causing that?" Selby wondered.

"It's probably an upwelling current," Dayton ventured. "This lake's well-known for it. Storm water run-off from the downs. Last March the whole area was turned into a swamp. When those two men were drowned."

"But any upwelling would bring up bottom sediment," one of the winchmen said. "That picture looks clear."

231

Selby switched the echo-sounder to profile. Instead of a downward view, the display showed a side view of the folds and slopes of the lake's bottom. The bathyscaphe was shown swinging towards the steep bank that they had been at pains to avoid when positioning the pontoon. Fogging around the bathyscaphe was possibly a cloud of sediment, suggesting that it had already been dragged through a fold. "Let's get her up," he ordered urgently, jumping to his feet. "We don't want her getting buried."

Even before he finished the sentence the echo-sounder's screen suddenly went blank. All five men on the pontoon felt the simultaneous shockwave that punched up from the depths. Tony Selby yelled an expletive. Before the two winchmen could reach the winch, the lake erupted all around them. A column of water exploded through the central hole in the raft and geysered into the air with sufficient force to tear away the steel "I" beam that had been supporting the bathyscaphe's weight.

Roger Dayton was the only man not thrown clear into the water as the pontoon was tipped up by the massive bubble exploding beneath it. His seafaring experience taught him to stay with his ship at all costs, so he clung grimly to the winch with all his strength as the world about him suddenly seemed to be standing on end.

During a particularly savage storm in the Indian Ocean he had been running before a banshee gale under bare poles with only a drogue sea anchor to maintain the yacht's heading. He had been about to inspect the drogue's straining sheets when a tremendous sea had thrown the vessel on to her beam ends before he had had a chance to secure his quick-release safety harness. He had wrapped his arms and legs around a deck stanchion rail as the raging seas boiled up to meet him – praying that the iron tonnage of the yacht's keel would assert itself. After moments that had seemed like hours, the keel had asserted itself and rolled the vessel upright. Roger Dayton had clung on then and he clung on now. But this time it was his seafaring experience that killed him. That and the "I" beam that crashed down on his head.

Fifty-Two

M alone's major concern as he stood before the 150 of his officers crowded into the operations room on that hot Saturday afternoon was how many of them were one hundred per cent trustworthy. He knew most of them by now but the number of recent recruits and the law of averages suggested that there was likely to be at least one among the gathering who, although not a supporter of Adrian Roscoe, would not be averse to receiving the cult leader's shilling in return for information. One was all it would take for Adrian Roscoe to be party to Malone's operational details to ensure the security of the coming evening's carnival. To minimise the consequences of a leak, Malone had appointed a hand-picked twenty-strong armed unit under the command of Russell Norris as the "special protection unit". They had already been briefed and knew their duties.

"To recap," he said, using a pointer to indicate the buildings around Market Square on a large-scale wall map of Pentworth town. "All those I've assigned to roof coverage are to be in position by eighteen hundred hours. The search units covering all the roads and passage ways leading into Market Square are also to be in position by eighteen hundred. I stress that everyone entering the square must be searched. Members of the public already in the square when you go on duty must also be searched. There can be no exceptions, even if they're carnival organisers. The same goes for vehicles and wagons. All must be subjected to a thorough search. The carnival committee have given me a list of transports that will be bringing in barbecue supplies." He paused and added wryly, "Don't be put off checking sacks of charcoal. No one's going to have a go at you for looking scruffier than you usually are."

The comment was greeted with laughter.

"Any questions before we move on?"

"How many are expected, sir?"

"I can only go on the May Day carnival figures. About one thousand three hundred. Any search unit that's under pressure can call on back-up from the Delta unit."

Carol Sandiman slipped into the room and passed Malone a note: *Serial 55. Fatal accident at the lake. Deceased: Roger Dayton. Chairman would like you to attend asap.*

"I'm being called away," Malone told the gathering. "Russell will fill you in on dealing with the shops and the security arrangements for public buildings."

On the short drive to the lake, Malone picked up a radio interview with Adrian Roscoe. The poor quality of Pentworth's telephone system had little effect on the sonorous quality of the cult leader's voice, and, for once, he was talking in moderate tones that would be certain to impress listeners.

"All I know is what you've told me," Roscoe was saying. "But Pentworth Lake is, as we all know, at the exact centre of the Wall and is therefore the centre where God's almighty powers are concentrated. To probe or challenge those powers in any way is to invite retribution, and that seems to be exactly what has happened. I can only express my deepest condolences to Mr Dayton's widow. It seems that her husband was an innocent party who was cynically exploited to further the evil machinations of others."

Malone swore and turned the radio off. Everyone seemed to know what was going on except the police. Had anyone visited Mrs Dayton or had she learned about her husband's death on the radio? The lake came into view and his anger was forgotten. It was the same sickly mustard colour of churned sediment that he recalled from the previous March after the storms that had turned the lake's margins into an expanse of dangerous swamps. The artificial beach had been scoured by a wave that had nearly reached the road. The watchman's caravan was tilted at a crazy angle. The pontoon had been beached and there were several figures standing on it. The structure looked undamaged apart from the missing "I" beam.

The ambulance that was leaving the parking area stopped

beside his Range Rover. Millicent Vaughan leaned across and confirmed that they had Roger Dayton's body on board and that he had been killed by an explosion under the pontoon.

"Mrs Dayton left five minutes ago," Millicent concluded. "She seemed OK – taking it very well, but these things don't hit home until later. Delayed shock."

Malone thanked her. He left the Range Rover at the entrance rather than risk the heavy vehicle on the soft sand. The watchman standing nearby had a theory concerning the explosion.

"My dad told me about this Heinkel bomber, or it may have been a Junkers, that got shot down – 1941 or 42. Pilot tried to land on the lake. They found some bits of wreckage. Wing and tail but most of the aircraft were never found. Lake too deep. So I reckon it was one of the 'plane's bombs that got set off."

Harding was tight-lipped and pale when he greeted Malone. Tony Selby and his men were examining the shattered remains of the bathyscaphe. Only a third of the original filter housing had been recovered. The rest had been blown out of the lifting harness and lost. The bright yellow glass-fibre housing lay on the pontoon like a fragment of a bizarre egg.

Malone listened to Tony Selby's account of what had happened.

"Did the bathyscaphe touch the bottom?" he asked when the engineer had finished.

"We think it may have done. But only briefly as it was swinging. Did George tell you about the Dornier?"

"He said it was a Heinkel or a Junkers."

"No – it was a Dornier," said Selby. "1941. My grandfather was in the Observer Corps. It was heading for London when it was hit by Pentworth's one anti-aircraft gun. The only thing it did hit in the entire war. So the chances are that the bomber had a full payload of bombs on board."

"There was nothing that looked remotely like aircraft wreckage on the bottom," Harding observed. "You saw the echosounder's display, Mike. You were with me when I found the anomaly."

Malone made no reply. He asked Selby's men to prop the

remains of the bathyscaphe on the winch so that he could take a close look at it. He tilted what was left of the base around so that it was in full sun and spotted a gleaming fragment of metal embedded deep in the glass fibre's yellow gel coat. He teased it loose with a penknife and slid it into an evidence bag. Several more fragments of the same material caught his eye and they, too, were added to the transparent bag. He passed the bag to Harding.

"They look like aluminium. About the right weight, too."

"That's what I thought," Malone replied. He took the bag from Harding and wrote some details on the paper tag. "This is one of those times when I feel nothing but envy for those TV cops who used to say, 'We'll run it by the lab boys and see what they come up with,' except that I don't need a forensic lab to tell me that the Germans didn't make their bombs out of aluminium, and if they did, it wouldn't remain bright and shiny after nearly three-quarters of a century underwater."

Harding was nonplussed. "You think someone made a bomb?"

"I don't know what to think," said Malone wearily. He took Harding to one side. "All I know is that Roscoe was already making quiet capital out of this on the radio without histrionics or rhetoric. That this place is the centre of God's omnipotent power and that what happened here is divine retribution because we sought to challenge those powers."

"Shit," said Harding softly.

"Just what we wanted, today of all days," said Malone wryly.

Harding stared at the fragment of his bathyscaphe. "I've asked myself if this could be due to some sort of defence mechanism used by the Visitors."

"My first thought," Malone replied. "But on past form, something as crude as an explosion is out of character for them. If they'd taken a dislike to your presence, they could've used their spyder to punch holes in the pontoon's oil drums, or something like that. I don't think they'd harm people permanently. In fact I know they wouldn't."

"We think alike, Mike. If the explosion was due to an

external cause, the big question is whether or not it damaged the Silent Vulcan and whether or not the Visitors might construe it as a hostile act."

"How else would they construe it?"

"And whether or not they're still alive," said Harding.

"The echo-sounder was wrecked?"

"Totally."

"There's not much point in worrying about the Visitors right now," said Malone. "If they're alive, they'll probably let us know."

The police officer was being less than honest with Harding. In truth, Malone, having encountered the formidable powers of the Visitors at first hand the night before, was very concerned about the Visitors – about their welfare and how they might react to this latest development. To what extent did Vikki's insistence that they could not harm people cover self-defence? How could he be sure that she had correctly interpreted that they had a code that prevented them harming people? The lives of 6,000 people was an awesome responsibility that could not be left to chance and surmise.

"You could help a lot, Mr Chairman, if you went on the radio asap to explain about the German bomber and that the possibility is that one of its bombs may have been accidentally set off during the test dive."

"I suppose that could be considered near the truth," said Harding doubtfully.

The comment irritated Malone but he didn't show it. "It's probably a damn sight nearer the truth than the story that Roscoe is promulgating."

Malone returned to the beach. Ted Savage and his Radio Pentworth gig had arrived. The radio reporter was interviewing a group of six angrily chanting demonstrators. Malone tried to ignore them but Ted Savage, his Uher tape recorder hanging from his shoulder, buttonholed him before he had a chance to get into the Range Rover.

"Michael Malone, the Chief of the Police, is with me now. Mr Malone, do you share Father Roscoe's view that the death of Roger Dayton is the result of God's retribution?" The microphone was thrust under Malone's nose.

"Of course it is!" a woman demonstrator yelled. There was a loud chorus of agreement from her companions.

"What happened here is that there was a tragic accident that resulted in Roger Dayton's death," Malone replied, knowing that he sounded ineffectual but unable to think of anything more positive off the cuff.

His comment provoked a storm of catcalls.

"Thou shalt not suffer a witch to live!" the woman shouted. "It's God's command in Exodus and we are paying the price for ignoring it!"

The hell of it was that a tiny but vociferous group of demonstrators would sound like a large crowd on the radio. Malone knew that attempts to reason with them would be futile.

"So what would you say in answer to Father Roscoe's assertions, Mr Malone?"

"I would say," said Malone, getting into the Range Rover and starting the engine, "that Mr Roscoe is prone to jumping to conclusions that don't fit the facts. The best thing is for everyone to listen to Bob Harding on the radio later today. He'll be making a full statement as to the likely cause of the explosion."

He drove away leaving Ted Savage's follow-up question unanswered. His black mood was not alleviated when he passed another knot of demonstrators heading towards the lake. From their placards, they weren't Roscoe supporters but those who liked the new life and resented attempts to interfere with the Visitors and their Wall.

Rather than use his radio, he found a public telephone and alerted the police station that a small crowd was gathering at the lake which required the cover of two officers. Diverting police on the one day when they were all being assigned was a damned nuisance.

The next problem was to get in touch with Vikki during the hours of daylight. The best thing would be to do it openly. Surreptitious behaviour was more likely to be noticed. Anne Taylor had warned him that her neighbours were incredibly nosey.

He parked outside her front door and rapped sharply, knowing that his knocking was probably stopping a few hearts inside. Anne opened the door. Before she could speak, Malone gathered her into his arms and gave her a net-curtain-twitching passionate kiss. To his relief, she made no attempt to repulse him but returned his investment with interest.

"That's my reputation buggered," was Anne's rueful comment when Malone pushed her into the hall and closed the front door behind him. "Although it was pretty well wrecked by your leaving early this morning. Vikki was quite mortified. And I'm certain that nosey old Mrs Johnson across the lane saw you leave."

"The woman who thinks Himmler is her cat?"

"That's the one. She misses nothing. You're not due for several hours."

"You've heard the news on the radio?"

"About the yachtsman? Yes – it upset Vikki."

"I need to talk to her." With that Malone went up the narrow stairs, two at a time and climbed the second flight to Vikki's attic bedroom.

Ellen, Claire and Vikki had heard his voice and were looking up expectantly when he entered the tiny bedroom. All three were sitting on Vikki's bed playing cards – in compliance with Malone's strict instructions that they should not move about the house unnecessarily and risk being seen. The women had willingly accepted the restriction, knowing that the hour of their freedom was now close. The soulful eyes of Dario in his Zulu finery followed Malone from the life-size wall poster.

"Vikki," said Malone without preamble. "A word with you in your mother's bedroom, please."

"Of course. You know where it is, don't you, Mr Malone?" said Vikki tartly, following Malone down the stairs.

Malone sat the girl on Anne's double bed. He ignored the reproachful look in her green eyes and sat beside her. "Your mother says you've heard the news about the explosion at the lake?"

Vikki nodded. "That man who sailed around the world with his wife was killed."

"We think it may have been an unexploded World War Two bomb."

"Well it's exploded now."

239

"We don't know what effect it may have had on the Visitors or how they may react. Vikki – it's imperative that you get in touch with them and tell them it was an accident."

"Why?"

"In case they decide that it was a hostile act and react accordingly.

"They won't. I've already told you that they can't harm people."

"I have to be certain of that. So I want you to tell them that it was an accident."

"How?"

"Well, I don't know. How do you normally get in touch with them?"

"I never have. They've always made contact with me."

"Well try."

"How?"

Malone checked an impulse to get angry with the girl. "I don't know, Vikki. Perhaps if you tried concentrating on them, they might hear you. Just try – *please*."

Vikki closed her eyes tightly and screwed up her face. She opened them again after a minute and shook her head. "Nothing, Mr Malone. Perhaps the explosion killed them all?"

"Don't say that. We could be stuck with the Wall for ever."

"I've usually heard them clearly when the spyder's been near. And they've always been clear at the lake."

"Then we'll go to the lake," Malone decided.

Vikki looked worried. "Now? In daylight?"

"Now," said Malone firmly, standing. "Put something dark on. Black trousers. Strong shoes. Cover your hair."

"Mrs Johnson is sure to see us."

"We'll have to take that chance."

Anne was more worried than Vikki when she heard that Malone wanted to take her daughter to the lake but she accepted that it was necessary. She stood at the front door to wave goodbye to Malone as he started the Range Rover and executed a three-point turn in the lane. As he reversed close to the front door, Vikki darted out of the cottage, bent double, and

240

dived into the vehicle through the tailgate. She wriggled under the rug that Malone had spread out and was hidden before he had engaged forward gear to complete the turn. He waved to Anne as he accelerated away. The whole operation had been neatly performed in less than three seconds.

"How was that, Mr Malone?" asked Vikki from the back of the Range Rover.

"Brilliant, young lady. Well timed. Stay out of sight."

Anne remained on her doorstep until the Range Rover had gone. Mrs Johnson's net curtains had twitched but it was unlikely that she had seen anything amiss. She resisted the temptation to give her nosey neighbour the finger and went indoors.

Malone arrived at the lake five minutes later. The pontoon had been partly dismantled and watchman's caravan had gone. He was alarmed to see that the numbers on the beach had swelled to about a hundred. They were all standing silently, hands clasped together, heads bowed. One of the two morris police keeping an eye on the gathering strolled across to the Range Rover.

"Adrian Roscoe was here when we arrived, sir," he said in answer to Malone's questions. "He left about five minutes ago. He didn't do any preaching. All he said was that everyone should pray for their salvation. We thought it best to leave him alone."

"Probably the best thing," Malone replied and wound up the driver's window as a gesture of dismissal. The morris policeman seemed uncertain at first and rejoined his colleague.

"Vikki?"

"I'm thinking hard," Vikki's voice answered from the back of the vehicle. "But there's nothing."

"Keep trying."

Five minutes passed. New arrivals joining the small crowd on the beach were outnumbered by those leaving. At least the crowd was dwindling.

"I'm sorry, Mr Malone. I'm concentrating as hard as I can but I can't hear a thing. There's nothing. Why are all these metal plates fixed to the doors?"

"Just keep your mind focused on the Visitors. It may be

241

that you're getting through but they can't or won't answer. Keep saying that the explosion was an accident."

"But *was* it? I don't know how to think lies. I can't help myself thinking that it might be a lie. And the harder you try not to, the more you think about it."

Her comment reminded Malone of the children's unicorn game in which contestants were promised a prize if they didn't think about unicorns. The prize was always denied because it was held to be impossible to concentrate on not thinking about unicorns without thinking about them. "Just keep trying," he replied.

After a further five minutes Vikki complained that she was getting cramp. There was nothing for it but to take her home.

Fifty-Three

A t 6 p.m. the final touches were being put to the preparations for the evening's celebrations.

In his early days as a uniformed police officer, Malone had
often been assigned to duties outside nightclubs and at football
matches. As a result of that experience he had developed an
indefinable sixth sense that told him when trouble was likely
to erupt without warning. It was a sense that depended on an
ability to identify and summarise seemingly inconsequential
clues. Very often the clues were hardly apparent but they were
there nonetheless; their presence added up to something that
could only be described by that inadequate word "atmosphere".
The atmosphere in Market Square was hardly electric yet there
was that strange sensation that caused Malone's sensitive
antennae to respond and a prickling of the hairs on the nape
of his neck.

The public address system riggers, working up ladders to
make last minute checks to their speakers, weren't whistling
as they normally did when setting up the sound for discos.
Maybe it was the cloying humidity which was the worst it
had ever been. Other groups were subdued as they prepared
their stands. Maybe it was the news of Roger Dayton's death?
Unlikely. From his personal experience of the yachtsman's
abrasive, forthright manner, Malone knew that he wasn't
particularly liked.

The Crown's waiter brought Malone his beer but he didn't
make a start on it. He would need his wits about him, therefore
the one drink he had allowed himself would have to last. He
settled the radio earphone more comfortably and listened to the
cryptic exchanges between Carol Sandiman and various police
units. As with previous operations, they were using callsigns

that primarily identified coded locations rather than individual officers.

Everything was going smoothly. The Woman's Institute barbecue supplies wagon was given a thorough search by two morris police. It was still fairly quiet in the square so the two men helped the women heft the sacks of just-lifted second early potatoes. The easing of the food-rationing restrictions for carnival and disco nights was becoming a Pentworth tradition.

The square was starting to fill when the Bodian Brethren's mobile canteen entered. It was driven by Helen, the senior solar sentinel that Malone had interviewed on the night of the raid on Pentworth House. A carnival marshal assigned the converted Winnebago to its parking spot on the north side, and four morris police gave it a close going over. Mindful of Malone's watching eyes, they poked into everything, even to the extent of using probes to investigate the oil in the vehicle's deep-fat friers, and rapping the bright orange propane gas cylinders. The rear half of the canteen's interior was an empty compartment containing sound equipment and the rear-projection video player. There was nowhere to hide anything; nevertheless they shone lights through the ventilation slots in various pieces of equipment and took up the floor panels to inspect the bank of batteries. One of the morris police gave Malone a signal to indicate that the vehicle was clean.

The tempo of activity increased as evening shadows crept across the square. Plastic chairs and tables appeared. The rear of the Winnibago opened to expose the video screen. Children gathered in excited anticipation. Helen appeared holding a microphone with a routine that had always been performed by a male sentinel at discos and village fêtes. But the children loved it, regardless of the sex of the presenter.

"Do you deserve a Tom and Jerry cartoon?"

"*YES!*" the thickening crowd of children demanded as one.

"Oh, no you don't!"

"*Oh yes we do!*"

Malone noticed that it was a woman sentinel who entered the Winnibago's side door to operate the video projector. Hitherto it had always been a male. His unease mounted.

"I don't think we've got a Tom and Jerry tape!"

"Oh yes you have!"

"Oh no we haven't!"

"Oh yes you have!"

"Oh yes we have!" Helen looked pleased as her audience dissolved into laughter.

The screen glowed and the delighted children were soon hysterical at the antics of the cartoon cat and mouse.

By 7 p.m. Market Square was dimly lit by a series of small spotlights that were powered by a generator parked in a nearby street. Malone estimated that there were five hundred people in the square. Music was pounding from the disc jockey's consoles on the steps of Government House, drowning the cartoon's soundtrack but the children didn't seem to mind. The Woman's Institute barbecue was filling the air with the smell of hotdogs. Family groups were busy commandeering tables and chairs, lighting candles that imparted a cheerful glow. Waitresses dressed as Elizabethan serving wenches were taking and delivering orders. Some people had noticed the unlit floodlights and were speculating about the time of the promised big switch-on. Malone sauntered across the square to the far corner where Mrs Williams ran her little shirtmaking shop. Originally the premises had been one of Pentworth's many antique shops that had now disappeared. Seats at tables around her shop were occupied by the twenty-strong force of Malone's special protection unit. All were in plain clothes. Anyone trying to use a spare table and chairs in the corner were advised that they were reserved.

Mrs Williams came bustling out of her shop to greet Malone. A small, pleasant-mannered, greying woman who knew Vikki and her family well. Anne Taylor had assured Malone that she could be trusted implicitly.

"Everything all right, Mrs Williams?"

"All ready, Mr Malone. There's your phone." She indicated a telephone on a low ledge by the table where it was out of sight. It was permanently connected to Carol Sandiman in the operations room. "When will they be here?"

"Soon," said Malone non-committally, sitting at the table and not acknowledging the existence of his men.

"Have you noticed how few men there are here from Pentworth House?"

"Yes, Mrs Williams," said Malone evenly. "I had noticed." His .45 Smith and Wesson was a solid presence in its armpit holster as he adjusted his earphone.

Fifty-Four

It was dark when the delivery-collection cart stopped outside the Taylors' cottages. It was crewed by Russell Norris and Carl Crittenden. Their timing was near-perfect – they were within thirty seconds of their ETA. Carl jumped down and inspected the cart's offside wheel with a flashlight. He grasped it by the rim and worked it back and forth as though he suspected that there was something wrong with it.

"Bearing's working loose on this one," he reported. "It needs tightening." He released the drop-down side panel and found a toolbox. As he did so, a crouched figure clad in black slipped silently from the shadows at the side of the cottages and climbed nimbly aboard the cart. The figure wriggled under blankets and sacking, squeezing to one side, and was joined by a second figure who did the same. Two more figures boarded the cart while Carl was tinkering with the wheel. "Okay," he called up to Russell. "Should be all right now."

Carl returned the toolbox and latched the side panel closed. He jumped up beside Norris. They were about to move off when they heard a sound above that they had heard before. It was faint but there was no mistaking the beat of the spyder's rotors. The two men looked questioningly at other.

"We'll report it from a TK," Norris decided and flicked the reins. The cart moved off at a sedate pace.

Vikki's heartbeat had returned to normal by the time the cart left the rutted lane and turned on to the smooth asphalt of the road.

"Well done, ladies," said Russell. "Can't think that anyone saw you. But best you all stay hidden."

"I bet old Mrs Johnson saw the cart stop," Anne's voice answered from beside Vikki. "Nosey old cow."

247

"She wouldn't have seen you," said Carl reassuringly. "Didn't even see you myself. You all OK back there?"

Ellen and Claire answered that they were fine. Claire complained that the blanket smelt of horses.

"Vikki?"

"I'm OK," Vikki's voice answered from under her sacking.

"You all got your changes of clothing?"

"We've got everything," Ellen answered.

The cart lurched and creaked on through the night. Its motion was a bleak reminder for Ellen and Vikki of the time when the Bodian Brethren had paraded them naked through the streets of Pentworth on a dogcart, their wrists manacled to a crossbar.

They were assailed by a sudden overpowering scent of water hyacinth as they passed one of the sewage treatment ponds that Asquith Prescott had initiated. They stopped for a couple of minutes while Norris phoned in a brief report from a telephone kiosk and resumed their journey. Vikki sensed the slight increase in gradient which told her they were nearing the town. She heard voices of passers-by exchanging greetings with the two morris police.

"Still a lot of people heading for the carnival," Russell reported in a voice loud enough to be heard by the concealed passengers. "Not far now. Just passing Baldock's Field."

"What's that noise?" Ellen asked from under her blanket.

"Test-running the big jenny. And that hissing and clattering racket is David Weir's old rust bucket."

"Her name's 'Brenda'," Carl reprimanded. "Show some respect. Me and dad have put a lot of work into that old lady."

"It's a rust bucket," said Ellen. "David thinks more of that bag of rivets than he does of me."

"People near," warned Russell.

The light-hearted exchanges did little to allay Vikki's mounting fear of what lay ahead. Mike Malone had emphasised the importance of surprise. But how surprised were Adrian Roscoe and his sentinels going to be? Just after Malone had left following their visit to the lake, she had seen Himmler from an upstairs front window, heading for home with a robin in his mouth. Knowing that her mother would have a

248

screaming fit, she had pulled the net curtain aside and banged on the window. It had been intended as a quick warning, and she had been horrified to see Mrs Johnson in the lane, also threatening Himmler. She had looked up at the window just as Vikki dropped the net curtain. At that the old lady had come storming up to their front door and banged furiously. Vikki had heard the conversation, hidden at the top of the stairs.

"I just saw Himmler with a robin, Mrs Taylor."

"Really? I'm surprised. Himmler and robins don't usually hit it off together."

"He'd killed it!"

"Robins are getting so vicious these days. They're displacing starlings as the skinheads of the avian world."

"Himmler's lost his collar. The bell used to stop him catching birds."

"I'll get another one if I can find one. That's a promise, Mrs Johnson."

"Is Vikki back? I thought I saw her."

"Not yet. Even my husband couldn't always tell the difference between us. Must dash – I've got something cooking in the garden. I'll try and hunt down a collar for Himmler next time I'm in town. Goodbye, Mrs Johnson."

"I'll phone around for you if you like. They just given me a phone."

"That's very kind of you, Mrs Johnson. Goodbye."

With that Anne had closed the front door and gone off muttering to herself about Mrs Johnson being a prying old biddy.

Vikki had darted to a front window and watched the old woman leave, staying carefully hidden this time. Mrs Johnson had walked a little way and stopped to turn and stare back at the cottages before returning to her own cottage. There was a notice on the wall beside her front door that Vikki hadn't seen before: "TELEPHONE AVAILABLE HERE FOR EMERGENCIES."

Carl's voice intruded on her thoughts. "Journey's end coming up, ladies. We'll be turning into the alleyway behind the shops in a few minutes."

Vikki's heartbeat quickened and a cold knot of fear writhed like a trapped demon in her stomach.

Fifty-Five

M alone waited for the disc jockey's record to end before
calling Carol Sandiman on the telephone that Mrs
Williams had provided. The policewoman answered immediately. "Mr Malone?"

"Good evening, Carol. I've been listening to PMR. Have you
had any landline reports on Adrian Roscoe's whereabouts?"

"Nothing, Mr Malone. Hardly any sentinels up and about.
Looks like they're staying in their HQ."

Damn!

"Russell Norris has just landlined to say that everything's
OK. He says that the spyder's stooging around at a considerable
height."

"Does he know its course?"

"He said that it's too high and that he and his company will
be with you in about ten," said Carol. "Do you want them
delayed until Roscoe shows up?"

Malone glanced across to the steps of Government House.
There was activity around the rostrum that had been prepared
for Bob Harding's switch-on. One of Tony Selby's engineers
was talking into a telephone while trying the big main switch.
He gave a thumbs up sign to a colleague. The cartoon videos
being shown by the Bodian mobile canteen had stopped. "No.
We'll carry on as planned," Malone decided.

"I'll call you on this landline the moment Roscoe's seen."

"Thank you, Carol." Malone hung up and was lost in thought
for a few minutes. That the spyder was around offered little
comfort; he doubted that it would or could interfere in any
way. He rose for a word with the nearest morris policeman
in the group sitting at the corner tables. "There's no sign of
Adrian Roscoe," he muttered. "Pass it on to the others."

The officer looked concerned. "Do we scrub, sir?"

"No. Maybe it'll mean everything passing off without trouble. We might as well carry on." Malone returned to his table and ordered five soft drinks.

"Five?" queried the waitress.

"I'm expecting friends."

The girl returned with the drinks. Malone was positioning them in the centre of the table where they wouldn't get knocked over just as Bob Harding emerged from Government House to be greeted by an assortment of cheers and catcalls. There were some hostile yells from members of the public on Malone's side of the square. He heard a woman cry, "Kill the witches!" He turned and saw that it was the same woman who, that afternoon at the lake, had shouted a phrase from the Old Testament at him. Exodus chapter 22, verse 18: "Thou shalt not suffer a witch to live." It was an admonition that had caused the most terrible suffering down the ages. It was "EX2218" spray-painted on Ellen Duncan's shop window that had marked the opening of the vitriolic hate campaign against her by Adrian Roscoe and his followers. And now Roscoe's message had spread from the confines of Pentworth House to gain a hold over a sizeable percentage of the populace. Just how sizeable, Malone wished he knew.

The woman stood and pointed an accusing finger at Malone. She uttered a single word:

"*Mekhashshepheh!*"

It wasn't the first time that Malone had heard the ancient Hebrew curse in Pentworth but it was the first time it had been uttered so openly. The plain-clothes morris police seated around Malone's table became tense, expecting trouble to erupt. They relaxed when the woman's embarrassed companions pulled her down into her seat. She continued to glare at Malone.

"Good evening, ladies and gentlemen, boys and girls," said Bob Harding over the public address system. He was standing at the rostrum, wearing a radio-microphone headset, a small spotlight was trained on him. "On behalf of the hard-working organisers, it gives me great pleasure to welcome you all to our August carnival. First the bad news: the Women's Institute

251

are confident that they have plenty of their home-made hotdogs and hamburgers to last the evening."

There was some laughter; the WI ladies manning the barbecue joined in, some shook their fists in a good natured manner at Harding.

"But the good news is that we've plenty of cider and malt beer, and enough soft drink to drown a hippo in. The arms of those living around the square have been seriously twisted so that the music and dancing will go on until 4 a.m., but please don't expect me to stay with you that long. Not at my age. But the really good news is that from today, we will have enough electricity to keep essential services going throughout the coming winter and there will be sufficient for shops and workshops around the town centre to remain open after dark. It looks as if the production capabilities of the methane well in Baldock's Field will exceed our wildest expectations."

Loud cheering greeted the news.

Harding held his hand up. "And just to give you an idea of the power that is now available to us, we're going to have a little switch-on demonstration. Firstly, everyone please remain seated. We don't want any accidents . . . OK . . . Can we have all lights out, please?"

The electric lights went out save for the single spot on Harding. People blew out their tablelamp candles. Market Square, apart from the rostrum, was plunged into a semi-darkness. It was virtually total in the corner where Malone was sitting.

"On the count of ten," said Harding. "Ten . . . Nine . . . Eight . . ."

The crowd took up the chant. "Seven . . . Six . . . Five . . .

Malone saw the brief flash of a penlight torch in Mrs Williams' shop. Figures brushed around him. A glimpse of white. The scrape of chairs.

"Four . . . Three . . . Two . . . One . . . *Zero!*"

The dazzling explosion of light in the square was like a nova. Not only did the previous lights come back on but all the additional batteries of lights burst into life, including the street lights together with arrays of suspended Christmas illuminations – a riot of flashing, racing neons. To complete the shock effect, all the shop fronts and windows overlooking the square also spilled light into the square. The crowd was stunned into silence for several seconds, and then it seemed that everyone was on their feet, clapping and cheering.

The disc jockey's timing was excellent. He came in with "Stayin' Alive!" at full volume, drowning the excited shrieks of children and their parents pointing up at the lights. It was a stunning spectacle for a people who had become accustomed to the dim light of candles and charcoal lamps after dark.

Malone raised his glass to his four women companions who had appeared at his table during the ten seconds of darkness.

"Your health, ladies."

Fifty-Six

Ellen was wearing a long, chunky jumper, pulled low over a pair of Anne's jeans to hide the big safety pin that was holding the fly closed. Vikki was wearing jeans and a T-shirt. Claire looked sensational in one of Anne's short summer dresses, and Anne was wearing the absurdly small white dress that she had worn at the May Day carnival. Russell and Carl had taken up positions nearby, their eyes scanning the crowd that was too intent on applauding Bob Harding at the rostrum to notice the new arrivals.

"I feel frightened," said Vikki apprehensively, glancing around at the crowd.

"I think we all do," said Ellen.

"There's a lot of people here, so it's only to be expected that you feel intimidated after having been shut up for so long," said Malone, resenting having to watch the crowd instead of looking at Anne. "But you're surrounded by friends."

"So you see, ladies and gentlemen," Bob Harding was saying, "things are looking up for us. Crops are looking good – we've already started lifting potatoes and we'll be cutting brassicas soon. As predicted, our Mediterranean climate is going to give us a glut of melons and other fruit. The telephone network is going nicely – every household should have a phone by Christmas, and soon Selby Engineering will be producing iceboxes now that the ice-making plant is gearing up. Next year we start work on a major water hyacinth water purification scheme that'll bring main drain sewage to outlying areas."

Sporadic applause greeted each statement.

"Anyway, that's enough from me. And these lights are hardly conducive for a smoochy evening, so let's have them back to normal, and light your table lamps. I declare this carnival well and truly open. Have a great time, everyone."

The floodlights and shop lights went off. The disc jockey faded up a lively number that tempted some couples on to the dance floor. Malone saw that the woman who had shouted the curse was staring across at his group, her expression one of frozen incredulity. She eventually nudged her companions. Several pairs of eyes turned towards the corner table and all looked thunderstruck.

"Sighting Number 1," said Malone phlegmatically into a microphone that he pulled from his jacket pocket. "Stand by."

The music stopped abruptly. There was a sudden buzz of conversation from the surrounding tables. An assortment of derisive calls and whistles assailed the disc jockey as he checked the connections on his equipment. Bob Harding stood to say something but there was no sound from the overhead speakers. He unclipped the radio microphone from his belt and checked that the battery pack was snapped home.

"Something's up," said Vikki nervously.

Malone signalled to Carl. "Find out what's happened to the PA system."

The morris policeman pushed his way through the crowd.

"Ladies and gentlemen!" It was Adrian Roscoe's sonorous voice booming from his mobile canteen's public address system. The big video screen was flickering. "Despite the efforts of myself and the Bodian Brethren, the accused abominations – those disciples of Satan – that have brought the wrath of almighty God upon us – are free and among us to wreak their evil upon us even as I speak!"

The video tape shot by Nelson with his camcorder of Ellen and Vikki manacled to the dogcart before they had been taken to the Temple of the Winds, appeared on the screen. Someone had done some clever lip-synch dubbing because Ellen seemed to cry out, "Satan! I beg you, Master! Deliver us from your enemies!"

"And Satan heard her plea and she was delivered!" Roscoe's voice echoed around the square.

Tables and chairs were overturned as people swarmed forward, pressing together around the mobile canteen for a better view of the screen. Vikki started sobbing. Anne gathered her protectively into her arms. The special protection unit were alert, awaiting Malone's signal.

"And Satan answered her prayer!" Roscoe triumphed. "He used his terrible powers of darkness to defeat God's Wall so that his witches could escape to Farside. We have the irrefutable proof! Watch!"

The picture on the screen changed to the sequence of Vikki chasing after Himmler, her long, blonde hair blowing in the wind. She was naked apart from the sabre-tooth tiger's skull, her body marked with the charcoal runes that she had drawn on her body when she had been bored. They were little more than rings around her breasts and navel but the effect on the crowd was electrifying, particularly when the shot tightened to a close-up of her face and the fearsome skull of the sabre-tooth cat, the huge incisors in front of her cheeks, as if the skull was a primitive headdress intended to ward off evil spirits.

"Oh, no!" Vikki wept. "How can this be?"

"Is that not an acolyte of Satan?" Roscoe thundered. "Is that not Farside in the background? What more proof could you want – but watch!"

Malone was stunned. He roundly cursed himself for being duped by Faraday when the video cassette had been handed over in the field by the Wall. In retrospect he realised that Faraday's cloak and his fumbling due to the plaster cast on his arm had made it easy for him to swap the tape cassette. For once Malone's ability to think fast and make snap decisions deserted him in the face of these wholly unexpected events that saw all his careful planning come to naught.

A great gasp went up from the crowd when the sabre-tooth cat came into shot. The video editor had even dubbed on sound effects: the crouching cat gave a mighty snarl that brought Vikki to a standstill before it. The low growls rumbling from the sabre-tooth were at just the right volume. Ellen and Claire appeared over the brow, with Ellen in the lead, running fearlessly straight towards the cat. The video editor chose that exact moment to cut to a close-up of Vikki's terrified face. They were frames copied from earlier in the tape and enlarged. The shot lasted only two seconds but it was sufficient to bridge the editing out of Ellen throwing the rocks at the cat. She was heard to scream as she rushed at the cat, "Satan! O Master! We beseech you! Banish the enemies of your followers!" The dialogue was absurdly biblical and melodramatic but its effect on the crowd was profound. Everyone was bludgeoned into silence by the incredible scene unfolding on the video screen. Hardly had the dubbed fake voice of Ellen finished speaking, when the sabre-tooth cat gave one last, mighty snarl and bounded down the slope and out of sight. The final sequence was of Ellen, Claire and Vikki embracing. The image shrunk and the fake soundtrack was not of three women expressing tearful relief, but hysterical, triumphant laughter.

"Those witches are among us now!" Roscoe's voice ranted. "They escaped the just retribution that was due to be meted out to them. *They must not escape again!* Find them! Bring them to me so that they can receive almighty God's justice!"

On a signal from Malone, all twenty morris police in the special protection unit jumped to their feet and formed a tight phalanx around the corner table. "All Mike Sierra units!" Malone barked urgently into his radio's microphone. "Get to the mobile canteen! Disable it! Arrest Roscoe if he's inside. Go! Go! Go!"

The special protection officers around Malone's table stood firm while about fifty other morris police on duty in the square surged towards the big Winnibago but could make no progress through the throng. Malone was about to bundle the four women into Mrs Williams' shop and their escape route when he heard the sound of distant gunshots coming from the direction of the police station. He snatched up the telephone.

"They're over here!" yelled the woman who had seen the four women. "*Mekhashshepheh!*"

Ellen's anger triumphed over her common sense. She jumped on to a chair. "Who said that?" she challenged the crowd.

"*There she is! That's one of the witches!*"

"Carol? Carol? For Christ's sake answer!" Malone was trying to talk into the phone and pull Ellen off the chair at the same time. Russell scooped her up. He was about to push her into the shop but Malone grabbed him by the arm.

It was an open line to the police station. Malone could hear shouting, running feet, a gunshot which came over loud on the phone and could be heard in the distance. A woman's scream was cut off by the blast of a shotgun. Malone slammed down handset. "Russell! Something's happening at the nick. Get down there asap. Take some back-up."

"What about Roscoe, sir?"

"A recording. It has to be. Get moving!"

Russell signalled to two morris police. They charged through the line of morris police and into the gathering crowd. The horde made a path for them as they closed in on the corner of the square, urged on by the curse-screaming woman. The phone call had cost Malone valuable seconds.

"Into the shop! Come on!" Malone yelled. Anne was nearest. He grabbed her by the arm and hurled her into the shop doorway just as the mob, mostly yelling women, were thrust back by the circle of morris police.

"*Mekhashshepheh! Mekhashshepheh!*" the curse-shouting woman continued screaming. She was standing on a table, drawing an even bigger crowd into the mêlée.

About fifty determined men with more piling into the affray stormed the police line. It held for a moment and it collapsed. Tables and chairs were scattered. Malone's martial art skills were no match for the sheer weight of numbers. For an insane moment he thought of firing his .45 into the air but he was thrown backwards against the wall. A fist connected hard with his temple.

"*Mekhashshepheh! Mekhashshepheh!*"

Momentarily stunned, Malone heard Vikki and Claire screaming as they were seized, and he caught a glimpse of Ellen swinging a chair before she, too, was overpowered by the mob. Six morris police who tried to save the women were forced to defend themselves. They and Malone went down under the savage onslaught. Suddenly the crush diminished, the crowd pulled back. Malone staggered to his feet and nearly slipped over in a pool of blood from an injured police officer who was lying still, brought down by a chair. Someone was yelling his callsign in his earphone. Vikki was screaming hysterically as the mob bore her and Ellen and Claire in triumph to the Winnibago. Anne tried to dash after them but was pushed away. Sobbing, her rage and frustration boiled over. She hurled herself forward again. This time she was grabbed and pushed back so hard that she almost lost her footing.

"*Mekhashshepheh! Mekhashshepheh! We have the witches!*"

Malone leapt for a street light standard and had shinned up four metres, enough to give him a clear view over the crowd that was packed around the Winnibago. He saw the side door open and had a glimpse of Vikki's and Claire's blonde hair as they were forced inside. Ellen was last in, fighting and kicking. The door was slammed shut and the vehicle started nudging its way through the throng. Malone realised that there was no chance of him having a clear shot at its tyres. Even if he had, he would need both hands to hold the .45 steady, which he couldn't manage while clinging to the lamp standard. There were fights all over the square as enraged bands of Pentworth's citizens battled to prevent police officers getting near the mobile canteen that was now crawling through the heaving mass, heading towards the road that led to Pentworth House.

He jumped down and saw that Anne was tending to the wounded police officer, whom she had helped to a sitting position.

"Look's like Roscoe is calling the shots after all," she said listlessly, not looking up at Malone.

The calls clamouring in Malone's earphone that Carol Sandiman wasn't acknowledging stopped when he gave his callsign. "All units head for Pentworth House!" he ordered, not bothering to use the mansion's code name. "Stop the canteen getting through the gates, and I want everyone on board that vehicle unharmed and in custody, but I want it stopped!" He propelled Anne into the shop, told her to stay there, and darted through the premises and into the back alley. He broke into a run and emerged in the side street where he had parked his Range Rover. He thought he heard the spyder overhead but was in too much of a hurry to listen.

Anne caught up with him as he was unlocking the vehicle. "I'm coming with you," she gasped.

There was no time for argument. Malone knew how strong willed she was, so he bundled her into the front seat and drove off, accelerating hard. He switched on his main set in time to catch Carl Crittenden's report that the power lead to the public address amplifier had been cut.

"Bit bloody academic now," Anne observed.

Now that he had a more powerful radio than his handset, Malone repeated his order that all units were to head for Pentworth House. He slewed the Range Rover around a corner, determined to use the vehicle with its extra weight of armour plate to ram the Winnibago if necessary. Anything to stop it getting to Pentworth House.

Russell Norris came in with his callsign, sounding unnaturally strained. "There's been a raid on the nick . . ."

Jesus bloody Christ!

". . . Ten men. They've stripped the armoury . . ."

Fuck!

"Anyone hurt?" Malone demanded. "What was the shooting?"

"WPC Sandiman's stopped some shotgun pellets in her leg. They threatened to kill her unless she handed over the keys. She's badly shaken but OK. They've killed Jerry Hamilton. Paul Henley and Des Rowley were supposed to be on duty at Baldock's Field. They must've heard the shooting and went to investigate. They're also dead."

The rest of the report was drowned by Malone burning rubber as he slewed the Range Rover through a 180-degree handbrake turn in the narrow street. He gunned the engine and headed south, inwardly cursing the heavy vehicle's sluggish acceleration.

"What about Pentworth House?" Anne demanded. "What about Vikki?"

"Three of my officers have been killed and several others injured!" Malone snarled. "We're going to the nick!"

A few seconds later Anne was thrown forward when Malone braked beside a parked police Commer. The driver was standing beside the vehicle, holding his head. The Commer was on its rims, its tyre slashed. This had been a well-planned operation.

"You OK?" Malone demanded.

"Just about, Mr Malone. Three of them. They—"

Malone didn't wait to hear the end of the sentence. He hammered the Range Rover into the night and out of the town.

"There's no sign of the mobile canteen at Pentworth House," an officer reported over the radio.

Malone snatched up the microphone, abandoning radio procedure. "What the hell do you mean? It's got to be there!"

"Sorry, Mr Malone. It took off around the back streets. We've got about fifty units at the gates waiting for it, but it hasn't showed up."

Another police officer requested permission to break in. PC Conrad Hardy was a member of Pentworth's original police force and one of Malone's most capable officers. "A member of the public has just stopped me," he reported, "and said that he saw the Winnibago turning into Baldock's Field about ten minutes ago. I'm in the vicinity now."

"Baldock's Field is the next turning on the right!" Anne cried. "*Please*, Mr Malone! God knows what they're doing to Vikki and the other two."

Malone thought fast. The whole point of his leaving the town was because he thought his officers would be at Pentworth House in force to deal with the Winnibago. Not only had Faraday duped him over the video cassette but Adrian Roscoe had outsmarted him, too.

"OK," he muttered. He lost speed, and killed the headlights. The powerful lights that lit the generating station were a glow above the field. He switched off the engine and allowed the Range Rover to coast to a standstill beside a high hedge before the turning into Baldock's Field.

"Aren't you going in?" Anne demanded.

"Not yet," Malone replied. There was no one about. It was best to await Hardy's report than rush into the field. He wound down the window and presumed that the sound of the Centrax generator covered the sound of Hardy's arrival. First the road was deserted and then the police officer seemed to materialise from nowhere and was crouching at the driver's window.

"Weird set-up in the field, sir," he reported, in a low voice. "Roscoe's in there, sitting on that steamroller thing. Other side of this hedge. It's not a very thick hedge so best keep our voices down. I reckon he's on the steamroller because it's the highest spot for a kiddies' radio he's using and it's a good lookout point for covering the entrance. They dragged three women out of the

261

canteen, all gagged, and have tied them to the fence around the well-head down the bottom of the slope."

Anne gave a little gasp of horror.

"How many men?" Malone demanded.

"Ten, as near as I could judge. They've got David Weir and three of Tony Selby's men in the canteen."

"Are Roscoe's men armed?"

"Four shotguns, maybe more, and Roscoe has the Sterling from the armoury."

Malone swore under his breath. The ex-army submachine-gun and some loaded magazines had been handed in by a woman during an arms amnesty held just before the emergency.

"They had a lookout near the entrance," Hardy concluded. "But he's now sleeping off a right hook. A bloody hard one."

"Well done, Hardy," said Malone, picturing the layout of the field in his mind. He fell silent, trying to work out a plan.

"Mind if I make a suggestion, sir? You know the old saying about making thunder in the south, and attacking in the north? You make some thunder in the south with this thing, and I reckon I could deal with Roscoe and his Sterling." He grinned. "I can move real quiet at night. My dad used to be a poacher."

Malone nodded. It was a good plan. "This is where you get out, Anne."

"Not a good idea, sir. That dress might show up through the hedge."

"I'm not driving into the field with her if Roscoe starts blazing away with a Sterling or anyone lets loose with shotguns!" Malone hissed.

"She'll be all right if she stays down, sir. Mr Prescott had this vehicle lined with steel plate, as I recall."

"In that case, I'm staying," Anne declared. She climbed over the back of the passenger seat and sprawled on the floor in the rear of the vehicle.

"Give me three minutes from now, sir," said Hardy.

"I'll hook left when I enter the field," said Malone. "Give Roscoe less of a target with that fucking Sterling."

"You give me three minutes, sir, and he won't have that fucking Sterling." With that Hardy melted into the shadows.

262

Fifty-Seven

The three minutes seemed to pass with agonising slowness.

Malone released the flap on his .45's holster while watching the luminous hands on his watch. With ten seconds to go, he started the engine, snicked into four-wheel drive, switched the headlights on to main beam, and roared into the field, his horn blaring. He skidded to the left, the Range Rover's tyres spinning on the soft ground. A shotgun blasted nearby and shattered the rear window. He squeezed off a shot in the direction of the flash and heard someone cry out. Next he took a calculated risk and yanked the steering wheel around. The headlights spoked across the field, momentarily picking out the Winnibago and the three women tied to the fence around the well-head. Malone straightened so that the headlights targeted Roscoe standing on "Brenda", his blue eyes twin chips of hate. He aimed the Range Rover straight at the showman's engine and had to swerve to avoid Hardy who materialised out of the shadows, clutching the Sterling. Roscoe remained on "Brenda"'s driver's platform, screaming abuse and calling on his God to wreak divine vengeance on his enemies.

"Three sentinels with Roscoe took a dive into the hedge when I tackled their leader," Hardy panted, offering Malone the Sterling. "Didn't have time to flush 'em out but they're not armed. Do you want this thing, sir?"

Someone fired both barrels of a shotgun from behind the Centrax generator although the targets were out of range.

"You keep it," said Malone. "Use it to keep that clown behind the generator pinned down while I free the women."

"You better hurry, sir." Hardy pointed down the slope. Two sentinels were frantically adding to the bonfire that had been

263

piled up around the three women. They were using the dry brushwood that Tony Selby and his team had cut away from the concrete plinth when they had discovered the well-head.

"Light it! Light it!" Roscoe yelled into his walkie-talkie.

Malone hurled the Range Rover down the slope. The chain-link fence and its three captives loomed in the windscreen. He spun the wheel so that the sentinel who was about to light a torch caught the full force of the door when Malone shoved it open and rolled on the grass. Hardy galloped down the slope, weaving left and right, and threw himself flat when he was within the Sterling's useful range. There was a sharp *rat-tat-tat* accompanied by muzzle flashes as he fired a short burst to deter the gunman behind the generator from trying to shoot at Malone.

The second bonfire-builder came at Malone with a shovel and keeled over, screaming and clutching his arm, when he received the full benefit of one of Malone's deadly kicks.

Malone could hear Roscoe in the distance, yelling at his men to drag the railway sleeper chocks clear of the showman's engine's front wheels. He glanced up the hill, couldn't quite make out what was going on, and turned his attention to the three terrified women. Their faces white, their eyes imploring, their mouths bound with duct tape. A shadow came rushing out of the darkness and keeled over in response to a burst of fire from Hardy.

Ellen kept still while Malone examined her bonds. A stout cable tie had been used to fasten each of her wrists to the chain-link fencing. Vikki's and Claire's bonds were the same. Malone was considering searching the Range Rover's toolkit for wire cutters when he looked up the slope and saw what Roscoe's plan was with "Brenda". His sentinels were using a railway sleeper to lever the showman's engine off its hard standing of pine logs. The great machine was rocking back and forth. It was only a matter of seconds before the mighty machine came charging down the slope. Small wonder that the cult leader was staying aboard – he intended to steer it straight at his victims.

There was nothing for it but to use the .45. "It'll make a helluva a bang," he warned Ellen, "but it won't hurt. For

264

Christ's sake keep absolutely still." He pulled the cable tie hard across the revolver's muzzle and fired. The tough plastic parted easily and the deflected round punched harmlessly into the ground.

Roscoe gave a demented cry of triumph. Malone looked around. The sentinels had succeeded: the showman's engine was rolling and gathering speed as it lurched down the slope.

Faraday abandoned his position behind the big generator and worked backwards, keeping the machine between himself and whoever it was who had got hold of the Sterling. Firing the shotgun with any accuracy with one arm was impossible anyway. He slipped his last two cartridges into the barrels and kept moving. If he circled right around and came up close behind Malone, accuracy wouldn't be a problem.

Malone's second round was as successful as the first, and Ellen was free. "Get clear!" he yelled.

Claire's hands were trembling. Malone held her left wrist, pulled the cable tie across the muzzle and fired. Her wrist came free.

The great traction engine was less than seventy metres away and still piling on the speed. Roscoe could be seen spinning the steering wheel. The steering chains were slack, causing him to over-correct but his mean course was straight at Vikki.

Claire was free after the second shot. "Get clear!" Malone yelled. The girl didn't need the warning. One look at the monster pounding down the hill was enough.

Vikki closed her eyes. Malone's first shot was good; the cable tie parted, freeing her left wrist. The ground was shaking beneath the onslaught of the ponderous, clanging machine. Malone's second shot only partly severed the cable tie. He pulled trigger again but the hammer fell on an empty chamber. He dropped the gun, grasped her wrist, and sawed the hang of tough nylon back and forth on the chain-link's rough galvanizing.

"Brenda" was only thirty metres away when the cable tie parted. Malone grabbed the terrified girl and dragged her clear. "*Run!*" he yelled. "*Run!*"

And Vikki ran with Malone hard on her heels. He heard the traction engine's front wheels hit the fencing and threw himself and Vikki flat. He twisted around in time to see the charging machine rip through the fencing and hit the well-head's concrete plinth. Both front wheels were shattered by the tremendous impact but the momentum of the machine's mass was enough to keep it going. The huge boiler sloughed across the concrete, raising a great blaze of sparks, and smashed into the squat methane valve.

It needed only one spark, but "Brenda" provided them by the million.

Fifty-Eight

The blast's concussive blow swept over them, making their eardrums ring with pain, and a tongue of blueish-white flame thundered around the traction engine. Roscoe's screams were drowned by the tremendous roar from the mighty flame that was reaching higher and higher into the night sky, lighting up the field as though it were the middle of the afternoon. It was as if a hatch leading to the crucibles of hell in the depths of the earth had opened. It was on such a colossal scale that the destruction of Adrian Roscoe was a mere nothing in the flame's fearful presence. He danced, his mouth opening and closing, and then slumped over the steering wheel and was still, the heat searing the flesh from his body. In a way it was fitting that he should die in the manner that he had planned for his victims.

"Why didn't he jump clear?" Malone asked.

"Blame me," said Hardy. "I handcuffed him to the hand-brake shaft. I didn't think he was going anywhere with a hundred tonnes of steamroller attached to his wrist."

"Well he's certainly gone somewhere now," Malone observed. "Wonder if he'll be made welcome?"

Deprived of its methane fuel, the Centrax had stopped but several emergency site lights remained on, powered by the generator's batteries. A power failure alarm was bleeping.

The sentinels who had sent the traction engine on its final journey and their master to his death, were thunderstruck and helpless, standing on the slope and staring up at the mighty column of roaring blue fire lancing into the sky. Malone and Vikki backed away from the appalling heat. Eventually not even a hundred metres was far enough away. They were joined by Ellen and Claire. They had pulled the duct tape from their mouths and yet were still unable to speak.

Malone pointed to the Winnibago. Its paint was starting to blister and bubble. "David and the others are in there!"

Ellen rushed to the mobile canteen and disappeared inside. She emerged a minute later with David Weir and the three power engineers, all rubbing their wrists. They backed away from the widening sphere of the flame's terrible heat and stood gaping. The Range Rover suddenly burst into flames.

Malone realised that he had forgotten all about Anne. He uttered a cry and started forward but heat had already been working on the vehicle's methane tanks and it was torn apart by a cataclysmic explosion. Debris rained down, forcing them even further back. He said nothing to Vikki – indeed speech was virtually impossible.

They all moved further and further from the hellish epicentre. The remains of David Weir's traction engine collapsed and the terrible lance of flame and thunder now had unimpeded access to the heavens. The silent witnesses stood in a loose group, enmities forgotten as the now leaderless sentinels contemplated the scene of Adrian Roscoe's last stand against his God's imagined enemies. David with his arm around Ellen's waist, Vikki clinging to Claire, Malone thinking about Anne.

The Winnibago finally burst into flames. Its aluminium roof melted and collapsed and it, too, caught fire, sending clouds of heat-driven sparks spiralling upwards.

There was a sudden cry from behind. Malone wheeled around just as Faraday pitched forward, dead from the mortal blow that Anne had delivered to the back of his skull with the Range Rover's jack. A quiver of nerve impulses caused his fingers to tighten on his shotgun's triggers. The barrels roared and the twin blasts of shot sprayed harmlessly into the ground.

Conrad Hardy knelt and examined the still form. He looked at Anne in respect and admiration. She was standing legs apart, breasts heaving, eyes wide with a mixture of triumph and shock, clutching the heavy jack like a talisman.

"He's dead, miss," said Hardy. "Not much left of the back of his skull."

"I'm a misses," Anne pointed out hollowly.

Malone took the jack from Anne, and dropped it on the ground so that his arms were free to hold her close. She accepted the security and extended the same to Vikki. The three stood together, not moving.

At that moment something extraordinary happened.

For six months they had become accustomed to warm, humid nights. Even as far back as March, when the Wall had first appeared, the nights had been consistently warm – nothing like the normal, variable but rarely balmy nights of southern England. They all felt the strange tingling sensation that they knew from the many times they had touched the Wall. It lasted a second and was gone.

The rapidly shrinking Wall had swept over them. In that moment, the bubble of warm, humid air that had been their atmosphere was also gone. The temperature fell with a suddenness that had Anne clinging even more closely to Malone. Her tiny white party dress was hopelessly inadequate. Malone placed his jacket around her shoulders. A chilly wind blew from the south-west. This was not the nightly zephyrs of convection currents within the Wall but a stiff and sustained breeze that bore the scent of the sea.

"The Visitors are coming!" Vikki suddenly cried out, pointing at the sky in the direction of Pentworth Lake. They all looked up but could see nothing beyond the glare.

"What can you see?" Malone shouted.

"Nothing. But I know they're coming! The Wall has gone! They said that the fire would consume all our oxygen!" She pointed. "There! There they are!"

They all saw the Wall's arrival just as Vikki had finished speaking. It was no longer a mighty sphere of an invisible force ten kilometres in diameter but had become a faintly glowing orb that drifted silently from the direction of Pentworth Lake. Only when it was silhouetted against the mighty flame could the watchers see how small it was – a mere fifty-metre diameter replica of what it had once been. It rose rapidly to the very top of the flame, centred itself over the terrible column of fire and descended. The flame was not deflected but was absorbed into the sphere. The noise diminished and ceased altogether when

269

the Wall touched the ground and kept sinking so that it became a hemisphere. The flame had vanished completely. The Wall lifted, changing from a hemisphere back to a globe of energy, leaving behind a mass of fused metal where the well-head had been and the now cold remains of the showman's engine. The Wall had created a merciful silence apart from the crackling from the burning Range Rover and the Winnibago. It remained hovering over the well-head's concrete plinth.

We must go now, Vikki, before there is any more killing.

"Why did you come?!" Vikki cried out so that everyone turned to look her.

We cannot say.

You owe us that much! All the suffering you've caused!

We did not mean to, Vikki. Please believe us. What has happened here has been terrible. Beyond our understanding. Goodbye, Vikki. Your child is our gift – a part of ourselves that we understand; a part of yourselves – a people that we don't understand. But he can only be those things if he wants to be. We will leave behind a monitor – what you call a spyder. It will wait until your son is an adult when the monitor will enable his powers, but only if your son wants them enabled.

I will have a son?

Yes. A normal, healthy boy with far above average intelligence. You will be proud of him. You must tell him about us. Tell him that the monitor is waiting and that it will come to him when he is old enough to understand. If he so decides that he wishes to talk to us as you can, the monitor will ensure that he will be able to do so. Not merely him, but the generations that will follow after him. It is a new monitor and is very different from the one you know. It will not be possible to find it and will remain dormant and always near your son until he calls it. We have ensured that he will have the wisdom to make the right decision for your people – our laws do not allow us to make that decision or to interfere. We can only provide a helping hand in the hope that when the time comes, he will consider us worthy partners. Do you understand?

Vikki remained sunk in silence, not answering the Visitors while watched anxiously by her mother and her companions.

Do you understand, Vikki?

270

Everything except one thing. Why did you come?

One day your son will know – if he wishes to know.

I want to know! If you don't tell me why you've come, I will kill myself and the baby! Vikki projected an honestly held vehemence into the terrible thought.

There was a pause before the Visitors answered the girl.

You would do that, Vikki?

Yes!

Yes – you have that ability. Very well. We will tell you. We did not want to because our reasons for coming expose our shame.

What shame?

A finger of ethereal light detached itself from the now shrunken Wall. It was little more than a glowing point attached to its parent body by a shimmering thread that seemed to shrink to almost nothing as it lengthened, but the light swam with myriads of coalescing colours and moved purposefully towards Vikki. She didn't flinch when it stopped a few centimetres from her face, illuminating her features. It was so small that it was reflected in her green eyes as twin spots of luminescence.

Don't be afraid, Vikki. It is easier for us to tell you this way.

Anne was about to drag her daughter away from the phenomenon but her hand was stayed by Vikki saying aloud: "I'm not afraid." There was a faint, enigmatic smile playing at the corners of the girl's mouth. She reached out to touch the light with the forefinger of her left hand but it withdrew a little way and hovered, as though uncertain.

"I promise you I will try to understand," Vikki whispered. "This is the hand you gave me. I know I hated it at first, but it is the most wonderful gift you could have given me. Touch it. Please touch it and forgive me for being ungrateful."

The point of light made a whirling circle around Vikki's finger. It stopped, touched it, and was gone – absorbed into the darkness in an instant.

Vikki gasped as the kaleidoscope of images and concepts flooded into her mind. Anne sensed her daughter's distress and tightened her arms, crooning gently to her as she had done when Vikki was a baby. Vikki started trembling. Her

271

fingernails dug spasmodically into Anne's shoulders. The young girl's body was trembling uncontrollably. "Hold me, Mummy! Hold me!"

The Wall rose slowly into the sky, gathering pace. It would have been impossible to see it but for the faint glow that suffused its boundaries. It dwindled rapidly to a mere point high above the group and disappeared. Vikki brought her trembling under control but her legs were weak. Malone and Anne eased her on to the grass and sat beside her, Anne gripped her daughter's hands and felt the tension draining away. Vikki tried to speak but was unable to make any sound.

"Don't try to say anything, darling," said Anne softly.

"They've gone," Vikki blurted. She marshalled her thoughts and spoke with more confidence. She was helped by the concerned faces of her loved ones as they gathered around her. Ellen and David joined Claire, sitting on the grass. "The Visitors have gone. The Wall has gone."

There was a silence for a few seconds that was broken by Malone.

"Did they say why they came?"

Anne wanted to tell Malone that his questions could wait but Vikki sensed her mother's concern and said, "It's all right, Mummy. I want to say . . . Just give me a moment . . . The Visitors said that they had been to many planets, visited many peoples. In all cases they discovered that God had appeared to the peoples. Sometimes early in their histories. Sometimes recently. But always to offer guidance and salvation. But God has never appeared to the Visitors. It has tormented them for many of our millennia since they became travellers. They have wondered if they are . . ." Vikki hesitated. "The nearest word I get is 'unclean' but I don't think it's the right word. They have wondered if they are unclean in any way and do not understand why or how if they are. So they study other peoples, hoping to discover the answer to why they are so different. What is it that makes them so different from the peoples of other worlds."

The group digested this, each silent with his or her thoughts.

"But why the Wall?" Ellen asked. "Why imprison us?"

"It wasn't to imprison us," said Vikki. "It was to imprison them. A self-imposed quarantine. They didn't want their

272

presence on earth to contaminate the earth. The Wall was as small as they dared make it so that we could live."

"Did they tell you why they chose Pentworth?" Ellen asked.

Vikki nodded and said simply, "They sensed the presence of a person they thought they could talk to. Just one person. Me."

She talked for another five minutes, answering questions as best she could.

They all heard the distant beat and turbine whine of a helicopter approaching from the south. They turned and saw the brilliant lights in the dark sky. The blazing quartz halogen lights were mounted on an army Westland Scout helicopter. The beams picked out the field. It hovered directly overhead, and then climbed so that its beams of light widened to encompass the entire field. As the sound faded, so they heard the roar of diesel engines and the heavy crunch and clatter of caterpillar tracks grinding on asphalt.

Bathed in the light from the Scout, the group rose to their feet and trudged up the steep slope, stepping over the deep ruts caused by "Brenda"'s last journey as they converged on the entrance to the field, drawn by the harsh sounds and lights of the military convoy.

A Challenger battle tank turned into the field, roared forward and lurched to a stop, its engine idling, clouds of exhaust fumes whipped away by the strong breeze. Behind it were two armoured personnel carriers. Their fat tyres sank a little into the soft ground and they also stopped.

The group gathered before the Challenger, oblivious of the menace of its long, intimidating 120-millimetre main gun. The commander's hatch on the tank's turret clanged open and the head and shoulders of a man in his mid-thirties appeared. He was wearing a combat jacket. From within the tank could be heard the crackle of radio messages and the harsh hiss of white noise. The young officer studied the group for some moments before speaking in a cultured accent.

"Good evening. I'm Captain George Halliday, Seventh Armoured Brigade. Who are you good people?"

"I'm Mike Malone. Acting Chief of Pentworth's police,"

Malone volunteered. He was about to list all the names of those in the group but the tank commander held up his hand and leafed through a clipboard crammed with papers.

"Detective Sergeant Michael Malone?"

"Guilty as charged."

Captain Halliday folded his arms and looked quizzically down at the group. "Well, DS Malone. Perhaps you'd be good enough to tell me what the hell's been going on here?"

Fifty-Nine

C aptain Jack Weismann of 21 Army Intelligence Corp
was a genial, mild-mannered, 45-year-old who, it was
rumoured by his colleagues, could be obliged to wear a
uniform but only at gunpoint, and sometimes not even then.
He was a skilled interrogator whose preferred technique was
the amiable chat, rarely asking direct questions, but seeding
his conversation with observations that would often prompt
those he was questioning to volunteer information rather than
allow such a likeable person to get things wrong. His tools
were his fast shorthand, his urbane manner, his quick wit, and
an ability to sum up people within a few minutes. He had an
uncomfortable feeling that Mike Malone was the real master
at the latter.

He was seated at the table in Anne Taylor's large kitchen,
with David Weir and Ellen on one side, and Mike Malone,
Anne and Claire on the other. Vikki sat at the far end of the
table, watching him intently. It was three hours since the inci-
dents in Baldock's Field and Captain Weismann appreciated
that everyone was tired. He had been asking Vikki casual
questions for ten minutes and had sensed that her reserve
could easily become hostility if he pushed her too hard. The
hissing charcoal lamp hanging above the table dimmed slightly
and required a few strokes from Anne to restore its brilliance.
It gave him a chance to ease the pressure on the girl.

"Remarkable," he said, standing to take a closer look at
the lamp when Anne explained how it worked. "And you say
Selby Engineering made several hundred of these?"

"At least six hundred," said Ellen.

Captain Weismann's mobile telephone trilled. Hardly five
minutes had passed during the interview when it hadn't rang.

He answered, listening carefully and saying little other than an occasional grunt or an affirmative. He ended the conversation and looked at each in turn. "It's been decided to allow Pentworth a winding-down period. No one other than army jobsworths such as myself will be allowed in or out of the exclusion zone for twenty-four hours." He smiled. "After that the ban will be eased to allow essential service teams in – phones, electricity. It may sound harsh, but it gives us time to debrief key people such as yourselves, it gives the press hordes time to select a team to represent all of them, and, most important of all, it gives the people of Pentworth time to adjust."

"It seems a sensible move," said Malone. "Will I be able to phone my kids?"

"Of course, Mike." The army officer turned to Ellen. "Your car's outside, Ellen. Do you still want to return to your shop?"

"Try and keep me away," said Ellen with feeling, rising. "Can David come?"

Weismann spread his hands. "But of course, Ellen. You two have a good night's sleep. I'm sorry to be such a pest when I realise how tired you all are. Maybe I won't seem such a pest in the morning."

Anne followed Ellen and David to see them out.

"He's clever and damned dangerous," said Ellen in a low voice to Anne. "Do you think Vikki will stand up to him?"

"She's done well so far," said Anne.

"Vikki's not a very good liar," David observed, pulling the kitchen door closed.

"She's a bloody useless liar," said Ellen. "Anne – you've got to call a halt if it looks like he might worm anything out of her about Trinder. But try not to make it too obvious. If they learn the truth, the poor kid will become some sort of guinea pig."

Anne nodded. "I realise that."

They embraced and kissed, bidding each other good night. Anne returned to the kitchen and sat at the table. Weismann gave her a warm smile. "Mr Malone is a good friend, Anne – he won't let me question Vikki unless you're present."

"He's a very good friend," Anne confirmed, catching Malone's eye.

"Did you see the Visitors as friends, Vikki?"

Vikki looked puzzled at Weismann's question. "How do you mean? What else could they be?" She held up her left hand. "They gave me this."

"Yet you said that you hated it at first?"

"I couldn't control it. I had to really concentrate just to open and close the fingers."

"But all is well now?"

"Oh yes."

"And yet imprisoning some six thousand people within the Wall was hardly a friendly act, was it?"

"The Wall never hurt anyone," said Anne.

Weismann raised an eyebrow. "Yet it has separated you from your husband, and Mr Malone from his children. There must be countless similar stories in Pentworth."

"The Visitors didn't understand us," said Vikki. "They wanted to find out what made us so special in the eyes of God. That was why they came. To find out about us. It was a question I thought at them and they answered. As for the Wall, I think they were surprised at why we moved about so much – why we were always in the wrong place."

Malone smiled at that. "A good point. Take a look at a busy intersection on a motorway any morning or evening and ask yourself why we condemn ourselves to always being in the wrong place. Or why we spend so much time and money on transport systems to ensure we're always in the wrong place. We accept it as normal because we can't see it from the perspective of an alien philosophy."

Weismann had already come to the same conclusion. He decided that he liked Malone. Although the police officer had often answered questions directed at Vikki, the army officer was skilled at reading body language and gauging what questions Vikki seemed relieved not to have to answer.

"Curious," said Weismann reflectively, making a note in rapid shorthand. "They know enough about us to grow a new hand for you shortly after their arrival, and yet you say they stayed for as long as they did to learn about us."

277

Malone intervened again. "There's nothing curious about it, Captain Weismann. It's possible to learn much about the physical characteristics of a people from a tissue sample as simple as a nail paring. Learning about sociological, political and religious structure is a lot more complicated. I've been struggling with it for years. Let's not mess about any more. We're all tired. This Twenty-first Army Intelligence Corp of yours. I confess I've never heard of it."

"We've been around a long time," said Weismann carefully. "Since the Crimean War."

"Let me guess. Among your responsibilities is assessment of enemy weaponry?"

"Not necessarily enemy weaponry, Mr Malone. Weaponry outside our control." Weismann was about to ask Vikki a question but Malone intervened again.

"Your principal concern is whether or not the Visitors have left behind anything that could cause harm or might be of military value. Correct?"

"A technology that can produce such high levels of radio frequency radiation that it can kill foxhounds at a distance is something we'd like to know about," said Weismann guardedly.

"Which we'll have in twenty years anyway," Malone replied. "Once we know that something can be done, we'll pull out all the stops to do it. That in itself is useful intelligence and a more useful line than chasing after philosophers' stones in Pentworth. It would've been better had you come clean right from the start as to what you're really interested in, Captain Weismann. Furthermore, your intelligence training ought to tell you that the chances of the Visitors leaving anything behind are small to vanishing. They gathered up all their belongings and left. They've left nothing behind. So, can we all go to bed now?"

Weissman regarded the police officer thoughtfully. "I think I'll get you to write my interim report, Mr Malone. You're in the wrong job."

Sixty

The long day was over.

For the first time in over a month Vikki was safe and secure in her little bedroom, free from fear. Her mother and Mike Malone downstairs, her arm around Benji, her threadbare bear, Himmler a dead weight at the foot of the bed having gorged himself senseless on the remains of a chicken he had been given. Dario looking down at her as she tuned her portable radio up and down the band, searching for a pop music station that wasn't obsessed with news bulletins about Pentworth.

Tomorrow she would have to face more of Captain Weismann's endless questions but at least Mike Malone would be at her side. The army officer had been friendly enough but there had been moments when his probing had driven her close to tears. Tomorrow she wouldn't have the excuse of tiredness.

Vikki decided that she liked Mike Malone. To have someone on hand who was strong, trustworthy and protective towards her was something she wasn't used to. She now understood what her mother saw in him. That she was a little jealous of her mother was one of those uncomfortable little truths to be banished and dealt with another day.

She found a foreign station that didn't seem to have heard of Pentworth. She closed her eyes and lost herself in the music, wondering how she would face up to the inevitable questioning the next day.

There was something that she had not disclosed and would never disclose to anyone – not even her mother or Mike Malone: that her baby was very special; that he would have the power to change the world if he so decided. The Visitors had said that they would return to earth in a thousand years in the hope that they would find a world with many people like Vikki – people they could talk to in their endless quest for understanding.

THE END

Appendix One

"The Phantom Hand of God in the Placing
of the Planets?"

The German-born astronomer Johann Bode (1747–1826) was an undoubted child prodigy – a self-educated mathematical genius who started publishing star catalogues in his early twenties that are still in use today. He was in his twenties when he popularised a "law" based on the work of Johann Titius that has astronomers at daggers drawn to this day. It was a wholly arbitrary law that hinted at divine intervention in the placing of the planets of the solar system in their orbits around the sun. At a time when astronomers were peering through their telescopes and making new discoveries every day and seeing only chaos, Bode's Law came as bit of a shock. Strictly speaking, it's not Bode's and it not a law, but the principle is easy to grasp, requiring only an understanding of what an Astronomical unit (Au) is. Quite simply, one Au is the Earth's mean distance from the sun of ninety-two million miles.

Bode's first step was to write down the following string of numbers:

0 3 6 12 24 48 96 192 384 768

The relationship is obvious: from the 3 each number is double the preceding number. Next he added 4 to each number so that we have:

4 7 10 16 28 52 100 196 388 772

Finally he divided each number by ten so that we end up with:

.4 .7 1 1.6 2.8 5.2 10 19.6 38.8 77.2

And here's where what many astronomers dismiss as coincidence creeps in. Mercury, the closest planet to the sun, is .4 Au from the sun; the second planet is Venus at .7 Au, and Earth is, of course, 1 Au from the sun; Mars is 1.6 Au.

Those eighteenth-century astronomers who were jealous of Bode's reputation rubbed their hands in glee. "Okay, Herr Bode. So where is this planet that's supposed to be 2.8 Au from the sun between Mars and Jupiter? There isn't one."

Then, in 1801, the first of many asteroids were found in what is now known as the asteroid belt located at approximately 2.8 Au – exactly where Bode thought there would be a planet. Another boost for the Titius-Bode Law was in 1781 when Uranus was found at 19.2 Au – the distance predicted by Bode was out by only 0.4 Au.

Neptune, the planet that Bode predicted would be found at 38.8 Au, was not discovered until 1846 – 20 years after his death. Its actual distance from the sun is 30 Au, so Bode's prediction was starting to wobble a little.

It wobbled still further in 1930 with the discovery of the ninth and last planet, Pluto, at a distance of 39.4 Au – a long way short of Bode's anticipated 77.2 Au. But, to be fair to him, Pluto is a bit of an oddball planet. Its orbit isn't concentric, and it's not even in the plane of the ecliptic like the other planets. Many astronomers now believe that Pluto is a captured body that wasn't part of the solar system to begin with. Or that it may have been a moon of Neptune. One noted astrophysicist has suggested that there might be a small, dark body orbiting the sun at Bode's predicted distance of 77.2 Au, the mythical tenth planet that has yet to be discovered. Stranger things have been known, but none so strange as the formula proposed nearly 250 years ago by a gifted German astronomer that hinted of a divine hand in the placing of our planet and its neighbours in their paths around the sun.

James Follett
Godalming, Surrey

Appendix Two

From: *Daily Mail* newspaper.
Date: Saturday, February 3rd, 1996.

FINDINGS OF THE JOINT AIR MISS
WORKING GROUP (BRITISH AIRWAYS)

A UFO? Actually, it was just our alien
friends in the North.

By Michael Harvey

It flashed past silently in seconds. Illuminated by white lights like a Christmas tree, it came shudderingly close as the British Airways Boeing 737 approached Manchester Airport.

The Boeing's bewildered pilots knew they had seen something. They weren't sure what.

Yesterday, officials were also scratching their heads after a year-long investigation failed to come up with a convincing explanation.

But there were knowing nods at the British UFO Research Association. Members are sure the mysterious craft was the Silent Vulcan – a triangular shaped craft that has been reported cruising northern skies for 20 years.

Captain Roger Wills and First Officer Mark Stuart were almost ready to land British Airways flight 5061 from Milan when the craft hurtled towards them on January 6th last year. They radioed traffic controllers at Manchester and filed a formal air miss report after landing.

Yesterday the findings by the Joint Air Miss Working Group said: "To speculate about extra-terrestrial activity is not within the group's remit."

But morale at the British UFO Research Association rocketed. Members believe the report practically confirms what they have known all along – there is definitely something "out there".

"The report is remarkably open-minded," said director of investigations, Phillip Mantell. It is a milestone in official recognition of the phenomenon of UFOs.

"We have always contended that there is something out there which is beyond accepted science and now this is being reflected in the corridors of officialdom."

Mr Mantell said the Silent Vulcan – named because it is shaped like the old British Vulcan Bomber – has been seen all along the "Pennine Corridor", from the Midlands up through Derbyshire and into Yorkshire. There was a surge of sightings in the 1970s and then again in the late 1980s. One came from a Sheffield Police Officer.

The Silent Vulcan widened its horizons in 1989 and 1990, with a spate of reports in Belgium. The airforce there even scrambled two F-16 fighters, which tracked the object by radar.

They failed to find any UFO but their readings showed it accelerated and lost altitude at speeds that would have turned any human pilot into pulp.

"This latest report is the first officially recognised sighting of the Silent Vulcan along the Pennines," Mr Mantell said. "British Airways are to be complimented for treating this incident seriously."

It seems that not all at the airline appreciate the gravity of the situation. Captain Wills of Normanton, West Yorkshire and First Officer Stuart, from Congleton, Cheshire, are said to have been constantly ribbed by colleagues.

"I think they're both fed up with hearing about it, although they're glad the CAA took them seriously," one said. "Both are level-headed guys but they have had their legs pulled unmercifully over this business."

284